# THE SOUL'S RECKONING

# THE SOUL'S RECKONING

## *The Q'Zam'Ta Trilogy, Book Two*

Shireen Anne Jeejeebhoy

# ADDITIONAL TITLES BY SHIREEN (ANNE) JEEJEEBHOY

Lifeliner: The Judy Taylor Story

The Job Sessions: Why Do The Innocent Suffer?

She

Eleven Shorts +1

Concussion Is Brain Injury

Aban's Accension

Time and Space (Relaunched in 2025)

Concussion Is Brain Injury: Treating the Neurons and Me

Louise and The Men of Transit

Brain Injury, Trauma, and Grief: How to Heal When You Are Alone

The Soul's Awakening (The Q'Zam'Ta Trilogy, Book One)

The Soul's Turning (The Q'Zam'Ta Trilogy, Book Three, forthcoming in 2026)

# ONLINE PRESENCE

**Central Hub**: shireen.link

**Bluesky**: bsky.app/profile/shireenj.bsky.social

**Website**: jeejeebhoy.ca

*Psychology Today* **Blog**: psychologytoday.com/ca/blog/concussion-is-brain-injury

**Mind Explorer**: shireenjeejeebhoy.substack.com

**Patreon**: Shireen Jeejeebhoy

**Political Blog**: pario.blogspot.com

**Brain Injury Website**: concussionisbraininjury.com

concussionisbraininjury.ca

**Flickr**: flickr.com/photos/pario/

**LinkedIn**: Shireen Jeejeebhoy

# PRAISE

"Executed with grace, compassion, wit, and vulnerability, this is an innovative and potentially life-changing read."
– *SPR* on **Brain Injury, Trauma, and Grief**

"With the author's well crafted, distinctive, and narrative driven storytelling style, "The Soul's Awakening" is raised to an impressive level of literary excellence....especially and unreservedly recommended for personal, community, and college/university library."
– *Midwest Book Review* on **The Soul's Awakening**

Winner of Literary Titan's Gold Book Award for Fiction, for exceptional storytelling and creativity, a compelling narrative, memorable characters, and a story that captivates readers.
– *Literary Titan* on **The Soul's Awakening**

"Author Shireen Jeejeebhoy blends an entertaining mix of satire, action, and time travel adventure to deliver an absorbing thriller that you simply can't put down."
– Pikasho Deka on **Time and Space** for *Readers' Favorite*

"Time is an inspiringly fearless explorer of these bizarre but recognizable timelines. Brazenly ambitious from start to finish, the novel challenges the present we're pursuing and warns against the future we're inviting, for a work of speculative sci-fi that acts as a fiercely urgent call to arms."
– *SPR* on **Time and Space**

"What an amazing journey into the future!"
– Ana on *Time and Space* on *Goodreads*

"Jeejeebhoy is a passionate advocate for patients, and a sympathetic narrator."
– *SPR* on **Concussion Is Brain Injury: Treating the Neurons and Me**

"Put simply this is the best urban fantasy story that I have ever read period."
– Shane Porteous, Writer, gives **She** 5 stars on *Smashwords*

"A compelling story....Reading [**Lifeliner**] will make you laugh, smile, cringe, cry and most importantly, think."
– Diana Rohini LaVigne, Online Editor, *Indian Life & Style Magazine*

"I had a hard time stopping reading."
– **Aban's Accension,** featured on *Wattpad* in 2013

"An inventive second chapter of Shireen Anne Jeejeebhoy's post-life saga. This series offers an expansive and detailed vision of Heaven, souls, and the afterlife, amplified by a wealth of metaphorical creativity....All told, this epic spiritual odyssey is a unique and inspiring read, complex in its storytelling machinery, but steadfast in its poignant and powerful messaging."
– *SPR* on **The Soul's Reckoning**

# AWARDS

**Best Biography, Reader Views Reviewers Choice Awards, 2008**
Lifeliner: The Judy Taylor Story

**Finalist, The Word Award, Novel–Futuristic Category, 2012**
She (A Fantasy)

**Featured, Wattpad, 2013**
Aban's Accension

**Finalist, The Word Award, Books–General Market Non-Fiction,
Life Stories, 2018**
Concussion Is Brain Injury: Treating the Neurons and Me

**Finalist, The Word Award, Books–General Market Non-Fiction,
Culture, 2023**
Brain Injury, Trauma, and Grief:
How to Heal When You Are Alone

**Finalist, The Word Award, Writer of Colour, 2023**
Brain Injury, Trauma, and Grief

**Winner, Literary Titan, Gold Book Award, 2025**
The Soul's Awakening

**Winner, Literary Titan, Gold Book Award, 2025**
Time and Space

**Winner, The Word Award, Books–General Market Fiction,
Speculative, 2025**
The Soul's Awakening

**Winner, Writer's Digest Self-Published E-book Awards–
Prescriptive/Informative Category, 2025**
Brain Injury, Trauma, and Grief

*For my Aunts, Sophie, Adi, Pat, and Joan. Hong Kong. Indonesia. UK. And Canada. Long lived and abounding in humour.*

*And to my Aunt I never met, Aban, lying in a desecrated grave, dead in Burma in an era when fever took many children, and whom I honoured in my second novel* **Aban's Accension**.

# THE SOUL'S AWAKENING RECAP

At the moment of my death, my life began.

I was upset. Angry. Horrified.

And confused.

Looking back to that moment in the Solar Age, I found the voices the most unsettling, certain my dying brain had created them and not daring to ask who they were.

I ran an accounting firm, my own one-woman office. I interacted with clients only when needed, saw my one-year-older sister as little as possible, attended my cardiologist appointments when required, and knew no one else. I didn't need anyone else. My existence had ended because I'd met a doctor who understood me. *Why then, voices?*

"Why is she surprised?"

Chimes, like tiny silver bells, slivered the air.

"You know why, Blair."

"I know, I know, Bailey. I'm frustrated with her decision."

"We're not here to decide for her."

"I know, I know."

I regained consciousness on the ceiling, hearing these two voices intermingled with chimes, as I spied below me my physical self lying in the bed under the blanket and sheet, the blanket's mounds outlining my legs lying straight together, my hands clasped over each other on my stomach while my head stuck out, denting the pillow, eyes closed, reminding me of a guillotined head. The face, my face, reflected peace. So still. I'd never seen such an unmoving face before. I squinted. *That's what death looks like.*

THAT'S HOW CHARLOTTE Elisabeth's story started in *The Soul's Awakening*, the first book of *The Q'Zam'Ta Trilogy*, winner of the 2025 The Word Award for Books—General Market Fiction: Speculative. If you haven't read it yet, what are you waiting for? Go! Do that now!! You won't regret it. As one reader reviewer wrote, "I was stunned by this book!" After all, I don't want to give away the first story to new readers of this trilogy!

For the rest of you who have read the first novel, I wrote this recap to aid your recall as you read this, the second novel in the trilogy.

As you may recall, Charlotte Elisabeth died and woke up alive. It's no secret she chose MAiD. That, for non-Canadians, stands for Medical Assistance in Dying, aka euthanasia aka a doctor shooting you up with drugs to kill you. Why, you ask, did Charlotte Elisabeth want to die? Well, it's the age-old issues. Unexpected health problems. What passes for medical care these days. Fractured relationships (which we'll get to in this book). And loneliness.

As she lay in the Dying with Dignity Suite at a Toronto hospital, waiting to, well, die, Charlotte Elisabeth's soul family arrived to welcome her into the afterlife. To be clear, her soul family—who you'll meet again in these pages—once lived on Earth. Triplets Bailey, Blair, and Blake, the last one speaking in silver chimes when we first meet them. Charlotte Elisabeth first saw them when she died and her body released her soul. That's where *The Soul's Awakening* starts.

Charlotte Elisabeth couldn't believe her senses. Life is physical life on Earth. Since she was still conscious, she refused to believe she actually died, that her life continued after her first death, that she had a soul family who accompanied her through the Earth-Heaven Interdimensional Expanse, which was more than a simple life review.

In the Expanse, Charlotte Elisabeth must answer tough questions. She was less than thrilled. She wanted to die, dammit! Dr. Veritas, her euthanasia doctor, the only one who'd listened to her, had promised an end to her existence. And there she was, living an existence she'd never heard of before and didn't understand. Worse, there was some sort of living light that hovered over the dark Distortans—the first part of the Expanse she entered—which are both places and beings.

But it's not only the Distortans she must answer to; she must also find her way out of Hell Track when she plummeted into it and ended up learning a seductive, unpleasant truth.

But her struggle didn't end.

Somehow, she landed in Flower Power Track, where she must endure the life review postcards sucking her in to experience others' emotions and thoughts within key scenes from her past from a ceiling perspective.

The Flower Power Track's one happy spot is Greeter. The Golden Lab. The dog guides her, comforts her, keeps her company when she's not sucked into one of the postcards.

Whether battling the Distortans, being seduced in Hell Track, or experiencing life scenes within each postcard, Charlotte Elisabeth was never alone. Her soul family accompanied and supported her as she learned astonishing new things about herself, her father, mother, and half-sisters Sally and Sincerity.

Those scenes form the backdrop for the tasks she must complete in this book.

*The Soul's Awakening* ends at the Barrier, where this book, *The Soul's Reckoning* begins.

Are you ready? Don't worry, I've scattered breadcrumbs from the first book throughout the second to help you remember. Turn the page and enjoy Charlotte Elisabeth's second adventure!

# Chapter One

# THROUGH THE BARRIER

*M*eow.

An unknown cat's call punctured the prickling, metallic static as we hurtled through photons: me, Bailey, Blair, and Blake.

*Where are they taking me?!*

My soul family, who'd brought me safely through the Earth-Heaven Interdimensional Expanse, were now transiting me into an unknown world through the Barrier.

*I'm alive*, I gulped, reminding myself.

A fusillade of light bombarded my retinas.

*I want to be alive, and that's all that matters*, I told myself as I fought the fear building in me.

Joy from without shattered my control, deepening, widening, and subsuming me. I folded into myself. I hadn't experienced joy before and suspected it when I'd seen it in others. How could anyone feel that happy? *What is this joy? An emotion, a state, or a sensation?* Whatever it was, its intensity was drowning me.

Prickles thrummed my outer skin-type layer like particles sweeping in and calling the hairs on the back of my neck to rise. Except I didn't have hair anymore in this version of myself. *Version? What am I?* Although the limitless, perplexing joy didn't leave me, I forgot about it as these questions lanced my mind.

Then the stinging began. Countless wasp-type stings peppered me.

*Am I dying again?*

I squeezed into myself. I reminded myself that I hadn't died, unlike what I'd hoped for, longed for. I'd continued to exist. I tucked my head tighter into my chest as I gripped my arms.

*Meow.*

Pressure formed on my back, building, building, building, forcing me to let go of myself, bending me into a taut bow.

*Meow!*

*Who—no—what cat is inside my mind!*

An emotion.

A state.

A sensation.

An eye-blinding golden light.

Hugged me.

Flowed into me, comforting and protecting me.

In my first moment in Heaven, in the Solar Age, I still didn't understand this kind of existence, these feelings surrounding me. During my journey of fear, anger, and resentment in the Earth-Heaven Interdimensional Expanse, I'd admitted to existing after death. I'd admitted I wanted to live and had approached the Barrier with anticipation. *But...but is this existence?* I shrank against the pressure-wave accelerating me forwards through the Barrier.

Bailey's words penetrated my fear, like bells in my ears. "This love you feel overwhelmed all of us, Charlotte Elisabeth, the first time we felt it. It's okay you can't identify the emotion, state, or sensation. You've controlled and locked away your emotions, hidden from relationships because, as you saw, your early childhood hurt you. But Heaven is a safe place. You don't have to revert to your old ways."

*Safe? Is anywhere safe?*

We burst through the white, prickling, stinging Barrier and soared into flowers, tumbling and somersaulting into a kaleidoscope of reds and blues, velvets and silks, sugar and tart.

*MEOW!!!*

The hidden cat's greeting belled my mind as petals flew up around us, showering us with colours, sensations, and scents I hadn't known existed. I landed face first in the flowers. I lay stunned. I sensed no time as I lay unmoving. *Does time move forwards here?* I flipped over.

Spit, spit, spit.

I spat petals out of my mouth. I didn't know how petals had crawled in. *How do I have a mouth again?*

"Meow?"

I turned my gaze towards the vocal inquiry, no longer in my mind but outside of me.

Sitting next to Bailey, Blair, and Blake, a calico cat blinked and smiled at me, its tail waving like a languid snake. This cat was the source of the meowing in my mind. It purred words into my being.

*O Death, where is thy sting?*

I stared at the cat's serene face.

*What strange words*, I thought. *Is this the second death Blair had warned about in Hell Track before we reached the Barrier?* I scanned beyond the calico cat: flowers of every hue and saturation overpowered my vision. *Am I back in the Expanse's Flower Power Track? No, I can't be! I refuse to visit my Earth life again!* I lifted my head, frantically searching for the postcards that had sucked me into my life review.

No postcard in sight.

I sagged back into the flowers. Transiting the Barrier had disoriented me.

I turned and pushed myself up on my hands, opened my mouth to object, a purple petal hanging off my lower lip, and gasped. The sight before me boiled away my confusion.

Flowers stood tall and short around me, far into the distance. Fields of flowers in three-sixty extended into the distance all around me. I didn't know how I grasped this three-hundred-and-sixty-degree vision. *Am I an owl now?* I twisted my head to double-check my vision. The Barrier had vanished. In its stead, flowers waved in a lazy breeze. Their vibrancy halted my gaze. Such colours, more real, more saturated, more energetic than previously in the Expanse's Flower Power Track. Sepia tinged the edges of some. Others shone in black and white, in grey scale like silver tones and nickel highlights. No, this wasn't Flower Power Track.

The golden light that had invaded me intensified, electrifying my tongue, bursting my heart, shattering my mind.

I flung myself forwards into the red, yellow, blue, purple, sepia, silver flowers, throwing my hands over the back of my head. Petals enclosed my face as I smooshed flower heads and their stems, releasing intoxicating fragrances of rose, lilac, and lily of the valley and tastes of vanilla and saffron. Tears flooded my face, and snot drained into the petals' colourful bed.

A hand patted my head awkwardly. "What should we do?" Blake whispered. Her hand stopped patting.

"She's overwhelmed," Bailey replied. "Like we were. Let her be." Blake removed her hand; I felt its absence.

I bawled.

"Meow." Calico—for that was its name I sensed—vocalized as it purred. Comfort and understanding rumbled into me.

I wailed and flung my hands forwards, my fingers scratching into the soil, grasping the colourful cacophony, unheeding of the dirt invading my fingernails. I hated dirt. I hated working in filthy soil, not knowing if a raccoon or squirrel had used it for its business. Yet here I was digging my nails into dirty soil, and how was I able to do that?

*Am I in physical form again? Hadn't death changed me into that strange energy form while I fought the Expanse's Distortans and escaped its Hell Track? And this endless flow of—*

I shook my head. *No!*

A soft, small paw touched my left forearm. The cat's toe beans roughened my skin as the calico cat padded at me, claws sheathed.

"Meow." *Calico is here.* The words entered as thought, simultaneous to my ears registering a cat's meow while my skin registered the soft hairs of its paw.

Purrs rippled my skin and vibrated the tears off my face. My nose stopped draining into the beauty I'd crushed. Yet the emotion, state, sensation that I couldn't name didn't let up. I dared not allow myself to believe that the inexplicable joy that had subsumed me in the Barrier had powered up in Heaven.

I focused on the cat. No cat existed in Flower Power Track; Greeter, the dog, had accompanied me there.

I missed Greeter.

I hitched up onto my right side to rub my chest where my heart hurt. Maybe I could stop this joy and erase this inexpressible feeling out of me. I wiped my face and opened my eyes. My left forearm lay on the flowers' velvet surfaces. Calico's claw-sheathed paw rested on my arm. I adjusted my gaze and looked into unblinking green eyes. *Calico?* Hadn't my soul family told me about a cat called "Calico"?

*Yes*, it replied. *And I'm not an "it." I'm a "they." The English neutral pronoun for living beings.*

*Cats are rude*, I remembered.

*I'm not rude. I'm blunt.*

*Greeter talked to me. Why is this thing thinking to me?*

*You're in a mood.*

*Yes, I am! That...that...thing! That stinging thing has sent me back into Hell Track! And this golden light, this joy, whatever it is, is too much! I need it to stop! Stop! Stop!*

*You're not in Hell*, Calico replied into my mind. *The sensation you can't identify is unconditional love.*

I smashed my lips together and dug my fists into my eyes.

"What are they saying?" Blake whispered to Bailey.

I expanded my chest, dropped my hands, and pushed myself up to sitting, forcing the cat's paw off me, and stared up at Blake. I sniffled. "You can't hear our thoughts? Why not? I thought we spoke through thoughts?" I couldn't stop myself from whimpering.

Bailey hunkered down so that her eyes were level with mine. "Calico has the ability to speak in a way that only those they want to hear them can hear. No one else can hear them. Calico is..." Bailey sent her eyes left towards the cat sitting placidly with their unblinking eyes staring at Bailey. "Calico is ornery."

The cat, no, Calico, grinned. I'd learned my lesson to remember and use names back in the Distortans.

The picture of the Cheshire Cat popped into my mind. I shook my head free of that memory and fell back. I stared up at the endless blue. I laid one palm over my other hand and rubbed my torso up and down, up and down. "Where am I?" I asked it. *No, they. The cat is a they*, I instructed myself.

"You call it Heaven," Blair said.

"What do you mean, I call it 'Heaven'?"

"She didn't go to church, remember, Blair?" Blake simpered.

Blair growled.

I heard a swat. I raised my head to look. The cat was glaring at Blair, who was glaring back and rubbing her leg. I guessed they were speaking to each other, and the cat was keeping me out of the conversation. I didn't like this...this unconditional love, this body-invading joy. Too much. Too much. I let my head fall back as tears salted my face and I drowned my vision in the seamless grey above me. I contemplated it. *What happened to the blue? Why grey? Why not sunny? Or still blue, like in Hell Track? Is Heaven an endless monotonous scene of flowers and grey with a cat bossing people around and this overwhelming emotion, state, sensation?*

A swishing sound reached my ears, like legs carving a path through flowers.

"Stand up."

I lowered my eyes towards the flowers. Calico had spoken. Behind the cat stood a man. Dressed in a white robe, with white hair crowning his head. Unfelt wind fluttered his garment, and his hair waved in all directions.

"Stand up for the elder," Calico commanded again.

I grumbled, "Cats are bossy everywhere." I stood up. I faced the man as I towered over the cat and tears dripped down my cheeks. *What's an elder here? An old man?*

"Enough crying," the elder adjured me. "It's time for you to complete your Soul Track."

*A boss*, I thought, as I tightened my lips and shut down my emotions. *Don't I get to rest?*

His face, lined yet unlined, almost as white as his robe, tensed as light the colour of a blushing sunrise flooded the surrounding air.

"Not yet," Bailey countered to the elder. "She must first learn about this place and her new form."

"She chose to end her Soul Track prematurely. She had relationships that hadn't ended yet as they'd been destined to. Consequences must be experienced. She must reconcile." The surrounding light intensified from blush to rose pink. The elder's face pinched against the light. My tears stopped, and I cocked my head to watch this fascinating challenge to the elder's authority.

"She will experience the consequences. She must reconcile her relationships," the elder croaked against the magenta light.

"Heal them, yes," Bailey agreed. "But not yet. She'll flounder and fail if you force her now."

*Reconcile?* I thought. I swallowed hard. I thought existence after death meant I never had to see my family again. I missed creating a friendship with my client. That hurt. But those postcards in Flower Power Track, that life review, had fixed my relationships, hadn't they? I'd seen my family's and others' perspectives and had understood them for the first time. *Isn't that understanding...what's the word?...forgiveness...doesn't forgiveness mean reconciliation? What more must I do? Why do I have to go back? No, I can't!*

The elder bowed, his torso parallel to the ground. The surrounding light softened into ruby pink. Remorse flowed out of the elder and into me. I gulped. He said, "Your failing is not my concern. Euthanasia is abhorrent—"

"It's not euthanasia," I interrupted. "It's Medical Assistance in Dying. It was my choice. I have a right to choose when to die." I muttered, "I thought it would end my existence."

"That was your first death. But first death does not end your existence, and your death is meant to come when you've finished your time on Earth. You did not do that," he told the soil and flowers beneath my feet as he remained bowing.

Confusion at his unending bow, and over what I thought I'd been told, harshened my voice. "I've been through this already!"

"You have not."

"She already did!" Blake snapped. She stepped around Bailey to stand in front of the old man and straightened her spine. I stared at her. Something was different. Blake continued, "She faced the Distortans and saw through Hell Track's seduction. She saw the truth. She accepted she exists. What more do you want?"

"Yes, she won against Hell Track's seduction, but second death still threatens her."

"Why can't she learn the rules here?"

"Rules?" He swallowed. "I apologize. Please forgive me. I'm on Welcoming duty at your entry time and you are my thousandth that I must explain dissatisfactory news to. I put my dislike of this chore onto you. Like the prodigal son in the pig sty, you must experience the results of your abominable actions and self-denying thoughts, and I am deeply sorry that I cannot be kind in telling you this. Only blunt."

I angled backwards. I edged my right foot backwards, then my left. Bailey drew abreast of Blake. "She will learn but not yet. God wants her to succeed. She needs to learn how to exist as an energy being. She needs to learn the concepts of spirits and ghosts and what she can do here and on Earth before she leaves for Earth." Bailey turned to look at me over her shoulder and instructed, "Accept his apology so that he can end his bow."

I ducked my head as I said to her back, "I accept your apology."

The elder straightened up.

"She'll be in danger on Earth if she goes there now," Blair said, drawing abreast of Bailey's other side, making the elder turn slightly away from me. I stepped backwards again, away from this terrifying elder, away from this confusing entrance to Heaven, away from the demands to reconcile. Hadn't I reconciled my past? I didn't want to face reconciling my relationships. *How can I reconcile, with me in Heaven and them on Earth? No, I'm not returning to Earth!*

Careful step by gentle backwards step, I crept into the infinite field of flowers. Flowers, I understood, even these strange flowers with their intense hues and real-time growth. Calico sat on their haunches and regarded me from behind the elder. As I walked backwards, the flowers seemed to grow taller.

I bent my knees to shrink myself and swivelled silently on my toes. I fought against running from this…this unconditional love, the ruby light, and the elder's message. With practiced ease, I blended myself into the background as the adults squabbled. I felt like a child next to these…humans? Not an adult in my sixties. I duck-walked below the level of the flower heads, trying to ease between their vibrant green stems so I wouldn't cause them to sway. I pushed the words "second death" out of my mind. I had no idea where I was going. I didn't care. Away from the challenge was what mattered.

*Is it?*

I jerked my head around. *That cat! Where is it? Them!*

Stems of every green blocked my view of the group. They hid the cat, too.

*My name is Calico. But I'll forgive you.*

*Forgive? Who are you? Why do I need your forgiveness?*

Flowers danced above my head. I was talking to myself, I decided.

Purring rumbled through me. *I'm the one who greets you at the Barrier exit and guides you in this Solar Age place most call Heaven.*

*Heaven?* I twisted and turned my head. I couldn't see the cat—

*No, Calico,* I remonstrated with myself.

I stretched my hearing and vision. Nothing. I couldn't hear my soul family or the elder. Calico had vanished from my mind. I turned to face forwards again and resumed walking away from them. The flowers leafed and blossomed in front of me as their stems grew. I straightened my legs, and I strode. I relaxed briefly. Thoughts squeezed past my control. My mind tensed.

*Danger? Ghosts? Spirits? I'm an energy being?*

I halted my escape and scanned myself. I didn't feel the same. *I'm not transparent anymore.* I played my fingertips on my face. It felt like myself before Dr. Veritas had killed me in the Dying with Dignity Suite. *Killed me.* I mulled over those words as I meandered through the flowers. Yes, I'd requested it. I'd signed the forms. But he'd seduced me into believing MAiD trumped the medications my cardiologist had prescribed. *No, those medications had killed me, too. They'd robbed me of my energy. Fatigue had ruined my life. Neither doctor had listened to me, to my needs and wants.*

I dropped my head as I admitted that the Distortans, Hell Track, and the postcards had shown me that not even I had known what my needs and wants were.

I contemplated the brown-black soil wafting petrichor between the crowded stems as these thoughts settled into my mind. Neither doctor had had my best interests at heart. One had listened to me and offered me death, believing it'd bring me the end of existence and pain. Yet he hadn't heard my innermost desires. How could he when I didn't know what I desired? I shook my head. I won't think about that. The cardiologist appeared in my memory. He had spent no time with me. I was only a biological entity with one organ that deserved his attention. A biological organ. With no desires. He'd cared only about how it beat. Not how his treatment beat my innermost self with his prescription interfering with my ability to work, sapping my energy, making me prone to unusual errors in my clients' business accounting reports and tax filings. Memories of those errors assailed me. I shoved the pain away. That was in the past. No need to remember all that now.

My mind didn't listen to my desire to block the pain. Thoughts kept coming. Neither doctor had thought my existence, my value to my clients, worthwhile.

I hiccupped.

I clapped my hand over my mouth and hunched down. I waited frozen until I felt safe to move again. I straightened and dragged my hands down my face. I hadn't wanted to die; I'd wanted health, energy—not to be fatigued from doctors' treatments. But I'd feared life; quelled at knowing people and having them know me. Would Dr. V have succeeded if I hadn't been afraid? I didn't know.

That overwhelming sensation Calico had called "unconditional love" stroked softening tendrils over my back as it left me and faded into the background.

I sighed, thinking it's too late now, and began walking again, unheeding of the beauty that inflamed my senses. *I'm not returning to Earth.*

Chapter Two

# THE WOMAN AND THE LIONESS

"Hello."

I STUMBLED, my arms whirling as my mouth fell open. I caught my balance and gawked.

"So sorry, I didn't mean to startle you."

I snapped my mouth shut and stared up at a tall woman with straight black hair and mischievous brown eyes glinting down at me.

"Who are you?" I asked.

She turned her head this way and that as if seeking an answer. She paused. Her eyes slid towards my face, and her lips twitched as she examined me. "What do you see?"

"What do I see?" I frowned at the growing flowers all around me. "Ummm. I see flowers. What do you see?" I raised my eyes to her straight nose.

The woman pointed in random directions. "Lovely tea roses, there. They remind me of David Austen roses I used to grow. Or tried to," she laughed. "Over there foxgloves blossom. Deadly, you know. And there, in the far distance, can you see through those bobbing daisy heads, the peonies? Isn't it wild how these disparate flowers bloom all at the same time and in such gobsmacking colours, here?"

I goggled at her, my eyes drawn to hers.

She returned my gaze; her brown eyes pierced me. "You feel flowers, too!"

*I feel flowers?*

*Yes!*

I wrinkled my brow.

*Oh, you're new here. I forget. I love meeting new people. They're so shiny and ignorant.* She grinned.

My lips curved against my will.

*It's wonderful here, isn't it!*

"I guess so," I spoke out loud.

"You and I seeing the same thing, our nascent minds creating the same environment, it must mean we're simpatico."

"Simpatico?"

"Absolutely. Come, let's go explore." She reached for my hand; I retracted both my hands behind my back, my hands gripping my wrists.

Her brow wrinkled. "You don't want to explore?"

"No."

"Mmm..." She hummed, staring into the distance.

I stepped sideways and paused. Her eyes remained fixed on the horizon where sky met far-off blooms. I slid my right foot backwards. She tilted her head up to scan the endless grey above us.

*Why grey?*

I froze. *That wasn't my thought,* I thought.

*No, it's my question. Why do you see grey?* she thought into my mind.

*I don't know. Because the sky here is grey?* I answered in my thoughts as I sidled my left foot to meet my right.

She shook her head, her straight hair swishing against her back. *You're the one who sees grey. I see blue. Endless blue with white puffy clouds.*

I blanked my mind and edged one foot, then the next, away from her.

"You see," she spoke out loud, startling me to a halt. "I can see what you see. It's taken me awhile to figure out how to see another person's environment. It's not easy. Well, not for me, anyway. I met this guy—a guy on Earth, but we're all genderless here. It's glorious. So freeing!" She glanced at me and then back towards the oppressive grey above. "I understand some non-English languages don't have gendered pronouns, while some have only male. Isn't language fascinating?"

Her brown eyes glinted, and her lips lifted as she side-eyed me.

*Uh-huh*, I thought. I feared my voice would croak if I spoke out loud while trying to escape her. I didn't want to have anything to do with anyone. I craved solitariness, to leave behind the overwhelming emotion that wasn't an emotion, the one Bailey had called, "love." I didn't want to be bothered by Red Robes, cats, people, Distortans, and old men. I shuddered as the image of the elder appeared in my mind.

"I know," she said. "The elders can be a bit...pretentious. And bossy," she added as an afterthought, craning her neck towards the sky.

I waited as she scanned the grey above us. *What did she mean she sees blue and I see grey?* I shivered to shake that question out of my mind. Knowledge wasn't always power. The woman's eyes squinted under their Elizabeth-Taylor-arched black brows. Shaped to capture all hearts. *Is this woman trying to capture mine? Why?* I bent my head to consider this idea and stole a glance at her through my half-closed eyes. She didn't seem unaware of me. I resumed my silent sidling away from her towards a narrow path through the tall flowers.

"I wouldn't go that way," she said.

I jerked. "What?"

She lowered her chin and faced me. Concern filled her eyes, and her mouth lay in a straight line. "I wouldn't go that way."

"Why not?"

"You'll end up back where you started."

I frowned at her.

She sighed. "You'll be back with your soul family and the annoying elder. His name is Samuel, by the way. He thinks he knows everything. Just because we're in Heaven and can hear each other's thoughts—that is, the ones we want others to hear...though they do tend to leak out, you know—

"Anyway, that doesn't mean the elders or others can't be annoying. We—" She considered me. "Well, I'll let your soul family teach you. Bailey is amazing. I really like her."

*I do, too.* The realization shocked me into halting.

"I'm glad you do. They've been waiting for you for a long time. They were so worried when you made that decision to end your life. There was lots of talk here about how to interrupt Dr. Veritas, but Jesus said we were not to interfere. Free will and all that, you know." She waved her right hand dismissively. "We're reconciled with free will here. But some still get their knickers in a knot, saying as how Jesus should interfere. The elder Samuel was most put out they were assigned to Welcoming duty as you entered Heaven; they believed you needed to be shot back onto your Soul Track. But Jesus knows God's plan." She grinned as her gaze shifted to the ground. A chuckle left her.

I cocked my head. *What's so funny about Jesus knowing God's plan? I don't understand this God thing. And who is Jesus, anyway?*

The woman flung back her head and roared. Through her laughter, she choked, "Jesus is the only one who keeps Samuel in check. Jesus's love overpowers Samuel's holiness and is why Samuel bowed in apology to you. You saw it, remember? The pink light?"

All thoughts drained from me.

She stopped laughing and pursed her lips. "I think that was the elder's third heartfelt bowing apology during their Welcoming stint." She chortled and shook her head. "Anyway, as I was saying, we all believe God should tell evil men like Dr. Veritas off. But you can't do that, can you? You gotta let the material living ones learn their lessons, like we all did over millennia of our existence. We hope they can hear their guardian angels—"

"Their what?" I exclaimed.

"Oh, you don't know?" Surprise darkened her eyes.

"Guardian angels?" I snorted. *I understand I still exist. I understand I have a soul family, even though I don't understand where they came from or why they chose me. But guardian angels? I snorted.*

She nodded.

This eavesdropping on my thoughts annoyed me.

"I get that," she said. "Bailey, Blair, and Blake will teach you how to not be eavesdropped on." She leaned in and said in a stage whisper, "Except I'm real good at it. Few can hide their thoughts from me." She giggled. I gawped, expecting to see the same predatory expression Mom had had when I was a child and she was out to catch me in doing something against her ideas. Instead, a combination of mischief, amusement, and curiosity sparkled in her eyes, the kind of curiosity that wasn't about catching people. It was...

I contemplated her face.

"I like people," she stated. "I'm endlessly curious about what makes them tick. It's heavenly here being able to be as curious as I want to be. Yeah, I try to respect people's boundaries, but you'll find the whole idea of boundaries doesn't really apply here. We get to live the way we're made. Well," she paused and bent her neck to the right as she pursed her lips and scanned my face. "Eventually. We have a lot of learning to do here. I think Bailey was going to explain that to you."

Suddenly remembering where I was, I hastily surveyed my surroundings. Stems marching close together held up waving blooms of reds and purples and pinks, with yellows and blues intruding here and there.

Silence fell.

"There's only us here, Charlotte Elisabeth."

I swivelled my eyes towards her. "How do you know my name?"

"I told you. Your soul family has been telling us all about you when they were eagerly awaiting your death so they could greet you."

"They wanted me to die?" I ejaculated.

She shook her head violently. "No, no. I didn't mean it that way. I meant they didn't want you to die when you did and in the way you did. They wanted to meet you. You know, how you can't wait to meet a friend or relative for the first time."

I stared at her. *What's she talking about?*

She bit her lip. *I'm sorry.* Sorrow filled her face.

I winced. My heart hurt. She laid her hand on my shoulder, and I recoiled. I blundered through stems and stumbled into a clearing. The woman followed.

I sensed padding coming towards me. This tall, strange woman shifted to put herself between me and the source of the padding. The flowers had heightened while we'd been talking; their blossoms danced above her head. A menacing presence approached, disturbing a trail through the flowers. The woman glanced at me over her shoulder. "Don't worry. Shelagh won't harm you. We're not yet at the point where the lion lays down with the lamb. That'll come in the Resurrection, one elder told me. The less filled-with-holiness elder than Samuel."

I couldn't see through her, and so I watched the flowers as they parted in a line drawing closer to us. Red rose heads at the edge of the clearing we stood in, parted. I peeked around her shoulders. Large golden eyes in a golden furry face stared into me as if I was lunch. I grabbed the woman's shoulders, hiding behind her back. *The lion's head Mom had mounted on our living room wall! It's come alive! Followed me here!!* Like bile, terror rose into my throat as I relived the day father had left and Mom had nailed the stuffed head on the wall, my sisters and I trying to hide from its angry golden eyes and Mom's fury.

The woman reached behind and patted my right arm. *It's okay,* she thought to me. *It's a lioness, not the head.*

I gulped. I peeked around her arm. This one didn't have the massive mane of the one Mom had defiantly displayed.

Another lion with a magnificent mane padded through the roses to stand beside her. I lurched and clung to the woman's back, unable to take my eyes off the lions.

We stood in that tableau. The roses swung back into place. The lioness sat on her haunches, her unblinking eyes on mine.

The woman nodded and stepped one step to our left, put her right arm around my waist, and pulled me forwards to stand beside and slightly behind her. "It's okay," she said. "Shelagh is here to tell you her story."

I glanced up at the woman. "Her story?"

"Yes."

I gazed into Shelagh's eyes. A kaleidoscope flashed into my mind. Images, sounds, emotions, and thoughts. Like a movie playing every scene all at once, the avalanche inundated one part of my mind, while the rest comprehended what I was seeing, hearing, feeling, smelling, and thinking in sync with the kaleidoscope. I was living the experiences and feelings of the lioness, the lion whose head decorated my mother's wall, and their cubs and young lions who hadn't yet left the pack. Bewildered, I let myself be swept into another dimension. Not a life review, not my time nor my lifetime, but...I wrinkled my brow at this familiar-yet-unfamiliar experience.

*It's a backstory,* the woman thought into my mind. *We share memories through our community in this form of time.*

*What?*

*Never mind, just experience.*

The lion was the grandfather. He'd arrived at their pride with his last surviving collaboration partner, the one standing beside Shelagh amongst Heaven's flowers, standing so still, watching me, watching me. And then I remained no more in Heaven.

GRANDFATHER LION WAS nearing the end of his last years. He and his collaboration partner decided that this pride would be his last one. The two males anticipated dying together.

The cubs cavorted through the tall grasses of the plains they lived on, safe in the lion's protective watchfulness as he lazed under the sun. Only his ears twitched as insects hovered too close in his watch place. His eyes saw every blade, every tree, every movement. His roar frightened off intruding hyenas, leaving the lionesses free to hunt for their food. The day he left them began like any other day.

The sun blazed as it did every day. Heat built up as the morning awakened. Predator birds soared overhead, and the lion heard the stamping of hooves. The cubs had nursed and were dozing, hidden in a thick patch of grass. The young lions eagerly trotted off to help the lionesses hunt. The lion's ears flicked as he reclined in his spot. The wisdom of his long years let the hunters know Shelagh and her sisters could lead the young ones to the hunt.

He was the one most familiar with the deadly growl that signalled the humans coming.

Shelagh couldn't distinguish between the good humans, with strange black things slung around their necks, and the bad ones who killed and roared off with one of their own. But the grandfather lion could. They relied on Grandfather to distinguish which was which.

He yawned that morning and flicked his ears again. Smiling and secure, the females and the juveniles left the cubs to follow the hoofbeats. His partner strolled in the heat to a thicket to doze in the shade.

The shot blasted the air, startling the birds out of the trees, the hooved ones into a run, and the lionesses and their young ones to freeze. They sensed Grandfather remained no more with them. They galloped towards their shaded home and halted when they saw the reflecting white of that which had brought humans to their home. They restrained the young ones from attacking the two-legged ones.

"You'll die," Shelagh warned

The juveniles didn't believe it. "We're the ones who rule," they rumbled. "We need to find grandfather!" One sister bit them to hold them back. They snarled but obeyed.

Shelagh lowered herself to hug the ground and crept forwards until she had a view of Grandfather's place through the concealing blades of grass. Grandfather lay on his side. Blood flowed out of his neck as a man cut off his head, sunlight glinting on his blade as blood dripped from its exposed sharp edge. The metallic taste of fresh blood flickered on her tongue. The man lifted the head away from the prone body as the cubs trembled in their concealing grassy patch, their frightened eyes widening. The man stood, hefting Grandfather's head by the mane, and strode to a tall white man who held the long killing thing against his shoulder. The cutting man held Grandfather's head out to the tall man, who handed the killing thing to a man who appeared then disappeared. He grasped Grandfather's mane and stared into Grandfather's dead eyes, blood escaping from his severed neck.

The tall man grinned and lifted the head high as his companions cheered his victory.

"One shot!" one of his companions crowed.

A girl stepped out from behind the noisy white beast, holding a killing thing, its blasting end aimed at the ground. The man strode towards her and clapped her on the shoulder. He nodded towards another man who retrieved the killing thing from the girl before disappearing behind the white thing. The tall man's teeth gleamed and his stretched lips elicited a tentative answering grin from her. He offered her the head. She grabbed a chunk of Grandfather's mane, the tall man let go, and she staggered under the weight. The man laughed and grabbed Grandfather's ears. He stood behind the girl, his holding hands hidden so that the girl simulated holding Grandfather's head by herself. Man and girl, standing together, blood oozing from Grandfather's decapitated head to redden the dusty soil beneath their feet.

Shelagh snorted with contempt. *These humans have no courage. All they have is the ability to hold a killing thing while safely snugged in their white, roaring, shiny thing. But why hadn't they heard it coming?* Grandfather knew its sound from way off.

Shelagh squinted into the now-silent white shiny thing's depths. Inside sat men with those strange black contraptions slung around their necks, watching the fatal celebration. *Had Grandfather mistaken the sound for the good humans, the ones who left them alone to live as a family?*

The cutting man shouted at the men inside the shiny thing; one of them climbed out and raised the strange black thing to his eyes and spoke incomprehensibly. The man and girl stood still as a click reverberated into Shelagh's listening ears. Another click. Then the man lowered the black contraption and signalled to the two grinning humans with his hand, palm down, waving up and down.

The man and girl with the killing things, who needed no family, no natural ability to hunt the lions' pride, unlike they who hunted the hoofed ones, hunched down. The man posed the girl with the head in her arms as if cradling a child, sorrowing at its death. The one with the black contraption moved around them. Clicks accompanied him.

Helpless rage filled Shelagh as she witnessed the ignorant humans desecrating Grandfather. She held back, knowing she could not compete with their killing things. Grandfather's collaboration partner gritted his teeth as he hunched within the cloak a nearby bush gave him. He knew, too, he couldn't kill the two-legged ones who hunted them. Those long, narrow things blast shot faster than his leaps.

THE HEAT-SOAKED plains vanished.

Grey sky and nodding flowers filled my vision.

I was shaking. I'd experienced the story as Shelagh had experienced it. Her revengeful spirit, the collaboration partner's mourning spirit, flooded my heart. Sorrow drowned me. I couldn't separate myself.

She said, "Your grandfather slayed my grandfather."

The partner rumbled, "It was the girl."

Shelagh drew back her whiskers. "He and your mom ended our family's wisdom for the sake of sport. Your grandfather and your mother denied our grandfather's collaboration partner their dying time together. It's a sacred time to be near the dying, to be with them in their last breaths."

The collaboration partner roared, vibrating my being. "You denied us our sacred time!"

My mind buzzed. My thoughts broke apart.

The two lions spat, "For sport."

Shelagh's whiskers twitched. "When your grandfather died, I found his energy being." Her whiskers lifted as she snarled, "I chased him. Without his killing thing, it's him versus me. His spirit versus mine. I claimed the right to end him. He fled." She purred-growled, "He." She snapped her head sideways towards the collaboration partner. "He reserved the right to kill your grandfather's descendants as they deserved."

The collaboration partner jerked his cheeks up and dropped his jaw. His eyes blazed. I gulped and stumbled backwards.

"Enough!" the tall woman commanded. "Forgiveness reigns here!"

Shelagh and the male, suddenly placid, blinked at me. *It doesn't mean we can't terrorize them into remorse.*

*We grow into mercy here. Remember who has the right of vengeance? Not us!* The woman answered.

*Our wounds remain unhealed!*

The woman nodded. *And so are hers. But we are here to let Jesus's unconditional love nurture us into healing our wounds and repairing our relationships.*

*We have no quarrel with you, Shireen Anne.*

*Mercy, forgiveness, reconciliation. Remember?*

*When will she reconcile our relationships?!*

I faltered. *Reconcile? With the lion's head on the wall? Wait, the girl was Mom? The man who shouted triumph, Mom's father? My grandfather? Shelagh and the male want my head! A head for a head.*

I lurched sideways and, hidden behind the woman, I turned in the opposite direction to Shelagh and my original path and fled into the concealing flowers.

# Chapter Three

# NIHIL AND SCRUFFY

*I* stretched my right hand forwards and eased aside the flower stems so that I could sidle through them. I stretched my left hand to the next group of stems to push them aside unobtrusively. I didn't want the flower heads swaying and giving away my position. I'd been walking this careful way through the flower field for hours. *I'm tired, weary. No!* I adjured myself. *Don't think yourself into fatigue. My being...*

*Am I physical or energy or spirit? What is spirit, anyway?* I shook my head free of these thoughts. I feared active thoughts might give away my path. But, oh, how I longed to rest.

I stretched my right hand forwards, and it entered empty air. I halted. I leaned one way then the opposite, but I couldn't see through the stem forest. I bent forwards at the waist and poked my head through the stems. An olive tree, old and gnarled, abided on the side of a small ragged circle of thick grass, the tree-high flowers acting as a circular concealing wall. A bench of wooden slats waited beneath the tree.

I rushed through the intervening stems and collapsed on the bench. My legs splayed out; my head flopped against the rough bark of the tree. A rush of air exited my mouth. *Air? Breath? I can't be back on Earth! Can I? No, the elder said I had to be sent back, and no one had sent me back. I'm safe.*

I let my eyelids drift down, vanishing the sight of my corner of Heaven hidden from the elder, the tall woman, my soul family telling me I had to return to Earth. I closed my eyes against the overarching grey and joyous colourful riot before me.

A rustle.

I half-lifted my eyelids.

Grey, like that of slate, filled my vision. My eyes snapped open. I followed the grey up to a sharp-angled face. Eyes, cold and hard, stared into mine. I froze.

After a while, the face, so close to mine, retreated three centimetres. Another woman. Chin-length straight black hair framed her features. She straightened up, and her hair swung with her movement. Clasping her hands behind her back, with twisted lips, she scanned me from my feet to the top of my head. I followed her gaze. I was wearing what I'd died in. *Do people exist for all eternity in the same clothes they died in?*

"No."

Her voice sliced through me. I scrabbled backwards, but the olive tree held firm.

"You're Charlotte Elisabeth," she stated.

*Does everyone here know who I am?*

"Bailey, Blair, and Blake talked about you endlessly. Whoever was near them heard about you. Why'd you run away just now? It's futile. Calico knows where everyone is all the time. Calico has a ninth sense. You can't escape the cat."

I blinked up at her. *Who is this person?*

"I'm Nihil."

"Uh, nice to meet you?"

Nihil cocked her head and squinted at me. "Is it?"

I didn't know what to think or say.

"Good. That's the truth. You can't lie here. Don't try."

"Okay."

Nihil nodded, her mouth relaxing into a straight, tight line. Her hands let go of themselves behind her back, and her arms fell forwards to her side. She turned her back to me and craned her neck to observe the flower heads. "Interesting environment you've created here. Why grey sky and pink daisies?"

"I don't know."

She swivelled her head around to contemplate me. "You don't know? Did you run away before anyone had a chance to explain Heaven to you?" Her lips stretched. Her eyes remained hard. "No one escapes Calico before the cat can explain the 'rules.'"

"Rules?"

"Yes, the rules."

"Why are there rules? Do they have laws here?"

Nihil tsked. "Not legal rules or parent rules. Heaven rules are about existence."

She'd lost me.

"If you hadn't been a coward, you'd've understood."

I shot up. "I'm not a coward."

Nihil faced me fully, leaned into my face, and said, "You are."

My fingers curled into my palms, but alarm shut my mouth and my thoughts.

Nihil raised her eyebrows.

Dragged into answering, I whispered, "Why are you bothering me?"

Nihil straightened, crossed her arms, and smirked. Her grey eyes, like mirrors of the sky, bore into mine. "I wanted to see for myself this person-being who'd escaped Calico."

I blinked.

"You're not on Earth. It's not like you can hide here. We all have our environments." She waved her hand at the sky. "You know, you created this grey sky."

"I did."

"I can see other humans' environments, too." She growled, emphasizing the pronoun, "She isn't the only one who can do that."

*She? Oh, the tall woman.*

"Your thoughts. The way you are, you know, you created this." She stared at me until my eyes lowered under hers. "Even so, here, in

Heaven, we're all connected, whether we like it or not. We learn to keep our private thoughts barricaded against eavesdropping." Nihil frowned. "Except that one person who somehow knows how to eavesdrop on private thoughts, too. I hate her." The venom in those last words shocked me. Was this Heaven no different from Earth?

I stared into the distance and wondered: *Is she talking about the woman I'd met?*

"Yes, her, Shireen Anne!" Nihil spat.

Silence descended. A breeze ruffled my hair and lifted her fine, black strands. She dropped her arms. "Heaven is peculiar. You'll learn about it. It's not as bad as the Distortans—"

"You experienced those, too?" I interrupted, shocked to meet another survivor.

"Yes."

"Did you have a soul family to guide you?"

Nihil's face stilled.

I puckered my brow, searching for a hint of her thoughts.

Suddenly, I felt less lonely. I wanted to know more. This strange person intrigued me. I didn't know why.

Nihil snapped her head around and stared into the forest of fresh green stems. The blue snapdragons in the distance swayed. Then, the burgundy roses afore them bounced left, then right. The pink daisies that bordered this grassy rest area parted. A dog emerged. Fur stood out from its rectangular snout like a derecho had stormed it. Smaller than Greeter, it trotted up to Nihil and thought, *There you are.*

I gaped. Scruffy. I knew its name was Scruffy. *How do I know its name?*

Nihil growled, "Dogs have special powers to communicate their essence to you sans thought, instantly. It's annoying." She turned her back on it. It sat on its haunches, like it was used to being ignored.

"It's just a dog. Ignore them. They think they're God's special creatures, above us all, because of their special powers."

I stared at her. I lowered my gaze guardedly towards Scruffy. Their brown eyes loved her. I blinked. *How do eyes love?*

"You're hallucinating," Nihil said brusquely.

My eyes jerked to her face. "That's what Dr. V said about near-death experiences. But he was wrong."

Nihil's face pinched in on itself.

I had a sudden idea. "Did Scruffy accompany you through the Distortans?"

"Yes."

My eyes widened. I'd thought only humans accompanied humans through that terrifying landscape. "Did you see the Red Robes, too?"

Nihil frowned at me. "Who?"

I shook my head. "Never mind. I don't want to go back to Hell Track or see those rationalizing liars again."

"I told you. You can't lie in Heaven. God sees all, and Jesus reveals all."

My behind landed abruptly on the bench. I tired of all this talk of God and Jesus. *I want to rest!*

"You can't."

Scruffy stretched their back legs, then their forelegs. They lowered their rump to the grass and rested their chin on their forelegs.

I steadied my head against the comforting rough bark of the ancient olive tree and closed my eyes. "Why can't I rest?"

"Because you have work to do here. You have to learn the rules first. You know, the ones about your new type of existence. You're not material anymore. You're...well...you'll learn about your new form and how you have to continue your Soul Track like the rest of us."

"What if I don't want to? I had no choice but to go through the Distortans, Hell Track, that endless life review—" I opened my eyes and stared into her grey garment. "Why can I remember every detail of my life from my birth on in crystal clarity?"

"You're not a physical being anymore."

I raised my arm and examined it. "I can't see through it like I did while in the Earth-Heaven Interdimensional Expanse. So I must be physical again."

"You're not."

I set my mouth. "Physical means not being transparent. I'm not transparent. Reality here is strange, sure. I've never seen these kinds of flowers grow as tall as sunflowers or trees. Nor colours so vibrant they feel like they're vibrating my retinas. But I can feel my arm." I stroked it. "It's like my flesh again. I'm not on Earth am I? They didn't send me back without me knowing, did they? That elder was—"

"I know. That was Samuel," Nihil said, cutting me off. "You're not on Earth. You're in Heaven, the second stage of reality. You can't escape it, no matter how hard you try." She muttered, "I know because I tried."

"Why did Scruffy accompany you through the Distortans?"

"Scruffy's not my dog."

"But—"

"No buts. Stop trying to avoid the reality of your situation. Go back to Calico. Learn about Heaven." Nihil turned away from me and stepped towards the flowers. Scruffy didn't move, and she had to zigzag around him.

"Science teaches us about reality," I said to her retreating back.

Nihil stopped. She spoke over her shoulder. "Are you certain?"

I stood up. "Yes."

"Then how does your science explain this?" She gestured to the giant flowers and seamless grey above me. "Or the Distortans?"

"I don't know. But there must be an explanation. I accept Dr. V was wrong. I accept first death and that I died in the Dying with Dignity Suite. I accept I continued to exist after I died. But I don't accept that I'm not physical when I'm as opaque as when alive. We're made up of atoms and molecules. I don't know why I was transparent while in the Expanse and why I'm not here. But...nothing else makes sense scientifically, so I must still be physical."

Nihil turned back to face me. Her glacier eyes scraped me. "Why?"

I faltered. "Wisdom of Wrath judge said I'd killed my body. But here it is." I raised my arms at her. "My body exists. I exist."

"Is that enough?"

"What?"

Nihil stared at me.

*Will I never escape questions?*

Nihil smiled with her lips. She raked my face with those icy eyes. "Bailey is advocating for you not to go back to Earth yet. Samuel is relentless. That elder gets their way every time. But I'd put my money on Bailey. She's formidable. Those three—your soul family," Nihil drawled. "They'll return to Earth with you for the next stage of your Soul Track. You're lucky, and you don't know it."

"If you believe I'm lucky, then why must I return to Earth?"

"To reconcile with your family."

*That's impossible! My Soul Track is done! Why do I have to face my family? How can I reconcile with them? That's impossible!* A command rose from deep within me: *Flee! Flee further into Heaven so no one can find you!!*

Nihil raised her right eyebrow. I hated people who can raise one eyebrow. They liked to show off their superior physical skills. *Boastfulness is the worst human trait,* Mom used to lecture me. *Never boast.* Amusement shone out of Nihil's eyes as she canted into my face.

I reared back. The bench hit the back of my knees. I fell hard onto the wooden slats, yet my bones and muscles communicated no pain, only pressure. Nihil bent down to my level, her nose centimetres from mine, her arms crossing, her eyes glinting triumph.

"Bark," Scruffy voiced.

Nihil scowled.

Scruffy stood and trotted over. They wedged themself between her legs and mine and pushed against her legs. She frowned down at Scruffy's chaotic fur and dropped her arms as she staggered backwards until the dog stopped pushing her away from me. Scruffy raised their head and barked up at her.

I understood their bark. *How's that possible?*

The dog sat down, facing Nihil, separating her from me.

"All right," she groused. "All right. I get the message."

She straightened and explained, "Heaven is about completing your Soul Track. You learn some things on Earth, and some things in Heaven. You didn't finish your Soul Track on Earth. You were supposed to have reconciled with your family before you died. I don't know how. I can't read God's mind. If I could, I wouldn't have this mutt following me everywhere I go. But it is what it is. Accept it."

She stared at me for a moment, an eternity. "Return to your soul family, listen to Samuel, learn the rules, and return to Earth. You can't escape." She rolled her eyes. "They let you run away from the

Barrier and the Welcoming Place to give you space. But they only have to focus on you to find you wherever you are in Heaven. And, if they can't," Nihil shrugged. "Calico will rat you out." Nihil paused and stared at me like she was thinking. But I couldn't read her thoughts.

*Why not?* I wondered. *Is it true we can keep some of our thoughts private? Doesn't that mean we're physical beings like on Earth? We are physical!*

"I'll go with you."

"What?"

"I'll go with you and the three 'Bs.' I'll go with you to Earth. I want to see how you reconcile with your family. If you can," Nihil smirked. "I may even help you. You intrigue me. This place has been deadly dull for ages. You're like a new puzzle I can play with."

I didn't like the sound of that. Yet...

Nihil nodded. She swivelled on her heels and stomped off, Scruffy trotting behind her. Nihil crashed through the stem forest, flinging blossoms higgledy-piggledy, their petals scattering down like rain. Scruffy followed, and they disappeared. The flowers stopped swaying. I rested my head against the tree. It comforted me. I fell asleep.

# Chapter Four

# FREDERICK

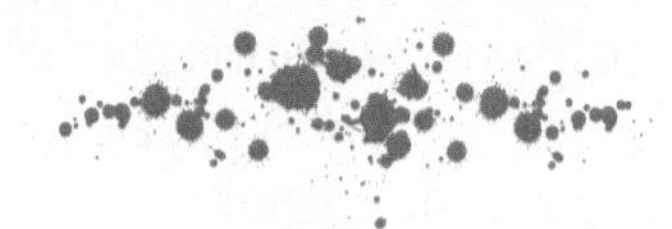

Eyes bored into me. Their intent nudged my eyelids up. I resisted.

*Resistance is futile.*

*Who said that?* I grimaced and opened my eyes.

Nihil and the man from the Earth-Heaven Interdimensional Expanse stood in front of me, eyes on my face. Or rather, Nihil was glaring at me; the man was switching his eyes from glaring at her to looking at me with...

I rubbed the thought out of my head and sat up straight.

Scruffy scratched themself.

Their rhythmic scratches sounded loud in the still air. He tilted towards his scratching foot, moaning. Tilting and tilting, yet not falling. Nihil followed my fascinated gaze. She rolled her eyes, saying, "That dog won't fall. They's like that Leaning Tower of Pisa."

Scruffy fell.

And woofed-squeaked.

They hastily leapt up and shook their whole body, their stumpy tail at attention like a stiff flag. I wrinkled my nose against musky-dog smell.

"Ahhh-choo!" Scruffy's nose hit the dry grass. They blinked in confusion. Wobbling, they sat down again.

I choked back a laugh. Somehow, Scruffy's fur stood on end more chaotically than before. The flowers swished behind me, and the scent of roses flourished the air. I glanced behind me. *Had the roses shrunk?* I squinted at them, rotating to survey them all.

Scruffy lifted their left hind leg and dug their claws into their ear. Scratch, scratch, scratch. They were off again, fanatically scratching at a hidden itch.

*Has to be fleas, otherwise why the incessant scratching?* I decided.

I stood up, skirted around Nihil and Scruffy, avoided Scruffy spraying dandruff and fleas, and approached the swaying roses, now shorter than me.

*No fleas. No dandruff. I like scratching,* came the thought flaring into my mind. I batted it away because who likes scratching? Scruffy scratched louder.

I scanned the distance. Flowers created a colourful blanket that met the seamless grey sky at the horizon. *This place has horizons, too,* I thought.

"Are you done sleeping?" Nihil asked my back.

"Let her be," said the man in a rich baritone. His rumble comforted me. I refused to dwell on why.

"You don't like to think about a lot of things, do you?" Nihil asked.

I kept my back to her. I drowned my gaze in the colours before me, a tapestry of red dots in yellow and blue fields, with purple lines and burgundy squiggles. The tapestry swayed. In some places, the flowers circled like helicopter blades were disturbing them. In other places, they waved back and forth. I fixated on the shapes and movements. Fixation kept thoughts at bay.

Nihil blocked my vision. Her sharp-angled face frowned down at me. "Don't you want to know the rules?"

The man said from behind me, "There's time enough for Charlotte Elisabeth to learn them."

I let Nihil's grey top blur in my vision, letting the colour be all that I perceived.

She waved a hand in front of my eyes, but I'd long since perfected the art of blurring what I was looking at so that I perceived only it in my mind while being aware of what Mom was doing and yelling. One needed both to stay safe.

Nihil huffed. "Does she even know who she is?"

"Does it matter?" the man asked.

"Of course it matters," Nihil exclaimed as she stepped around me. The two argued behind my back. Scruffy stopped scratching and trotted up to my right leg. Coarse, sand-coloured fur tickled my calf as they lay down with a sigh.

"You can't reconcile with family unless you know yourself," Nihil stated.

"You may be right, but sometimes it's better to reconcile first."

"That's sophistry, Fred."

"Frederick."

"Fred. Frederick. Whatever."

"Do you know yourself?"

"Of course."

Silence. I sensed him raising his eyebrows. *Three-hundred and sixty vision is real!* I didn't know whether I liked it. *So his name is Frederick. It suits him. Feels solid, dependable.* I caught myself and refocused on the shifting flower tapestry. *I don't think they're picking up my thoughts,* I reassured myself.

"She's barely accepted she exists. Why the rush, Nihil?"

"Time waits for no one."

"But time doesn't exist here."

"Not as we know it, you're right." Nihil exhaled in one sharp blow. "Only God exists outside of time."

I heard the irritated swish of an arm slicing through the air and saw it, too. *I see what's behind me! Maybe this three-sixty vision isn't so bad.* I mentally batted away liking anything, for then I'd have to agree with resuming my Soul Track. I glared at a fat red tea rose, silver outlining its generous petals. The silvered red rose filled my vision. I remembered roses like that in a neighbour's garden. They had had no scent. *Sterile beauty,* I thought. *Here, too?* I wondered. I buried my nose in its lush centre and inhaled. Intense rose fragrance tinted with silvery chimes and a clean smell surged into me. I reared up, stifling an insistent cough and an insistent sneeze, and stumbled backwards, my arms pinwheeling. I caught myself. The fragrance faded from my senses as I put distance between me and the rose.

"Time exists on Earth, and we're connected here," Nihil said coldly.

"Only when we go down there do we experience familiar time," Frederick retorted.

"Which you do a lot. What are you looking for, Frederick?" Her smarmy tone hunched my shoulders. I forced them down. I avoided looking at the rose and focused instead on a streak of midnight blue daisies. The calm of a twilight with scents of the ocean wafted through me.

"You know who, Nihil. My father. He's lost," Frederick answered.

"Have you ever met him?"

Scruffy snorted in their sleep as Frederick replied, "You know I haven't. Why do you pepper me with the same questions every time we meet? Are you trying to distract me from your nihilistic viewpoint of existence?"

"Existence doesn't end. We must endure. Charlotte Elisabeth must go on her Soul Track, just as I was forced to. There, you know my viewpoint."

"But you haven't finished your Soul Track, Nihil."

"Have you?"

Silence descended. The absence of sound stretched and lengthened. *Frederick, like many men, manipulates the art of silence to silence women*, I thought. I sympathized with Nihil. *It's like arguing with Mom. You can't win. It's best to leave. Can I leave? I'd left the elder, Calico, and Bailey and company. Then I'd left that woman...what was her name...Shireen Anne...yes, Shireen Anne, and I'd left Shelagh and the male lion. Nihil had left me because I'd driven her away. But she'd returned and brought this man with her. Frederick. The man who'd known me at university. Do I remember him? I squinted into the grey sky. I do...only now...I don't want to. The past—my Earth existence—it's over! Why had he helped me with my knapsack?* I pressed my lips together at this errant question.

"Death is final," I blurted to the blue daisies. Their blue heads pirouetted and leaned in. "I may exist, but death ended my life. All there is are flowers and grey sky. Why argue?"

Two sets of eyes drilled my back. I refused to turn around. *I have three-sixty vision*, I thought. *I don't have to obey the rules of Earth here.* A dawning understanding of what that meant lifted a weight off my heart.

"Death isn't final," Frederick said in soft tones. "It doesn't even end our time on Earth. We're in the Solar Age, and it will last beyond our ability to understand. God is the only one who knows when. God has created—"

"Enough about this God," I interrupted.

"Okay," he said. "Let's agree we are still alive."

"I agree we still exist," I said to the rose stems gathered closely together in front of me.

"I agree with you," Nihil said. "We exist, and existence is infinite and to be endured."

"We can do more than endure it," Frederick said. "We're here to grow. Like those flowers. Like characters in a story, except we're not fictional."

"What happened to the flowers?" I asked.

"You slept," Nihil stated.

I turned around. I lifted my face to look into their two faces. One sharp-angled, with cold grey eyes. The other with its defined jaw, soft brown eyes, and wavy chestnut brown hair.

They watched me, Nihil like a predator eyeing its prey, Frederick like he wanted me to...I shook my head. Scruffy stood up, stretched their forelegs, and trotted around me to sit beside Nihil.

"Why do you dislike Scruffy?" I asked Nihil.

"They's always there."

I frowned up at her. She shrugged and looked away.

"I have to return to the entrance, don't I?" I asked, hoping they'd say I didn't have to.

"Bailey, Blair, and Blake will find you when they believe you're ready to hear them," Frederick consoled.

I shrugged and stared at the ground. Grass grew thick and vibrant green. Greener than the grass on Earth. Yet grass green. *Hadn't the grass been dry?* Confusion knitted my eyebrows.

"Reality messes with your mind here, doesn't it?" Frederick said.

I raised my eyes and contemplated his face. "Yes. Why are we here?"

He wrinkled his brow. "I don't know. I believe we're like…"

A whoosh startled me. I jumped and turned one hundred and eighty degrees. Shireen Anne vaulted through the silvery-red roses as if they had no guarding thorns and thumped feet on the ground in front of me. I reared back and bumped into Frederick. His solid chest startled me, and I flung myself forwards.

"Whoa," Shireen Anne said as she grabbed my upper arms. She released me. "I can answer your question. God created us. We're like the characters in a novel. Our author created us, and we're in storytelling time now. Writers decide what we do…well, some writers claim that their characters create the dialogue and action. But who knows, really, eh? I have some theories about where characters come from. But, anyway, we are real. God created us, then God set us free. Though we're supposed to end up where God intended us to…eventually, anyway." She shrugged, eyes sparking with mischief as she wound down.

I needed to sit.

I back-walked to the bench and collapsed onto it, knowing exactly where it was even though I'd kept my back to it. This new vision discombobulated me, yet I liked it. *There!* I thought. *I admit I like this vision!* And somehow I can use it as if I'd always seen that way.

"It's freaky, isn't it?" Shireen Anne chuckled.

I nodded. "But. I don't like the idea of being a character under someone else's control. Why can't death be final?"

"Where's the fun in that?" Shireen Anne asked. She gestured to the other two. "We all landed here, wondering what had happened. When I was alive—alive on Earth, that is, not like vibrantly alive here." She stretched her arms wide and flung back her head. Dropping her eyes back to me, she continued, "When I was alive, I thought—no, I'd hoped—but wasn't sure death isn't the end. I'd read all the scriptures and stories about what happens after we die, but—"

She shrugged a shoulder and let it drop. Her eyes darkened in memory, and her mouth straightened. "Personally, that emotion that's a state and a sensation, that greets us, it overwhelmed me." The other two nodded in agreement. "I bawled like a baby, I have to admit. I bawled and bawled." Shireen Anne's eyes lit up and her lips quirked. "They ran around not knowing what to do with me! I'd never cried so hard in my life, feeling that unconditional love and strange joy. It was like coming home."

Frederick added, "It was. I hugged everyone."

"Even Samuel!" Shireen Anne choked on a laugh.

"Even Samuel," he admitted.

"How about you, Nihil? What did you do in the face of that overpowering love?"

"I left," she said shortly.

*Like me*, I thought.

I contemplated these three strangers, who knew me and treated me like a...I averted my gaze then stole a glance back up at them. The three loomed before me. Nihil's face expressionless. Frederick's concerned. Shireen Anne's vibrating with energy. *She's exhausting*, I thought.

*People say that about me a lot*, she thought to me. *I don't mind. I am who I am. What about you?*

I dropped my eyes to the grass. I thought I'd left questions behind when I'd escaped the Distortans' hold on me. *Where are you going human-killer?* I gasped as that repetitive question ricocheted in my mind. I slapped my head repeatedly against the Distortans' question.

"You're not a human killer. Don't believe those Distortans. You faced them down and left them behind in the Interdimensional Expanse. Forget what isn't worth remembering." Frederick's voice snapped my head up. He repeated those words. "You are alive. You have a soul family. You have us."

"You?" I frowned. "What do you mean 'us'?"

"We're your friends." Shireen Anne said. Scruffy swished their tail back and forth. Nihil stared at me, eyes shuttered, face blanked.

Since Dr. V had tried to heal me through life-ending death but had succeeded only in sending me into the Distortans, Hell Track, and those endless postcards of my life review, I felt like I'd been on a treadmill sped up to beyond my capability. The treadmill had flung me off, spun me out of reality, and hurtled me into a surreal existence.

Frederick leaned down and grabbed my hand. "You're not spinning off. You're not alone."

I pulled my hand out of his grasp. "I'm always alone." I paused as part of me rejected that thought. I had to admit my soul family hadn't left me.

*You see*, Shireen Anne burbled in my thoughts. *You're not alone.*

"You have work to do," Nihil stated. "Stop stalling, learn the rules, and return to Earth."

*No!*

"Yes."

I glared up into her stony eyes. "If I can do what I want then I'm not returning to Earth. Those relationships are over. It's not possible to reconcile with Mom. Yes," I nodded, "I regret not spending more time with Sincerity. But there are no second chances once you're dead. And I'm dead. Yes, I admit I exist. I still exist. But that doesn't mean I'm alive. I don't even know how to reconcile. Shelagh is out for my end. I wanted to end my life, enter sweet oblivion, be done with pain of every kind. I didn't want to live anymore. The Expanse got me to admit I was lying to myself, that the truth was, I wanted to live.

"But if I have to exist, I don't want some lioness angry at my grandfather taking her revenge out on me. What did I do to her? I had nothing to do with what happened! I didn't like his head on the wall. It scared me. It terrified and repulsed my sisters and me. But Mom does what she wants, and we three have no say. You say I can do what I want? Then I want to be alone like I always have been!"

The three humans and one dog didn't move. Scruffy yawned and sat, sighing-singing as they closed their jaw and leaned against Nihil's leg. Their eyes drifted closed. Nihil didn't move.

The silence screamed into my mind. The scentless air sucked my breath.

"I want to reconcile with my father," Frederick said. "My mother didn't tell me who he was. She wouldn't let me meet him. She had so many lovers she may not have known who my father was. She used to tell me, 'At least I kept you. I could've aborted you, you know.' But she thought a cute son would keep her boyfriends longer. She was the one who got bored with me when a new one caught her eye. I may not know who my father is, but I believe this next stage of life will guide me to him. We can then reconcile. Don't lose hope."

*Hope?*

*Yes, hope,* he replied in my thoughts.

I rubbed my head. I sagged against the gnarled olive tree. The scent of old wood and fresh fruit hugged me. I desired sleep. I yearned never to wake up.

"Let's let her be," Frederick murmured. Through my slitted eyes, I saw him herd the other two towards the rose entrance to the flower field. Scruffy trotted after them.

Peace settled my limbs.

My eyelids drifted down. The sight of this place I didn't want to be in vanished.

# Chapter Five

# FOUND

*S*lurp. Ice cream slid into a sundae glass with a plonk. Desire Distortan stood in front of me, their green gelatinous blob jiggling with merriment. They pushed the fluted, frosted sundae glass at me. My mouth watered at the scoops of chocolate and burnt banana ice cream nestled in whipped cream clouds with a ribbon of chocolate fudge sauce weaving through it to pool at the bottom.

I screamed.

My eyes shot open. *Am I dreaming? Is this reality? Am I back in Desire?* I choked on a silent sob. *Where am I?* A line from Romeo and Juliet played in my mind. *Wherefore art thou Heaven?* I giggled. *Am I delirious?* The ancient olive tree's rough bark scratched my back through my dress as I stirred. I straightened up and noticed the flowers. They'd shrunk. Their heads bobbed below my seated eye level.

I remembered.

My Soul Track isn't over.

Calico sauntered through the flower stems, stirring them gently as their sleek calico-coloured body undulated in tune with their waving tail.

Calico padded towards me until they reached my feet. They stopped. They sat. They blinked depthless green eyes up at me in ecstasy. Scruffy bounced through the flower stems, flinging rose petals upwards and dragging daisy and peony blooms with them where they fell onto the flattened grass.

"You're awake."

*Where had Nihil appeared from?*

"One of the wonders of Heaven. We don't have to use our feet to move if we don't want to." Nihil smiled with her mouth.

Calico purred, and Scruffy braked next to the cat, flinging soil onto my calves.

"Woof!"

My eyes widened. *Aren't cats and dogs natural enemies?*

Calico's whiskers twitched up as they smirked. Scruffy jumped up, all four paws airborne. They landed, pushing suffering grass into the messed-up soil. "Bark!" Scruffy snuffled Calico's cheek. Licked Calico from chin to ears. And sat.

Smugness oozed out of Calico's eyes. Desire clung to the vestiges of my dream state. *Had I been asleep? Is it possible to dream when existing but no longer alive?*

*You're alive,* Calico thought into my mind.

I shook my head. "I exist. I admit it. But life? Life was material on Earth. That was reality. What you can see, touch, hear, smell, and taste. I dreamed of ice cream, but where is the food?"

"You don't need any," Nihil said.

"Then this is not life. It's not reality. We all know we cannot live without food and water. I haven't drunk water in..." I frowned. How much time had passed since I'd died?

*Time moves differently after death and before the Resurrection,* Calico thought. *What matters is your growth. You can't escape that.*

"Why not?"

Calico's furry brows pulled together. Then they rolled their eyes up. I sensed impatience. I sensed they'd heard this a million times before, and it bored them.

I said, "I can't help it if it's the truth. And others before me knew it."

Calico lowered their gaze and pulled my attention into them. *You don't know the truth about this place yet. Or life. Or reality. You have work to do. Samuel is obnoxiously insistent. So, you must return to the Barrier Welcoming Place. Now.*

I flattened my back against the tree. The bark with its cracks and ridges dug into my back, yet I felt no pain. The sensation swept me into the tree's life. Through touch I saw the grooves time had wrought into the tree's trunk and sensed branches twisting with age; I heard the sap slipping through the tree's cells; I smelled herbaceous olives as their incubating flowers fruited. Physical yet not physical sensations through an unearthly three-hundred-and-sixty vision. The gnarled olive tree comforted me. *I'm not leaving this place—this eternal rest. It's all I need and want. Why must I complete my Soul Track?*

Scruffy raised themself up to balance on their back legs and laid their paws on my knees. I leaned forwards and stroked the coarse fur on their head. *Maybe I won't see Greeter again,* I sniffed, *but this dog also seems to know what I need.* My face lowered towards Scruffy's forehead as I stroked between their ears, front to back, front to back. The fur I was stroking wettened.

"It's no use crying," Nihil said.

Tears sloshed down my cheeks, and Scruffy raised themself a little and licked them. I blubbered. Their soft tongue dried my cheeks like a mother wiping away a child's tears. *I wish I'd had a dog. I could've used this comfort through those long childhood years. Where's Frederick?*

"He's off looking for his father. It's his obsession. His concern lasts only as long as he takes a short break from his search."

*Oh.*

Scruffy's brown eyes exuded warmth, and my tears dried. I sat up, letting my hand fall to my side. Scruffy lowered their front paws back to the ground.

Calico stood. Arched and bowed in yoga's cat pose. Shaking each paw free of soil first, they turned towards the flower field. Against my will, I stood and followed. I wiped tear residue off my cheeks with the backs of my hands as I threaded my way through the cypress-green stem forest. The blossom tapestry had changed. No longer full-blown flowers swayed above my head. Now buds reached for the grey sky in the breeze-less air as far as my vision saw.

*It's not air,* Calico said. *You don't need to breathe anymore. Your energy comes from the particles of the universe. Photons feed you. Electrons quench your thirst. You're no longer atoms and molecules, as you know them. You are mind. A particle-mesh that physicists and cosmologists have yet to discover. They call it dark energy.*

*Dark energy? No, Charlotte Elisabeth, don't ask. It doesn't matter if I don't know that term. What matters is I'm solid, unlike in the Interdimensional Expanse.*

*Can you see through intense light?*

I frowned. *Can I? Nooo...I'm not sure.*

*Then you have your answer.*

I frowned. *I do?* I sidestepped the question. It hurt too much to think, to understand. *Maybe I can return to the olive tree's rest.*

Nihil snickered behind me. "There's no rest for the wicked."

I twisted my head around to stare at her.

"We're not perfect just because we're in Heaven. We're the wicked."

I scowled. *I don't consider myself wicked.* I turned back to face the direction we were walking in.

Nihil guffawed behind me. "You think you're not wicked? But you don't want to reconcile with your family?"

I halted. She bumped into my back. I shrugged her off me and spun to face her. "It's not that I don't want to. It's not possible!" I howled.

"What's impossible is your attitude."

"And your attitude is A-okay, is it?" Anger boiled in me. *Why can't people leave me alone?*

Calico bumped into my knees, buckling my legs and pushing me into Nihil. Nihil didn't react. She stood there, her arms at her side, as I grabbed at the grey cloth of her top and tried to stay upright.

*Don't stop!* Calico's forceful thought clanged through me. I stopped scrabbling for purchase and fell against Nihil's unyielding chest. I rested my head briefly on her shoulder. I cried silently, *I can't face that overwhelming emotion, sensation, whatever that love is. I can't face it again!*

Calico jolted my legs. *Unconditional love from Jesus will not kill you. God's breath-love created Heaven and sustains all of us. Face it!*

I gripped Nihil's shoulders. Pushed myself upright. Dusted myself down. Turned and followed Calico's undulating flag tail. Nihil followed with Scruffy trotting beside her.

"What is Heaven, anyway?" I grumbled. "Bailey said she'd tell me after the Barrier. I've crossed the Barrier, and I still don't know what this place is."

Calico thought, *This place is where souls travel to after death. But not all souls. Many peoples created versions of the after-first-death story. Storytellers like Star Trek's—*

"I'm a fan," Nihil interrupted. "Are you, Charlotte Elisabeth?"

*—their own versions to imagine what is unknown. Ancient people spoke of it in metaphors. The good go to Heaven; the bad to Hell.*

"Hell Track," I muttered, shivering and faltering.

Calico stopped and faced me. *It's not that simple. God wants all their Creation to live with them. God doesn't want to say goodbye to anybody. God created this place as a way station on the way to—*

Calico lowered their eyes as if someone had spoken to them. They bowed their head. *I apologize. I've overwhelmed you. Right now, all you need to know is that Heaven is connected to Earth. It's a place where you continue your Soul Track or, if you've completed it, continue to grow towards the next stage for humans. Not all arrive here. Not because they're bad people but because they don't want to.* Calico's thoughts loudened. *They hang onto their resentments, spewing their jealousies, pettiness, greed, and unbridled desires like viruses.*

"They created the Earth-Heaven Interdimensional Expanse!" I ejaculated.

Calico snarled. *Yes. They resisted being pulled towards Heaven. They remained stuck in the Expanse, and some boomeranged back onto Earth. But you'll learn more once we return to the Welcoming Place.* Calico stomped through the daisy buds, head high, tail waving, body weaving in sync, like a Sphinx.

The flower field vanished. We arrived at the Barrier-exit-slash-Welcoming-Place and the group I'd fled from. I braced myself against that overpowering love state, which had earlier torn apart my emotional stability. A whisper of it gentled my arms, caressed my face. I gulped against another geyser of grief and—

I averted my mind from emotions I didn't want to identify. Bailey, Blair, and Blake turned in unison from their argument with Samuel. Blake skipped towards me. She hugged me hard, assuaging the weeping threatening to swamp me again. "There you are! Bailey's winning." She grinned and looked over her shoulder at Samuel. He looked put out.

"I concede," he said and stomped off.

Blake let go of me and stuck her tongue out at his retreating back.

*This is like Earth,* I thought. *People argue here. They get upset with each other here. But they're telling me I have to reconcile. Don't reconciled people always get along?* I sighed. I didn't want this kind of existence. Struggle defines life. *Does it have to define existence as well?*

Calico thought, *Heaven is mistaken for a place of harps and boring paradise. Humans cannot grow without conflict.*

Bailey walked over to me and placed her right hand on my shoulder. She leaned into my gaze. "It's okay, Charlotte Elisabeth. We're here with you. Always. You'll see. It's not as hard as you think. Your life hasn't ended. It's begun."

I pressed my lips together. That dream or vision of Desire had reminded me otherwise. Life had ended.

Bailey shook my shoulder and smiled. She let go. She gestured to Blair and Blake. "We're going to teach you about Heaven. The crucial lesson you must learn is to pray."

"Pray?" I wrinkled my brow as I tried to remember. "Isn't prayer that thing people say doesn't work and they dropped it because of that? Thoughts and prayers became thoughts?"

"Prayer works," Blair said.

I blinked. I didn't know what prayer was and didn't want to. I'd left learning behind, or so I'd hoped.

Blake threaded her right arm through my left and hugged me to her side. "Hey Charlotte Elisabeth, you'll like prayer. "

"I will?"

"Uh-huh. You'll like learning it. It's like talking to your best friend."

"I don't have a best friend."

Blake hugged me to her side harder. "I know. But we are your family and your best friends, all together. We won't let you go. And we're going to teach you about prayer. It's how you'll stay alive."

I yanked my arm out of her grasp. "What! You mean I can end my existence?"

Blair remonstrated, "Now you've done it, Blake."

"I have not," she pouted. She said to me, "No, you can't end your existence. But without knowing how to pray, you'll become prey. It's *très* unpleasant."

I shot my eyes this way and that. *I don't want to see those Distortans again! Not here, too!*

"No, no," Bailey soothed. "You're done with those. And here in Heaven, none can harm you. But you have work to do on Earth, and you need to learn how to live fully in tune with your actual self, your mind, and how to protect yourself. Earth can be—"

"Earth is dangerous," Nihil stated.

I blinked at her. She shrugged.

*More reason not to go to Earth*, I thought.

Calico said into my mind, *You must. But not yet. Come. You have lessons to learn. Follow me to Heaven school.*

*Heaven school? What am I, a child?*

Calico pulled me along like a strong magnet attracting a helpless iron filing. I strained backwards. No use. My feet kept stepping forwards like they didn't belong to me. The calico cat ruled.

Blake giggled behind me. "Cats always rule."

I gave in. Scruffy trotted behind me, snuffling, their nails clicking a staccato beat. I looked over my shoulder. Like a line of soldiers, Blake, Blair, Bailey, and Nihil followed Calico and me, with Scruffy wending back to Nihil's side.

*I guess dogs comfort strangers but never leave their owners.* I turned to face Calico's tail ensign.

*I'm not owned*, Scruffy thought-barked. Their thought jolted me. *I'm her companion.*

Keeping my eyes forwards, I refused to contemplate how I'd heard words in Scruffy's bark.

"You're learning languages. It becomes automatic here. It's like being a toddler again where you pick up words by hearing them over and over," Baily explained to my back.

Against my will, I followed the waving orange, black, and white tail and blurred the rest of the environment out of my mind.

"It's okay to be upset," Bailey said. "Growth isn't easy. But you'll like where you end up."

*I escaped the Distortans*, I thought. *I still didn't like where I ended up.*

"This isn't the end," Bailey said. "Heaven is the second stage in your—our—journey of life."

Calico stopped.

I looked past their tail.

A wide space opened up in front of us with semi-circles of stone lining a steep hill. A wooden platform filled the bottom of the hill. Behind the platform, endless grey waves surf-splashed underneath the seamless grey sky. Grey stone. Grey wood planks. Grey sea. Grey sky.

Calico thought, *You have a lot of grey in your mind.* They turned to look up at me. Concern filled their green eyes.

*A cat cares about me?* I fluttered my lips at the idea that this cat who had exerted its will on me cared about what I saw.

*What you see is what you feel*, Calico replied.

*Yes*, I nodded. *That feels true. Misery fills every cell of my body.*

Calico lead me to the stone tiers. They stopped at the second one from the top and gestured. I filed onto the tier and sat; the stone in this wide open empty space pressured my being.

Calico disappeared.

Me, my soul family, Nihil, and Scruffy were the only beings here.

# Chapter Six

# HEAVEN SCHOOL

People appeared in the distance. Led by calico or glowing human-like beings, they arrived from north, south, east, and west. I shut my eyes against the brilliance of the human-like beings; yet longing to rest my eyes on their essences, I opened them again.

Blake nudged me. "They're angels. You'll get one."

I raised my eyebrows. *Angels?*

Blake nodded.

I opened my mouth. And shut it. Another thing I knew nothing about because Mom hadn't taught me. I flashed to the building coronated with two crossed poles. The memory, like the life review postcard had, hurtled me back into that scary drive with Mom. But it didn't explain angels.

From behind me, Calico said into my mind, *God created angels to serve humans.*

*Oh.* I pushed myself to say, "Thanks."

Bailey angled towards my left side and spoke sotto voce, "Angels may look like human beings on Earth. You may have seen one unknowingly when they took physical form. But God's primary purpose for them is to be God's messengers, to obey and praise God. Unlike us, they have no free will."

I turned to stare into her eyes. Bailey smiled. "The elder who'll teach you will explain."

Someone bumped me on my right side. People had filled my tier without me realizing it.

"Time for us to go," Bailey said as she stood up.

"What?" *They're leaving me?*

Bailey patted me on the shoulder. "Don't worry. We'll meet you after school is done. You won't notice we're gone."

"Try to keep up," Nihil said as she vaulted the steps ahead of Bailey and out of the amphitheatre.

"Good solar day, everyone." The voice boomed from below me. I jumped; my eyes shot forwards. I strained to see the voice's source. A being stood on the platform. I squinted to see better. *I don't need to squint*, I reminded myself. *Why do I do that? Habit?* It made no difference. Wherever I looked or thought, I saw the focus of my gaze clearly, no matter how distant or close.

A woman in white robes with white hair flowing around her head like a Medusa crown stood on the platform. An elder. I smiled to myself. I knew my Greek gods and myths, at least.

The person next to me snickered.

*Oh-oh. Everyone can read everyone's thoughts here.*

*You betcha. Your mind is so interesting. I've never met anyone who knows nothing about God or angels before. You're a real newbie, eh?*

I turned to stare at this person. I frowned. *Why can't I read her thoughts?*

The elder's voice boomed from below. "We've covered the amphitheatre with a thought-transmission-prevention blanket. You're all so new here, we know you cannot control where and who can read your thoughts and emotions. It'll be cacophony if we don't temporarily suppress their egress from your mind. Plus you won't pay attention to me! What I'm about to teach you is critical for your survival. We don't want any of you experiencing second death, now, right?"

A murmur of agreement rose from the crowd. *What's second death?* No, I didn't want to know. My first death had confused and troubled me enough when I'd discovered I hadn't died, only changed form. I shifted backwards on the stone tier. My seatmate nudged me with her left elbow. I didn't respond.

The elder had somehow increased in size. She appeared as clearly as if she were standing right in front of me. I saw the entire amphitheatre in one glance. I squeezed my eyes shut at the strangeness of seeing the big picture and her close up all at once. I opened my eyes. The sight hadn't changed.

I sighed.

The elder raised her hands until everyone stopped moving and murmuring. Quiet sank into us. No breeze disturbed our hair; no birds chirped, nor squirrels squeaked. I missed the familiar hum of constant traffic. A hush so profound it vibrated through the amphitheatre and drew my attention towards the elder.

"The first lesson, and the most important one, to learn about Heaven, is to pray."

*Pray?* There's that word again. I'd heard and read so often that prayer doesn't work. Action does. Politicians dropped "prayers" from "thoughts and prayers" in their condolences after people lost their lives or hurricanes blew apart coastal towns. *Prayers are for people who want to pretend they're doing something while not, aren't they? Yet here, prayers work?*

"Shhh," my seatmate hushed me.

"Sorry," I said hastily. I hadn't realized I'd scoffed out loud.

"Yes, pray!" The elder insisted.

"Why prayer?" she asked rhetorically, as she walked to the platform's left side. As she pivoted and walked towards the opposite end of the wood-slatted platform, she clasped her hands behind her back and raised her eyes to the top tiers, to where I was sitting.

*Yes, why?* I bit my lower lip.

"Prayer is how we talk to God. You know God as the one who created the universe—"

*I do?*

"—know God as Love. When you arrived through the Barrier into the Welcoming Place, you felt that unconditional love communicated to you through Jesus. Some of you may have felt it for the first time; for others, it's as familiar as a constant friend. You talk to Love, and Love will listen, hear, guide you along the path Love has created for you, and protect you. This last is most important. It's important when you lived as a material being. But your mind has now shed its first physical manifestation. You're starting to experience living in your raw mind-matrix form. In your raw mind state, you communicate through thoughts and prayers. It's critical you learn how, especially for those who must return to Earth to complete their Soul Track." The elder paused and bent her head as she looped back to her left.

The elder raised her head to scan our faces. "Some of you have not yet completed your Soul Track. You've come through the Earth-Heaven Interdimensional Expanse, having resisted the Distortans and rejecting Hell Track. But your Soul Track remains incomplete. It's usually reconciling relationships that remains yet to be done. Reconciliation requires you to return to Earth to finish the pre-Resurrection part of your Soul Track. But, listen. If you don't learn to pray, you'll become prey to those souls whom the Distortans flung back to Earth when they refused to grow as they transited the Expanse. Or souls who returned there to complete their Soul Track but got lost along the way. These souls want you to join them in their misery. Anger, resentment, jealousy, envy keep them roaming Earth. Their emotions expand the Distortans. Humans created the Distortans when they first traversed the Earth-Heaven Interdimensional Expanse. Every human who felt anger, power lust, hatred of those not like them, desire to remain material and keep their wealth, and judged all others as morally inferior to them, created the Distortans and grew them. They're like unquenchable coals."

The elder paused and glanced down at the wooden slats. "Let me clarify. When I say 'souls,' I mean the heart of who you are. You're actually mind-matrices, each created from nascent mesh God harvests from the universe's raw energy, which structurally organizes similar to your Earth-bound neurons and neural networks as you learn, experience, develop, and follow your Soul Track on Earth, in Heaven, and beyond. The way it—"

I swallowed against the tide of information. *I'm a numbers gal. I know accounting and budgeting and how to grow a business. Minds? Souls? Love?* I hugged myself. *Do I have to learn all this?*

The person on my right leaned forwards and grabbed my upper arm. "Ghosts!" she breathed.

*Huh?*

"—resisted the Distortans, made it through the Barrier, but didn't learn how to pray to Love. They didn't believe the Word—Jesus, Christ, Saviour—the names many of you know the incarnation of Love as from your time on Earth."

*No, we don't!* I tried to stop listening, but the elder's words penetrated my barrier.

"These didn't learn to connect with the Spirit—the Holy Spirit as some of you learned on Earth."

*Holy Spirit? Another term I don't know. Why do they assume we all know what they're talking about? The elders may not be posing the confusing questions the Distortans had, but they're just as dominating. Like Mom.*

"That left them vulnerable to being seduced by anger and resentment all over again. The life review leads to growth in Heaven, but back on Earth, the memories of your life review may fade, especially if you encounter your ancestors or close relatives who died not long before you. And what I mean about not long is a few decades, maybe up to three generations before you."

The elder paused. She stroked back her Medusa hair, letting her hands fall to her sides as she rolled her shoulders. Tears slid down her cheeks. "I grieve for all the ones who made it through the Barrier then lost themselves again as they returned to finish their Soul Track on Earth. The struggle is real, everyone! The danger is real! Prayer, staying connected to that unconditional love, will protect you. Your companions who accompany you on your Soul Track—the ones you met in the Expanse—your soul family or ancestors—will support you like they did as you journeyed through the Distortans. But you must learn how to ask for help, for guidance, for protection. Use prayer to ask God, Jesus, or the Holy Spirit for protection!!" The elder shouted this last part, blasting my being.

I didn't know what to make of it. *How could prayer, that thing everyone claimed didn't help, keep me safe?*

The elder looked up towards my tier.

"I shall teach you now how to pray when they attack you."

I blinked. Did I need to learn? I'd lived for over 60 years on Earth without knowing about prayer. I'd reconciled myself to returning to Earth after Calico had dragged me here. Earth, I understood. I'd lived unmolested for decades by invisible beings. Why was my seatmate giddy about ghosts? I'd never met a ghost or an angel on Earth. *Why now?*

I became conscious of voices harmonizing all around me. The thunder of a thousand voices repeating after the elder, vocalizing the same words together, shook my inner self with its power. *What is happening?*

The voices stopped. The elder smiled up at us all and clapped. "Let's try that again, and this time, those of you who tuned out, join in. I cannot emphasize enough how much you need these words ready in your mind the moment you need them."

My seatmate inclined towards me. "You scoff a lot," she whispered. I ducked my head in apology, avoiding her serious eyes. "You're going to be in trouble."

"—after me." The elder's voice burst into my hearing. "I want to hear all of you speak these words out loud with your voices. I want your lips and tongues to form the syllables. You'll hear me in your native language, and you'll understand each other in your own languages. We'll sound like we're uttering the same phonemes. You'll experience the harmony you need to resist the obdurate souls who'll cajole, threaten, intimidate, and entice you to join them in their endless ghostly roaming on Earth." The elder scanned the tiers, stepped back, and raised her arms. "Are you ready?"

I sagged and listened.

"Jesus loves me."

I grimaced.

My seatmate joined the others in eager repetition.

The elder looked towards me. "Jesus loves me. Repeat after me. Jesus loves me."

I complied.

"Love is with me."

"Love is with me," I repeated in a monotone to the stone beneath my feet.

"Protect me now!"

"Protect me now," I said with the others.

"Spirit guide me and buffer me from these who wish me ill."

"Spirit guide me and buffer me from these who wish me..." I frowned. The words slipped away as I remembered the Distortans, how futile my answers to them. I forced that memory out of me.

The elder raised the volume of her voice. "Spirit guide me."

"Spirit guide me," we repeated in unison. *But your soul family helped*, a voice whispered into my mind.

"And buffer me from those who wish me harm."

"And buffer me from..." the others repeated as my voice faded into forgetting.

"And buffer me," the elder boomed. *Remember the light that watched over you?*

"And buffer me," I repeated with the others as I wondered where that voice in my mind was coming from.

"From these ghosts."

"From these ghosts," I said in unison with the rest.

The elder nodded. "The Spirit has inscribed these words in your mind. But I recommend you repeat them to yourself a few times so that when you need them, you'll remember them automatically. When you're in danger, muscle-word memory will save you."

I nodded politely.

"The second thing you must know is that every human being ever created is a child of God. Love wants to save all of their children. Every single one. That includes you and those you like and love—and those you resent and hate. This knowledge will guide you on your Soul Track." She paused. Her eyes punctured each of our minds in turn with the seriousness of her statements. I straightened my back.

"Mercy, forgiveness, and reconciliation exist in a triangle. In reconciling with those you know you need to, whether family or friends, or coworkers or neighbours, remember the triangle's points. Reconciliation requires two people. One shows remorse; the other forgiveness. Only God offers both mercy and forgiveness simultaneously before we express our own remorse towards God, others, and ourselves—that unconditional love that greeted you upon your arrival through the Barrier brings out our remorse and ignites gratitude for God's forgiveness and mercy. But we human beings extend hands one to another, and together we experience reconciliation.

"Those who've completed the Earth section of your Soul Track will now embark on your life here in Heaven. Heaven is the second stage of the Solar Age. It's as much about growing as the first stage on Earth. Your angel guides will accompany you."

A murmur arose around me.

The elder waved her hands, palms down. "Yes, yes, I know. Many of you have seen angels on Earth or felt them. Or maybe you heard about guardian angels, seen that famous movie."

Tears of confusion prickled my eyes. I breathed in the non-air and whooshed it out.

"—already met them. But your angel guides in Heaven are different, as you'll discover during your second maturation stage. Those of you who must complete your Soul Track first won't meet your angel guides until you finish reconciling your relationships and return here."

*Thank Heaven for that!* I thought.

"The third thing is trust God. Trust Love, the Word, and the Spirit. You're never alone. They're always with you. Remember that light you saw when you were in the Distortans? That light, whether you can see it or not, is the Love that created you and doesn't want to let you go."

I preferred to forget all about the Distortans. I was relieved I'd made it through the Barrier. I'd rather forget that terrifying time. And I couldn't contemplate anyone wanting to know me that much.

"The fourth thing is God created the universes, every living thing, every particle and wave, the matrices of your minds. But God set Creation in motion to follow its own choices. Love built a plan for Creation to follow, like an author creates an outline for their novel. But the paths Creation follows are of its own choosing. All of us will ultimately end up where God in their Love intended. But some of us may take circuitous routes; it may seem like we never will find joy. What you choose to serve will determine your path. Do you choose to serve possession? Possession isn't just about money, material wealth, and material things. It's also about controlling others to your will. Or being controlled. Allowing others to possess your thoughts, words, and actions. To do their bidding unthinkingly."

The elder paused as she regarded us seated in the amphitheatre tiers.

*Isn't that what they're doing here, though,* I thought. *Controlling me, deciding for me where I must go, whether I like it or not. If I really have free will, why can't I stay here?*

"The second choice is evil. Spirit beings you know as demons exist. The Accuser exists. If you want to know more, I recommend C.S. Lewis's *The Screwtape Letters*. We elders all devoured it when it was first published. Such an imaginative truthful reading of the situation. We also recommend the Book of Job. It requires much contemplation as it's harder to understand.

"And the third choice is to follow Love. To listen to the Word. To ask the Spirit for guidance and believe their advice. Which choice you make will determine your Soul Track."

The elder stopped. She interlaced her fingers and walked to the centre of the platform. The elder scanned each tier in turn, starting from the bottom and ending at the top ones where I was sitting.

"Remember entropy and conservation of mass-energy?"

*Oh boy, physics!* I'd hated physics in high school. Pulleys and levers. *Math was cool, but physics...*

My seatmate nudged me and whispered into my ear, "Isn't that cool? Each universe is a closed system, and the total energy God created cannot be destroyed, like entropy cannot be destroyed. Our minds are forever!"

I doubted it, but I tuned back in.

"—you end up, you determine. But remember, you cannot be destroyed. Not yet. Will you choose to follow possessions, listen to resentment, fear, jealousy, obey the charming blindly, the ones who speak what you want to hear, who stoke your fear and cause you to look on others as out to get you, hinder your goals, destroy your dreams? Will you listen to the Accuser saying you're not good enough, you don't work hard enough, you're lazy, you don't love, you're guilty and unforgivable? Or will you adhere to Love, follow the Spirit and think on the Word, no matter how challenging and how much courage you must draw on? What and who you listen to will lead you back here to Heaven or keep you stuck on Earth until the cataclysm creates another opportunity to choose God. Your choice."

My thoughts spun like an out-of-control carousel, poles ripped out of their anchors, grinning horses banging into each other, careening them off. *Entropy? Conservation of mass-energy? Can't be destroyed...yet? Cataclysm?* Images of my high school physics teacher writing equations on the blackboard. Chalk breaking in his zeal to explain entropy. *Wasn't that disorder? And what did the elder mean about conservation of mass-energy and cataclysm? Do they mean nuclear war or the climate catastrophe?*

I shook my head free as my seatmate rose. She stooped and patted me on the shoulder. "Whew. That was a load, eh? Glad I completed my Soul Track and know all about prayer. Well, that prayer was a new one for me. I won't forget it." She passed me, sprang onto the step beside our tier, and vanished upwards to the surrounding ground. The elder walked off the stage, and people rose to follow my seatmate.

I remained seated.

# Chapter Seven

# RETURN TO EARTH

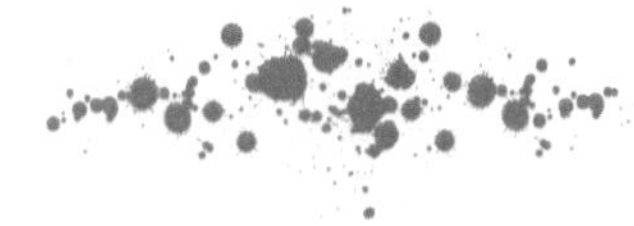

*I* stood on a strip of grass before a two-storey white building. Sash windows marched like soldiers across both storeys. A slanted four-sided roof topped a square tower, and a rusted weather vane perched on its point. I squinted to see it better. Then I remembered: I have three-sixty vision and can see the object of my desire by looking straight at it. The weather vane's rooster swung its side to me. Then squeaked-screamed back around. The world looked faded, like colours had leached out. *Why are colours lifeless?*

"Hey! Are you coming up or not?" A voice boomed above me.

I jumped. But gravity didn't pull me back down to earth. *Earth?* I stared between my feet as the ground slowly moved away from me. Nihil walked underneath me and raised her grey eyes, her face a mask. She said, "It's Earth. After visiting Heaven, colours here are boring."

Scruffy sauntered to her side, sniffing the grass. Frederick joined them.

*Where are we?* I wondered.

"We're visiting your grandmother," Frederick called up.

"I've been waiting ages for you," the voice above me shouted. I curved my back and neck back. Shireen Anne was grinning at me, her head on this side of a closed window a few metres to my right, her body hidden inside of the window.

My lips parted, and I panted.

Bailey spoke from behind me. "We're back on Earth. We're with you like we were in the Earth-Heaven Interdimensional Expanse. There's nothing to fear."

I faced her. "Why are we here?"

"Your grandmother resides here."

I gawped.

"She's close to death," Shireen Anne shouted down. "Hurry!" She beckoned us up.

I snapped my mouth shut. I'd met my grandmother only once. When I was a child. When my father had left. I'd seen my grandfather a few times, but not my grandmother.

Blair said, "Remember? You're here to reconcile with your family."

"But why her?"

"She's your family."

"I guess." I stared up at the window as Shireen Anne retracted her head through the glass and vanished. I pointed at it. "How do I enter?"

"You go through the window," Nihil said, levitating to match actions to words. Scruffy raised their head to watch and sneezed, as if to say Nihil is alright. Scruffy recommenced sniffing, following an invisible trail along the wall towards the corner of the building under my grandmother's window. Frederick hovered next to the second-storey window, waiting for me.

*When had he risen?*

Bailey touched me on the shoulder. "Think of yourself as photonic energy. Wherever light can go, you can go. You're a mind here. You are what you think you are. Descartes had it right, in a sense. It's like in the Expanse, except you control where you go here. You decide."

"I didn't decide to be in Heaven School one moment and here the next."

Bailey nodded as Blake stated, "Truth."

"Samuel felt you needed to start with the generation that's about to die."

I continued to stare at the closed window, reluctance weighting my heart. My shoulders drooped. *How do I pass through glass?*

"It's easy," Frederick said as he straightened his right arm, his hand open, palm up. He reached towards me. "Take my hand, and I'll lead you through."

I raised my eyebrows at him. He smiled and canted towards me.

*How does one walk on air?* He lowered himself and grasped my hand. Warmth enfolded my palm. I looked down at our joined hands and blanked my mind. He tugged. We rose up towards the window. Cold molecules scratched my skin as I followed through the window.

I was in the room, standing on the laminated oak floor. Shireen Anne waited on the left side of a hospital bed. A wizened woman lay in it. Dark blue eyes glared at me. I scrambled back.

Into Bailey.

She grasped my shoulders and said into my ear, "It's okay. She can't harm you."

"She can see me," I whispered back.

A door slid open. A nurse in her pink uniform strode in.

"I hate pink." *Hoarse and piercing, the voice cannot belong to such a tiny woman,* I thought. But her eyes also didn't match her shrunken form, which barely raised the blankets covering her.

The nurse halted. Her mouth dropped open. She turned on her heel and hurried out.

Shireen Anne blurted, "Your grandmother hasn't spoken in months. She's in the last stages of Alzheimer's. Your mother visits her once a month. Today is her scheduled visit." She gestured with her head towards the door. "She'll be here soon."

"You!" The hoarse voice grabbed my attention. The wizened woman with the fleeting hair glared at me. "Who are you?"

I pointed at myself. *Am I alive? How can she see me?*

Shireen Anne replied, *She's in terminal lucidity. She can see the dead at this stage.*

"What?" I gabbled.

The voice bellowed, "Get out!" at the same time as Bailey came to my side and said, "It's time to reconcile with her before she dies. It might be too late if you can't. For awhile anyway."

I frowned at Bailey. Chaos had infiltrated my mind; it had snatched reality out of my hands.

Mom banged the door open and hustled in. She braked beside the bed. The wizened woman glared at her then addressed me. "Stop calling me the wizened woman. I have a name. You'll use it!"

I stumbled backwards.

Mom said, "Who are you talking to?" as she looked in my direction.

Her appearance slayed me. Hair wild around her crown; features drawn harshly across her bones; eyes sunken in. *Mom, you've aged! How did this happen in only one day?*

"Time is not—" Bailey began.

"There are interlopers here," my grandmother barked. "They waltzed in without asking. Have you accepted Jesus Christ as your Lord and Saviour?" she rasped.

"Mother, you can talk! When did you wake up?"

"Answer my question, you ungrateful child!"

Mom stepped back and dropped her head.

"This is my...grandmother?" I breathed.

Those dark blue eyes pierced me. "You!" she said with disdain. "You are my granddaughter? This poor excuse for a daughter's daughter?"

I averted my eyes and hunched my shoulder against her hostility. Mom cowered. I'd never seen Mom cowed before. *Flee!* The goading from my core pushed me to step back. I bumped into Blair standing behind me.

Shireen Anne urged, "Now's your chance. Hurry!"

"My chance for what? For reconciling with this person I don't know. She hates me. How can I reconcile with her?"

"Tchuk." Grandmother's throaty contempt strangled me. I'd met her only once. *How does one reconcile with instant hatred?*

Bailey said, "We can't tell you how. Only that you must try."

My eyes darted here, there, anywhere but at those accusing blue eyes. Frederick hadn't let go of my left hand. He squeezed it now. Calm flowed into me. I gazed up at him. His brown eyes smiled down. He nodded. He pulled me forwards, towards the bed, and let go of my hand. From inertia, I floated forwards until I hit the rails at the foot of Grandmother's hospital bed. Her mouth thinned. Her eyes narrowed. Her almost invisible white eyebrows angled down towards each other. Her white wrinkled skin, like a city map, sunk into hollows below her bones. Only her eyes blazed with life, dark and foreboding.

She gestured her head slightly towards Mom; the movement released scent. It tickled my memory. Her hoarse voice ground out, "This one won't accept Jesus as her Lord and Saviour. What about you? Do you believe? Or are you going to hell like your mother here?"

*Lavender! Yardley's? Yes, that was it,* I remembered. Her words surfaced memories of Hell Track. I blurted, "You don't want to go there. It's not a pleasant place."

"I," she drawled out, "won't be going there. You and your mother will if you don't accept Jesus Christ as your Lord and Saviour."

"I don't think it matters if we do or not. It's how we lived our Soul Track."

"You know nothing. It's only those who've attended church faithfully and accepted Jesus Christ as their Lord and Saviour who will go to heaven. You won't," she ended maliciously. I didn't know much about church attendance or her mantra, but I recognized the bitter hatred dripping from her mouth. She, like me, was heading to the Distortans. Suddenly, I didn't want this awful woman experiencing them. I didn't know why because she deserved to experience their torturous questions.

I glanced at Mom's bowed head, her half-shut eyes, her silent attention fixated on the floor.

"Mother," Mom whispered. "Who are you talking to?"

"Your daughter and her friends," she spat out.

Mom lifted her head and surveyed the room. Her eyes went right past me.

Grandmother pulled a wrinkled, emaciated, crooked forefinger out from under her blankets and pointed at me. "Can't you see her, you stupid child?"

Mom moved her head from side to side. "It's okay, Mother. You have Alzheimer's. I know—"

The nurse bustled in with a doctor on her heels. He strode to the side of the hospital bed and lowered the rails. He examined my grandmother swiftly: checking her pupils, asking her where she was, asking who was standing beside him and in her room. Grandmother snapped out short answers as if he were the most unintelligent person she'd met.

"Are you done?" she barked.

The doctor straightened up and turned to Mom. "She's in terminal lucidity. Sometimes, these patients can see dead people. But we know she's lucid because she sees you and is talking with you and us." He added, "I'm sorry. This phase happens usually hours before death." He laid a gentle hand on her shoulder. "Would you like to call someone to be here with you?"

Mom shook her head.

He nodded. He gestured to the nurse to follow him. They left the room.

Silence blanketed us and them.

Grandmother's hoarse voice cracked it. "I have no fear. I shall meet my Lord and Saviour. He shall carry me triumphantly to heaven."

"He won't," I stated.

Grandmother smirked, "What do you know?"

"I know," I sighed as I gestured to my again-transparent self. Returning to Earth had transformed my being from opaque to transparent. "You'll be like this when you die. You'll enter the Earth-Heaven Interdimensional Expanse." I gazed around the room. "I don't see anyone to greet you. These," I gestured to Bailey, Blair, and Blake, "are my soul family. They greeted me when I died. They'd been by my side, they said, before I died. But I didn't see them until I was dead. Since I'm dead, I can see who's waiting for you. You can, too, if you can see us. The only people here are my soul family, and the three people I met in Heaven."

Grandmother interrupted me. "You?" she guffawed. "You in Heaven?" She laughed, phlegm gurgling as her lungs wheezed.

Mom stepped to the rail. She pulled it back up, locked it in place, and rested her hands on its top. "Be careful Mom. I don't want you falling out of bed."

Grandmother eyed her, amused. "You only want my money. You...you...atheist." She vomited out that last word.

"Be careful," murmured Shireen Anne to my grandmother. "If you keep hardening your heart against others, God will harden your heart until you face your second death, and last-minute regrets won't save you."

"Who are you to talk about God," snarled Grandmother. "Get out!"

Frederick said, "Jesus came to save. Even her." His soft baritone stroked reassurance along my limbs and back. Yet I couldn't relax.

"I'm supposed to reconcile my relationships, Grandmother. But how am I supposed to do that with you?" I said, clutching my abdomen.

"Jesus separates us like goats and sheep. The goats will go to hell," Grandmother lambasted me. Or was she spewing her judgement at Mom? "The sheep will go to heaven. You're a goat. Sheep cannot reconcile with goats. I will not tolerate the likes of your Mom and her progeny. We must remain pure for our Lord and Saviour."

"I don't think hatred is pure."

"It's like the fire of hell. If you don't like the burning, get out of the atheist kitchen." She chuckled. Coughs wracked her bony form.

Memories again. The judge in the Distortan Wisdom of Wrathful Person. "Destroyer of realms and human killer," the judge had called me. As I stared at Grandmother, I thought, *She's killing Mom and trying to kill me.*

"Of course. There's no room for atheists in the Lord's kingdom. They shall burn in hell fire."

"No. They won't. I don't know where they'll end up, but you're wrong."

Nihil laughed. Startled, I twisted to face her. I'd forgotten she was here as well. "I don't think that's how you reconcile," she grinned, white shards brightening her grey eyes. "Why don't you appease her?"

I blinked. I usually did appease people. I didn't like conflict. Yet here I was, arguing—no, I was pushing back against this harridan. I gulped. I shouldn't have thought that about her.

"It fits," Nihil stated.

"Is that how you reconciled?"

"Reconciled with whom?" Nihil shot back.

"I...I thought Soul Tracks were about reconciling?"

Nihil's expression, like icicles, stabbed me. "We're here for your Soul Track, not mine."

Bailey touched my shoulder, a gentle gesture that warmed me and recalled my focus to her. She said, "Reconciliation takes two people. Do you remember what you learned in Heaven School about the triangle?"

I hesitated before nodding.

"You do your part. That's all you're responsible for. Do you believe you're doing your part?"

I looked into her eyes. "You're not an orb."

Bailey smiled. "No. We're staying in our human forms this time round."

*Why?* I shook my head free of the question and massaged my forehead. My face felt like the magnetic skin I'd experienced in the Expanse. I examined my hands, turning them this way and that, examining the translucent versions of my Earth-bound physical fingers and palms. I saw the floor's oak planks through them. *I guess I'm able to stand on the floor because light can't penetrate blond wood laminated planks. I can't move through it willingly or unwillingly.*

My legs gave way. I landed on the floor, my legs folded underneath me. Frederick hunkered down beside my left side as Blake knelt down on the right. She patted my arm. "It's okay, Charlotte Elisabeth. It's a lot! I believe in you!"

Frederick glanced at Blake, nodded once, and said, "I have to go."

He stood up and walked through the window.

Nihil spoke above me. "He's looking for his father. He does this."

I let my vision blur out the empty space beneath the hospital bed.

"Your daughter has gone into hell." The hoarse voice penetrated my tired, overwhelmed mind.

"She has not!" Shireen Anne stated. I looked up and over at her. She was bending towards the dark blue eyes aimed at her.

"Be quiet," Grandmother commanded Shireen Anne.

"You can't scare me," Shireen Anne replied. "Your granddaughter is sitting on the floor. She can't believe what she's seeing and hearing from you. She's never seen her mother cowed before. But you're quite something. I'm rather fascinated why you emerged from behind the barrier Alzheimer's created and the first thing you think of is to tell your daughter and granddaughter that they're going to hell. Haven't you been in hell all this time?"

"Silence!"

"You can't go to Heaven until you face your reality and repair your relationships."

"Wait a minute," I interrupted. I stood up. "I was in Heaven, and I haven't repaired any of my relationships."

Shireen Anne nodded thoughtfully. "You're right. But you realized you had made mistakes. Until you did, you were stuck in the Expanse." She waved towards Grandmother. "I'm not sure she'll be able to do that. She's experienced separation from humanity and wants that for you and her daughter. It's fascinating. I want to learn more."

I goggled at her.

"I know, I know. I'm weird. Endless curiosity here. You should go. I'm going to wait to see how long her lucidity lasts and how she dies."

Grandmother pointed at me, her hand shaking, as she glared at Mom. "Is she your aborted one?"

"I was sixteen," Mom whispered to the floor, her features twisted in agony.

"You were also twenty," Grandmother accused, her finger unwavering. She sucked in her cheeks until her cheekbones looked like shelves. She thrust her head forwards along her pillow like a chicken lying on its side. "Jesus saw into your heart! I saw because Jesus revealed the truth to me. You can't hide from our Lord and Saviour!!" she sputtered. "That boy—"

I staggered back. *Wait a minute. I had aborted siblings?*

"You and your monstrous lies didn't go unnoticed by the one who sees all." She thrust her finger upwards. "Baby killers go to hell."

Her malice paralyzed my thoughts. But my feet swung me around and barrelled me through the window.

"That's right!" Grandmother shouted after me. "Run away. But you can't run from Satan. He knows his own. He already has you in his hands. I won't be seeing you again. I'm going to join my Lord and Saviour in heaven and..."

Her voice faded as I fled further and further away from that white building.

# Chapter Eight

# ESCAPING THE SPIRITS

"Hey chicky!"

AS I fled through my grandmother's window, a force like two hands yet flatter and wider shoved my back and spun me. I smacked into the oak tree towering by the corner of the white building. The tree sang sympathy from the back of my head to my heels.

"Nursing home!" a soprano voice tittered off to my side somewhere.

A baritone voice rumbled, "She doesn't know nothing."

"You'll have to mansplain. Cuz she's not a man," an alto voice giggled above me.

"I will," said the baritone.

As I gripped the tree behind me, I thought, *I'm transparent yet physical. How can I go through glass yet not solid matter? Why can't I disappear into this tree?* I dug my fingers into the thick bark and pulled myself around the tree to my right. The voices remained close and hidden.

"Who are you?" I yelled.

"Who are you?" mocked a tenor voice.

"Wouldn't you like to know!" said another.

"You want to join your Grand-ma," drawled a third.

"She does!" tittered the soprano.

"Come join us. We're fun," said the tenor. "We're not like those tired old goody-two-shoes."

I hadn't heard that term in a while. *How old are these people?*

Laughter rang around me, its force rippling my mind then my skin. *They're going to tear me apart!* I clutched the solid bark, sucked air in through my mouth, and scrabbled around the tree, away from these voices.

"Remember the prayer!" a shout came from far away.

*Who's that?*

"Who was that?" mocked the voices.

"Who was that?"

"Who was that?"

"Who was that?"

"Who was that?"

"Do you know?" the baritone leered.

"Do you know?"

"Do you know?"

"Do you know?"

"Do you know?"

I let go of the tree and slapped my hands over my ears. My slight inertia floated me forwards like a balloon in a stream. But the voices kept ringing and clanging, repeating the questions over and over, over and over, into my mind like a bonging bell banging my skull.

I screamed. Its sound wave reflected off the tree onto me. I sailed through the air, away from the nursing home—

"She's figured out what the building is."

"Good for her."

"You didn't need to mansplain, Archie!"

—over the sidewalk, arcing higher and higher across the road, flipping and somersaulting.

Splat!

The rough brick of the opposite building stopped my motion.

I stuck there spreadeagled, upside down, and face against the wall.

I slid.

I clawed at the mortar on either side of me.

*I can't go through solid matter*, I reminded myself. *And I'm not Spiderman.* Dizziness assailed me.

Molecules rushed up, down, and around me. The voices overran me. *Who are they?* I twisted my head to see the voices' origins, and an electrical field snapped my nose against the brick.

"No peekies," said the alto.

I forgot I had three-sixty vision—and I almost saw them—but the voices rat-a-tat-tat ripped it away.

"Who are you?" The brick muffled my voice.

"Wouldn't you like to know?"

"Remember to pray!" Was that Bailey's voice?

"Don't listen to her."

"She's so boring," said the soprano, dragging out the vowels.

"She's not," I said.

"Well, is she here for you?"

"She isn't, is she, Archie?"

"Nope," replied the baritone. "She's telling you what to do. Aren't you fed up with people telling you what to do?" He guffawed. "You're back on Earth. Free as a bird. Come join us! We have fun!"

I didn't feel very fun-like.

"Get off me," I said weakly.

A melody ribboned its way into my hearing.

"What's that?" squawked the tenor.

"They're singing that song!" squeaked the soprano.

*What song? Who is?*

The electrical field sticking my face against the brick weakened. I flattened my palms and pushed against the wall, ignoring the brick's sharp eruptions grooving my transparent skin. A tiny space opened up between my face and the brick. If my new vision was failing me, I'll use the Earthly way. I wrenched my neck and slanted my eyes far to the right. Human forms hovered there at the edge of my vision. They were retreating from my soul family. The forms' faces were like blurred photographs. Translucent like me, yet not defined.

I pushed harder to get a clearer look.

"Jesus, the Word made flesh, loves Charlotte Elisabeth," Blake's voice chimed as the three pursued the hostile translucent mockers.

*Jesus? Is Jesus a word?* I scowled in an effort to remember. My brow lifted. Jesus was the source of that overpowering emotion, state, sensation. Unconditional love. *And what had the elder said in Heaven School?* I grimaced.

"Charlotte Elisabeth doesn't know God exists, but you do. God is watching you," said Nihil as she hovered above everyone, arms crossed, looking down with her cold grey eyes and inscrutable face. Scruffy wandered across the road, nose glued to the tar-ribboned asphalt, until they reached Nihil. Lifting their head, they floated upwards and sat in mid-air next to Nihil. Their brown eyes enswathed the unearthly group.

The electrical field let go, and I shot down. I landed on the sidewalk, palms down, hands breaking my fall. I stayed in the handstand as my mind caught up with my body's fall.

The translucent humans backtracked away from my soul family, following the sidewalk, away from Nihil. I remembered how I used to lower myself from my handstand as a child, and I was standing. I stared hard at the disappearing group. I confirmed their forms and faces were blurry, as if their magnetic skin couldn't retain its integrity. I lifted my hands to my eyes. Their edges were blurry, too, but sharpening as I studied them.

Shireen Anne sang out, "Jesus loves Charlotte Elisabeth. The Word will never let her go! She's a child of God, and you're messing with her. Parents don't like bullies!"

The group eased around the building. I caught glimpses of black hair, blonde pigtails, wind-stream-looking blue, and brown eyes, before they vanished, catcalling as they fled.

Shireen Anne dashed towards me and grabbed my hand. "How could you forget, Charlotte Elisabeth? You gotta remember to pray! Lesson One, eh?"

"Pray?"

"Yes! Pray!" She gestured to the corner of the building where the blurry people had disappeared. "They're bad spirits. Ghosts! Remember what the elder taught? They want you to join them, and they'll keep coming after you if you don't pray."

"Lucky for you, we were here," Nihil said, sinking down to my level, her arms still crossed. Scruffy wandered downwards to sit beside her.

Blake rushed up and grabbed my other hand. "Silly you! We have fun, too! Loads of fun!!"

I didn't feel fun-like with them, either. Suddenly, I wanted to avoid this reconciliation work. If I have to be here on Earth, I wanted to go home. My home. The one I designed and lived in before Dr. V killed me—yes, with my consent, I admitted—ignorant consent—and sent me into the Distortans and Hell track. I squeezed my eyes shut, longing to be home again.

I opened my eyes, sighing.

My house appeared before me.

I blinked rapidly.

"Uh..."

I looked around me. I was alone. *What happened?*

I shrugged. I didn't understand nor care. I was home. That was all that mattered. I regarded my front door as I remembered I can't go through solid things. I stared at this obstacle. I thought about how I could move myself to my front window. *Does one think 'window' and you're there?* I swayed. With each sway, I advanced along the sidewalk. I compressed my lips. I wanted to cross my lawn, not walk down the sidewalk.

I looked down between my feet; my toes rested lightly on the concrete. I hunched my shoulders and bent my back; I imagined myself a boulder, a granite chunk falling off a cliff. My heels smacked the concrete, and I bounced up a little. I tried again, hunching gradually. This time, I sank gently until my feet rested, from toe to heel, on the sidewalk. I focused on the feeling. The solidity of the rough, grey material penetrated my perception.

I had bare feet, I suddenly realized, from when I'd lain in bed in the Dying with Dignity Suite. Yet the concrete's abrasiveness didn't hurt my soles like it used to when I'd been alive.

Someone had swept the sidewalk in front of my house.

I smiled. I'd done that weekly myself. I liked to keep my home and its environs looking cared for.

I straightened my knees. I paused. I straightened my neck and pulled my abdomen in until I stood upright.

Now all I had to do was walk.

I thought about my feet. I thought about the motion of walking. Imagining a long-learned ability as if I was a newborn strained my mind. My right foot shifted forwards. I cheered to myself. I imaged my left foot moving forwards and ahead of my right.

*This will take forever*, came the errant thought. "Shut up," I muttered to myself.

I clapped my hand over my mouth and surreptitiously scanned the gardens and sidewalks. The street remained empty. I paused to listen. When I'd closed my front door and locked it for the last time, the sparrows in a nearby cedar tree had been chattering like they were holding a party. Where were the sparrows? Did they sense me and had stopped their noisy chirping, waiting for me to leave? I sniffed the sharp air. I hadn't noticed until now that it was cold. I scanned the surrounding gardens. No snow. I shrugged. *What does it matter? I'm home.*

I returned to thinking about walking. My left foot shifted forwards, scraping across the concrete. Then my right foot. Then my left.

*I'm walking!*

I walked with conscious mind to my front walk. I sidestepped onto the grass. I walked forwards to my wide living room window.

*Now what do I do?*

I leaned forwards until my forehead touched the glass. The glass's molecules dripped against my forehead. I snapped my head back and rubbed my forehead. *Glass is a liquid*, I reminded myself. Still, I didn't like the feeling.

*You have to be brave, Charlotte Elisabeth, if you want to go home.* I nodded to myself. *I can do this.* I leaned forwards again until my forehead touched the glass. Cold molecules cut like an ice blade. I shoved my head through, and my body swept in behind.

I landed on my hands and knees and jumped up without consciously thinking as I emerged into my living room. I rubbed my hands together, my arms, my torso, my face, trying to rid myself of the cold burning sensation. Hugging myself, I looked around.

A woman sat in a stuffed chair, reading a book. A glass and metal round stand held her coffee cup. *What is this? Who is she? Why is she in my home?*

I stepped further into the room. The woman shivered and turned a page. *Does she feel me? Don't be silly, Charlotte Elisabeth. I didn't feel ghosts when I lived here.* I stopped my thoughts. *I'm not a ghost! Ghosts don't exist!* Horror encased me. My hands grabbed my cheeks. I dug my fingers into my eye sockets. The magnetic skin of my face repelled the magnetic skin covering my fingers, like how I remembered in the Earth-Heaven Interdimensional Expanse. I let go and dropped my hands.

The woman turned a page as she reached absentmindedly for the cup on the stand. She wove her forefinger through the coffee cup's delicate handle, raised the cup to her lips, and held it there. Using her thumb, she turned another page. She sipped. She lowered the cup. It hit the saucer with a tiny chink. Lavender scented the air as she lifted her hand from the cup to turn another page.

I bent my torso at the waist and screamed, "Get out of my house!"

The woman shuddered.

"This is my home! Not yours!"

The woman blenched, raised her eyes from her book, and raked the room. Her wide eyes raced right past me. She muttered, tucked her chin in, curled her legs up onto the chair, and recommenced reading.

I sagged.

*I want to go home.* Tears wet my eyes. One plopped down onto the carpet. I followed its trajectory. Transparent, its outline barely visible, it spread as it landed. It became one with the carpet. A horrid wall-to-wall grey carpet, its short pile flecked with purple. *Is grey to be the only colour in my existence now? What happened to the tasteful plush grey one I'd laid down after moving in?* I'd liked grey before, but not this much.

*Those scary blurry people were ghosts.* The thought dropped into my mind.

*I'm not a ghost. I'm still me*, I remonstrated myself. *And ghosts don't exist.*

I felt like I was lying to myself. *I just want to go home. I want to follow my routine. Be safe. Not think about family or Heaven or this puzzling God thing or...or ghosts.*

I scrubbed my scalp. Static built up, magnetic and electrical, raising my hair. Sparks exploded, and the woman's head flung up as her book tumbled to the carpet. Her alarmed eyes shot in my direction. I stilled my hands on my head. She stared hard. A clock in the hall ticked like gunfire. A grandfather clock. *Is that mine or hers?* I strove to see through the wall into the hall.

I looked back at the woman. She was still staring at me. Maybe I shouldn't move my eyes either.

Tick.

Tock

Tick.

Tock.

Tick.

The woman slumped, picked up her book with both hands, and began reading again, her eyebrows knitted, her eyes narrowed, her fingers white. She turned a page.

I leaned backwards in relief. Half of me plunged through the window. I welcomed the molecules knifing me along my arms, my shoulders, my neck, my head.

"You shouldn't stay in that position."

I straightened, yanking my head back in. I turned on my heel to stare out the window. A woman in a dazzling sari of gold and ruby reds stood on the other side. Gold earrings like miniature chandeliers hung from her ears. Her braided hair shone blue black. She smiled.

## Chapter Nine

# THE ANCESTOR

An automatic, tentative smile stretched my lips.

The woman in the sari reached through the window, seized my wrist, and yanked me. I flew through the window and fell, knees first, at her feet. I gasped. My joints and ligaments smashed into each other. *Except I don't have bones or muscles or ligaments, so how?* I clenched my jaw against the nausea and dared not look up.

The beautiful woman in the shining sari hauled me up.

I towered over her.

Her brown eyes blazed into mine.

I swallowed.

"What are you doing, child?"

"What?"

"Why do my children repeat themselves? You're all alike." She tittered, letting go of my wrist and covering her mouth.

I blinked at this apparition. I asked, "Who are you?"

"I'm your ancestor."

"My ancestor?" I knew no one in my family who dressed in such rich cloth, with bold jewellery, and braided blue-black hair. Her smooth skin shone white with tawny undertones. Kohl lined her eyes. Lashes long and matte black fell like a blackout blind when she looked down to study my bare feet. She tutted, "You weren't prepared, were you?"

"I was prepared for death," I replied stiffly.

She shook her head. "You were prepared for what you thought was death. But you were wrong, weren't you?" Her dark-chocolate brown eyes quailed me. I looked away, down the street.

"My feet don't hurt," I told the neighbour's young oak tree. My eyes widened. *Has the tree grown overnight?*

This strange woman turned her head to examine the tree. "Are you aware your time is not Earth time after your first death?"

I turned back to her. "What do you mean?"

She cocked her head and smiled. "You didn't pay attention in Heaven School, did you?" She reached her right hand up and patted my cheek.

I froze.

"Don't worry. All my children zone out. They like to think they know it all." She grinned. "Until they realize they don't." Her lips pressed into a horizontal slash above her chin; her eyes darkened to night black. "You are neither in time nor out of time. You're in storytelling time."

"What?"

"The stories we read don't progress chronologically, do they?" She lifted a querying eyebrow and waited.

"No," I eventually answered.

"You are the author of your storytelling time. Where you think, you go. See?"

I didn't.

She patted my arm. "Never mind. You'll get it...in time. What matters now is that you cannot go home."

I reared back. "I can, too." I flung my arm back towards my home. "That's my home!" I shouted.

Her eyebrows rose into her smooth forehead, creating fine horizontal wavy lines. "It isn't."

"It is!" Anger and grief flooded me. I stepped back. She crossed her arms and gazed up into my face. "You're not coping well, are you? Well, I've lost one child already. He's wandered off somewhere, and I can't find him. I'm not losing another."

"What do you mean?"

She didn't reply. Her eyes didn't leave my face. I took another step back.

A rock sailed over my head. I followed its trajectory, my mouth falling open. I turned to investigate its origin when another rock punctured my transparent self, shoving molecules this way and that, cascading energy waves inside me. The rock thudded on the ground. My ancestor neatly sidestepped a third as it thucked underneath the front paws of a fat, black squirrel sitting on its haunches, its front paws curled around a half-chewed acorn. I stared at the squirrel staring at me, frozen in place. I heaved. Every part of me was moving, like waves reflecting in all directions. I raised my hands to my mouth as my entire being wanted to vomit out through my entire skin. I didn't understand what was happening to me.

"Your first time?" My ancestor asked.

I strained to gather myself together. The squirrel dropped its acorn and bounded for the oak tree. I followed its path with my eyes as it leaped onto the tree trunk and flung itself upwards and around until it disappeared on the other side.

A wind blew up. Dead leaves scurried across the grass, tickling my feet, entering them along my edges. My ancestor stepped close to me and peered into my face. My heaving stopped. "What happened?" I gasped.

"A boy threw rocks at the squirrel." She gestured with her head towards my left side. I turned my head carefully to look over my shoulder. No one was in sight.

"He ran when he saw the rock land and the squirrel glared at him. An unmoving, glaring squirrel unnerves people more than one running."

I swivelled on my bare heel and marched towards my front window. "I'm going home," I stated over my shoulder.

Suddenly, she was standing in front of me. "No, you're not," she said. "There's no going home."

"Why not?"

"Your time as a mortal being is over."

"I'm here back on Earth."

"You know what I mean."

"No, I don't."

"Remember. You were returned here to complete your Soul Track, to reconcile your relationships. You didn't reconcile with your grandmother, and she's close to death."

"How can I reconcile with her? I don't know her. And she's an awful woman. I don't want to know her. Those...those...things! They can have her."

"Do you really want her to end up wandering the Earth with the lost spirits and the others?"

"I don't know why they are or what they want. But they can have her. But she won't stay down here, anyway. I tried to tell her she'll end up with those Distortans, with their snakes and lies. She just kept repeating something about Jesus and Lord and Saviour."

"I know. She's tough. She's stubborn. It's a family trait on both your sides. You know she'll avoid admitting her mistakes when the Distortans reel her in."

"I'm not interested."

She grabbed my hand and squeezed hard.

"Hey!" I yelled. "That hurts!" I stared at her. *How can this tiny, foreign-looking woman hurt me?* I shook my hand free and scrutinized it. "Why does it hurt?"

"Thoughts matter after first death. They decide your experience. You believed it would hurt, so it did. But right now, what matters is you must reconcile."

I craved my bed; yearned to return to my home, my bedroom.

I stood in my bedroom.

*This is my bedroom, isn't it?*

*How did I get here?* I twisted this way and that. *Why am I here?* Two familiar windows graced two walls. The room's door was in the same location. But pink-grey paint coloured the bare walls. *Where had my paintings gone?* A blanket lay askew on the bed, and the pillows lay helter-skelter on each other. I always made my bed. That final night, I'd left my bedroom neat and tidy.

Molecules zigzagged around me. I darted towards the window in front of me and exited it, barely feeling the glass's slow-moving molecules. I scraped my hands along the bricks, digging my fingers into the mortar joints to pull myself as quickly as I could downwards towards the ground and pulled myself around the corner onto the patio. I sighed. At least my patio looked the same. I flipped myself to land feet down. Brown, gold, and red leaves skittered along its concrete squares, piling up along the edges of the outdoor furniture. My furniture. I sank into one of the chairs and laid my head back.

"Are you done?"

My eyes flung open. The tiny woman, hands on hips, glared down at me. Her white skin shone under the scudding silvery and leaden clouds that blinked the sun on and off.

"It's autumn," I stated.

"Yes," she replied. "It's time to reconcile. What's the most important thing?"

I laid my head back and watched the clouds.

She waited.

I said nothing.

She waited.

"I exist."

"No."

"I think so. I didn't want to exist any more. That's why..." I turned my head and laid my right cheek on the chair's back pillow. I stared down the length of my garden. Weeds waved their dying fronds among the rhododendrons I'd planted along the perimeter fence. I frowned in thought. Three years of neglect, I estimated.

My ancestor nodded. "You're right. You were a good gardener, Charlotte Elisabeth." She bent towards me, her face closing in on mine. She wagged a finger. "But it's not yours now. You must let go of it and your mortal property." She straightened up. "What's the most important thing, Charlotte Elisabeth?"

"I admit I exist," I said to the wooden back fence with its vertical boards as clear in detail and colour as the cushion underneath my cheek. This new vision was remarkable.

"Focus, Charlotte Elisabeth."

I remembered Edwards Gardens. Its elegant flower beds and its winding paths.

I lay sprawled on browning grass near Edwards Gardens' formal fall chrysanthemum exhibit. Generous flower heads of small petals circling in layers filled my vision. Burgundies, golds, and...

I sat up. I'd become used to Earth's muted colours, but...

*What is that colour? Purple? Yet not purple.* Its hues played nuances of blues and violets and reds to create a deep royal purple. I refused to think about why I'd suddenly arrived in Edwards Gardens.

"Did you learn nothing in the Earth-Heaven Interdimensional Expanse?"

I jerked high into the air. I looked up, to my left, to my right, then down. I shot backwards. My ancestor's eyes bored into mine. Her brown eyes invaded me. All I saw was her.

"You cannot escape. You must complete your Soul Track." She grabbed my right upper arm and shook it. I tried to extricate it. But she clasped harder. "Why will you not listen?"

I heaved at my arm.

"You're in danger! Don't you see that? Why do so many of my children not listen!"

Her exasperation fluttered my face.

I twisted my arm this way and that. She didn't let go. I thought, *Home.* I remained hovering above the chrysanthemums.

She said, "You can't elude me this time. I won't let you go until you listen to me."

"I don't know who you are and I don't know why I have to listen to you. I want nothing to do with those things, with that hostile woman, or with the Soul Track. I want to go home."

"You're being a broken record. Do you even know what home is?" She puffed air into my face. I coughed. "First you don't want to stay alive. Then you accept you exist. But then you don't want to leave Heaven or listen to the elder or your soul family. Now you don't want to even start your task. Life isn't what you want it to be. Life is growth. Life is hard. While you lived, you didn't learn a healthy way to cope with suffering and manage your relationships." She paused. Her eyes softened. "All right. I admit. You didn't have it easy. Your parents failed you. But after first death, you experienced their emotions and thoughts during your life review. You experienced what you went through from their perspective and saw the big picture of your life on Earth. Didn't that teach you anything?"

"It taught me I exist."

She nodded. "Yes, it did. Don't you remember how you declared you wanted to live?"

I bit my lip and reluctantly nodded.

My ancestor shook my arm gently. "Darling, it should've taught you more. Look at you, you survived the Distortans. You saw through Hell Track's seduction and escaped through its Gates. You saw through the rationalizations of the Red Robes. Yes, it took you awhile. But you did it. You! You, Charlotte Elisabeth! And not only did you do it, but you accepted the love and help of your soul family. You may feel you're alone, but deep down you know you're not. Friends arrived and searched for you in Heaven."

Tears pricked the inner corners of my eyes.

"And why was that?" she asked softly. "Because they wanted to meet you. And they came here to Earth with you—with you, Charlotte Elisabeth—because they like you. Don't you recognize your true home?"

The distant caw of a crow shattered her mental hold on me. A squirrel chirrupped from its hiding place. A breeze waved the chrysanthemums. Soil exuded the richness of dying leaves.

My ancestor squeezed my arm. "Go find them, Charlotte Elisabeth. Complete your Soul Track. Reconcile with your relatives."

I said nothing.

Her hand loosened. "Take courage, Charlotte Elisabeth. We all fear the emotional torment of braving relations we fought with. We fear their continued rejection. We're scared of what we might find in ourselves. Reopening wounds we'd papered over terrifies us. But you can do it. I know you. Bravery flows in your being, from ancestors who faced the same conflicts and not only survived but thrived after reconciling." She paused. She susurrated, "You can do it, too. I—we—have faith in you." She jiggled my arm as if encouraging me.

"Look. You don't have to go back to your grandmother. Try someone easier. Choose any of your relatives. But just start. Okay?"

People here were like the Distortans, I realized. You can't avoid them until you answer their questions. Or, in this case, obey the elder.

"Fine," I said truculently. I didn't know why I was I thinking like a child. In my ancestor's presence, I felt like a naughty toddler, reluctant to accept responsibility to finish my Soul Track. *How far back is she in my genealogy?* I wondered

My ancestor smiled to herself and let go of my arm. "You're a child, like we're all God's children, like we're all children of our parents and ancestors. But we all grow. You'll see, Charlotte Elisabeth. It'll get easier. Now, go. Go find the relative you want to see the most."

*My sister Sincerity*, I thought.

## Chapter Ten

# THE FAÇADE CRUMBLES

Sincerity sat on the chair facing the entranceway, her back to one of the ice cream parlour's tall, etched mirrors, her companion on the other side of the round marble table, her back to me. They were sitting next to a closed rolling window-wall that stretched the full width and height of the dining space. Sincerity bent her head towards a fluted parfait glass and dug her long-handled stainless steel spoon into the mountain of whipped cream. Her parfait matched her companion's.

My mouth watered.

I imagined eating their ice cream.

I leaned over her companion's shoulder to check out the flavours. I frowned. Banana pudding filled the bottom of the glass. Little chunks of milky-looking cake rested on top. Mountainous whipped cream topped the parfait, a chocolate coin tucked into its sweet clouds. Sincerity and I dug roasted banana ice cream, caramel banana ice cream, but banana pudding? I shook my head. All three of us, Sally, Sincerity, and me, hated banana pudding. Mom had served us pudding cups every dinner in spurts. It didn't matter if we tired of them; she forced us to eat them for a month or two or three until another dessert type caught her attention. But a couple of times every year, she'd return to the marathon of banana pudding cups.

My mind repelled the oversweet taste memory. Nausea overtook me. I batted away the unexpected physical sensation and goggled at Sincerity as she plunged her spoon deep through the white whipped cream into the layer of cakes, nudged away a largish soggy chunk, then hoisted a tiny piece coated in cream. She put the spoon in her mouth and pulled it out between closed lips, like she was savouring it. *How can she eat that!*

"So how did your sister's house sale go?"

Her companion's question startled me. I sidled between the tables to study her face. A lanyard ribbon hung atop her shirt and underneath her suit jacket. I turned my head to see if Sincerity was wearing the same. She was. Colleagues. I knew little about Sincerity's work; I didn't know her friends or her colleagues. I hadn't been interested in her relationships. I swallowed down the prodding question: *Why not?*

I gazed around the mostly empty ice cream parlour. Our place. Demetre's on the Danforth. *Why'd Sincerity bring her to our place?*

Sincerity was speaking. "...the market is slow, you know. I don't know if we got a good price for it or not. Mom took care of it."

"Didn't you offer to pitch in, like I told you?"

"Yes. But Mom was adamant." Sincerity halted her spoon's downward thrust into the cake layer. "I don't know why. Mom rules, you know." Sincerity studiously gazed upon her slashed whipped cream. "She was unusually hands on with Charlotte Elisabeth's house and stuff. Every item had to be logged and tracked. She took months and months to decide on a real estate agent. Each one wouldn't do. I tried to take over, tell her I can do the work. Charlotte Elisabeth had bothered her. She didn't need to deal with her anymore. But Mom..."

Sincerity dragged a cake cube through the cream with her spoon. She paused its trajectory to her mouth. "I don't know. It was like dealing with Charlotte Elisabeth's things brought her closer. I mean, she controlled her more than Sally and me. But Charlotte Elisabeth had long since left and avoided her. In her later years, Mom refused to have anything to do with her. But since the day of her passing—"

Sincerity's companion leaned forwards, her unbuttoned jacket swinging dangerously close to dislodging the chocolate coin off her parfait's undisturbed whipped cream mountain. "Did she really choose MAiD?"

Sincerity nodded and hastily popped the cream-cloaked cake into her mouth. She chomped and pointed at her mouth.

Her companion nodded. "It's nasty, isn't it, this MAiD stuff. Mind you, I think if you're terminally ill or disabled—I mean, who wants to live like that? So undignified, and the pain must be unendurable. What is suffering good for? I see no point in it. I mean, to be in pain, to not have health, for no good reason. I'm with her," she said, nodding vigorously. She pointed her long-handled spoon at Sincerity's head bowed over her parfait glass. "I think it's wonderful we're giving disabled the right to die, don't you? Kevorkian was ahead of his time. He knew death is a right. And it's not like they can play and work like us. They must hate being sick all the time and want out. I would. I'd want to end it, wouldn't you?"

I watched Sincerity. As far as I knew, Sincerity didn't like suicide or euthanasia. We hadn't spoken about mine because Sincerity avoided conflict. *So did you,* a voice whispered from deep within me. I pinched my lips together. I'd faced my avoidance habit in the Earth-Heaven Interdimensional Expanse. Fearing conflict is why I hadn't told anyone about my choice until the last minute. That way, none would argue with me.

Sobs formed in my heart as the memory erupted of Mom wailing over my body in the Dying in Dignity Suite. I rubbed my cheeks hard to clear my mind and focus on this scene. I'm supposed to be reconciling with Sincerity, not regretting my fears and rationalizations.

Sincerity. The one who saw the best in people. I didn't understand her choice of parfait, though. I'd have ordered a sundae with salted chocolate and roasted banana ice creams dredged in chocolate fudge and oozing caramel. Sincerity would've ordered her usual strawberry and vanilla ice creams with plump strawberries, vibrant raspberries, thin banana slices, and purple-staining blueberries. My eyes half-shut in remembered bliss. I glanced down at my half-sister.

Sincerity nodded, eyes on her parfait, still chewing the cake I thought she didn't like.

Her colleague asserted, "I admire her right to self-determination. More people with chronic illnesses and disabilities should have her courage. At least she didn't burden you while she was alive, other than those ice cream dates. So what happened with the house? I know you were hoping to get a good price."

"I don't know. The proceeds don't come to me."

"They don't?"

"No. Mom said Charlotte Elisabeth's will had cut out the entire family. None of us get anything."

Her companion flopped back against her chair. "Well. Her death should've profited you at least."

Sincerity dug her spoon into the banana pudding, the metal clinking against the glass on the way down. Most of the whipped cream and cake cubes were gone. She scooped a tiny portion of the banana pudding and stared at the soft mound on the tip of her spoon. I thought, *Is she going to eat that?* I grimaced in distaste.

I regarded her regarding the hated pudding. *Didn't I tell her that none of the family was getting any part of my estate?* No one needed the money, not even Sincerity. We all earned enough to buy whatever we wanted. Mom had taught us how to manage money to make money. Yes, I had to admit, she did well teaching us how to live comfortably.

"Don't you think so?" her companion asked into the silence.

"I was hop..." Sincerity's voice faltered. She inhaled, air hissing between her teeth and over her tongue. "Charlotte Elisabeth suffered at the end. I brought her here for weekly dates. She loved ice cream."

"You'd think she'd pay you back for all the time you spent with her."

Sincerity nodded and placed the spoon on her tongue, closing her lips against it.

Nihil said from beside me, "Are you sure you want to reconcile with her?" Her forefinger appeared in front of me, pointing at Sincerity's nose. "She only wanted your money. That's why she arranged your weekly ice cream dates. Who paid?"

I turned my head to the right. *Where had she come from?*

"You paid?" Nihil stared into my eyes. I averted them. "Yeah, thought so. She was playing the kind sister to get at your money. She figured your heart disease would get you soon. I know the kind. They're not worth your time."

"Why not?" Shireen Anne thundered.

I jumped and smacked up against the ceiling.

"Sorry," Shireen Anne said, looking up at me. "Here, I'll help you back down." She reached up, grabbed my ankle, and gently pulled me down. She let go, and my feet touched the floor, back where I'd been standing.

Shireen Anne asked, "I wonder why she wanted your assets?"

Nihil replied, "Does it matter? She's agreeing with her colleague."

"Yes, but, why?" Shireen Anne stepped around my back and bent over to look nose-to-nose into Sincerity's eyes.

"What do you think of this parfait? It's one of my favourites," Sincerity's companion asked as she pushed her long-handled spoon through the pristine whipped cream mountain, through the cake layer, and into the banana pudding. She pulled up a spoonful of banana pudding with a cake cube hanging on and whipped cream clinging to the top. She stuffed the full spoon into her mouth. Her chipmunk cheeks expanded into a smile. "Banana pudding, my favourite. Yours, too, eh?"

Sincerity said, "Yes. It's good."

I blinked.

Shireen Anne straightened up. "I wonder why she'd say that?"

"She's a flatterer," Nihil said. "You can't trust people like that. They say what you want to hear, not what they're thinking."

"But why?" Shireen Anne considered Sincerity. My half-sister scooped up another portion of banana pudding and slid it into her mouth. She swallowed and smiled with her lips.

I shrugged. "I don't know how to reconcile, anyway."

"It's easy," Blake chimed from outside the rolling window-wall. I switched my vision towards the window. Bailey, Blair, and Blake were standing outside. *How long have they been there?*

Blake waved at me. I raised a tentative hand.

"It was easy to find you," Blair said. "We remembered how Desire enticed you. And we headed here."

"We tried the ice cream parlour next door first, but Bailey said, you'd be more likely to go to the one you'd been eating at the longest."

I puckered my brow.

"The triplets knew you when you were alive, remember? They saw where you went and who you hung out with," Shireen Anne said.

I stared.

Shireen Anne said, "Think of it like this. You're in a story, your story. You move through space-time along a web the Holy Spirit is and creates and had created. Your thoughts are like your transport system, like a GPS. You think. You remember. You move along the web through space-time to your destination in your story. Your soul family knows you intimately and have mastered the web's transportation system. So they can remember where you've been when alive physically on Earth in the first part of the Solar Age, find you in your storytelling space-time on the web, and take us there. See?"

I considered the scuffed floor. I raised my head, my mouth opening to ask her what she was talking about.

Stainless steel clanged on marble. Sincerity's companion had dropped her spoon on the table.

My questions about my so-called storytelling space-time and the strange idea of web travel fled from my thoughts.

"Well, I must be going. Will you sue your sister's estate? You know, get a lawyer to declare she was not of sound mind, and all. How could she be with all that suffering?" she asked rhetorically. "You could probably contest Dr. Veritas didn't know what he was doing since she woke up again and he had to try a second time. Maybe since he'd been incompetent—I mean, really, your sister deserved to die with dignity properly, the first time. You can sue on the basis that he didn't verify she really meant it. I mean, between you and me, she did. I wouldn't want to live disabled, would you?"

Sincerity shook her head, her mouth tightly drawn.

"Exactly. I'm liking how this law is being expanded. I really like the newest decision to sign up for MAiD in case we get dementia in the future. I mean, that's a no-win situation, right? You lose yourself and who wants that?"

"I wouldn't," Sincerity said tonelessly.

"Exactly. Look, I can get our legal department to look into suing her estate. You deserve a portion of her money, don't you think?" She looked hard at Sincerity.

Sincerity replied, "I do. That'd be great, if you could do that for me."

"Are you signing up for MAiD in case of dementia? I'm checking my Liberal Party MP is on board with this. We have a right to die, and I don't want the Conservatives coming back in and taking away the rights of the disabled to die with dignity."

"Ha!" Nihil guffawed, startling me. "This woman doesn't know what she's talking about. She's like you were! Stuck in useless chemical treatments, ignorant of Next-Gen ones that kickstart dying neurons." Nihil's wintry eyes penetrated my heart through my wide-open eyes. Scruffy barked. I jerked. Scruffy's chaotic wiry eyebrows bent towards each other; their eyes held Nihil's until she capitulated. "Okay. Okay. I get it," she said.

"I want my taxes going to support this." The colleague's authoritative voice grabbed my attention back.

"I know what you mean," Sincerity replied, her voice like a lead slab plummeting into the loaded silence.

Her companion moved aside her parfait glass and leaned forwards. She said sotto voce, "We need to support them. But accommodating all their requests is too much. I mean, what can they do for us, anyway? They're a drain on the economy and can't do anything. And," she leaned closer to Sincerity, her chest almost touching the white marble tabletop, neck arched as her eyes locked into Sincerity's, "I know we're not supposed to say this out loud, only through our taxes and policies, but," she pointed at Sincerity with her right forefinger then at herself, "you and me, we can talk freely, right? They're just lazy. You give them more money, and they'll spend it like it's their own." She lifted her chest a little. "Now, I'm for my taxes helping the middle class. We have to deal with so much, like inflation and rising real estate prices, while the ones who live off our taxes don't do much. I'm glad our party brought in the Canada Disability Benefit. It looks good, you know, but a couple hundred dollars per month for a qualified few is not a strain on our taxes. Rights matter more. No one would want to live like they do, you know."

Her eyes held Sincerity's. Moments passed. Sincerity's lashes fell as her eyes gave way.

Sincerity nodded. "It was hard on my sister. She had to battle fatigue and shortness of breath. I used to watch her having to catch her breath if she ate too much or too fast."

"That must've been painful for you. The pain is over now. And you can get on with your life."

Sincerity nodded at the tabletop.

My chest burned. My eyes stung. My mouth tightened into lipless pressure.

Sincerity's companion sat up, shot her chair back, and stood. "I'll get the bill."

Sincerity remained alone at the table. Her eyes followed her companion to the cash register, down the short entryway to the glass door, where she yanked open the door, strode through it, and disappeared around the building next door. Sincerity's spoon clattered to the table. Her shoulders collapsed, and her eyes closed as her body subsided against the chair back. Her head rested on the mirror.

Shireen Anne said, "Now we're seeing the real her."

"A phony," Nihil said. "Can you reconcile with her, Charlotte Elisabeth? Can you?"

# Chapter Eleven

# FALLIBILITY

ailey, Blair, and Blake huddled around me outside Demetre's. Bailey placed a hand on my back. Sunlight shone through me and warmed the concrete beneath my feet. Light reflected off Demetre's glass roll-up window-wall through Blair, whose back was to it, and into my eyes. And through them. I focused on the strangeness of staring straight into reflected sunlight and not squinting. Although the intense light didn't hurt my eyes, I felt the photons zip through me, like a rushing river of warmth.

Their voices rippled around me as I stared into the light.

"You can't reconcile with her." Nihil's voice crashed through my light fixation.

I blinked. "Is that your exp—"

"We're not here about me," she snapped.

*Am I this resistant to my Soul Track, to receiving support?* I shoved the thought away as Blair stepped sideways to face her. Bailey stopped rubbing my back. Blake hugged my arm and glowered at Nihil.

Nihil's frosty eyes held mine. "Sincerity's a hypocrite. You can't endorse that by reconciling with her."

"Why not?" Blake demanded.

I peered at her. I hadn't heard Blake speak like that before. Her silvery voice and chiming personality never wavered. Did Nihil's attitude call on some deeper, angry part of her?

"People are either good or bad. Phony people deceive us. They betray us," Nihil shot back.

*What undertone am I hearing? Some personal truth?* I pressed my lips together. Better not think about other people's pasts.

Shireen Anne spoke into my mind, *What's to fear about learning about other people? The more we learn, the closer our friendships, and the more fun we have.*

I raised my eyes to her. "Huh?"

She smiled and leaned against the glass wall. *How does she do that?*

*You'll see,* she thought towards me.

Bailey was speaking. "...good nor bad. People are God's creations."

*What had I missed?*

Bailey repeated, "Sincerity showed an aspect of herself you wish you hadn't seen. We all wish she was the way we saw in your life review. But people are both good and bad. Until we're fully formed, we are neither good nor bad—"

*What?*

"—People are God's creation."

"So what does that mean?" I asked.

"It means," Nihil replied tersely. "God wants us to judge the deed not the person. But I saw actions come out of people's thoughts. Their deeds are who they think. Their thoughts are who they are."

"They're not," Blair retorted.

"They are," Nihil stated.

*What is this? A schoolyard taunting argument?*

Shireen Anne laughed, her torso bending backwards through the window wall. "That's a good one, Charlotte Elisabeth! We adults are really children, aren't we? Is that why we're called children of God?" She straightened up, her face reemerging through the glass, mischief sparkling in her eyes. Her mind bored through those coruscant eyes into me.

*How would I know?*

She grinned, holding my gaze. *You should. But you will in due time.* Shireen Anne giggled. "Time!" she chortled out loud.

I frowned. "What do you  mean?"

"Time doesn't matter," Blair said.

"It's story that matters. Your story," Bailey added. "Your Soul Track."

I rotated three hundred and sixty degrees, gazing at my surroundings. People in light coats hurried along the sunlit sidewalks. Bikes whizzed past in their protected lanes. Cars pumped out exhaust at the red light a couple of shops away. A man zigzagged between slow-pedalling bicyclists and stopped cars to reach the opposite sidewalk in the shade.

"Time seems to exist," I said as I faced the others again.

Bailey nodded. "Yes, here on Earth, it does. But it doesn't matter to us. Your thoughts are what guide you, lead you. You are where you think. You're when when you think. The only time you cannot reach is before your death. Otherwise you move in space-time—you move in space and in time—according to your storytelling time."

I stared at her. *If thoughts guide me, then are they the same as actions? Is Nihil right?*

Bailey raised an eyebrow at me.

Blake hugged my arm tighter. "It's easy. Just think. And there you'll be when you be."

I switched my stare to her visage.

Nihil said, "She doesn't get it. The only thing you need to know is people are who they show you. Sincerity showed you she'll be whoever the other person wants her to be. She threw you under the bus. She buttered you up with ice cream to inherit your money. She's going to defy your wishes and grab a piece of what she considers her pie. You want to reconcile with a person like that?" Nihil's eyes hypnotized mine, defying me to argue.

I didn't.

Nihil vanished. Scruffy wagged their tail once and vanished, too.

I sagged.

"Don't listen to her," Blake said to my bowed head.

I examined the concrete. Grey texture. A tiny crack. The seam where two pours had joined.

"Charlotte Elisabeth!" Blair yelled in my ear.

My body convulsed.

"What is it you want, Charlotte Elisabeth?" Bailey asked.

"Remember why you're here," Blake said, shaking my left arm gently.

Bailey recommenced stroking my back. Neck to waist. Neck to waist. The soothing motion reminded me of brushing my hair at night, calming me, preparing me for sleep. My Mom-ordered blonde hair. My eyes shot open. Oh, how I wished I hadn't dyed my hair blonde to look acceptable, to merge in with other women, indistinguishable from each other. I wished I'd kept its natural colour, like my ancestor, like Shireen Anne had!

"It's not time to regret," Blair said.

"Give her space," Bailey remonstrated in a soft voice.

I raised my head to look through the shop-wide roll-up window. Sincerity hadn't moved from her position of leaning against the mirror inside. Her open eyes stared blindly at the ceiling. *What is she thinking?*

"If you like we can teach you how to read her thoughts?"

I turned to Bailey. I opened my mouth. I shut it. *Do I want to be able to read her thoughts?* "Isn't that an intrusion?" I asked out loud.

Shireen Anne replied, "It's how you develop closer relationships. It's the gateway to reconciliation. It's scary at first, but you'll get used to it. It opens up all sorts of exciting doors. You'll see!"

"I don't know..."

Bailey said, "You don't have to learn now. It's enough you can communicate with all of us through thought right now. But you have a decision to make. It's an important one. Remember why you're here. Remember you haven't completed your Soul Track. Whatever you decide now will either leave you stranded here on Earth like those torturing spirits and thence onwards to second death or one step closer to your ultimate destination."

"Heaven?"

"Sort of."

"What do you mean?"

"Bailey means that Heaven is part of the journey but not the destination. If we give you too much information, you'll get overloaded and disappear on us again," Blair said. "Billions learn these things over years of Sunday School or bible study or on their own through discussions on the forums. Even then, many don't believe it because it sounds too fantastical. Would you have believed you'd meet us at the moment of your first death? That we chose you and were eager for you to meet us and for us to be with you all through your journey through the Earth-Heaven Interdimensional Expanse? We told you over and over you weren't alone from the moment of your death; but only after you escaped Hell Track, just before the last stage of your life review, did you believe us."

I twisted my lips and cast my eyes down. I toed the concrete as Blake let go of my arm and hugged me around my waist.

"You're not alone," the three chorused.

"It took you your entire journey, us with you the whole time whether you saw us or not, before you believed."

I sighed. *They're right.*

"And now you have friends!" Shireen Anne chirrupped. "Me, Nihil, and Frederick."

"Don't forget Scruffy!" Blake pealed.

I smiled; sadness infiltrated my smile. *I had to die to not be alone.*

Bailey asked again, "What do you want to do, Charlotte Elisabeth?"

"I want to reconcile with Sincerity. But...is that person the Sincerity I want to reconcile with?"

"Yes, she is. She's flawed like all of us. She hasn't completed her Soul Track either. Can you say you're perfect, Charlotte Elisabeth? Should Jesus judge you for the actions you took while on Earth like Nihil wants you to judge Sincerity? Or do you want to focus on reconciling with a flawed human being? Like the unconditional love who embraced you when you exited the Barrier into the Welcoming Place? Remember what you felt during your life review."

I remembered.

Memory became present.

The present became memory.

I existed in the Earth-Heaven Interdimensional Expanse, felt my family's emotions during every scene in my life review. I existed simultaneously here on the Danforth.

I refused to contemplate how this strangeness occurred. I concentrated on my sister instead. I regretted not having a sisterly relationship like I'd seen other sisters have. *Were those emotions of hers I'd felt during the Flower Power Track life review false and her words today truth?*

"No," Bailey said. "It's the other way around."

I studied Sincerity through the closed window as I judged her betrayal. My attitude scratched my mind, grooving hard ridges and cracks. I relived the weariness and pain from Wrath's Wisdom's commands as he shouted at me from his high-up perch to answer his questions. I smacked my head. *I won't be like that judge!* "I'm not a human killer," I yelled. "I'm not!"

"So you'll reconcile with Sincerity?" Shireen Anne bounced from her position near the window and landed in front of me, her expression eager.

I smiled tentatively.

Shireen Anne shot her left arm in the air. "Awesome!"

My lips twitched upwards against my will. I said, "Don't get too excited. I don't know how. I also don't know which Sincerity I'll be reconciling with."

"We can show you," Blake said.

"Are you ready?" Bailey asked.

# Chapter Twelve

# SINCERITY'S BACKSTORY

Phones rang their electronic alarms. A photocopier in its room clicked-chuffed paper out in a relentless stream. Hushed footfalls hurried along the grey-carpeted corridors between cubicles.

"Where am I?" I asked a woman hustling by, clutching a sheaf of photocopies in white, pink, and blue. She kept walking, head down, and turned the corner of the end cubicle.

I appraised this place. It reminded me a little of the offices of one of my clients. *Am I there...? No, my client doesn't work in a hive.* I poked my head into the nearest cubicle. Bare grey half-walls enclosed a light-grey laminated desk that stretched from partition to partition. A black briefcase lay on top, half on the desk, half sticking off. A black office phone sat next to a beige CRT monitor scrolling through the Windows startup code. I reared back. "When am I?" I asked out loud.

No answer.

I wandered down the carpeted aisle.

*You're in storytelling time.*

"Who is that?" I twisted my head this way and that.

Men and women hustled past, carrying papers. *The feel is familiar, but the people aren't.* This scene reminded me of my time in the life review postcards, except I wasn't hovering over the scene like in the Expanse. *I'm in the scene. And this isn't my life. I don't recognize any of this. Where am I?*

"Yes, yes, we have your documentation," a voice exploded out of the cubicle I was passing. "We'll be getting it to you—no, don't worry. We have that, too. Yes, yes. Okay, bye, then." A phone receiver banged into its cradle. A chair spun backwards into the corridor, nearly taking me out. Except its wheel went through my foot. I yanked my foot back and studied my offended appendage. Grey carpet showed through it as my skin rippled back into form. When would I become used to existing and not being seen? I stared at the chair's owner as she back-pedalled her chair down the aisle.

*Sincerity?* My eyebrows shot up. *She's a young Sincerity!*

Sincerity rolled her chair into the next cubicle. I followed. "You wouldn't believe the call I had," she said to the cubicle's owner. I peeked over the top of the half-wall. The owner was a younger version of the woman from Demetre's. She spun her chair around to face Sincerity. *How long have they worked together?*

"Claimants expect us to hurry up. They never stop complaining. Did you get a bad one?"

"Yes. She wouldn't take my offer. I told her it was the best we could do. She said she had documents to prove her claim and asked if I'd gotten them."

"Those are the worst. The ones that won't stop. Did you take my advice?"

"I tried."

The woman beetled her eyebrows. "You need to do more than try, Sincerity. Sound sincere. You have that part down, don't you?"

Sincerity coloured. "Yes. I have to get home early today. Something's up with my sister."

"The accountant?"

"Yes.

"Well, we have our personal lives and our work lives," the woman reprimanded.

"Of course." Sincerity rushed on, "I don't want the two to interfere with each other." Sincerity's inner eyebrows quirked upwards as her eyes radiated apology.

"You excel at getting off on the dot of the clock, Sincerity. I think one day leaving early is good for you and for the company. They value us more when we take a rare early day."

"You think so?" Sincerity smiled; her smile wobbled as she glued her eyes to her colleague's expression.

*Why's Sincerity so eager to get this woman's blessing?* I wondered.

"Have you gotten that promotion yet you were talking about?"

The woman pulled her chair closer to Sincerity with her feet. She leaned into Sincerity's face. "Not yet. But Barry tells me it's in the works. Probably next week. I'll take you with me. But you need to remember my advice. This company likes solid workers with indisputable documentation who save them money. You know what I mean?" Her eyes held Sincerity's.

"I do," Sincerity whispered, nodding.

The woman jerked her head down and up once, wheeled her chair backwards with her feet, spun it around, and began clacking her keyboard.

Sincerity stood up and wheeled her chair into her cubicle. She exited her cubicle and walked towards the one at the end. She stepped in and grabbed the back of the man's chair sitting inside. I followed her.

"Hey Martin. How's it going?"

"It's a toughie, Sincerity. These claimants, their stories are so sad."

"I know. It's hard to follow SOP."

"It is. But we have to do what's best within our standard operating procedures."

"Best for the company."

Martin swung his head around to stare up into Sincerity's face. "No. What's ethical. What's legal."

Sincerity nodded and averted her eyes. "Yes, of course. I meant that."

Martin faced his CRT monitor and pointed. "This poor woman. She's had it tough since the rear ender. The police report says he was travelling at a hundred and twenty K-P-H in a forty zone. And she was stopped at a crosswalk. The hospital took care of the big bills. But she needs ongoing physio now. How can I say no to that? It's obvious she needs it."

Sincerity's hands convulsed on his chair back as she croaked, "Yeah. She does." She watched Martin type for a few minutes. "Did you hear anything about the promotions?"

"Nah," Martin replied, neck craned forwards, eyes glued to the form on the screen. His fingers typed furiously. "I'm going to quit soon anyway. I can't work for such an unethical company. Persuading gullible people to accept half of what they're entitled to for their car damage and denying their medical claims, is not my jam. You know what I mean?"

"I do, I do," Sincerity said as she stepped back, releasing the chair from her grip. "Well, I have to go. Something's up with my sister, and I need to see what's doing."

Martin stopped typing and turned his chair to face her. He looked up into her face. "I know how concerned you are about Charlotte Elisabeth. You're the best part of her family, Sincerity."

Sincerity blushed. "I don't know."

"You are!" His wide smile crinkled his eyes.

Sincerity ducked her head and hustled back to her cubicle. I stared at her retreating back and didn't follow. Martin seemed like a nice guy. And he liked her. *Why doesn't she respond?* She never married; I know she wanted to. I didn't. But she had.

"So!" Nihil said into my hearing.

I controlled my startle. This time, I jolted only as high as the top of the cubicle's half-wall. I spun around to object. Her glacier eyes assessed me. "You see where Sincerity's phoniness began, don't you?"

"I didn't know anything about her work."

"What?"

"I wonder why you didn't?" Shireen Anne mused as she floated up behind Nihil.

"I didn't ask," I mumbled.

"Why not?" Nihil demanded.

"It's best to keep oneself to oneself. Don't get involved."

Blair said behind me, "That's what got you into trouble with your relationships."

I whipped around. My entire soul family stood behind me, between me and Sincerity's cubicle. Sincerity half-jogged out of her cubicle behind them and ran down the carpeted corridor in the opposite direction of where we were standing. I moved to follow her, but Blair blocked me.

Bailey said, "Your desire brought you here. You've seen what you needed to see. Nihil was right. This is where Sincerity's puzzling behaviour began. You recognize it don't you? The rest you've seen."

"I have?"

Blake chirped, "Remember your life review? The day you left home when you were thirty-one?"

I nodded once.

"That's this day."

"Oh." I regarded Sincerity's disappearing back. "I didn't realize she came straight from work early."

"No, you didn't ask because you didn't care," Nihil said.

"That's harsh," Blake pushed back as she weaved around me to glare into Nihil's grey eyes. Nihil shrugged. "It's the truth."

"Is it?" Blake challenged her with her unwavering eyes. Nihil dropped her gaze.

"But..." I frowned. "This isn't my life review. I wasn't here. So how can I see it?"

"Storytelling time," Nihil drawled.

"What does that mean?"

"You remember your favourite novels, right?" Shireen Anne asked.

I shook my head. *Reading seems like another time.*

Nihil guffawed. "That's a good one!"

Shireen Anne bit her lip, but a grin broke through. "Haha! But, no, seriously, you're in your story, right? And stories have..." Shireen Anne eyed me expectantly.

I stared at the grey carpet for an answer.

"Oh, for Heaven's sake, just tell her!" Nihil huffed.

"Where's the fun in that?" Shireen Anne retaliated.

*Is this Heaven? Endless arguments? I want out!*

Bailey clasped my shoulder. I looked into her soft eyes.

*Flashbacks!*

Bailey smiled. *Almost.*

*Backstory?*

*Yes.*

"Now that you know storytelling time includes flashbacks and backstories," Nihil said. "Let's get back to what we all saw. Sincerity looked to see who had the power and made herself acceptable to that power. Promotion and money, that's all she cares about."

"I'm sure it's not that simple," Shireen Anne said. "I wonder why she needs to suck up to the power? Charlotte Elisabeth didn't. What makes one sibling a people pleaser and another hide from people?" Shireen Anne cocked her head and studied me. I felt like a lab mouse doing something unusual. I shuffled closer to Bailey.

Bailey encircled my shoulders. "She's not a lab mouse, Shireen Anne."

Shireen Anne gasped and covered her mouth with her outlined hands. "Oh no. I didn't mean to make her feel like one! I just have so many questions."

"We know," Bailey said. "But your gaze can be rather penetrating. Dial it down a notch."

Shireen Anne nodded. She let her hands fall and crossed her arms, grasping her elbows. "I know, I know. I've heard that often. I can't help how my eyes look. We are who we are. Aren't we supposed to learn how to accept people as they are, like Jesus does? And taught?"

Bailey smiled. "Yes, but—"

"How can she learn if we make ourselves acceptable in the way each person likes?" Shireen Anne interrogated.

"You have a point. You have a mind that won't quit. But give Charlotte Elisabeth time to get to know you. She'll become like us and not mind your infernal, I mean, eternal questions. They'll float past her," Bailey quipped.

Shireen Anne grinned back. "Okay, okay," she gave in, raising her hands, palms facing me. "I'm sorry Charlotte Elisabeth, I didn't mean to make you feel like you're under my microscope. I'm just curious about what makes people tick here on Earth and in Heaven. It's endlessly fascinating to me."

I couldn't understand that. The less I knew, the better.

"You can't reconcile without knowing more about the person you're reconciling with. Understand their origins, their ways of thinking, what they feel. Get to know them!" Bailey declared.

"I think we know all we need to," Nihil countered. "Sincerity chose to follow the ones who have power and to think, talk, and act like them. She's done it for decades. How can we know if she was sincere in her ice cream dates with Charlotte Elisabeth? We all heard her at Demetre's. She wanted her slice of Charlotte Elisabeth's pie. Money means more than family. And power means more than integrity."

"We are to love unconditionally," Bailey remonstrated.

"There's love and then there's being a patsy."

"How can Charlotte Elisabeth be a patsy to Sincerity now?" Blake implored as she rolled her eyes.

Nihil shrugged. "I wouldn't reconcile."

I kept looking in the direction in which Sincerity had vanished. I hadn't known she'd felt vulnerable until her interaction with her colleague communicated into me her insecurity, her desire to be liked and to avoid conflict. I'd sympathized with that. I avoided people because once your relationship crossed out of superficiality, conflict entered. *I hate conflict!* Fear bubbled up like a cauldron over a blazing fire. Her emotions while talking with Martin had overflowed into me, as well, but I couldn't understand those. *Had she felt…yearning?*

"Can we go?" I moaned to Bailey.

Bailey stepped back from me, letting her arm fall from my shoulders. She rubbed my back. "Of course. Are you prepared to reconcile now you know more?"

"I think you mean, still," Nihil harshed.

"No," Bailey replied. "I don't."

"I still want to reconcile with Sincerity," I asserted. *Although I don't know why she wants to please that woman. Does she have a hold over her?* I scrutinized the carpet, toeing it for an answer.

"Remember the life review postcard when you were three years old?" Bailey asked.

The terrifying scene flashed into my mind. I shivered and hugged myself. Blake flung her arms around me. "You're not there," she assured me. "But that's when it started."

I eyed Bailey from underneath my lashes. She nodded. I wrinkled my brow. I remembered: Sincerity had squeezed herself against the door frame to minimize herself in the face of Mom's rage; she'd feared the lion's head but felt better because Mom had smiled; despite her fear, she was the only one to talk to Mom like the whole thing was normal; she'd pleased Mom; then when Mom had left, Sincerity had placated me.

*A people pleaser,* Shireen Anne thought to me. *A natural-born one, maybe?*

Nihil snorted and winked out. I blinked. *Where had Nihil gone?*

"She's returned to the present," Blair said.

"I'll leave you to it," Shireen Anne said. "This is a family matter." She also winked out.

The bustling office sounds faded as Bailey, Blair, and Blake gathered around me. "It's not easy to reconcile with a living human being who cannot sense our energies. But if you're sincere in wanting to do it, you can. You'll have to learn more about existing as energy. Reconciliation requires listening. In this case, your desire flashed you into Sincerity's backstory, to the start of Sincerity's change in her work life. You already saw in your life review what set her up to become a people pleaser."

"It was that day, the day Father left, when Mom put the lion's head on the wall," I stated.

"Yes," Bailey affirmed.

"I guess it became more and more engrained in her. We were all so scared that day. She learned to please as a way to protect herself. But why did she cross the line to become someone with no integrity?"

"You'll have to figure that one out for yourself," Bailey replied.

"Some people do," Blake said.

"They're weak that way," Blair said.

"I think we could be more charitable," Bailey said.

"Why?" Blair said as she slid her eyes to the right towards her. "She is weak."

"Insecure."

"But even insecure people don't cross the ethical line."

"Perhaps. But some need others' approval so strongly that the more they abide by what others want, the more they rationalize the ones they please can do no wrong, and the more they edge closer and closer to crossing that line. They value the more powerful person's viewpoints and attitudes so highly that they consider them ethical. They don't want to think they're pleasing someone unethical or they're following someone who has no integrity. That'd make them believe they're unethical, too. Then they'd have to face the other person's flaws and face how they're not an excellent judge of character or how they allowed themselves to think, say, and do things their younger selves never would have. No one wants to believe they judge people badly or they're a bad person or they'd do unto others what they'd never—"

I interrupted. "I didn't judge badly. I thought I knew Sincerity. But my life review showed me how I missed so many things. I regret it now. I don't care why Sincerity—"

"You should!" Blair broke in. "You can't reconcile with someone unless you know them, understand them. You can't understand them by avoiding learning and caring about their flaws. Our work during this phase of our life is facing our flaws and others' flaws. Having mercy towards others who crossed the line because we understand their origins. Empathizing. And growing towards loving unconditionally. You don't fully see the people pleasing origins yet. You will, for you need to know a person fully, their foibles and their beauties, to love them unconditionally. To reconcile requires God's unconditional love, Jesus's kind, the kind you felt when you crossed the Barrier."

She lost me at "God." Even before that, I'd wondered, *Can I love another's flaws or only their positive aspects? What does my love feel like?*

"It feels like what you feel towards Sincerity. Regret. Longing. Wanting to reconcile with her," Bailey said.

"Does it?"

"Yes!" Bailey affirmed.

"Let's go!" Blake said.

I blinked at her. "Go where?"

"Back to present storytelling time."

# Chapter Thirteen

# POSSESSION

The wind shear from a cyclist racing along the path pushed me into Blair. She steadied me. I blinked and automatically twisted my head this way and that, taking in the two-storey shops, the black iron fencing of sidewalk patios, the people hustling through me. I shivered each time I felt them split my form. My mind struggled to reform my skin. Or what I thought of as my skin. *Is it skin?* I wasn't sure. *Enough of that! It doesn't matter what I'm made of.*

We were back on the Danforth, in front of Demetre's, in the present. *Whatever the present is. I need alone time. Time to think.*

An image of the Don Valley rose in my mind.

"We can walk in the park if you like," Bailey said.

I'll never get used to this intrusive thought-talking.

"You will. You'll learn how to keep your thoughts private, though not as private as in your first physical incarnation. But then you won't want to, either."

I sighed. Memories of a small ravine appeared like a moving picture show in my mind. Trees in golds and reds and resisting greens, towering above me as I walked along the muddy trail deep in the ravine. Messy green bushes bending towards the valley's path. The rain-swollen river rushing over its rocks. How I wished I was in that quiet place.

I glanced down at the grey concrete sidewalk and back up...

Young trees, denuded of their leaves, greeted my eyes.

"This is a lovely tributary," Blake rang out, dancing into the long grass, releasing earthy smells.

*I want to be alone*, I groused to myself. *I need to be alone to think!*

Blake stopped. Her arms froze in the air. She glanced over her shoulder at me. She dropped her arms. "Okay," she sang. "C'mon Blair and Bailey, let's leave Charlotte Elisabeth alone."

Bailey nodded. "I agree. Sometimes we need alone time to think. Let the trees and bushes settle you. I hope those who didn't complete their Soul Track will not find you." She patted my shoulder, took a step, then pursed her lips. Capturing my eyes, she said, "Remember love and relationships are the foundation of life. Love and relationships began with God. Remember to pray, Charlotte Elisabeth. It's the most important thing for you to stay safe."

Unable to look away, I blanked my mind and nodded.

My soul family winked out. I collapsed as thoughts raced into my mind, the first one being: *What's prayer got to do with anything? I don't understand this prayer stuff. Who do I pray to? Who's God?*

*Unconditional love*, came Bailey's voice from out of my memory.

I slapped my head to eject those thoughts. *Why does my form not break when I hit it but it does when living people do?* I batted that question away; I wanted to think about Sincerity.

I wended my way down to the narrow river, a runt leftover of the glacial age, and let my vision blur. White watery noise cascaded over birdsong and squirrel rustles as I trod to the edge of the river bank. I hunkered down and focused on the frothy waves as they hurled themselves over shallow, sharp-edged rocks, the mineral scent of cold water assailing my mind. I was starting to get the hang of moving around a physical world as a mind-energy being. I allowed myself a moment of triumph. *What had they called it...a mind-matrix? Who'd explained it? What to do about Sincerity?* I followed one thought after another in an unconnected path, replaying conversations in my mind. I focused on Sincerity's integrity, seeing each side of the argument.

"Hey!"

I ignored the voice. If I stayed still, it would pass me by. I smiled to myself as I cognized: *They can't see me!*

"Hey, whatchya doing?" The voice had closed the distance to me. I stole a glance over my shoulder, although I'd already seen with my three-sixty vision a person smiling at me from higher on the bank. A couple of others gathered around him...her? I wasn't sure. I rubbed my eyes and looked again.

The semi-transparent person laughed. "Yes, we're looking at you! We haven't seen you here before. Are you new?"

I nodded. *Who are they? Can they see three-hundred-and-sixty degrees like me? I must remember I do.* I watched them.

"It's a beautiful river, ain't it?" The others murmured agreement.

"Yes," I said tentatively. *That person is the leader. Who is...they?*

Led by the person, the group slid down the long grass to lean against the saplings on my left and my right. I stood up to face the first one. They seemed to have not advanced beyond Earth-bound vision.

"Did you come here when you were in human form?"

I nodded. "Who are you?"

Now that he was closer, I could make out his features well enough to see he was a he. He waved his hand dismissively. "We're the dead like you. Hey!" He pushed himself off the sapling. He snapped his fingers, and my eyes snapped to them.

*How did he do that?*

"I have an idea. Let's show you a secret place in this park. I bet you haven't seen it!" The others behind and next to me chorused agreement.

"I don't know..."

"Oh, c'mon," he said. "It'll be fun. We're all dead here. We might as well have some fun in our invisible forms, right?"

I ducked my head.

He scrambled up the slope, most following, one or two waiting for me. He skipped around the bushes that hugged the river's edge and stopped to gesture at me. I hesitated. He extended his arm towards me, palm up, and bent his hand towards himself in an upwards sweep. "C'mon! You'll love it!"

My right foot shifted forwards of its own volition. I'd wanted alone time. I got a group outing instead. My left foot followed; I climbed the slope.

Two brought up the rear, and we walked around the bushes with their higgledy-piggledy branches and leaves draped towards the water. As we hit the narrow dirt trail, he sped up. "C'mon slow poke!"

I dragged my bare feet along the trail, pebbles and twigs irritating my soles. *Why am I following this stranger?* He hadn't answered my question. *Who are you?* I thought.

The group expanded in number; their energy drew me along with them. *Didn't he hear my question?*

I narrowed my eyes in thought. *Are they not able to hear my thoughts?* My feet halted; a mud puddle oozing through my toes cringed my mind. The two behind me objected. "Hey! Don't stop. Why're you stopping?"

I shrugged.

Their leader skipped back towards me. "You gotta keep up to see the secret!" He danced in front of me, like a man inviting a woman onto the dance floor in those old black-and-white movies. *Is this a dream?*

He snapped his fingers to a rhythm I couldn't hear. I felt compelled to start walking again. "Good girl," he said as he twirled away. "Keep up!"

I looked over my shoulder back towards the river. It flowed below us. *Are we climbing out of the ravine? Where are we going?*

He didn't answer. Relief mingled with a sense of loss now I knew he and they couldn't read my thoughts. My eyes focused on his rippling back. He differed from them. I examined them. They differed from me as well. I returned my gaze to his wide shoulders and muscled back. He looked fully formed, like a semi-transparent version of his physical self, almost opaque, like I had looked in the Earth-Heaven Interdimensional Expanse; while the rest reminded me of energy images of their physical selves imprinted on 1920s' film. But now I'm...

The two behind me jostled me. I trotted in response. "Where are we going?" I asked.

"It's a secret!"

We seemed to leave the trees, but so many of these...ghosts? ...spirits?...surrounded me now, I couldn't see the bushes. I slowed to consider the white clouds drifting across the blue sky and think about this.

The leader bounced around and crashed through the crowd to face me. "You like secrets, don't you?"

"Not particularly."

"Oh c'mon. Everyone likes secrets. You're being a spoilsport."

The others jeered.

"I am not. I just want to know where we're going. I like to know."

"It's more fun not knowing. We wouldn't steer you wrong, right, guys?"

The growing group cheered in agreement.

*Where had all these people come from? And why are we exiting the ravine?* Concrete scraped my bare feet. Skyscrapers soared above me instead of trees. *How did we leave the Don Valley's tributary in such a short time?*

"You're so slow! Keep up!"

"I'm not slow."

"You are. You're not very good at walking. You probably weren't good at your job." The man's eyes glittered.

The others mocked me in sync with his words.

"I was!"

"No wonder Sincerity didn't like you."

"What are you talking about? She likes me!"

"Let's go find out, shall we?"

"What do you mean?"

"You're so slow," he taunted as he skipped in circles ahead of me. Hands pushed me forwards. Air rushed out of me as I struggled to stay upright. "Keep up," growled a voice behind me. I turned to see who it was, and a hand slapped my cheek. "Don't look back!" another voice commanded.

"If you don't keep up, the others will make you. You're so slow!"

I tried to duck away, but the group closed in. Feet swung at my legs. This was like Dark Distortan all over again, except I could see these creatures coming. Forces pounded me, and I tucked my head in between my arms.

"If you weren't so slow, you wouldn't be pounded, now would you? It's your own fault!"

"Your own fault," jeered the group.

Hands lifted me up high over their heads. I struggled against them. *How do I raise myself upwards?* I cast my mind about, to figure out how to escape from them. They threw me forwards. My arms and legs pinwheeled as I splatted against the stone wall of the original Bank of Nova Scotia building. I bounced off it and landed on the concrete. *Run!* I thought. *Get up, Charlotte Elisabeth. Run!* I scrambled up. Their feet thudded behind me. I threaded my way through the thronging lunch crowd. *When am I? Wasn't it afternoon in the present? What is time doing? Stop thinking, Charlotte Elisabeth, and move!*

Hands clutched my shoulders. Talons dug through my skin, rupturing my form. I thought of myself as existing within a protective skin; now my inner being was leaking through the punctures.

*They're tearing me apart!*

I panicked and twisted this way and that to release myself from their talons. *How do they have talons? Aren't they human?*

One waggled their fingers in front of my eyes; the fingers sharpened. They thrust their finger-talons deep into my forehead and temples. I screamed.

The leader leered into my vision. "We don't want you falling apart, now, do we? You haven't seen our secret yet!" He gloated as he grasped my neck and yanked me towards him. The finger-talons sucked out of me with a glop.

The others bantered, "We want a piece of her, too!"

"No! She's mine!" The leader slapped them away. "She hasn't seen my secret yet!"

"Oh come on! We're having fun."

"Later, guys, later, after she's seen my secret." He chuckled as his throttlehold held me. Laughter rang around me like I was back in Ignorance Distortan. He drew me against him. Energy like vicious lightning slashed through me. *Why am I not jerking like a tasered victim?* Suddenly, my skin ruptured like volcanoes spewing magma. He shifted his grip to my arm; I remained intact enough for him to drag me through the bank building, back out onto the street, threading our way between stalled traffic, towards a doorway in one of the older skyscrapers on the other side of the road.

"Stay here," he said.

I drooped. I couldn't move. Why bother trying to escape?

*Pray!* my memory demanded. *Why?* I asked my memory. *How? What good would that do?*

The group wandered off, leaving us two alone and one other whose unblinking eyes tracked us. She stood apart, her form, like an energy image, not semi-transparent like his. *Who are these energy images? Why can't any hear my thoughts?* I blinked. *I can't hear theirs either!*

I shifted. His clamped hand lanced me. I froze.

Sincerity walked up to the door and paused. My eyes widened. *Why is she here?*

"You recognize her, don't you?" the leader purred into my ear.

I bowed, not wanting to feel his grip tighten or be hauled deeper into his electrical being.

Sincerity stared at the door. She stepped back. She raised her head to scan the windows above us. She straightened her shoulders and took a step towards the door. Sincerity halted and stared at the door. *What's so fascinating about this door?*

"Can you see who this is?"

"What do you mean?"

"The door! Look at the sign next to the door! How stupid can you be?"

I scrutinized the wall next to the door and spotted the sign. I focused on it. Lawyer names. I stilled. *Is this the lawyer Sincerity's colleague told her about?* I swallowed. *How could she?*

He purred into my ear. "My secret will be revealed soon. You'll see."

*Is this his secret? To show me Sincerity's betrayal? Did she come straight here from Demetre's? How can I reconcile with her now? Nihil was right!* I shuddered.

The leader liked it and rubbed his face against mine, melding his form into mine where we touched, static like ants chewing my skin following his motion. He pointed at Sincerity. "Look at her."

I looked. Her right foot shifted backwards. Her left foot joined it. She turned towards the direction she'd come from. I concentrated on her and the weather. *Wait! It's lunchtime. Demetre's was after lunch. Sincerity can't go back in time. But I can!* I suddenly realized. *And forwards, too? This is the day after? A week after?* I watched as she hesitated, as she looked over her shoulder. She shook her head, dropped her eyes, tightened into herself, and walked away.

The leader lifted his face away from mine; my invaded skin reformed itself. He let go of my arm. "Now's the time for the secret." His being blurred as he rushed towards her.

Into her.

She arched and stopped.

I gasped and lurched towards her, my right hand outstretched. The woman who'd been watching us grinned. "This'll be fun." I stared at her.

Sincerity straightened. She swivelled on her heels, strode back towards the door, tugged it open, and strode inside. The woman pushed me towards the door, and I followed.

We stood in a lawyer's office, inside its closed door. Sincerity was sitting in the client chair in front of the desk. A young lawyer sat behind his faux-wood desk. Bookcases covered the wall behind him, each shelf stuffed with thick legal books. Document piles, edges lined up, graced one side of his desk. He was writing on his tablet computer as Sincerity was answering his questions. I couldn't hear what they were saying. Horror rushed through me. I didn't understand any of this. I didn't believe in ghosts. Yet here we three were, two of us standing next to his desk, and neither Sincerity nor the lawyer noticed us. I didn't believe in possession. Yet...

*No,* I objected. *This can't be happening!*

Sincerity stood up. She shook hands with the lawyer over his desk. The woman shoved me out of the way as Sincerity opened the door and walked out. I followed mutely. *This is not real. It's a dream. Another track in the Earth-Heaven Interdimensional Expanse.* I shook my head. *I'm not back in the Expanse,* I admitted reluctantly to myself. *I'm *here on Earth.* "How did he do that? Why'd she do that? It can't be real," I whispered.

The woman behind me guffawed, startling me. "You're so stupid! You don't even believe what's in front of you. People like you, denying what's real, are so stupid. How'd you make any success in the real world. No wonder you're wandering the Earth. Forget Sincerity!" I tuned out her taunts as I followed Sincerity to the elevator, down to the ground floor, and out the door where we'd started.

Sincerity paused. Her body undulated. The leader stumbled out of her and brushed himself off as if he'd chosen to leave her. Sincerity frowned and looked down at herself.

"She's as clueless as you!" the man laughed.

He and the woman high-fived. "That was fun!"

He leered into my face. "Now you see, dontchya? My secret? You can do that, too, you know. They won't teach you, but I will."

I quivered like a deer in a lion's sights. He leaned in closer, nose to nose. I didn't dare twitch. He grimaced. "You're no fun anymore." He gestured to the woman. "C'mon acolyte. We got done what I wanted. I'll treat you extra today."

She grinned lasciviously. "Hey, Charlotte Elisabeth, did you remember to pray?"

He roared with laughter.

The woman doubled over. "Both as clueless and stupid as each other."

*Well, your vocabulary is stupid. You're so repetitive.* I didn't say my thoughts out loud. Sincerity, meanwhile, was ogling the building, chewing her lips. She checked her watch and frowned at it. She shrugged. I watched her head towards Bay Street. *What will she do now? What do I do now?*

# Chapter Fourteen

# THE BUTTERFLY MESSENGER

I reappeared at the river's edge where those ghosts had found me. I realized now the spirits were ghosts, like the ones outside my grandmother's nursing home. The leader must be an über ghost...

I shrugged. I didn't know their purpose and didn't care to know. I searched the riverbanks for a thick bush I could snuggle into and hide from them. I slipped and stumbled over long green grasses, muddy patches, and hidden rocks to a denuded bush with branches crossing and twisting to the grey sky. *When had the clouds joined and greyed the sky?*

I averted my gaze from above and squeezed my way through the tangled bush, its dead leaves releasing mustiness, its branches scratching my skin, sending fuzzy messages up and down my arms. Dead twigs cut into my bare feet. I yelped when a tiny stone punctured my heel. I inspected my offended sole as I balanced on my left foot. Pain didn't seem to bother me. It was the sensation. I lowered my foot and pressed my sole into the ground to assess this stone's effect. It dug into my skin, dimpling my being where it jammed into my foot. My mind read its shape, its size, its edges. Every detail etched itself into my heel, and my mind gathered the intel and created an image. Yet pain did not accompany the sensation. How odd.

I lifted my foot and flicked out the stone. I crept into the bush's centre, lowered my behind to the ground, and hugged my knees to my chest. The river tumbled by, its waves thrashing the razor-edged rocks. I watched its noisy, rushing course through the screen of branches and let my thoughts float down the rapids like flotsam in a storm.

Sunlight cracked through the clouds, lighting up a patch on the rapids. The waves' froth transformed from grey to white as they entered the patch. The light called to my mind a memory. Sincerity talking to the lawyer in his artificially lit office.

I shrunk into myself.

*Had that ghost, that not-a-ghost, truly possessed Sincerity? Had he really made her decide to see the lawyer?* She'd walked to his building of her own free will. My mind argued with my mind that her colleague had planted the idea in her head.

*But she didn't have to listen,* I argued back.

*She likes to please people,* came the excuse. *Remember the scene at her work?*

*Yeah, but, again, she didn't have to please that woman. She could've been polite but not chosen power over ethics.*

*Not everyone has the strength.*

*What strength? How does it take courage to not defraud people?*

*Groupthink.* Long-forgotten university knowledge erupted the term into my memory. I grumbled to myself, "This is tiring."

I refocused on the river. The clouds had closed up against the sun's rays. The slate-coloured rapids hurtled over charcoal-grey stony slabs. Churning, churning over and around the boulders that cloaked the riverbed. Splashing onto the muddy bank. Releasing spring scents.

*Spring?*

*What season am I in now?* Climate change had shifted the seasons before I'd died. Some autumn days smelled like spring, with its fresh loamy scent and birds chirping at each other. Some spring days leadened from soaking snow. And winter stalled for months then suddenly blew polar vortexes and blizzards over us. *Storytelling time changes seasons?* I mulled that over in my mind. *What does that mean? Am I in the same day as when I saw Sincerity? Or am I in the hour before the ghosts found me?* No, I reminded myself, *the sky was blue with white puffy clouds then. Can I use the seasons made unpredictable by climate change to anchor me in time?* I sighed. *No, I can't,* I conceded. I gave up trying to figure out when I was.

At least I knew where I was.

"Why are you here?" purred a voice behind me.

I jerked and dug my fingers into the soil to keep myself from shooting upwards. *Calico?*

The cat padded around the bush. I stared at this apparition from Heaven. Calico settled onto their haunches between me and my view of the river and wrapped their tail around their furry front paws. Green eyes blinked at me.

My jaw dropped.

"Do you remember the mercy-forgiveness-reconciliation triangle?

"Yes," I gulped.

"Tell me."

"To reconcile, I must show mercy and forgive...I think. They must think remorse...or feel it...or maybe express regret...or maybe tell someone they're sorry for how they treated me...or maybe they forgive me after I expressed my remorse in the Expanse? ...Reconciliation can't happen if only forgiveness or only remorse happens...no, that's not it. It's if only forgiveness happens without apology...or the other way around...that reconciliation can't happen, right?" I fell silent in the maze of my thoughts.

Calico's eyelids slowly lowered and raised again, their vertical pupils constricting. "What fuels your reconciliation?"

"Fuels?"

Calico's green eyes nictitated while they waited for me to churn out an answer. Blankness spread like a confusing void through my thoughts.

"God's love, Jesus's presence, their Spirit activate this triangle and your forgiveness of others. They forgave you with unconditional love. That's what you felt when you entered Heaven."

My eyes widened.

"Do you remember why you were sent back? Have you understood the consequences if you don't?" Calico asked, their dilated pupils mesmerizing me.

We stared at each other.

Calico growled low. A rush of air fluffed my face. I involuntarily closed my eyes and reared back. I half-opened my eyes, letting my lashes protect them. Calico's slitted eyes pierced my mind.

My eyes widened. I ejaculated, "I'm to reconcile with my relatives. I don't know the consequences."

Calico closed their eyes and smiled.

"But..." I dropped my eyes to the disturbed soil. "Is it right to reconcile with a hypocrite, someone who chooses power and currying favour over doing the right thing with their clients? Someone who chooses to go against their sister's will for the sake of money?" I paused. "Chooses money over their own sister?" I whispered. "Aren't the consequences better if I don't reconcile with a hypocrite?" I sank into myself. "Did she really only meet with me to butter me up so I'd leave her my estate or a part of it?"

I wrinkled my eyebrows and raised my eyes to Calico's beaming face. "Is that right?"

Calico twitched their whiskers up.

I pressed my lips together against the slow, thrusting burning in my chest.

Calico blinked that slow cat smile.

I waited. My grief sharpened into defensive anger.

"Well?" I demanded.

Calico purred.

I slammed my right hand on the ground. "Answer me!" Stones rammed into my palms and shot out the top of my hands. Their trajectory smashed molecules together in the space between my palms and the top of my hand. Twigs needled me. And mud oozed between my fingers and into their edges. Revulsion spasmed my mind's image of my stomach. I lifted my hands and brushed them against each other, hard. I felt the skin of one hand repulsing the skin of the other like two magnets pushing against each other.

Calico's purr loudened.

I huffed and rubbed my offended fingers. I studied the holes in my hand and thought, *Why won't the holes close? I shouldn't have holes in me. I'm not physical anymore!* My skin rejoined over them. My eyelids froze in the open position as I ducked my head closer to inspect this strangeness. I turned my hand this way and that, seeing it whole again, seeing the ground beneath it. I adjusted myself to sit cross-legged and let my hands drop into my lap. I looked into the distance and let the rushing rapids fill my hearing. Like white noise, my thoughts defocused. Calico and I sat silently for a while.

Unknown animals rustled dead, dried-up leaves in the bushes behind me. A woodpecker drilled a tree trunk nearby. Traffic hummed in the background. The rapids dominated the soundscape. My head drooped, and my fingers, as if on their own, played with dead maple leaves, turned brown with cold and loneliness.

"I guess," I said to Calico. "I'm supposed to reconcile with Sincerity regardless."

Calico's purr filled my being, vibrating me like a well-tuned violin.

"How do I do that?" I asked, my eyes staring sightlessly.

"You send a butterfly."

My head shot up. "What?"

Calico stopped purring and blinked at me. "You send a white butterfly. White butterflies are known messengers from the dead to the living. We're not dead, but that's how they see us. You send a butterfly."

"How do I do that?"

"Did you pay any attention in Heaven School?"

I averted my gaze.

Calico unwrapped their tail and swished it across the long, wet grass. Back and forth, back and forth, faster and faster. I gulped. I stole a glance towards them. Their whiskers twitched. Their lips pulled back. Sharp white teeth glinted. I leaned back as far as the bush would let me go.

"I'm sorry," I whispered.

Calico narrowed their green eyes at me. They held mine prisoner. Energy poked and prodded my thoughts. My mouth dropped open. I bit my lower lip hard, trying to avoid Calico's invasion. Suddenly, they blinked, widened their eyes, and smiled. "I believe you are sorry. So I'll teach you."

Calico raised their face to the sky. Presently, a white butterfly fluttered towards us. It landed on a high-up branch, facing the direction in which it had been flying, its back to us. It folded its wings. Calico trained their darkening eyes on it. The butterfly opened its wings, lifted off a millimetre, turned one hundred and eighty degrees, and landed, facing Calico. It opened and closed its veined wings as it rested its white legs on the branch. Calico's emerald eyes lightened, and the butterfly launched itself into the air. It flitted erratically as the breeze swung it this way and that along its path towards the city streets.

I watched its flight in disbelief then slowly returned my vision to Calico. I asked, "Did you speak to it?"

"Of course."

"How?"

"How else?"

"It's a butterfly."

"Of course."

"Butterflies don't have brains."

"So what?"

"They can't communicate like we do."

"Why not?"

I blew out air. "What do you mean? Butterflies do their thing. We do ours. We try not to kill them. But we don't talk to them!"

"You haven't tried." Calico thrust their pink triangular nose close to my nose. "Second death is the consequence if you don't try."

I glared. *What's this second death? Do I care?* I thought rebelliously, refusing to move.

Calico settled back and blinked placidly at me. They lifted their left front paw and licked it. They bit into their pads and pulled on their nails. They licked their claws and toe beans with their rough pink tongue. The scraping sound jarred on me. I gritted my teeth. Calico paused. Resting their paw back on the ground behind their protective tail, they turned their darkening green eyes on me. Although I averted my gaze, my vision filled in every direction with emerald green fire, igniting the molecules within my skin, hurtling them in every direction.

I grabbed my shoulders against the invasion.

Clenched my arms.

Rubbed futilely at my chest.

My world turned green-red as if resentment, envy, justified rejection had become colours and distorted my vision, my very being. A cicada hum grew into a deafening whine.

I swallowed. "Okay. How do I tell a butterfly..." I furrowed my brow and lifted my eyes. "What did you tell it?"

"I showed it an image of Sincerity and told it to find her and stay with her for the day."

I eyed the branches to my left then my right. The cicada hum faded. I sucked in my lips then pursed them. "Uh, okay. How do I do that?"

"You call a butterfly to come."

I blinked rapidly.

Calico hissed.

I jumped and banged my head against a cross branch; the branch reflected me back to the ground. I rubbed my head. Maybe it hadn't been such a good idea sitting in the middle of a thick bush.

"Uh, here butterfly. Here, nice butterfly," I called, raising my face to the sky.

Calico rolled their eyes. "Use your thoughts! See a white butterfly in your mind. See it as you see yourself. Focus on that image."

I didn't understand the allusion to seeing myself, but I obeyed. I imaged a butterfly in my mind, outlined in black, like a sketch. I painted it white and transformed its black legs and antennae into white. A white butterfly zigzagged into view. It landed on a branch above me. It wasn't facing me.

"Now what?"

"You saw what I did."

I admitted reluctantly to myself that I had. I fixated on the butterfly. It opened its wings, fluttered to a branch at my eye level, and stepped up and down the branch, up and down, before turning around to face me. I shifted my gaze to Calico. "Now what?"

"Now you image what you want the butterfly to tell Sincerity."

"Tell her?" I laughed, one short bark. "No human can understand butterfly language!"

"No, but she'll notice a second white butterfly hanging around her."

"That's it?"

"No. Put all your feelings in your image of Sincerity. Your desire to reconcile. You missing her. You wanting to have your weekly ice cream dates with her again. Your regrets. Every emotion and thought you have with her, bound up in the wrapping of reconciliation, like a present."

I chewed my lips, twisting them this way and that. I stopped. I pressed my lips hard against each other, feeling the magnetism of their surfaces pushing against each other. I let out a sigh. *Okay, I'll try.* I brought an image of Sincerity into my mind.

"Don't forget to look right into the butterfly's eyes when you do that!"

"What?" *Its eyes?*

"Yes!"

I considered the butterfly, cocking my head this way and that. My vision drew every detail into my mind. *I see its eyes! How bizarre. Okay,* I told myself, *I can do this.* I didn't know how I'd image Sincerity as she looked at the lawyer's office while simultaneously looking into the butterfly's eyes, but if Calico said I must, then I must.

I opened my lock against my emotions. Regret, missing, and desire to be with her streamed out. Their intensity mingled with the belief I must reconcile with Sincerity; I swayed under their combined force. I struggled to focus on having a relationship with her, a sisterly one, one suited for us, not copying others but having our own...

I averted my thoughts from loving.

Calico huffed.

I gulped. I forced the word "loving" into my thoughts as my stomach caved in. I kept my eyes glued on the butterfly's as I felt and thought these foreign emotions. I let go all of a sudden. The white butterfly vaulted off the branch. I followed its flitting and fluttering until it disappeared into the distance.

"You've now reconciled with Sincerity. One down. Go. Rejoin your soul family for the rest."

# Chapter Fifteen

# HORRIBLE REUNION

*I* crab-walked out of the bush. I straightened up and slid down to the river's edge. Its ASMR of water rushing, rushing, rushing towards the wider Don River blanked my mind. I shook my head. *Stop dilly-dallying and go find Sally! That butterfly...how did it...*

I stared into the rapids, not understanding how a butterfly had reconciled me with Sincerity. Maybe I'll find out later. Right now, I needed time to process what had happened. Next on my reconciliation list was Sally, my oldest sister. My other half-sister.

*Where would she be?* I queried the sky.

Its flat greyness didn't respond.

*When is she?*

I turned and hiked up the grass-slippery slope to the muddy trail path. I walked along it until I came to a set of stairs. I climbed them and exited onto a quiet suburban-looking street. *Where am I?*

I shrugged and kept walking. *I suppose there are quicker ways to find Sally,* I said to myself as I walked along the clean white-grey concrete sidewalk. I observed my bare feet alternate in their forwards motion.

I was getting used to seeing the material world through my feet and hands. My legs' rhythm soothed me.

*Honk!*

I looked up at the familiar sound of a Toronto driver.

I'd neared a wide street. Cars rumbled impatiently as they crept-braked driving west next to me. Cars sped east along the far lanes. I didn't know how much time had passed since I'd died, but I felt comforted that Toronto drivers hated stalled traffic impeding their way as much as ever.

Like Sally had.

Sally drove hunched over the steering wheel, like a vulture scanning its surrounds for food. Mom told us about this building in Bombay—I corrected myself, Mumbai—where vultures lived. The people there laid out their dead on the top of the tower, and vultures ate their flesh. Apparently, the vultures dropped human bits on nearby balconies, to the residents' consternation, who hadn't been told their flats sat near a sky gravesite.

I giggled.

I clamped my hand over my mouth. I eyed the sidewalks left and right. *Had anyone heard me?* I rolled my eyes at myself and dropped my hand. No one walked along the sidewalk on this busy street, and they couldn't hear me, anyway. *But what about **them**? Can they hear me? Or their leader? They can't hear my thoughts, but...*

I hustled across the street, zigzagging between the cars, beating speeding ones and ones braking hard at the red light they couldn't beat. I didn't want to learn what a car moving through me would feel like.

I bounded onto the opposite south-side sidewalk and considered how to find Sally. So far, except for my first landing back on Earth, whenever I thought about where I wanted to be, I found myself there. I was certain Sally lived near Lake Ontario on the south edge of Toronto, but walking there seemed like a long hike and would consume too much time. Maybe I could try finding Sally by thinking about her, since I didn't know where she lived. I thought: *Sally.* Simultaneously, an image of home rose in my mind.

Home appeared before me.

Its windows faced the street like blank eyes. The front door's unwindowed solidity warned people to keep away.

I turned my mouth down. I inhaled. Molecules of oxygen, nitrogen, and carbon dioxide flowed in through my mouth and out through every millimetre of my skin. Molecules rubbed against my mind's energy. I shuddered. I exhaled hard. Air molecules streamed out of my mouth. I shoved the sensations out of my mind and focused on the front door.

*How do I get in?*

I contemplated the house. My home. My original home, but never my home. Its walls warned me to stay out. Their energy spoke of death and emptiness. I shifted my right foot back. My heel fell off the edge of the concrete sidewalk onto a drain. The drain's slats tattooed my foot with its pattern. I leapt up and yelled, "Ouch!" as I grabbed my tattooed foot, hovering over the offending drain. I glared at it. *Why had I yelled, 'ouch'? It hadn't hurt. It'd just felt...*

*No!* I told myself. *Don't think about this weird body, this alien way of existing. Earth is familiar. Find Sally! Focus on Sally, not on this unfamiliar life, Charlotte Elisabeth!*

I wiggled myself downwards and forwards, touching the sidewalk with my toes. I tippy-toed to the front door. *I can't walk through doors*, I reminded myself. *Find a window, Charlotte Elisabeth.* I lowered my heels to the concrete path, stepped onto the dying grass lawn, and walked towards the living room window. A sensation of a pounding heart I no longer had subsumed me. I patted my chest. *It's the easiest thing to climb through, Charlotte Elisabeth. You're invisible. The lion's dead head can't see you.*

I lifted myself onto the windowsill and dove head first through the glass. I no longer noticed how cutting glass molecules are. My hands broke my fall, and I somersaulted.

I leapt up and found myself face to face with Mom's lion head screwed into the wall.

I careered backwards and slammed into coarse fur.

I froze.

Fur scratched the back of my head. Long, rough fur.

I gulped.

I slid my right foot forwards.

The fur growled. My mouth trembled as my mind froze. My skin undulated under the baritone rumble.

*You're in my territory now.* The snarling thought, thrust into my mind, raised my hair. Fear transfixed me. *The lion's head? No! It's dead!*

*Yes. I'm the one your mom nailed to the wall. I'm the one your mom shot. I shall have my revenge.*

*Shelagh!* I remembered. *It's Grandfather behind me!*

Teeth scraped the back of my neck.

I screamed.

The Lion's jaws snapped into my neck. I shot forwards, as the Lion's canines scraped the molecules inside me and its carnivorous teeth dragged through my shattered skin. I whirled around.

The Lion's blond eyes bored into me. *How dare you call the name of my granddaughter!*

I gulped.

*My coalition partners and I roamed the Earth until your kind killed me for no reason. What did you do with them?* The Lion lunged forwards, and I thrust my arms up and pushed my open palms down, shooting myself up onto the ceiling.

The Lion mocked, *Your kind can't murder my coalition with your fire! They were young and virile! Too strong for your cowardly ways, hiding behind your long tubes of fire.* He thundered, *Shelagh's not your prey! You will not hunt my granddaughter!*

I shook my head violently. "No, no, no! I don't hunt. It's disgusting. I don't kill animals! I'm not hunting Shelagh! I'm not hunting your granddaughter."

The Lion bared his teeth; light flashed off the canines Mom used to polish fortnightly, which somehow shone in his spirit form. He padded forwards. If I hadn't been staring at him, I wouldn't have heard his footfall. I shivered and crab-walked along the ceiling. I knew I was being silly. With one leap, he'd reach me. But I couldn't help it. *Should I tell him?*

*Tell me what?*

*It's none of my business. I don't get involved. Relationships are messy. Better to stay out of things. Besides, I can't remember. I'm supposed to reconcile with my family, not other families, not animals!*

The Lion thrust himself upwards. I screamed and hustled sideways towards the living room window. My feet hit the decapitated lion head on the wall. The Lion's roar blasted me, shocking my mind, tearing my skin into shreds.

*How dare you disrespect my body!*

*I'm coming apart!*

*You deserve it.*

Atoms leaked through the rips in me, and air molecules rushed in, splitting my shredded self apart with their force. *How do I pull myself together? Am I supposed to reconcile with animals, too? With the Lion and Shelagh? I can't! That's not possible! I didn't do anything to them!!* I whined. My mind sobbed. My fingers floated off towards the Lion's opening jaws, canines dripping in anticipation. My feet fluttered to the ground in anatomical pieces. I dared not look at my torso. *Had Heaven School taught us how to keep ourselves together? Why, oh, why hadn't I listened? Is this second death? My denial and avoidance is my second death!* I blamed myself. *I want to live!!* I remembered when I first admitted that, how I'd rejected it, how I'd come to claim it. *Don't give up now*, I admonished myself. *Think, Charlotte Elisabeth! Think!!* I strained to capture pieces of my memory. *Shelagh! I'll tell him what Shelagh said. I should call him by his name. Grandfather.* But fear smothered my memory.

The Lion snarled in my face. I reared back, but the wall wouldn't let me through. I felt my head flattening.

"Shelagh," I breathed. "She, she found me. She...she...was..."

*What?* The Lion's golden eyes dominated me.

"She said...she said...I don't remember," I gasped.

*Try!*

I gulped. I focused on the roses that had undulated in Heaven's breeze. Their image quietened my mind. Shelagh's face and her story flooded into me. "I'm so sorry," I gasped. "I'm so sorry about what happened to you. But I wasn't even born then. I had no say. I didn't know about it until Mom..." I gulped, "until Mom...she...."

The memory powered into my mind, his name like a flashing sign, and Grandfather blinked. Had he seen the story of that awful day when Father left and Mom had torn down the painting to replace it with...

Grandfather floated backwards. "What did Shelagh say?" he growled.

*Help me*, I thought towards someone, anyone. A murmur of that unconditional love that had greeted me at the Barrier's Welcoming Place warmed me. Fear's tendrils slid out of me.

Energy flowed from the islands of my skin, like magnets pulling towards each other. I envisioned myself as the person who faced me in the mirror each morning as I'd dressed for work.

I coalesced into one, unified form.

I didn't understand how that had happened, but relief sagged me. *Remember Shelagh, Charlotte Elisabeth*, I counselled myself. Straightening up, I faced Grandfather. I blurred my vision against his hungry eyes. Memory of the day Father left edged into me and sparked Shelagh's last words into my thoughts. I snapped a locked lid against them.

"Vengeance isn't satisfying," I said.

*Isn't it?* he growled.

"No," I said as I sidled towards the window. Emptiness blanketed this place. Grandfather, the Lion, is not mine to reconcile with. Only the Lion's energy filled my mom's home. Sally wasn't here. I reached the window.

Shelagh's intent of human life for lion life blasted through the lock restraining my memories.

The Lion's eyes widened.

I hurtled myself through the window, thought *Sally*, began running, heard the Lion screech through the window, its paws thudding on the lawn, and thought *Demetre's*. The houses vanished from my view. Cars roaring by replaced the Lion's roar. I collapsed flat on the sidewalk.

# Chapter Sixteen

# ANOTHER FAÇADE EXPOSED

*I* huddled up to the wall of the corner restaurant near Demetre's, as living people paraded past, their shoes brushing my edges, rippling my knees through my white dress.

*I exist.*

*I know I do.*

*Yet I'm separated, not alive, like these men, women, children, anonymous people strolling by, striding by, biking by. How do I find Sally?*

I squeezed myself tighter against the wall. I blinked. *Does it feel like the wall is softening?* A child thunked their basketball through my bare feet, and I gritted my teeth against the nausea. *How do I feel nausea?* It's like my mind believes anything brushing me, or thudding through me, is poisonous food. I closed my eyes against this confusing, chaotic existence and reflected. *Thinking about Sally had taken me home.* I shuddered. *I can't go back!* I pushed my forehead onto my knees.

Danger still stalked me in this new form of existence. If anything, existence scared me more in this form. I hadn't confronted lions in my living room when I'd been alive! My lips twitched upwards. I leaned my back and relaxed my head against the wall. I let go of my legs. They straightened, and my feet relaxed sideways. I studied my bare feet. They looked young. Not veiny and bony like when I'd last seen them as I'd slid under the sheets in the Dying with Dignity Suite.

*That was not a dignified exit,* I admitted. It probably had looked like it to Dr. V, but death didn't complete itself on the visible plane. I grinned. He didn't know that, though. Smug in his certain science, he didn't know what awaited him. I waggled my feet. Someone walked through them. My mind was less upset. These rules confused me. I can't go through solid matter, yet a person can walk through me, shove their molecules into my being, and exit, allowing my skin to reseal itself.

*Sally,* I told myself. *I must find her. How?*

An image. That building on the corner Mom had yelled at me about, the one with the cross rising from its steeple. I squinted at my waggling feet. *Why had that mental image entered my mind? Am I to find a church? That church? What day is it?*

I looked about me from my vantage on the ground. No date appeared in the air, no calendar hovered in the sky, to tell me when I'm existing. I lifted my right arm to inspect my wrist. No watch. *Of course not,* I remonstrated myself. *Watches don't belong on dead people.* I screeched and whooped, rollicking over the sidewalk, rocking off it onto the bike path as a black-clad courier pedalled through me. I grasped the concrete edge, unheeding of its sharpness grooving my skin, and hauled myself up, as I cackled and chortled and tried not to vomit. *What would I vomit? Molecules!* I screamed with laughter.

I smacked my right cheek. *Wake up! I'm not dead! I exist...I exist.* I slumped against the wall, my head lolling down, staring at my pristine white dress covering my thighs. *My task is impossible.*

Voices. Sounds. Penetrated my mind.

Soprano, tenor, child-high.

Bicycle bell.

A bass shout.

Car brakes squealing.

Acrid diesel exhaust.

Coughing.

Wings fluttering.

Geese honking in harmony.

A door hissing open and sighing shut.

A flash scent of sweet waffles.

A skittering candy wrapper.

Winter air enwrapping me in its cold scent.

I faded out of my thoughts. The sun punctured the endless grey clouds and slanted onto me. The ray moved on. The sun set. Streetlights splayed their intense white light all over the Danforth. Warm-coloured light spilled out restaurant windows and glass doors. Phone displays highlighted their owners' faces with bluish tints as they hurried by, looking for directions and their companions. I remained separated from this passing life.

*Sally*, I remembered.

Using the wall as a brace, I stood up. Swaying, I sighed. It feels like November, like the day I thought I'd died. November grey with biting cold that blew sporadically. Snow had yet to arrive. *What building do I look for? Where is Sally?*

Bloor Street bustled behind me as the imposing grey edifice of St. Paul's on Bloor materialized.

I blinked. *Will I ever get used to thoughts as transport?* I giggled and clapped my hand over my mouth. *I'm not losing my mind! Not now! Not after I'm dead.*

I let my hand fall, inhaled a steadying breath, and held it as I thought: *I don't need to breathe, so why do I inhale? I feel the molecules entering me. I know their structures, their names, but they do nothing for me.* I decided that it's my mind's habit to deep breathe to calm myself.

Letting go of...*what do I call it...breath? Molecules?* I deflated and studied the stone building with its square towers before me. I knew its name because the sign said so. I didn't know who St. Paul was. *Is Sally here?* I shrugged and trudged towards the front doors. The centre ones, I decided. A few people straggled past me. I sped up to catch up with them and enter the doors when they opened them.

I found myself in an echoing space. Grey stone columns soared heavily in arcs above me. Stained glass filled the tall, narrow arched windows. The bright indoor lights darkened the windows' colours as they reflected off the white-grey walls. Shoes squeaked on the red and grey stone tiles. I hesitated. Sally rushed by. My mouth yawed, and my eyes widened.

*Sally's here? Does Mom know?* I snapped my mouth shut and hustled after her. She slid onto a long wooden bench halfway down the right side of the cavernous space. Music filled the air. I wasn't sure what to do. *Do I sit next to her? Stand in the aisle between the two sides of long benches?*

"What pew are you going to sit in?" I whirled at the voice behind me. I skipped out of the path of a man and woman peering along alternating benches.

"All the same to me. You choose."

"Let's sit in the pew behind Sally."

"Okay."

They slid into the...*pew? Is that a fancy term for bench? Why ask myself these questions? I don't know the answer. Does it matter? I can't sit behind Sally, anyway, with that couple there. Maybe in front of her? But then I'd miss her when she left.* I wandered back down the aisle and found the last pew empty. I sat next to the aisle. I stretched my legs and slid down. I stared into the ceiling high, high above me and zoned out.

Sally, head down, reading a thick book, wandered by me. I shot up and followed her.

"Hey Sally!"

Sally stopped, snapped the book shut, and smiled. "Hi."

"Good service tonight, eh?" A woman drew up to Sally.

"Yes."

"Are you going?"

"I'm not sure if I can make it. I have my mission work downtown."

"Yeah. That must eat up a lot of your time."

"It does. But it's what God calls us to."

"Yeah. The homeless will always be with us."

"The unhoused."

"Oh, of course." The woman speaking with Sally laughed briefly. "I can't keep up with the buzzwords."

"It's important to try. We mustn't let them feel neglected or unheard."

"You're right. You're right." The woman paused, then asked, "So, what do you think of the NDP's universal basic income idea?"

Sally shook her head. "I believe in hard work. The unhoused have been dealt a bad hand with their addictions. The government should be funding recovery services not wasting our tax dollars on people who don't want to work."

"I know what you mean. I have barely enough left over after I pay my mortgage and food. Inflation is crazy expensive these days."

"It's getting harder and harder to find the funds to help the unhoused. Too few shelter spaces. Too little political will. Too little health care. They're in desperate need, and no one seems to care."

"Yeah. But you do, Sally. You do so much for them, and the disabled."

"I try. My sister..."

The woman patted her shoulder. "You don't have to talk about it. She was disabled by her heart disease, wasn't she?"

*Disabled? Me?*

Sally nodded, lips pressed tight.

"Yeah, it's hard. You're doing well in her honour, helping out the disabled. I wrote to my MP about the Canada Disability Benefit."

Sally released the pressure between her lips and touched the woman's left arm. "Thank you. It's important work we did, hosting that letter writing campaign."

"That was a celebration when they instituted the benefit. The Liberal government did a good thing there."

"Yes. The benefit will help so many Canadians. I'm proud of the two hundred dollars per month."

"I heard talk," said a man who'd come upon the two silently, "that that amount isn't enough, that UBI would help them better. Universal basic income includes the disabled as part of the general population. A disability benefit leaves room for the government to discriminate against them and impoverish them."

Sally nodded. "I've heard that rationalization, too, but I want my tax dollars to go to those who need it, not to people who should know better."

"But is it?"

Sally pulled her eyebrows together, dropped her chin a little, and raised her sharp eyes to his blue ones. I stepped back. I usually avoided Sally; I used to find a reason to leave when she became like this. She was saying, "...government is helping the disabled in the best way."

The man shook his head as the woman reversed from them, one step, two steps, three. And then she turned on her pump-shod foot and was gone. He said, "The Ontario government takes away their portion for those on ODSP. The rest on CPP Disability also get less than the poverty line. It isn't enough."

Sally said, "The new federal benefit is a good thing. Disability groups were advocating for it. I merely came alongside and listened to them. I don't think it's for you to decide for them."

Nihil snorted in my ear, making me lurch. "Progressives and church types always know what's best for us."

"Where'd you come from?" I exclaimed.

Nihil shrugged. "I've kept my distance. That was quite the fight you had with Grandfather Lion."

Scruffy bumped their whiskery snout against the back of my knees.

I quivered.

Scruffy trotted around to sit beside Nihil. I squeezed my mouth shut. I turned to face Nihil fully. "You saw that?"

She smiled with her lips and nodded.

I glared at her. "You didn't help me?"

"Nah. You had it under control. A good experience for you." She gestured to Sally. "This one is interesting. Another hypocrite like your other sister. Two peas in a pod."

"How is she a hypocrite?"

Nihil erupted, "Euthanasia!"

"What? What are you talking about? How does euthanasia connect to disability benefits? And, anyway, Sally didn't know about me until after."

"How? What happens when your income is so low in the midst of plenty your teeth fall out? You want to die, don't you? Besides, she knows now about eu-tha-na-sia," Nihil drawled. "She knows Jesus now, too. She claims to be a follower." Nihil shoved her face into mine; I reared back, eyes widening. Nihil spat, "Has she seen what Jesus lived? He healed the sick. He didn't kill them. He raised Lazarus from the dead. From. The. Dead."

I stared mutely.

"Jesus helped the lame walk. He restored sight to the blind. He even fixed a blind man's brain after he fixed his eyes so he could recognize people. Jesus wept for the disabled. Yeah, he never talked about euthanasia—"

"MAiD," I said automatically.

"—but he showed us the way, right? He showed us we're meant to heal. Heal!" Nihil shouted. Molecules stormed out of her mouth and pitter-pattered my face. I tried not to move.

"No one healed me." Nihil jabbed at her chest. "They pretended they cared, but they didn't. You can't care if you don't want a relationship, right, Charlotte Elisabeth. You know all about that." She railroaded my attempt to answer. "Keep people at a distance so they don't know about you, and they don't have to spend any time or energy on knowing others. Hands off. Don't get involved. Did Jesus ever not get involved? He crossed a sea, for blank's sake, to get involved in a demon-possessed man!"

"Jesus cares?" I asked, wondering if the unconditional love I'd run from was caring.

Nihil screamed, "He didn't kill the living on Earth! He doesn't kill us after first death!!"

Nihil straightened and crossed her arms. "Your sister wants to decide for the disabled how much and what kind of health care they deserve to get. She wants to keep them separated from the middle-class mainstream so she can feel good about herself helping the less fortunate, showing how progressive she is. This here—" She tossed her head at the pews. "—is a social club. You get to belong if you do the right kind of volunteering."

*Huh?*

"With universal basic income—liveable," Nihil emphasized the last word. "Liveable income. Universal liveable income," she repeated. "No one would be able to single out the disabled. But then they couldn't feel superior." Her vicious grin made me cringe. "What criteria could these people use then to decide who gets to belong in the social club? UBI makes people equal."

"I know how UBI works."

Nihil eyed me.

I didn't understand her talk about social clubs and belonging. I ignored it and focused on the UBI. "I disagree with Sally," I said. "Where it's been instituted, it's saved tax dollars and created a more productive and educated workforce. But she's entitled to her opinion."

"Sure she is. But she's patting herself on the back and receiving accolades she believes she's due for helping the unhoused," Nihil inserted a mocking tone into the last word. "Her unhoused and disabled ready to accept benefits that keep them separated from the mainstream are deserving of compassion and her help. But the rest..." Nihil shook her head and dipped her face close into mine. My pupils expanded as her glacier eyes filled my vision, but I didn't pull back. "She decides who deserves help. It gives her the power, you see. Hypocrite. Like all these church types who want to fit in with the left-leaning. How are they different from Hitler, eh, with their endorsing MAiD?" Nihil sneered. "Different hands-off rationalizations. Same results."

I blinked and turned my head. Scruffy's rough tongue wetted my right hand.

"Don't they declare Christ lives in them?" Nihil blared into my ear.

*Christ? Who's Christ?* I wrinkled my brow at her.

"These church types say Christ lives in them, but they're afraid. Fear not, Jesus declares! But they do!"

"I'm afraid," I said. *You're afraid, too,* I thought.

Nihil glared. "I didn't say Jesus's spirit lives in me."

"What?" I looked down at myself. *Is someone else living in me? Where?* I rotated my hips and shoulders in opposite directions, looking, searching for another being. No, it's just me.

Nihil smirked, "You're alone, all alone."

"Then why are you here?"

Scruffy licked my hand, distracting me, warming me.

"Do you really want to reconcile with such a hypocrite?" Nihil asked.

I hunched my shoulder against her and wondered if she'd failed her Soul Track because she feared relationships like me and found reasons not to reconcile. *Am I avoiding the truth like I did in the Expanse?* I stepped sideways, away from Nihil, and returned my attention to Sally. Scruffy trotted to Sally and stared up into her face. They barked at Sally's reddening cheeks. The man wasn't giving way to her as Sincerity and I used to. His blue eyes transfixed her eyes, yet she didn't back down. Typical man, exuding tolerant calm, while her anger suffused her words with volume and speed.

"I'm here to reconcile with my family," I recited as Sally and the man's argument raged louder.

"Yeah, but does she deserve it? Like she said, the lazy don't deserve help. Don't you think she's being lazy in her thinking?"

Scruffy trotted back to Nihil and barked, their whiskered eyebrows drawing towards each other.

I kept my attention on Sally while with my three-sixty vision I eyed Nihil. "How so?"

Folding her arms and ignoring Scruffy, Nihil said, "You know."

"No, I don't. Explain it to me, Nihil."

"She follows a set pattern. Feed the unhoused like the church says. Advocate for the disabled, acceptable groups tell you, the ones who claim to represent them but keep them caged in old ways. Attend missions in long-established patterns. Don't question how your help changes nothing. Keep your thoughts in the right troughs so that you can retain power and be seen to be doing good. You know Jesus said to not go about with trumpets. Modern church goers don't use actual trumpets. They trumpet accepted tropes."

I stared at her. *Is her cynical tone warranted?*

She blinked cat-like back at me.

"Mom doesn't know what Sally is doing." *Why had I said that?*

Nihil laughed, throwing her head back, glee sparking black highlights in her grey eyes. "Of course not. That'd mean stepping out of the do-good pattern. It'd mean she'd have to face questions and have her faith challenged." Nihil straightened. Her grey eyes hardened. "It's easy to help 'the poor' when the poor have no choice but to accept what you're prepared to offer for fear that even that will be taken away. It's not so easy to face questions about how you're helping and who you're affiliated with."

*Had I known Sally in life? I hadn't known Sincerity.* Samuel's command to reconcile had forced me to learn about Sincerity's work and her need to please. Sally had always been Mom's henchwoman, yet here she was inhabiting the type of building Mom had banned us from entering or learning anything about. *When are we? I don't even know the date.*

"A year to the day of your appointment with Dr. Veritas," Nihil stated.

*A year? Is this how storytelling time works? Shuttling back and forth along some timeline, my mind dragging me higgledy-piggledy wherever I think?*

"Your mind can't travel on its own."

I puckered my eyebrows. "What do you mean?"

Scruffy thought to Nihil as they placed their paw on her foot, *Easy does it.*

"I mean," Nihil sighed, "that we're all connected through God's Spirit, through the web that ties us together and provides highways to travel along."

I blinked at her.

"Never mind that. The question for you, Charlotte Elisabeth, is why you want to reconcile with a hypocrite and a half-sister who bullied you and is now taking credit for honouring you. Did she ever honour you in life?"

*No, I thought. She hadn't.*

# Chapter Seventeen

# THE WEEK OF MY DEATH

"I wonder where my soul family is," I muttered. "They always hung out with me."

"Hey!" Blake shouted as she flew towards me through the last of the diminishing church crowd. "We wanted to give you space."

"You had enough alone time?" Blair asked, braking alongside.

I nodded.

"Why is Sally in church?" I looked around for her.

"She's gone," Nihil stated.

"Oh. Should we chase her?"

"No need," Bailey said behind me.

I whirled around. "Why?"

"You asked why she's in church. We can show you. You can return to this moment in time, if you wish, afterwards."

"I can?"

"Yes. You really should've paid attention in Heaven School, Charlotte Elisabeth. Those elders drone on like the worst chem professors. But their information is useful."

I sucked in my lips.

"Here we go into a backstory, a week after your first death," Bailey said.

MOM'S FRONT DOOR slammed open. Sally vaulted from the couch, and the magazine she'd been reading tumbled to the floor.

"Mom," she gulped. "I'll have dinner ready. I swear."

"I don't care about dinner."

Sally stared and tiptoed away from the couch as Mom flung her purse against the wall.

*Bang!*

It jangled and bounced to the floor. Sally's eyes almost popped out as she followed its ricocheting trajectory. "What happened?" she whispered.

Mom bent at the waist and screamed.

Sally screamed, stumbled backwards, and fell over the coffee table, arms pinwheeling. She thrust herself back up, brushed at her chest, and stared open-mouthed at Mom, who white-knuckled the corner of the couch, screaming into soprano pitch.

Mom stopped screaming.

I let go of my breath.

Sally rocked back and forth, from foot to foot.

"A week. For a whole week," Mom moaned, "I tried to get answers from that quack and the hospital. But they said it was her free choice. Free!" she exclaimed bitterly. Mom's legs gave way, and she folded in onto her knees. Her car keys fell from her tight-fisted hand.

Sally clutched the couch arm, legs resisting as she handed her way across the couch's back towards Mom.

"What's going on?" I whispered to Bailey.

"It's quite a scene, whatever it is," Nihil said as Scruffy licked her hand.

"Hush!" Blair said. "This is serious."

Scruffy nuzzled my hand. I absent-mindedly rubbed their head as I eavesdropped on the tableau. Sally was helping Mom up as tears and snot gushed down Mom's face. Sally guided Mom to the couch. Mom sat down. She fell onto her side, her head hanging over the couch's arm. She wailed.

And wailed.

And wailed.

Sally sat next to her and awkwardly patted her shoulder as she scanned the opposing chairs and wall for answers they couldn't give.

Silence erupted.

Sally stopped patting and bent her head to look into Mom's face. "Mom?"

"Charlotte Elisabeth killed herself."

"What?" Sally gasped, jerking up. "What do you mean? She suicided?"

"Yes! That silly girl went and got herself killed."

Sally puckered her brow. "You mean, she did something Charlotte-stupid and was murdered?"

I pressed my lips against yelling at Sally that I'm not stupid. Bailey touched my right shoulder as Scruffy licked my hand. Calmness flowed into me.

"...was him!" I'd missed what Mom had said.

"Who was?"

"That so-called doctor!"

"A doctor murdered her?"

"With her permission! What was he thinking? What was she thinking?" Mom exclaimed, emphasizing the pronouns.

"I don't know, Mom. Tell me what happened."

Mom told her about my first death in the Dying with Dignity Suite.

Sally collapsed back against the couch's back. Colour fled her cheeks. Her arms became flaccid. Her voice died into a rough whisper. "Why'd she leave us?"

"Why do they care?" I asked Bailey. Suddenly, I shouted, "Why?" Anger and frustration poured out like magma from the locked box of my emotions, the box I thought I'd opened in the Expanse, which somehow here on Earth had relocked. "You never cared when I was alive!" I yelled at an unheeding Mom and Sally. "Why now?"

"Anger won't help. Dig into the emotions underneath your anger, Charlotte Elisabeth, and keep watching."

"I'm so angry!" I hissed. "They act as if they loved me. They didn't love me!"

"That's the truth, isn't it?" Nihil said. "Why reconcile with people who get upset at your choice?"

I nodded hard.

Bailey sighed, grabbed the sides of my head, and turned my attention to watch their fake sympathy act out.

"It's not fake," she stated.

Sally slumped unseeing as Mom lay over the couch's arm, her arms as limp as Sally's.

"I can't believe it," Sally whispered. "I can't." Silence ticked along. "I can't." Suddenly, she shot up, strode towards the front door, bending to pick up the car keys along the way, and slammed open the door. It bounced against the wall and swung back to latch itself as Sally ran to Mom's car.

We were in the car. Sally pressed the accelerator down. I was glad to be in this form, my neck no longer subjected to her accelerating-braking mode of driving. Her tires screeched as she turned the corner, the car canting steeply to the right; her brakes squealed as she closed in on a red light.

Her fingers tapped the steering wheel while the light remained obstinately red.

Green flashed on.

Sally jammed her foot down hard on the accelerator. The car shot forwards.

I flew backwards through the rear window, and the car disappeared down the road with the others yelling at me from the back seat to come back as Scruffy leapt out, raced down the trunk, jumped into the air, and barked madly, galloping towards me. *How had they stayed in place?*

Frederick grabbed my hand. "C'mon," he said.

Startled, I swivelled my head and blinked up at him. Tugging me along, he sailed after the car. Scruffy executed a U-turn and raced ahead of us, tongue lolling in the car's slipstream, legs a blur. Frederick stretched my right arm forwards until it reached its full extension. My body followed. I let myself go slack, and we zipped along faster and faster, closing in on the speeding car. I felt like I was stomach-skiing on air.

Sally braked the car hard in front of the church we'd just been in. The drivers behind her squealed their brakes, their cars' back ends rising before lurching back down, and honked. She flung herself out of the driver's door, leaving the door wide open, causing the drivers in the passing lane to swerve. Yells, honks, screams, screeching whipped the air as she raced up St. Paul's steps towards the front doors. She yanked on one door after another. Locked, they resisted her efforts.

Sally shrieked, bending over, clutching her dyed-blonde hair.

A man in a long black frock hurried out the glass doors in the low building next to St. Paul's imposing grey stone edifice. He grasped her shoulders. "It's okay, it's okay. Is that your car? Give me your keys. I'll have someone move it for you."

A woman, who'd followed him out the door, said, "The car's still running. I'll go park it."

The frocked man nodded and gently led bent-over Sally to the glass doors.

I stayed outside, near the car. Frederick squeezed my hand. "It's a shocker, isn't it, seeing how others react to our deaths?"

"Is this what happened to you?" I asked him, turning to face him.

"Something similar, but I didn't stick around to watch them."

"Why not?"

"I had to find my father."

"Is that your Soul Track?"

He didn't reply.

The woman slammed the driver's-side door shut and drove off.

"When are we? The past?" I asked.

"This is a backstory in your storytelling time," he reminded me, without taking his eyes off the man and Sally.

"Yes," Bailey confirmed. "This is a week to the day you had Dr. Veritas kill you. Sally's reaction is confusing you, isn't it? Death is hard to take for anyone. Grief irrational. None of you told each other what you felt. You kept hidden inside your locked hearts the love you felt towards each other. Death strips off these barriers. Facing and defeating the Distortans in the Earth-Heaven Interdimensional Expanse unlocked your heart, Charlotte Elisabeth. But your desire to avoid, the pain of learning things you know you ought to have known when still alive physically on Earth, is relocking your heart. Add to that, suicide, euthanasia, or violent death traumatize the survivors. Deep down no one can reconcile themself to the killing of another human being. Whether suicide, murder by persuaded permission, or murder."

"Persuaded permission?" I frowned at Bailey.

"Yes," she stated. "We believe we're individuals, free to make fully independent choices, because we exist on Earth in separate corporeal bodies—"

"Except Siamese twins," Nihil said. Scruffy rumbled. Nihil rolled her eyes.

Bailey carried on as if she hadn't spoken. "That false sense of full independence masks how those around you can persuade you to do what you otherwise would not if you opened yourself up to experiencing the full love of God in them. No one wants another human being dead. Death is against the law of nature."

"Death is part of nature," I remonstrated.

"It is now. But it wasn't meant to be. It's why we exist after death but not in the bodies we were meant to live in. Those will come later."

"Huh?"

"Your family loves you. They couldn't show it. They feared to show it, just as you did. It made them and you feel weak, vulnerable. But buried in all your hearts, locked away like how you locked your emotions in that box, is the desire to express that love. To be truly free to show emotions and love. Without fearing repercussions—"

"Like mocking or rejecting," Blair finished.

"You missed out," Blake said, her hand reaching out to stroke me.

Bailey added, "At some point you so successfully shut down that you didn't know you had those feelings, what love feels like, and so God's unconditional love—Jesus's loving-care for you—at the Welcoming Place, overwhelmed you with its healing power."

I considered the glass doors through which Sally had vanished. "He seemed to have compassion for her," I mused.

"He did and does. Whatever flaws Sally revealed when you found her, the priest and his assistant, freely showed her compassion and Jesus's love. For the first time in her life, she received unfettered love. She hasn't reconciled her grief. She's buried it in her good works. They know this—"

"The congregation doesn't," Blair interrupted.

"True," Bailey said. "But they've befriended her. Some are the usual church superficial friendships, but there's one who's real. That man."

"The one who questioned her?" I asked.

"Yes," Bailey replied. "Good friends aren't afraid to question one's choices while showing love and compassion."

Frederick's energy warmed my hand. I liked it. I felt balanced, reassured, calm...loved? At that thought, I tried to pull my hand out of his. But he tightened his fingers around my palm. I stopped trying to pull away. Blake eyed our hands and grinned. When she saw me looking at her, she whipped around to point at the glass doors. "We can follow if you like?"

I shook my head.

"Then we'll return."

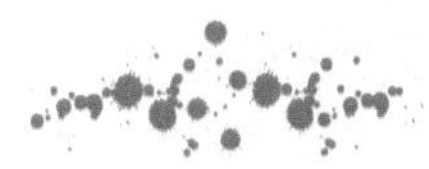

STARS TWINKLED ABOVE the city's painfully white streetlights.

"I'll have to leave you," Frederick said. I tightened my fingers around his hand. "Why? Are you also on your Soul Track?"

"I haven't found my father yet. You needed my help; I sensed it. But not anymore in this present of your storytelling time. The others are here with you. I've done my part."

I wanted to ask if I'd see him again. *What are you thinking, Charlotte Elisabeth?* My fingers loosened. He slipped his hand out from mine and vanished. *I'll never get used to this*, I thought.

"You will," Blair said.

"I don't understand men," I said. "I thought they didn't have emotions, like us."

"They're human, too, you know," Blake giggled.

"After all that, do you still want to reconcile with Sally?" Nihil asked me, refocusing me on my assigned task.

"What do you mean?"

"She didn't show any love to you but wants others' sympathy for her 'loss'." Nihil mimed air quotes. "She only wants to help people in a way that's visible, you know, through 'good works'," Nihil said, again miming air quotes. That was the second time I'd heard that phrase, "good works."

I asked "What are good works?"

Nihil's cold eyes scraped mine. "They're what church people call their deeds. They say it's what Jesus asked them to do. They're meant to help people, but really, they're mostly about making themselves look generous because helping people like us works best through governments with their pooled resources who can lift unhoused and disabled and working poor alike with homes and food in a way no megachurch ever can."

"Megachurch?"

Nihil fluffed her lips. "Don't you know anything?"

Blake said, "She can't help it. Her mom hid from her everything and anything to do with God. It's weird. But that's one reason we were attracted to her, why we adopted her."

I turned to face Blake. "What do you mean?"

"Don't get distracted," Bailey said. "You need to focus on your Soul Track. Reconciling your relationships. Remember? Samuel won't let you back in to Heaven unless you make an effort on Earth before the Solar Age ends."

I heard the discipline of my strictest teachers in her voice. I opened my mouth. I closed it. I swallowed. "How?" I asked. "I don't think a butterfly will do it." I paused. "I still don't understand how a butterfly reconciled my relationship with Sincerity."

"You put love in your relationship through the butterfly. Messengers like white butterflies carry love, compassion, thoughts of the other. That energy transmits at a subconscious sensory level to the recipient. They may not fully understand it, but a butterfly or bird hovering near them in an unusual way attracts most people's attention and comforts them."

I mulled that over. "I don't think that'll work for Sally."

"Probably not," Blair said.

Nihil death-stared at my soul family.

"Why don't you want me to reconcile with them, Nihil?" I asked.

"It's fake. It's not real," she said.

"Why do you say that?"

"Because I know," she replied, crossing her arms against herself. Bitterness roughened her voice. Scruffy pawed at her shin until she released her arms.

*Do I want to know?* My question fazed me, exhausted me. I didn't.

Nihil eyed me. "You're not ready, anyway. You find thinking about others exhausting. So why do you want to reconcile with them?" she asked, emphasizing the pronouns.

The others waited for my reply, too.

# Chapter Eighteen

# WHY DO I WANT TO RECONCILE?

*Why do I want to reconcile with them?* Nihil's question echoed in my mind as I gazed upwards, towards the light-smothered stars. And counted. Three. How many stars versus humans? One hundred billion humans. Over one hundred billion have lived and died on this planet for tens of thousands of years. Eight billion in material form today.

Numbers soothed me.

I hadn't thought about numbers since the last day of work, when I'd handed over the last accounting reports to my most faithful client.

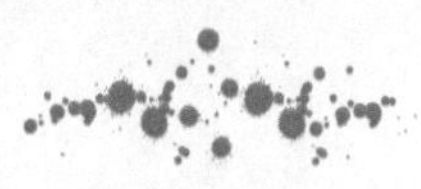

I ENTERED A reverie. My client's face as she last looked at me appeared in my mind. Her face came closer and closer.

*Whoosh!*

I entered her reverie. A hospital room. With four beds. And pastel-striped curtains drawn between them. Did she visit me in the Dying with Dignity suite? No, my suite was a large, private, soft-lit room. Harsh sunlight shone through the windows.

Now we inhabited her flashback. Somehow, I knew my client was flashbacking to a memory of guilt. Regret tinged the memory. The yellow vinyl of the hospital chair stuck to our legs; the curtain hid her from the other patients and them from her as we waited for her friend to return from her CT scan.

Voices penetrated.

A social worker spoke loudly and slowly to the man in the next bed.

"We've done all we can for you."

An alto voice responded. "Don't you mean you've done all for my husband what the funding will allow?"

"It's what we can afford. We allocate so much for each patient. We can't give you everything you want."

"How is living at the poverty line and receiving daily home care a want? My husband has MS and can't walk anymore. You know that."

"You tried that unproven treatment, and it didn't work."

"It worked," a baritone voice replied.

"You can't walk, can you? It's difficult to accept reality, but not everything we want we can have. You have to accept your condition."

"My condition is a disability not a death sentence."

The alto added, "The treatment worked, but we ran out of money. The three-step photobiomodulation therapy and audiovisual entrainment kept him in remission far longer than any of you predicted."

"Please mind your tone."

"My tone?"

"I won't be disrespected."

"You're offering my husband MAiD, and you think you're the one being disrespected?"

I felt a stirring in my chest. I sought the source. My client's heart hurt. Her metaphysical heart.

"We've tried, Dorrie. We couldn't afford neuromodulation treatments long enough for permanent effects."

A sob broke. "We did try! But they haven't, and now they want to save a buck by killing you off! We never asked for MAiD. Why does she bring it up every time she visits?" A sob broke the alto's voice. "We've said no to you over and over."

The social worker replied in cool tones, "People change their minds."

"We haven't!"

"Most of my clients do."

"It's to be expected," the baritone said dryly.

"Exactly!" the social worker crowed.

"When you barrage them daily and keep them on below-poverty-line income and withhold necessary support." A pause. A cough. Rough inhalation morphed into wheezing. "Didn't Jesus cure and restore life? Why don't health care professionals focus on curing and restoring instead of negating and killing?"

Fabric rustled. Footsteps strode off.

"She'll be back," the alto wailed.

"I know," the baritone answered. "Let's see what the doctor can do for me, and then talk about MAiD."

"I don't want you to die!"

"Neither do I. But we must face reality, Dorrie. The local LHIN isn't going to pay for the community care that I need, and our Ontario, CPPD, and this new Federal disability benefit isn't enough. We've mortgaged our home and maxed out our credit cards, and we still can't afford all the neurostimulation therapies I needed. I can't work anymore without the personal support worker."

"An hour a week," the alto said bitterly. "What good's that?"

"It is what it is," the baritone sighed. "I, too, wish it was more. I'd dearly love to contribute again. At least the entrainment device helps me sleep better."

"We'll find a way. We always do."

"Not this time, Dorrie. And after a decade of fighting them, I'm tired."

Soft crying drowned the silence.

"And I worry about you losing the house and how you'll pay off our debt. Maybe when we go home our children can fight for permanent palliative care rather than the short consult we got."

A bitter laugh cracked the crying. "In our small town? What is life when death is cheaper and quicker?" she asked rhetorically.

Thoughts flew in my client's mind. I caught snatches of them. *Why is the church silent? Should I intervene? This is a one-off. Yes, a one—*

*Our governments wouldn't offer death, not health—*

*Health care is a right—*

*I believe in choice—*

*Free will is what Jesus gave us. They have freedom to say no....right? What's neurostimulation?*

*Forget it! There's nothing I can do!*

The reprimand shot like a bullet through my mind and blasted me out of my client's reverie.

NUMBERS SOOTHED ME.

As I tried to recall how many stars are known to exist, I wondered why I'd forgotten about numbers. Steady, certain, yet challenging, numbers didn't betray or abandon one.

*How many of us existing beings travel the Earth today?* I asked Bailey in my thoughts as I lowered my head.

"What's numbers got to do with it?" Nihil asked.

"That's fascinating that Charlotte Elisabeth answers your question with numbers!" Shireen Anne exclaimed behind me.

I jerked, spun, and growled. "Do you always do that?"

"Sorry," she said and hunched away from me, smiling. She straightened. "But I do find it fascinating you went to numbers. You were an accountant, weren't you?"

I nodded.

"Yes. That makes sense, in a way, that numbers would be your go-to distraction."

"Distraction?"

She blinked owlishly at me.

I raised my eyebrows.

"Oh, for heaven's sake. Answer the question," Nihil huffed.

"I'm one number in a hundred billion. Add on Neanderthals. Did you know they had social groups and were more...well...probably as intelligent as homo sapiens? We all have Neanderthal genes in us. They say fifteen percent of our genes is Neanderthal."

Nihil rumbled in her throat.

*Why's she so angry?* I turned to her. "I like numbers. They help me get answers. They're certain."

"And relationships are not," Bailey said.

I nodded. "I don't know why I want to reconcile. Samuel said I must, and I don't want to remain on Earth. There's too much pain, here. I left it, remember?"

I craned my neck to search for the stars above the lit-up buildings and streetlights. A jet plane flew high overhead, its twin white wing lights alternating with red flashes, like a speeding star. I felt insignificant yet one with the magnificence of the sky.

I dropped my head and blinked. I hadn't noticed the night sky like that before. *Magnificent.* I rolled that word around in my mouth. I gazed upwards again and longed to see all the stars.

DARKNESS BLANKETED US. Trees dwelt like shadows against a blacked-out landscape. Above us, stars multiplied across the sky like white-paint-spattered black cloth. I sucked in air. It filtered out through my skin. I'd never seen the stars like this before. Memory recalled me to that field trip to the Planetarium, the now-shuttered one next to the Royal Ontario Museum. We'd reclined in darkness in body-hugging seats arranged in circles as a narrator explained the heavens to us and stars appeared above us. Money and apathy had robbed today's children of that wondrous experience. Just like politics and money for businesses were depriving them of the

Ontario Place oasis and exploring the endless rooms, corridors, and cool teachers of the Ontario Science Centre.

I sighed. *Why now, when I'm not alive in mortal form, do I care?* I shrugged. No longer my concern.

*Isn't it?* Shireen Anne asked.

*Is that where Heaven is? In the stars?* I wondered. The stars' sheer number beholding this empty landscape of distant old mountains and endless plains enthralled me. Billions of people had struggled with relationships. Every one of us had to reconcile to be allowed back into Heaven.

"That's not quite right," Shireen Anne said.

Bailey nodded. "It's true."

"What do you mean?" I asked, dropping my gaze to them. I realized that they'd all arrived here in this dark-sky place with me. *Where had my thoughts brought me, anyway?*

"I don't know where we are," Bailey answered. "But your thought entered our minds, and in that connection, we followed you," Bailey explained.

*Oh.* "But...Do you mean...I mean...do I not need to reconcile then to leave this place and return to Heaven?"

"It's complicated."

I pressed my lips together against the words that threatened to erupt unbidden.

Nihil crossed her arms and stared at the ground. No moon lit the wild grass underneath her feet. The grass could be green or brown, for the darkness here was absolute except for the stars. Nihil dug her toes into the grasses and stared at it as if it held treasure. Scruffy bent their head to examine where her foot was digging. They lowered their head and snuffled.

*Ah-choo!*

Scruffy's sneeze ricocheted in the depthless quiet as their nose smacked into the ground. Nihil stifled a laugh. Scruffy shook their head and sat next to her.

"It's simple, really," Shireen Anne said.

Nihil's face flattened into expressionless.

Shireen Anne inserted herself between me and Nihil to face me. "Sometimes, it's not possible to reconcile. The Earth-living are too angry or abusive. Attempts go awry. In that case, Jesus lets us wait until the abusers and hate-filled are ready. But sometimes that leads to one of us not doing well. Jesus—God!—loves us unconditionally and has eons of patience. Literal eons!" Shireen Anne exclaimed, spreading her arms wide. "God instructs the elders to let the person in to Heaven like with you or to forgive failure and let them back in after they've tried. Even though they can't complete their Soul Track, God wants them to keep trying, keep giving them the opportunity to grow and learn and find a different way to reconcile. Relationships are key to existence."

"What about those ghosts?"

Shireen Anne cast her eyes down to the dark ground. "I'm not sure. They," she nodded at my soul family, standing close to each other a little apart from us. "They know the mysteries."

I cocked my head. "Why them and not you?"

"They've reached a level of growth I haven't yet." She waved her hand as if dismissing that topic. "That's why, no matter what and when, you'll have to reconcile."

"Why?"

"To avoid second death."

"Second death? Blake mentioned that, right? But you didn't tell me what it is. I didn't die when I thought I died. So," I narrowed my eyes and wrinkled my brow. "First death. Second death. What are these? First death is when I died in the Dying with Dignity Suite, right?"

Bailey nodded.

Blake asked Bailey, "Can I tell her now? She should know. Everyone who has read Revelation when in mortal form knows, anyway!"

Bailey nodded.

"It's easy," Blake grinned. "First death was when that Dr. Veritas killed you legally. You're alive but in a different form. So death is like a gateway from one form to another. First death from Earth life to afterlife." She didn't wait for me to nod. "But second death is a gateway to nothingness."

My eyebrows rose to my hairline. "Nothingness?"

Blake's eyes clouded. "Yeah. Nothingness. You won't exist anymore. It's sad." She fell silent for a moment. I couldn't contemplate this. *Why keep me alive only to void me?* A breeze ruffled the wild grass, releasing the rich scent of dying vegetation. "That's why Jesus wants to save everyone," Blake said. "And God gives us eons of time to complete our Soul Track."

"So you mean, I can do it another time? I don't have to now?"

"Yes, but your family is ready. Look at how upset they are! And we're," Shireen Anne gestured to everyone around us, "all here supporting you."

I peered through the consuming darkness but couldn't find Nihil.

"Yes, even Nihil is. And Scruffy supports Nihil. Questions help you dig deeper. They're not the way I'd put them—" She clapped a hand over her mouth and tittered.

"It's not enough for the elder to tell you you must reconcile. You must feel the desire in your heart as well," Bailey said gently.

I slumped into myself and nodded at the grass beneath my bare feet. *How many blades of grass used to grow here?* I rubbed my feet against the ground; sharp edges of long, dead grass ravaged my soles. The grass was dying under autumn's cooling blast. I'd died yet hadn't died. Mom and Sally had cried over my death. I didn't understand why. Perhaps I needed to see them again to understand. *Will reconciling with them help me understand?* I pondered this thought. I'd regretted not spending more time with Sincerity. Seeing hidden parts of her and how that man-ghost, whoever he was, possessed her, puzzled me. Regret remained. Did that mean I love her? *Do I love my family?*

"That question is a good one," Bailey said.

I lifted my head.

"Seeking to reconcile with them will help you answer it."

I exhaled. I wondered where Mom was.

THE SIDEWALK LAY empty before us. Darkness shrouded Mom's house. No light shone out the windows. The front door opened, and Mom emerged as Sally drove the car into the driveway beside us.

"This should be interesting," Nihil said as we observed the unfolding scene. Scruffy popped into view beside her like entering this time and place through a wormhole.

Bailey, Blair, and Blake gathered around me like a comforting blanket. I huddled closer to Bailey. She looked younger than me, yet her presence felt like what I thought a mother should be. I blinked at this new thought. *Am I developing...*

I shoved those thoughts out of my head.

"Where have you been?" Mom asked Sally, arms crossed, foot tapping as she guarded the front door.

Sally shut the driver's door with a click. She turned to face Mom. "Out."

"Where?"

"My usual place, Mom. You know," Sally hedged as she walked up the path from the driveway. None of us could lie to Mom. Sally never had to because she'd always been simpatico with Mom. I frowned as I remembered the life review of Sally with me when I was twelve years old. *Has Sally returned to that hidden rebelliousness?*

"Tell me exactly where." Mom's eyes bored holes into Sally's. Sally slowed to a halt. She looked away. "I—"

"I know exactly where you've been." Mom uncrossed her arms and pointed a bony finger at Sally. "I saw you," she accused her.

Sally's head snapped around. The streetlight cast her face half in shadow and half highlighting the paleness of her face. Grey glinted at her hairline. *Has Sally stopped dyeing her hair blonde?* My mouth opened in an "oh." I hadn't noticed that earlier. *How'd she dare?*

"You've stopped going to the hairdresser. Don't think I haven't noticed."

"I haven't stopped," Sally muttered. "I just don't want fake blonde hair anymore."

"What did you say? It was those people who put you up to it, wasn't it?"

"What do you mean, those people?" Sally asked the path.

"You know what I mean, Sally. With Charlotte Elisabeth leaving us like that and Sincerity doing her own thing behind that smiling mask of hers, you were my one ally. But you've betrayed me!" Mom's voice pitched high on her last words. I tucked my chin into my chest and glanced around from under my eyelids. *The neighbours will hear!* Mom forbade us to fight outside in front of witnessing neighbours. All obedience. All the time.

I gulped.

Sally half turned away from Mom, and defiance straightened her spine. "That's right, Mom. Those people welcomed me. They comforted me that day you told me Charlotte Elisabeth killed herself."

"That thing, that non-human who calls himself a doctor killed her. He betrayed his Hippocratic oath."

"I agree. He did. He betrayed life. He hastened death. Who knows what's happening with Charlotte Elisabeth now. I pray for her every day."

"Pray! Are you out of your mind? Prayer does no good. Charlotte Elisabeth doesn't exist anymore. She's gone!" Mom screeched the last word.

Lights turned on in the upstairs window next door. Neither Mom nor Sally noticed as Sally spun to face Mom and screamed in her face, fisting her hands by her sides, "She's not!"

"She is!" Mom screamed back, leaning in to Sally, her pointing finger curling into her palm, her right hand clenched. "You betrayed me. The one daughter who stayed with me has gone to those people!"

"Stop calling them those people. They're not vermin."

"They are! They should be eradicated. They fill people's heads with nonsense and fairy tales. You know that!"

"Not all churches are like yours was, Mom," Sally pleaded.

"You know what I went through! You know how they brainwashed me with their delusional Satan stories and—"

"I know, Mom. I know, but this church isn't like that!"

"You're being deceived, Sally! How dare you turn your back on me and side with those people! They fill your heads with snakes and fake history—"

I stepped forwards. Mom had gone off the rails. *What do snakes have to do with Sally and St. Paul's? Is Mom hallucinating?*

"She's referencing the metaphorical origin story in Genesis and confusing it as literal," Nihil stated.

"Huh?" I twisted my head around to look at Nihil. I wanted to face her; instead, I spotted those ghosts I'd seen earlier. They were gathering in the trees, their faces glistening with menace underneath the eye-assaulting white streetlights. "Um, Bailey," I said, pointing towards the trees.

Bailey replied, "I know. You can ignore them."

"I can?"

"Just pray," she said.

The ghosts, lead by that man-ghost, carved a wide arc around us as they rushed down and surrounded Mom and Sally. The man-ghost leader stood apart as his semi-transparent acolytes began mocking the two, screaming into their ears.

"Yeah, she betrayed you!"

"She's always telling you what to do. Time to tell her like it is!"

"You go, Mom. You get her under control!"

"Isn't she old! Pathetic! Why listen to her?"

Nihil gestured to Sally and Mom screaming at each other, their noses almost touching, as the ghosts prodded them. "This is better than I expected," she gleed.

I stared, horrified. Sally hadn't fought Mom like this before. None of us had ever dared to. We kept our intentions out of her sight. *Are the ghosts making them do it?*

"No, they can't make you do anything," Bailey said. "Unless you're already thinking that way. They'll exacerbate your thinking, tear at your control, explode your angry thoughts into words."

I blinked. The cacophony shrieked like a gale strengthening into a tornado. *Why doesn't Bailey do something?*

Bailey turned towards me. "They're your human family. We can tell you," she emphasized the last word, "that you must reconcile to return to and remain in Heaven, but you're maturing now. Part of maturing is to find your own motivation. What matters most to you? Do they matter enough to you for you to call on Jesus's unconditional love to help you forgive, to seek and recognize signs of remorse in them? Do you care enough *about* them for you to engage *with* them in a way you feared while living on Earth? You need to step up for them if you want to reconcile with them."

"Me?" *Why me? Why isn't my soul family helping me, then? They'd always guided me. What does Bailey mean about maturing? I'm mature! I worked hard to become independent from Mom!* I mentally slapped these thoughts away. I'd finished with self-analysis when alive.

*How had Mom found out about Sally going to St. Paul's, anyway?*

Sally suddenly fell silent. She echoed my question in a normal voice.

Mom hissed, "I saw you when I drove by. I almost caused an accident seeing you coming out of that godforsaken place. How dare you go to church! I've told you what a menace they are. How they abuse and prey on children."

"These people don't, Mom," Sally pleaded. "They cared for me that day, that horrible day. I'd have melted down if not for them."

"You go to them over your own mother?"

"You weren't comforting me, Mom!"

"We all have our cross to bear," Mom growled, the whites of her eyes a punctuation.

Sally held her ground. The ghosts beside her shouted, "That's right. Hold your ground. Tell her what's what!"

The ghosts crowding beside Mom yelled, "Show her who's boss. Do what you have to! Moms know best. You show her!"

"Stop!" I yelled, clapping my hands over my ears. The ghosts turned their faces towards me and scorned, "How're you going to stop us? You know nothing, little girl. You're useless and pathetic."

"Don't listen to them," Shireen Anne said behind me.

"I'm not!" I shouted.

Nihil rolled her eyes. "You really sucked at school, right?"

I frowned at her as the ghosts returned to mocking, scolding, and encouraging violence to Mom and Sally.

"What do you mean?"

Nihil smiled and returned her attention to my mother and sister. "Your mom's going to hit her."

"No!"

"Unless you do something."

Mom raised her fist, opening her palm to strike Sally.

Scruffy stood up, trotted to behind me, and bumped their wet nose against my calves. I stumbled forwards. Fear crowded my chest. I thought of Calico. Currently, nowhere to be seen. *Help me!* I thought. I remembered the light that had appeared in the Distortans. "Light, help me. Get those ghosts away from them. Chase the man-ghost away! Please."

A few ghosts stopped screaming and cursing at Mom and Sally. They turned their attention towards me. But they didn't come near me. "Stop that," said the leader.

"Stop what," I retorted, my voice trembling. "Asking the light to help me?"

"What can that light do? You don't even know what it is."

*God. Whoever that is.* I buried that last thought. Then I remembered they can't hear my thoughts. "God," I repeated out loud. The leader man-ghost slunk back. The ghosts fell silent and scuttled behind him. I broke away from my soul family and moved up the path from the sidewalk towards the side path to the driveway. I closed in on Mom and Sally. "God," I said, "will help me. That light stayed by me."

The leader hustled away from me. One by one, the ghosts fell away as I walked towards them.

Their voices faded.

They vanished.

Sally fell silent. Her shoulders slumped as Mom paused her striking movement in mid-flight and stared at Sally's drooping head. They remained statue-like for minutes.

Sally said, "I'm going to bed, Mom."

Mom dropped her hand, nodded, and followed her into the house. She shut the front door.

# Chapter Nineteen

# THINKING IN THE TREE

*I* shuffled back to the sidewalk, my eyes cast inwards on this God conundrum. Footfalls followed me. I bumped into a tree. Its bark burnished my skin; my eyes burned resentment at the interruption. I focused on an edge line and followed it upwards. Branches stretched over me, hanging on to their leaves, their fall-dressed colours bleached underneath the streetlights reflecting off the seamless clouds overhead. *When did those clouds roll in?* A breeze puffed up and rustled the dehydrating leaves. I yearned to hide in those leaves.

"You can," Bailey said from behind me.

"Yeah, we'll hang with you up there," Blake said. She shot up to the lowest branch and settled on it. Sparrows burst from the surrounding branches, chattering and swooping. Feet dangling, Blake stretched a hand towards me. "Think lightness. Think 'gravity doesn't hold me.'"

"Shhhh. She must learn on her own," Bailey said.

"I know, I know, but she's had a hard time. Can't we help her a little?"

I studied Blake's advice from all angles. *Gravity doesn't hold me? Do I imagine myself lighter than a feather? Lighter than an atom?* Nothing happened. Gravity pulls atoms towards it, I knew. Gravity bends light and space-time. *How do I defy gravity?* In turn, I considered Bailey, Blake above me, Blair, Nihil, Shireen Anne, their eyes on my face, awaiting me. Their neutral expressions revealed no answers. My mouth turned up as a line from Descartes entered my mind. *Cogito ergo sum. I think, therefore I am.* Mind. Thoughts. Reality.

My eyelids lifted into my eyebrows. I bent back my head and studied the branches. Blake smiled down at me, her legs swinging. *When I think, I move to a new destination. If my mind creates reality, does it create me? Does it not only transport me to another space but also move me?*

I dropped my gaze to the tree's bark before my eyes. Ridges and trenches zigzagged upwards. The tree grew against gravity. Humans do, too, though our feet—and this tree's roots—never leave the ground.

*I am not gravity bound.*

I thought it.

I believed it.

I knew it.

My feet lifted off the ground. The concrete sidewalk's energy pulled on my bare feet, magnet to magnet. I hunched my shoulders and turtled my neck. I fisted my hands. *I am superwoman,* I grinned to myself. The concrete gripped my feet. I let go of all my tension.

Nihil said as she zipped upwards by me, "You should've paid attention in Heaven School."

Frustration warmed me. "I'm trying!"

"What does not gravity-bound mean to you?" Shireen Anne asked.

Irritation prickled me up and down like ants racing along my skin.

"Hey, it's okay, Charlotte Elisabeth, you can do it!" Blake exclaimed from above me.

Vexation growled deep in my mind. My hands fisted.

"You won't get up there from here in that state," Blair stated.

I turned furious eyes on her. Her impassive face returned my stare.

Shireen Anne clambered up the tree and settled on a branch above Blake, her feet dangling close to Blake's head. Bailey stood impassively beside me.

Frederick's energy suddenly announced his presence. I didn't know how I knew this strange sensation of calmness and light and strength was him, but I knew. I turned around. He was standing on the road behind me. He walked towards me and took my hand. I looked down at our clasped hands. He said, "It's easy when you know how. But not when you don't."

I stared up into his shadowed face. *Why is a young man so interested in me?*

*I'm not young,* he replied in his thoughts. *I'm your age. I died young. Don't you remember me?*

I blinked up at him. Compassion and grief for him seeped into me. I didn't bat away these uncomfortable feelings. Instead, I let them flow and fill me. Somehow, it felt like I was not alone when I let them fill me.

"It's okay," he said out loud. "It was a long time ago when we met and when I died. It was the first day of your university classes. We were in line for coffee at Sid Smith. I helped you with your backpack."

"Backpack?"

His smile lightened his face as his eyes crinkled with amusement. He said, "Time is past and present and flowing time heals. I have a mission now."

"To find your father," I said.

"Yes. But also..." He paused and looked upwards.

"Also? Is finding your father your only Soul Track?"

He spoke to the sky. "My mother, for all her faults, and I got along. I had nothing to reconcile with her, but I was looking for my father when I died. An urge gripped me the month before I died. I forgot all else in the sense of urgency that drove me."

I stilled my molecules at this unaccustomed flow of words, hoping he'd continue these revelations of his mind and his Soul

Track. I studied his chin, his carved jawline clean of whiskers, a hint of his Adam's apple underneath his skin; I craved to see his face, his expression. His mind had created every detail of his dead physical body.

He turned back to me. "What is the feeling of defying gravity? For each person, it's different. You lifted off briefly. What were you imaging?"

Disappointed at no more revelations, I replied, "I wasn't."

"Okay. What were you thinking?"

"I know I'm not gravity bound."

He nodded. "What else is not gravity bound?"

I squinted up at him.

He nodded encouragement and squeezed my hand briefly.

"I...don't know...I wasn't good at physics."

"Neutrinos," he said.

*Oh.* "Gravity doesn't affect neutrinos? Do I think neutrinos?

"Yes." His eyes moved up and to the left as he searched his visual memory. "You had flowers in Heaven, didn't you?"

"Yes."

"Think flowers. Think neutrinos as flowers."

I raised my eyebrows and queried, "Flowers?"

He nodded. "Yes."

I looked down at my bare feet, at the concrete magnetizing them to it. I shrugged. *Okay, I'll try*, I thought to myself. I imaged a flower. A pink aster. I imagined being able to see neutrinos spinning it into being. That didn't feel right. I imagined neutrinos looking like pink asters flowing upwards. I smiled at the image. The concrete's roughness left my feet. Its energy pulled on them. I focused on the pink-aster neutrinos speeding upwards. The concrete let go, and I watched through my mental imagery, the tree sliding downwards beside Frederick.

*Bonk.*

"Ouch!" I rubbed the top of my head as Frederick teased, "Watch where you're going."

I smiled back. A giggle erupted out of me. I never had to think about hitting objects above me before. Ceilings, branches. What next? The sky? I laughed. He laughed. Bailey slid up beside me, her lips stretching wide. Blake shouted near me, "You did it! Come on, let's go higher, right into the leaves."

As the rest found perches on various branches, hiding themselves among the maple tree's fall-reddened leaves, I refocused on my image of pink aster neutrinos. Frederick and I rose and rose until I reached the top of the tree. I sat on the topmost branch. Sitting high up, I observed the residential neighbourhood laid out before me. The thickly gathered leaves below me hid the rest. Inordinately pleased at mastering this aspect of my new existence, I grinned. Frederick settled down next to me. "Why did you want to hide?"

"I felt overwhelmed. I don't know who God is."

He gripped my hand and swayed his feet and our hands back and forth.

"God is the light that—"

He frowned down at his feet, dropping his head. "No, tell me first who God is to you? I don't want to impose my experience onto you." He glanced at me.

"What do you mean?"

"God is both objective reality and personal. At this moment, you have only personal. Later, you'll learn the objective reality. But every person's experience of God is unique. I don't want your experience to be influenced by mine." He eyed me sideways, his long black lashes half obscuring his brown eyes. "We're social mammals. Even when we think we're fully independent, we're not. Each choice we make, each utterance, influences those around us, even making them choose or see their experiences differently than what they would have if completely left to experience and think about them on their own with no human or animal interaction at all. My mind-matrix supports and changes yours, and vice versa."

I stared at him.

He smiled. "Tell me about your experience with the light you saw in the Distortans."

I looked off into the distance and recollected. "Comforting. Challenging. Protective. Curious." I paused on that last word. My feet swung back and forth, back and forth. I gripped the branch hard with my right hand to feel its abrasive edges dig into my skin.

Frederick's warmth flowed into my left hand. No pain, only complicated sensation. I didn't like being curious. But my curiosity had awakened in the Earth-Heaven Interdimensional Expanse. I hadn't disliked it, I realized. Frederick squeezed my hand as a signal he was letting go. I tightened my hold. "Wait!" I said. "Why do you keep leaving?"

"I have to find my father."

"Why?"

"I need to reconcile with him."

"Don't you know where he is?"

He shook his head. "I didn't know who he was for decades. My mother wouldn't tell me. She couldn't because she'd had so many lovers."

I nodded, remembering, amazed at myself that I had.

"When I found out who he was, after I died, when such things become known to us, I began my search on Earth, thinking he was still alive. Then I learned he'd died. But I don't know where he exists."

"It's that important to find him?"

"Yes." He leaned into me, shaking my hand. "It's that important to reconcile our relationships. Our blood ones. Our friendship ones."

I opened my hand. He let go, levitated, and flew off. I watched him leave.

A shout filtered upwards towards me through the leaves. "Don't believe him!"

Another shout. "Believe him!"

I sat stiller than a dead branch. *How we've polluted our nights with artificial light*, I thought. *God isn't artificial*, came the thought. I pondered that thought. Its truth sank into me. I wanted it to be morning; I wanted to see the sun rise.

Sparrows dove for the branches beside and below me. They chirped at each other as they gathered. A gull shrieked overhead. Another answered. Craning my head to search for them, I spotted a hawk riding the high-up winds without a sound.

I stood up on my branch. A few sparrows objected and rocketed off. The rest chattered and chirped and called as I looked up at graphite clouds smudging the endless light-grey cloud ceiling, the horizon glowing, lightening the sky. I pondered Samuel's insistence

I return to Earth; the others talking about my Soul Track; and Frederick's decades-long search for his unknown father, who may not even know he exists, all to reconcile with him, someone he never knew and who'd never been involved in his life. *Why reconcile with such a person?* The glowing grey sky gave no answer.

A strange peace washed into me. Light accompanied that peace. *God is peace?* I blinked against that foreign idea. *What now?*

*Reconcile!*

*Who'd said that?* My three-hundred-and-sixty vision revealed nothing. I craned my neck, searched through the leaves below me.

Silence.

*God?*

Silence.

*My hallucination? My subconscious?*

Silence.

After straining my mind to the edge of its perceptions, I quit. I returned to what Frederick had said.

"How do I reconcile with Sally?" I shouted down to my soul family.

"Directly. Mind to mind," they replied as one.

# Chapter Twenty

# A SISTERLY POSSESSION

The room's walls closed in on me. After my soul family had told me about another way to reconcile, I'd closed my eyes and focused on Sally, anticipating opening my eyes in a different place—just not an office.

The tiny office housed a beat-up desk tucked against the window wall. The frocked man who'd greeted Sally outside St. Paul's sat in an old-fashioned wooden office chair on wheels, back to his desk, leaning towards Sally, elbows on his knees, hands clasped.

Sally was bawling.

Tears and snot drenched my half-sister's face in a way I hadn't seen before.

I averted my eyes.

I couldn't my ears.

Her sobs wracked the little room.

I studiously observed the office.

Bookshelves lined the two walls perpendicular to the window, and a table strewn with magazines, journal articles, books, papers, and errant pens snuggled up to the wall next to the shut door. I turned my head to look at my soul family. They gestured towards Sally as one. With my three-sixty vision, I somehow knew Nihil and Shireen Anne were hanging out in the hallway.

I turned back to face Sally. Her hands twisted her white, snot-filled handkerchief. Mom didn't believe in disposable tissues. Handkerchiefs ironed and folded had stuffed our sock and underwear drawers, one for each day, each day with its own colour. Sally's white handkerchief meant it's Monday. A fresh week called for a fresh white, Mom had declared every Monday. Somehow I felt comforted she hadn't broken the habit.

I shifted my right foot forwards.

Sally wailed, "She found out!"

*Is this the same day Sally and Mom fought on the path?* I drew my foot back.

The man didn't take his eyes off her. I noticed his black shirt's strange collar. A white square, centred within a stand-up collar. I glanced a question at Blake.

She said, "It's a priest's collar."

Blair added, "Pastors in the Anglican church wear them."

I studied this man. *A Pastor?*

"What's a Pastor?"

Nihil's sigh penetrated the wall.

"Hush," Bailey commanded. She said to me, "It's someone who's studied God, Jesus, and the Christian religion and who has been ordained, that is, anointed to lead a church and the people in the church. Pastors talk about God and Jesus and the Bible on Sundays, they pray for the sick and anyone who needs it, they counsel and comfort, like he's doing now with your sister."

"Half-sister," I muttered automatically. I studied the priest...pastor. His long black lashes framed his eyes above his pale cheeks. Tall, angular, and capable. Looking down at Sally's bent head, he looked like a rock she could lean on. Maybe I could...

"It's the only way to reconcile," Bailey said.

I pressed my lips together. Pressure between them built up, softness over unyielding teeth. Energy pulsed through the compression. As I sucked my lips in and pushed them against each other harder and harder, more and more energy flowed between them and spread outwards in a buzzing resistance. I let go.

Sally scrunched her handkerchief against her mouth. She dropped her hands to her lap, her right hand clutching the sodden fabric, and exhaled. The pastor's eyes didn't leave her face.

"I'm relieved, but..."

He waited.

"Mom wants me to move out. She said I betrayed her. But I didn't!"

"I know," he purred soothingly.

I blinked. *How can a man purr?*

"Don't be distracted, Charlotte Elisabeth," Bailey said.

"I can't believe she's going to kick me out! I'll be alone. I can't be alone! Sincerity has nothing to do with me. Charlotte Elisabeth is gone. Why did she kill herself?" Sally demanded, looking up and directly into his eyes.

He didn't answer. He waited, his eyes emitting patience and acceptance.

"I don't understand." Sally shifted in her straight-backed chair. She straightened her spine and slumped back down. "I've been good. I do what I'm supposed to do. I didn't tell Mom, and I went home and looked after her. I did everything she asked. No, demanded. Mom doesn't ask; she commands. She tells you what to do, and you don't disobey, you know. Never disobey. I did this one thing, and she gets mad. Why!"

"She's used to controlling her daughters. Some people are like that. They do it to keep their fear at bay," he said.

"It's like everything I've done didn't matter!"

"Now!" Bailey insisted.

I puffed out my chest. I took a long step towards her. I hesitated.

"Remember what we told you. Focusing on her allows you to enter her. You're not entering to control but to experience. She'll sense you, through her internal senses, and you can communicate your thoughts, your remorse, your love through them. Your mind to her mind."

I swallowed. Bracing my shoulders, I walked into Sally. Her body enfolded me. Muscles rippled into my energy. Her heart beat against my mind. I perceived every cell, every sinew, as I melded into her body, becoming one with her. One but two. Her emotions flooded me. Guilt, shame, fear, anger, grief. Unending grief.

I hadn't realized. I'd experienced all the emotions of different people—family to strangers—in the life review postcards, but nothing like this. I reacted instinctively with guilt. I sensed that my guilt wouldn't help her or me. And on that thought, compassion and love flowed out of me.

I sat forwards.

Her body sat up. I saw out of her eyes the pastor straightening, his eyes widening, his brow puckering.

"Be careful not to control her," Bailey warned.

The pastor scrutinized Sally's face as I gazed at him through her eyes, side by side with her.

"Are you all right, Sally?" he asked.

She blinked. Her throat constricted; my neck tightened. Her thoughts tumbled around in confusion. Her brainwaves tickled my mind like gentle electrical sparks. Behind them, I sensed her mind trying to control her thoughts. My mind reached out to hers through her manic neural networks to let her know she wasn't alone. I apologized to her.

Sally blinked.

"Sally?" The pastor reached out to touch her arm.

"Uh..."

"What is it?" he asked.

"I don't know," she whispered.

"Do you feel less alone?"

Sally frowned at him. "How did you know?"

"I've seen this before."

"Seen what before?"

"Your sister is with you isn't she?"

Sally reared back. The wooden slats of the chair's back dug into her back. Strange to feel solid physical sensations again, not molecular versions of them. Less real, yet more familiar. I tried not to control her movements and influence her thoughts. I only wanted her to know I loved her.

I gulped. *Love? Did I think that? Feel that? For Sally?* I jolted up, panicking.

Sally shot up.

Bailey said, "It's okay. It's okay. Don't think about what you feel. Simply feel. And try not to move, else you will control her."

I relaxed.

Sally dropped into her chair.

The pastor watched her, his arms crossing, his lanky legs crossing. "It's discombobulating, isn't it?"

"Yes, but..." Sally stared at him. "Are you saying...are you saying...she's...possessing me? Isn't that devil worship?" she whispered.

"No," he shook his head. "It's a way for the departed to support their loved ones. Yes, I should add demons can possess humans. Remember how Jesus threw demons out of the possessed, how they knew him before his followers did? But demons control humans. Some spirits with bad intentions can, as well. I've seen that, but spirits with ill intentions can inhabit only briefly, while demons can remain until someone throws them out. But what I see isn't possession. It's comfort. What do you feel?"

"I feel," Sally choked.

*Feel? What do I feel?* I thought, *Let the emotions flow and don't think.* I felt badly for Sally, for me, for the three of us. I reminisced, recalling what she did for me when I was twelve. Gratitude surfaced and burgeoned in her mind. Her fight with Mom elicited empathy for Sally. Unbidden, the image of her conversation in the church emblazoned itself on my mind. I didn't understand this church business. The word "hypocrisy" flashed before I could suppress it. Sally stirred.

"What is it?" the pastor asked. He uncrossed his arms, leaned forwards, and touched her arm. "Whatever you tell me, you know I won't judge. I've seen it all. Heard it all. Nothing you can say will affect my respect for you."

*Respect?* I let that word sink into me.

She said, "I heard...I heard...hypocrisy."

"Do you think that was your sister saying that about you?"

Sally nodded.

But I did respect her, I suddenly realized. Respect her for surviving and coping with Mom better than I had. I concentrated on the word "respect."

"Respect," Sally breathed.

"You felt that as well?"

She nodded.

"What else?"

"Love," Sally whispered so quietly, the pastor turned his ear towards her mouth. She repeated the word. "We don't say that word," Sally whispered.

"Who don't?"

"Our family."

My energy flagged. My mind lost my sense of self, and I exited her. Sally started as I lay on the floor, wondering if I was de-existing.

"Maybe we can talk about all the things you felt later. Right now, I think you need to process the experience. She's left you?"

"Yes," Sally said. She shivered.

"She didn't possess you to make you do her bidding. She made herself one with you to support you and to convey to you what she feels." He stood up and took a step to the bookshelf behind him. He ran his long fingers along the creased spines of tall and short, thin and wide books. "Ah-ha," he exclaimed as he pulled out a book. "Here, take this. It'll help you understand your experience and let you know you're not alone. You may not want to take it home since your mother believes vehemently that there's no life after death. I want to help you reconcile with Charlotte Elisabeth so that you two don't split apart in the afterlife, as well. You have your locker downstairs?" He handed the book to her.

Sally nodded as she took it.

"Read it here, and leave it in your locker until you're finished. Okay?"

"Okay," she said as she cradled the book in both hands.

"Sally, your sister came to you to reconcile. This personal experience is common yet not common between the departed and the living. They come to us to comfort us."

Sally gazed up at him. "Really?"

"Yes, really. I think once you process this, you'll find your spirit lighter. And your work..." He looked into the distance, across the short carpeted expanse of his office. "Your work here will change."

Sally smiled, hugged the book to her chest, stood up, stepped over me, and walked out.

"Thank you," the pastor said to the air. He stood smiling for a minute, then he abruptly swivelled his chair to face his desk, sat down smartly, and lifted the lid of his laptop, disturbing a pile of papers, a couple of which floated to the floor. He ignored them as Windows signed him in with his face.

I lay on the worn carpet like a beached dolphin. I needed time to process what had happened. When Bailey had suggested this as the way to reconcile directly, mind to mind, I hadn't believed it'd work. Nihil had said it was an invasion of privacy. Blake had mocked Nihil. Blair had given practical tips. Shireen Anne had questioned Bailey about practical details and the emotional fallout on me. I thought, *This method made more sense than the butterfly method!*

I stared up at the white ceiling with its round, frosted-glass fixture. And smiled.

# Chapter Twenty-One

# FATHER FOUND

Gasoline engines rumbled, electric vehicles whined, a cracked muffler thrummed, cyclists hit air horns and bells, pedestrians yelled, "Stop parking on the fucking sidewalk, ya moron!" I slapped my hands over my ears at the last eruption. Toronto's Vision Zero to protect people walking on the sidewalks wasn't working too well. I didn't miss the city's cacophony. *Why have I appeared here, where that man-ghost—demon?—had possessed Sincerity?*

Footsteps slapped on the concrete. I turned my head to look. A familiar-looking man. White hair shagged over his head and down his neck. Skin as white as wax. A prominent nose and full lips. Clouded brown eyes sunk into blue-brown puffy circles. I followed his stooped shoulders through the outer door and into the elevator. My soul family, Nihil, and Shireen Anne squeezed in beside me together in the elevator's small box. Toronto's Vision Zero pedestrian-cycling-driving rage faded into the background. The elevator creaked its way upwards.

*I remember!* I slapped my forehead. As I'd lain on the carpet, I'd asked Bailey if Sincerity had returned to that lawyer or if the butterfly had reconciled us. I'd then switched my attention back to Sally. Thoughts had flitted in and out of my consciousness, but this one must've stuck for it to have transported me to the lawyer's office building.

I scrutinized the man whom life had aged. *Why is he familiar?* The man leaned against the back of the elevator and stared at the scuffed elevator floor, his briefcase dangling from his thick, long fingers, oblivious to our presence. Bailey, Blair, and Blake somehow merged with the elevator walls to give the rest of us space.

Shireen Anne said in answer to my confused frown, "I don't know either. They won't tell me how they merge with walls like that."

I eyeballed her; she grinned; and the elevator dinged its arrival. The man detached himself from the elevator's back wall and slouched towards the end of the hall. We followed. Me leading.

He struggled with a ring of keys, dropping his briefcase, picking it up again with his left hand, jangling through the keys on their plain ring.

"Is it plain?" Shireen Anne whispered in my ear.

I eyed her and heard and saw the clunk of a lock unlocked.

I hastened to follow and almost bumped into the white-haired man's back.

"Sorry," I said and stepped back.

He swayed in the doorway, staring fixedly into space.

"Why's he standing there?" I asked no one.

No one answered.

With a long, long sigh, he shuffled into a square room with dented folding metal chairs decorating the walls perpendicular to the entrance and a weathered door with a frosted window directly ahead of us. He plodded past the empty chairs and turned the steel knob of the inner door. He rested a moment before pushing it open to enter a small office.

Two desks sat at right angles; bookcases lined every wall except the window one opposite the door; the larger desk occupied the space in front of the window. Below the window sat half-height filing cabinets. Plain beige and grey, as if bought and placed at random.

Paper stacked in neat piles on the smaller desk. Two flat-screen displays were the only signs of computers on either desk. Ordinary office black phones perched on the right-hand top corners of each desk. A notepad waited on the smaller desk, and a round soup tin covered in fabric held pens and pencils next to its phone.

The man sighed as he placed the briefcase halfway across the right-hand bottom corner of his desk as he rounded it to sit in the Air Chair behind it. He dropped into his chair, leaned forwards, and picked up a picture frame. He stared motionless at it for so long that I rounded the desk to peer at it, avoiding his briefcase.

A serious young child looked at the camera.

I blinked. I angled closer. I squinted. My sharp vision didn't sharpen; my three-sixty perception didn't improve. I glanced at Bailey. She nodded.

I recoiled and banged my behind against the top drawer of the filing cabinets. The pressure flattened me where I contacted the cabinet. The unpleasant sensation squashed my mind; I tried to tell myself, it's my mind's perception of reality, not reality. I cannot be compressed or squashed or pancaked.

Suddenly, I was whole again.

Relieved, I stepped back towards the desk and peered at the child in the photograph.

I pointed at the picture frame, mouthing an impossible question.

Bailey nodded as the phone rang. I jumped and bounced off the filing cabinet, landing legs akimbo on the floor. Time slowed; in slow motion, the old man replaced the picture frame on his desk, rearranged it with both hands, then reached over to pick up the incessantly ringing phone's receiver.

"Hello," he said, his baritone voice conveying disinterest. He listened for a minute. He said, "Yes, yes...You have an appointment? ...My assistant is away today...I understand...She handles the schedule. If you...Yes, I'm here. Who are you?...I see...Yes, she would have my file ready...You can come...I'll be here. What time did you say?...I see...Uh-huh...mmm...yes...okay...I'll see you in an hour. Good-bye."

He replaced the phone as if laying a baby in a cradle. He lifted his briefcase off his desk and placed it on the floor. It flopped against his desk.

My eyebrows lifted. I stared at my soul family. "No way," I breathed.

"So you figured it out, did you," Nihil stated.

I stared at her. "You knew?"

"We all knew. Remember, we've known you forever. They wouldn't shut up about you. We had to see your whole family."

My lips parted; my eyes widened.

Shireen Anne asked, "What do you think of your father? He looks like a defeated man. That's your photo there. When did he take it, Bailey?"

"When Charlotte Elisabeth was three. He snuck his camera in and shot the photo the day before her mom kicked him out."

Shireen Anne said, "He must've loved you very much."

I recalled my life review, the scene of him playing with me as a baby. I shied away from replaying the day he left. "Yes," I said, drawing out the word. "He did."

I turned to Bailey. "But I don't want to possess him to reconcile. I'm tired. Communicating mind-to-mind with Sally was tough!"

She nodded. "We understand. There are many ways to communicate with the physical in the Solar Age."

"I don't see any butterflies here. And how could I get one, anyway?"

"You don't need a butterfly," Blake chirped, skipping forwards. "Do this!" Standing at the side of the desk, slightly behind where the man had placed the frame, she focused on the picture frame. Her form seemed to coalesce, and she swept her hand against the back of the picture frame then immediately returned to her energy form. "Hey!" Bailey exclaimed as the frame slammed onto the desk, photo facedown. The white-haired man flinched and stared at the photo frame's back. He reached his right hand out, hesitated, then raised it back again.

"How'd you do that?" I asked Blake.

"She wasn't supposed to," Bailey said at the same time as Shireen Anne said, "Isn't it neat?" and Nihil huffed, "Show off." Scruffy barked, sat down, and scratched his left ear vigorously.

Blake stretched her neck and looked down her straight nose at Nihil. "No need to get huffy. We' re just more advanced."

Blair kicked Blake. "Ouch!" she yelled.

"What happened?" I asked, while the...my father...continued to stare at the frame as if daring it to fall.

"It's a time-honoured way to communicate with the living. You move things. Shireen Anne can do it, too. Nihil didn't want to learn how. But we three can interact with the—"

Bailey slapped a hand over Blake's mouth.

I eyed one then the other. Too many new and confusing abilities in this existence. I thought the Earth-Heaven Interdimensional Expanse was weird; inhabiting Earth in this way challenged me at every turn. Curiosity pinged me. I wanted to know: *How do they do that? How do the living know we invisible existing ones are communicating with them? If I can't do that, is it reconciliation?*

"Sometimes you can reconcile with your relatives through others like us when you don't have the skills yet. It's true," Bailey said. "Blake jumped the gun, but if you want to let your father know you're here, you can ask her to push the photograph of you down. Your father misses you. Do it enough times, and he'll get the message you're with him. And if he understands that, he'll know you hold no rancour with him because if you did, you wouldn't be pushing picture frames down, you'd be tossing papers around and throwing things at him."

"We can do that?" I asked, my eyebrows soaring into my hairline.

"Yes," Nihil said. "It's fun." I took a step back from the glint in her hardening eyes. *How had she been allowed in Heaven with such thoughts and desires?*

*That's a smart question,* Shireen Anne thought into my mind.

"Jesus wants us, all of us. Now, focus on the current quest and remember that Jesus's unconditional love ignites your courage to reconcile," Bailey interrupted, her voice loud, distracting me from Nihil.

I gulped, both wanting that courage yet fearing the overwhelming nature of that love.

"Do you want me to?" Blake asked, jumping up and down, grinning, her eyes sparkling silver and chimes. I nodded.

She coalesced slightly out of my father's sight. She extended her arm, watched the man's eyes, hovered her hand up behind the frame, and waited. He sighed and ducked underneath his desk to turn on his desktop computer.

*Slam!*

Blake jumped back and dematerialized.

He jerked his head up.

"Ow!" he ejaculated as his head hit the edge of the desk. Rubbing the top of his head, he pushed his chair back and hauled himself onto it. He stared at the frame lying facedown on his desk.

With both hands, he carefully raised it and positioned it to face him. After a while, he stopped staring at it and finished turning on the computer.

As he pressed the display's on button, Blake hit the picture frame hard. It slammed down and slid towards him.

He reared back. His mouth fell open; his eyes searched the room. With his shaking right hand, he lifted the picture frame up and set it down. Blake coalesced only her hand, smacked the frame, and dephysicalized her hand in less time than I blinked, while he was looking at it.

He covered his slack mouth and whispered, "Are you there Charlotte Elisabeth?" Tears filled his eyes and tumbled down his cheeks. Unconsciously, I wrapped my arms around him. "I'm so sorry, my dear. I didn't want to leave. Your mother insisted. She said I couldn't contact you again. My family had been against my marriage from the beginning. They'd wanted a nice Zoroastrian girl for me and didn't accept her, didn't accept you, my precious daughter. I should've been stronger, but my dear, I'm not. I missed you every day. What you did...what I heard you did five years ago...it broke my heart to hear you wanted to die. If only I'd been stronger. But your mother insisted. What could I do?" He babbled apologies and excuses.

I didn't care. The defeat that emanated from his sobbing form mingled with the vivid memory of him playing with me as a baby.

The comingling burned my heart with love. I was getting used to that word. *Love.* "Blake," I whispered.

She instantaneously and gently pushed the picture frame towards the edge of the desk near him.

He broke down. His forehead hit the desk next to the frame. Sobs heaved his stooped frame. His hands twisted in his lap, over and over. I rubbed his back and wondered at myself. *Is this the courage Bailey had said Jesus's unconditional love would ignite?* I was glad I hadn't refused it despite my fear.

Minutes ticked by. His sobs lessened. He sat up and, with trembling hands, he straightened the frame so that the photograph of me faced him directly. He croaked, "Thank you, my dear, for visiting me. Knowing you're still alive and aren't mad at me, fills me with hope. Perhaps I can see you one day. Thank you, my dear." He stretched out his right leg, reached into his pants pocket, and extracted a large striped handkerchief. He wiped his eyes, his cheeks, his chin. He blew his nose, refolded his handkerchief, and pushed it back in his pocket.

Shoulders straightened, spine taller, he grabbed his mouse, and logged in, a smile curving the edges of his mouth.

"Well, that was good, wasn't it?" Blake chirped.

My heart soared. I hadn't known I could reconcile with my father. *Two in one day...although...*

I pressed my right forefinger against my lips. Not one chronological day, but one storytelling day, a few years apart. *Sally and Mom weren't fighting five years after my death,* I scoffed. *Or...maybe they were?* I shook my head. *Don't think too much about irrelevancies, just thank Blake!* Nihil's expression stopped me. She was staring at my father, confusion clouding her grey eyes. She whipped around the desk and flew out the window, catching Scruffy unawares. With a short bark, they chased after her.

"What happened?" I asked.

"You reconciled with your father, silly," Blake said.

"I mean, about Nihil."

"Progress," Bailey said thoughtfully, looking after Nihil's disappearing form.

# Chapter Twenty-Two
# A MEDIUM GIVES A LEAD

Frederick sailed in through the window. He braked in front of me and grabbed my hand. I resisted his tugging.

"What?" I asked.

"You have to come. I have a lead on my father!"

I hadn't seen Frederick enthusiastic before. I held back.

"You do?" Shireen Anne asked eagerly. "What is it?"

"A medium."

She deflated. "You've used mediums before. What's so special about this one?"

"She doesn't know she's one, and an Aunt is trying to communicate through her."

"Your father's Aunt?"

Frederick shook his head hard. He grasped my hand tighter. "You have to come!"

"Why?" I asked.

"Come and see!"

I dragged my hand out of his. "Mediums are charlatans. There's no scientific basis for what they do. They ask for money and read your face and body language to make you believe they're speaking to the dead. There's no such thing," I ended emphatically.

He raised his eyebrows. "Really?" He gestured to the room and my father. "No such thing? Would you have believed before you saw Blake do it that 'the dead' can move objects?"

"You saw that?"

He nodded. "Yes. I stayed out of sight until you'd finished. I didn't want to interrupt your reconciliation in the excitement of finding the best lead I've had in years."

"Oh." I returned to his earlier comment. "You said she doesn't know. How is she different from you and me when we were...um...alive?"

He touched my hand. "Please come with me?"

I turned to Bailey. "I don't believe in this stuff," I said, but my voice rose at the end like I was asking her.

Bailey studied me and suddenly herded us all through the window. I gasped at how high we were floating above the sidewalk. Frederick hovered closest, and I grabbed his hand to steady myself.

"It's okay," he said, closing his fingers around my hand. "You won't fall."

I looked up at him to see if he was mocking me. His serious smile answered my questioning eyes. He said, "Momentum and inertia will help you navigate in three-dimensional space. And remember." He paused, stooping to hold my eyes. "You learned to defy gravity." He straightened up, his eyes crinkling, and said, "You don't need to be afraid, Charlotte."

"Charlotte Elisabeth," I murmured.

He smiled wider. "C'mon, Charlotte Elisabeth. Bailey has given us their blessing."

He swung his free left arm forwards, like Superman, and began flying. Faster and faster, he flew, pulling me along. The others kept up.

*How do they do this?* I wondered. *And why flying instead of thought? Isn't thought how we transit through Earth space?*

"We don't always have to use thought," Frederick bellowed over the rushing air. "It's funner this way. Besides, look down, you can see where we're going."

*No thanks!*

I slacked, letting Frederick pull me like I was a sack of flour, as I wondered why the air made a sound as we zipped through it.

*We're energy,* Shireen Anne thought into my mind from behind me. *But our skin contains molecules...and...ah, it's too complicated!*

I grinned. *For Shireen Anne not to understand something must hurt.*

She chuckled. *You got me!*

We halted outside a main floor window of a mansion. We entered through the bay window's mullioned glass. I felt the mullions scrape me, like they were trying to skin me alive. Frederick looked back at me when I squeaked. "Sorry. I forgot you're still not used to moving through matter. Think small or thin, and your form will reshape to move through narrow cracks or small areas." He didn't give me a chance to respond. He halted and released my hand.

I wandered into the knick-knack stuffed sitting room.

A buxom sofa faced an open floor space. A round table sat awkwardly on the sofa's side. I wondered where it usually sat. Two people perched on the sofa, while a third was standing in front of them, gesturing. A fourth person sat in a wing chair snugged next to the sofa, as if it, too, had been shoved out of its designated position. Flocked red fabric covered the walls. The ceiling and cornice mouldings brightened the place in a creamy white. My bare feet slid on the polished wide oak planks. I immediately longed to wear shoes and change into jeans and a T-shirt. Why had I chosen a frothy white dress to die in? I sighed.

Bailey, Blair, and Blake gathered around me as I parked myself near the table. Shireen Anne walked over to the wing chair.

I surveyed the two slim young things sitting on the sofa. They looked like siblings with their serious brown eyes, fine medium brown hair, and fair skin. Their lips spoke of generosity. I switched my attention to the man in the chair. Strands of grey laced his fine brown hair, which capped a thoughtful face creased with laugh lines and an amused smile. *Their father*, I thought.

*They don't believe in mediums, either*, Shireen Anne thought to me.

I studied the fourth person in the room, standing in front of the three, miming a movie camera. Dyed blonde hair. Hatred gripped me. All those years of being forced to dye my hair, hide my natural colour, choked me. Bailey touched my shoulder. "Your hair is your hair now." I squinted at her. "What do you mean?"

She tugged a strand of my hair around until I could see it and said, "Your mind creates you as you see yourself."

Black as blue black when I was a child. I grabbed a fistful of my hair and stared at it. I smiled back at her. Maybe this existence had a bright spot. It had returned part of me to me when I hadn't had the courage to do so when alive.

"So you admit you have no courage?"

I whirled around to see Nihil's grey eyes close up. I stumbled back. She shrugged. "It takes courage to admit you're wrong."

I frowned at her. "I didn't admit anything. You don't admit to being wrong, either. Are you a coward, too?"

I gasped at my effrontery and braced myself for the blowback.

She smiled with her lips. "Yes."

I blinked and turned back slowly to the tableau.

The young man and young woman were arguing about whether it was a movie or a TV show.

I felt lost.

The dyed-blonde woman, a medium who wasn't a medium, laughed. "C'mon guys, you know what this means!" She mimed an old-fashioned film camera again.

I clapped my hands. "They're playing charades!"

"Yup," Shireen Anne said. "I love this game." She settled herself down on the arm of the wing chair to watch.

Nihil yawned. Scruffy squeezed between her legs, unbalancing her. "Okay, okay," she muttered. "I won't ruin the show."

The young man said, "It's a movie."

The young woman riposted, "It's a TV show."

The dyed-blonde woman pointed at her. "Yes! You're right, Sophie. A television show!"

"Are you allowed to talk in charades," I asked, canting towards Bailey.

"Nope," Blake replied.

"What kind of medium is she, she doesn't even know what she's miming," I mocked.

"Hush," Frederick said, pointing to the far wall. I saw nothing but a wall and, high up on it, a narrow, rectangular window with squares of reds, blues, and greens. I was about to ask him what he was showing me when a woman careened through the stained-glass window and smacked herself against the back of the sofa.

"Oof," she said, dragging herself upright and dusting herself down. "Where is she?"

Frederick pointed at the woman now miming seven fingers on her left arm. Five, then two, repeatedly.

"Seven syllables," the two chorused together.

The woman nodded, smiling and pointing at them.

She tapped her right forefinger on her left arm.

"First syllable," the young man said.

"Are you sure, Jacob?"

"Keep up, Sophie," he replied.

"Cyrus, are you going to join in?" the woman asked the man lounging in the chair.

"Aunt used to play charades with us every Christmas. It's not Christmas, now," he replied.

"New Year's is close enough."

"New Year's Day is for sleeping," he chuckled.

"When are you going to make us your Dad's famous pakoras?"

"Okay, okay," he huffed, grinning and leaving his chair. He disappeared through a doorway near his chair. Stained oak framed the doorway.

The ghost woman flung herself at the dyed-blonde woman, her hands scrabbling at her shoulders.

The woman shook her head and slapped her shoulders as if trying to rid herself of spiderwebs.

Jacob frowned. "Are you okay?" he asked as Sophie watched expressionlessly.

"Yes," she said, shivering. "I'm fine.

The ghost woman stretched her neck forwards to bellow in the woman's ear, "I'm their aunt. Tell them I'm at peace. My death wasn't horrible like I thought it would be. They need to know. It's important. Please tell them." She gabbled along at a breakneck pace as the so-called medium fixed her eyes on the siblings and tried to mime an "A."

"You look like you're seeing a ghost," Jacob said. "Are you? Is that why you shivered? My Great-Aunt said when people walk over your grave, you shiver. Is that what happened?"

I stared at him. No one in my family talked much. Sophie hadn't said a word; she seemed used to his threaded questions. Mom would've shut me down if I'd pummelled her like that.

"Let's focus on the charades," she replied.

Jacob's eyes gleamed with curiosity. He opened his mouth—

Sophie said, "A."

Jacob shot her a look. "Okay, I give you that one."

The woman nodded, shaking her shoulders free where their aunt was grasping her, and tapped three fingers of her right hand on her left arm.

"Three syllables," the siblings chorused.

"C'mon, c'mon," the ghost woman exclaimed, jumping up and down, and running around the woman. *That poor woman,* I thought, *she's only trying to mime a television show title. Why won't their aunt leave her alone?*

"Tell them! Tell them Aunt is at peace. Peace! Peace, I tell you!"

"Peace!" the woman blurted. She clamped her mouth closed, her face flushing.

Sophie stared.

Jacob said, "Huh? Peace? Is that the title? Aren't you supposed to mime it? Or is that connected to your shivering?" He leaned towards her. "You're flushing. What happened?"

"Nothing, nothing, don't worry about it," she said, patting her cheeks. "It's just hot in here."

Jacob scanned the room, puzzled. "No, it's not. It looks hot because of our ancestors' knick-knacks, but we keep it cool."

I choked back a laugh.

Frederick exclaimed and strode over to the ghost woman. "Enough! It's my turn. I need her to ask them if they know where my father is."

*How will she do that?* I wondered. *Is he going to—*

Frederick spoke over his shoulder at me. "No, I wouldn't possess someone for this. But I know how to talk to people with the gift of perceiving our thoughts."

"Perceiving our thoughts?"

"Mediums."

I sidled closer to this so-called medium, no longer hating her, though still skeptical about this medium business. She'd repeated the word the ghost woman had yelled into her ear. Maybe there's something in this...?

The three were arguing over the three-syllable word, the medium soundlessly with increasingly impatient gestures, Jacob volubly, and Sophie with single words. "Korean," Sophie said.

"Yes!" the woman exclaimed, pointing at Sophie.

"That's because you're into K-Dramas, Soph. I'll give you this one."

Sophie rolled her eyes.

The pungent fragrance of pakoras preceded Cyrus as he walked back into the sitting room carrying a plate filled with freshly fried golden pakoras with veins of spinach green. My mouth watered. He handed around the plate, and they each took one, Jacob stuffing one whole into his mouth, Sophie nibbling hers.

"Thank you, Cyrus," the woman said. "I needed that." She brushed crumbs off her blouse and said, "We're working on the next three-syllable word. So far, Jacob and Sophie have guessed a television show starting with, 'A Korean'."

"Okay. That's Sophie's game," he laughed. He put the plate down on the table. "Help yourself." He walked to the wing chair and relaxed into it to watch the charades show.

This family, so easy with each other, seemed out of a movie. They teased each other and didn't try to control anyone. Cyrus, their father, cooked for them and didn't tell them how to eat. I didn't know where their mother was, maybe working. *A family like theirs,* I thought, *would have a mother, too. So if she isn't here, she must be working, sharing the financial load of supporting each other.* Amazement left me speechless. *Is this what family love looks like?*

Frederick cozied up to the medium's right side—*why and when had I accepted she's a medium?* She hunched her right shoulder.

"There she goes again," Jacob whispered to Sophie, leaning sideways towards her.

Sophie didn't acknowledge him.

Frederick spoke in a long, unbroken stream of words. His voice soft, like a purring cat. The medium, at first, focused on playing out the last word of her charades, tapping the first three fingers of her right hand on her left arm. But as he continued, her eyes defocused as if her attention was being drawn inwards.

"Cyrus is the son of my father's best friend," Frederick said. "I have a question for him. He knows the answer. You can ask him. Build it in your charades. Speak these words. You can do it. Cyrus is the son of my father's best friend. Start asking him about his father. His father is dead. Ask him how he learned to make the pakoras. Talk about the pakoras."

The woman dropped her hands. She walked with studied nonchalance to the table and picked up a pakora. She studied it and, too casually, said, "These are good, Cyrus. Your father made these, right?"

"Yup! He taught me how to cook."

"Where did he learn how to make these?"

"His mother. I don't remember Grandma cuz she died when I was little."

"I'm sorry to hear that. Did he make these for his friends?"

"Yeah, I think so. There was this one guy—"

Frederick, who'd stuck close to the woman, rushed in, "That's my father. Ask him about that guy, about what happened to him. You can do it. It's easy. It fits naturally into the talk about the pakoras. It's like an odyssey."

She said, "I guess that friend liked your father's cooking?"

"Yup," Cyrus nodded vigorously while Jacob and Sophie's heads swivelled from Cyrus to the medium as they followed their conversation. Jacob whispered to Sophie, "It's like she's listening to someone. I wonder who's talking to her?" Sophie side-eyed him. He raised his eyebrows at her.

"Did your father invite him over often?"

"Yeah, his girlfriend dumped him. Dad never found out why, but he felt sorry for him, so he'd make a bunch of these pakoras and invite him over to eat and talk."

Frederick interrupted, "Ask where he lived, where he hung out."

The woman bit into the pakora; her smile didn't reach her eyes. "I guess his home wasn't anything to stay in and why he came over. I'd come over often for one of these."

Cyrus grinned. "Thanks. I'll make more for you next time you come visit."

Frederick glanced at her and back at Cyrus. He seemed to inhale all the air in the room. His form glowed. I blinked. I hadn't seen that before. *What's happening?* Frederick pushed her, "Ask. Ask. Ask. Ask! Ask!—"

"Where did this man live?"

"Huh?" Cyrus replied.

"I mean they must've hung out together somewhere."

"Oh yeah, I guess it can't hurt to answer. Martin liked a bar. He'd hang out at the Shilly Shally. It was kind of apt because that's what he was like. Except for that woman, he couldn't commit. In fact, I'd say he went off the rails after she disappeared and he had to face that she'd had many men and he was as important to her as any of the others. In other words, not! He'd go there, play pool, bet, and lose money and make money. Whatever he made, he spent on beer. He liked stout." Cyrus shrugged. "I don't know why. His favourite place to live was up in the Yukon. He stayed in a small cabin there one year, roughing it. Not for my Dad, but he enjoyed the peace and quiet, he said the last time he came to eat Dad's pakoras. Don't know why because that bar was the last thing from peace and quiet. If he liked peace and quiet so much, he should've gone to a coffee bar." He chuckled and pinched his eyes. "Enough." Cyrus sat back in his chair.

Frederick gestured to the ghost woman that he was done and stepped back. She bustled forwards and chattered non-stop into the medium's ear, who shuddered, staggered, and resumed her place in front of Jacob and Sophie.

I picked up on her thought as she mimed: *Odyssey.*

Mom had forbidden television, and I'd never subscribed to streaming services. Why would I when I didn't watch television? But this title made me curious. *What is a Korean Odyssey?*

*It's a fantasy show,* Shireen Anne answered. *Super interesting. It's got a demon in it, called the "Monkey King." He contracts with a young girl to release him from a prison and makes a deal to protect her then promptly makes it so she can't call on him to do so. She can see ghosts and is a loner, the only family who loves her is her grandmother. Revelation—the book, you know, oh, you don't know—but anyway, Revelation makes clear nothing, not even God's love, can save evil. But I love these fantasies about love redeeming bad thoughts, words, and deeds, about overcoming evil intent and bringing forth compassion. It's an odyssey, Charlotte Elisabeth, like yours. It's addicting, and the male lead is hot.*

Blake choked back a laugh as I tuned her out.

Frederick left through the window. I turned and followed him, asking, "Didn't you want to hear what Cyrus said, or was it what Shireen Anne said?"

He folded his legs and settled cross-legged on the trimmed lawn. He yanked at blades of dying grass. "It doesn't surprise me," he said. "I thought he must've had a hard life, one that took him away from Heaven." He ripped more blades out of the soil.

*How does he do that?*

"I was hoping I was wrong." He stood up, brushed himself down. "I hope you see another path forwards to reconciliation, Charlotte Elisabeth. Use people like her to help you reconcile with your mom." He nodded towards the house as the others streamed through the window in our direction. He leaned down towards my right ear. "And get Nihil to use a medium, too. She needs help. I think you can help her." I raised startled eyes to his. His sad smile winked on then off. And he was gone.

# Chapter Twenty-Three
# THE CLIENT

Pedestrians congested the narrow sidewalk down Bay Street towards Lakeshore Boulevard. Traffic hummed the Gardiner Expressway's overhead bed as I entered the shadowed area underneath it where drivers drove fast, close beside the sidewalk. Few ventured underneath on foot, yet people clogged the cramped corners at the intersection. One person with a white cane was tapping in search of the traffic-light pole's rhythmically clicking button. My mind blanked as my eyes landed on him. Pedestrians in trench coats and puffy jackets and long coats glowered or ignored him. One let him through.

His trembling hand tried to press and hold the fat black button, but the light turned green before the beep sounded to indicate he'd activated the audio signal. The sighted flooded around him like a sea bashing and flowing around a rock, knocking him away from the pole. He swayed, caught his balance, and rooted himself, clasping his cane to his chest. The crowd surged across the boulevard underneath the Gardiner's struts, the crowd's tail end not yet off the sidewalk when the red-light countdown began on the pedestrian light. I looked around for cops. They took a dim view of pedestrians leaving the sidewalk after the countdown had begun. Resentment at their autocratic control strangled me. My mind flashed a memory: a walking advocate who'd explained the original agreement to add a countdown was to tell pedestrians how much time they had left to cross. After it was instituted, the cops changed their mind, declaring it the same as a red light, and ticketing those who dared to step off the sidewalk after the countdown had begun.

*Liveable city*, I groused. I watched the opposing crowd intersect the southbound one, sidling between the crosswalk-blocking cars, their drivers certain that endangering pedestrians saved them crucial seconds.

*Wait, I can cross whenever I want!*

I didn't move. I wanted to see how the blind man managed this dangerous intersection. He shuffled towards the traffic light pole; his hand hit it, palm facing, as if he'd found a life raft. His hand edged downwards, searching for the button. He huddled closer to the pole as the oncoming crowd tried to pry him away from it in their haste to get to Union Station with its waiting trains and buses.

The light turned red. He pressed the black button with all his might, using his body as weight against it. I counted with him. One. Two. Three. Four. Five. I heard the activation beep as if I was standing right next to it, not on the crowd's periphery. He'll get his audio signal to orient him to the opposite sidewalk, but it'll turn off when the countdown begins, stranding him in the middle of that four-lane boulevard, with drivers uncaring in their need to block his path for those precious seconds. A person cannot walk in a straight line when they cannot see. Only the audio signal would keep him safe.

*How will he manage to reach the tiny corner on the opposing side? The city has still not remedied that metal guardrail hemming people into a one-metre corner.*

*Hey Charlotte Elisabeth!* For once, Shireen Anne didn't startle me. I felt pleased I was becoming accustomed to my companions' sudden appearance and disappearance. *It doesn't apply to you anymore. You can levitate! You can cross above this mass, not jostle with people as everyone tries not to fall off the sidewalk onto the road in front of the impatient drivers in their metal death machines.*

*Metal death machines?* I chortled. I liked that term.

"You don't like cars," Nihil drolled beside me.

"They're conveyances. I have to use them."

"Not anymore!" Blake sang out, drawing abreast of us.

I smiled. "No, I'm free of...of..." I gestured helplessly as the pedestrian light changed and the crowds from both sides thronged the slivers between the cars blocking the crosswalk, dragging the blind man along with them like flotsam. As I predicted, the audio signal stopped when the countdown began. He walked into the side of a car. "Oof," he exclaimed. I winced. *Can I help him?* I asked Bailey.

"No need," Blake answered. "Look!"

An older woman spoke in the man's ear over the confined echoing of tires humming and engines rumbling. He nodded. She let him take her arm and guided him between the stopped cars safely to the other side.

"Are you ready to resume your—"

"Odyssey!" Shireen Anne shouted. "I like that term, don't you, Charlotte Elisabeth. It's like Homer. It's grand, and it's a story. Where are we in your storytelling time? Do you know?"

"I...um..."

I defied gravity and hastened to the waterfront above the stream of pedestrians. I didn't recall noticing street life before. When alive, I'd stayed in my inner life, avoiding the outer life of others. I pondered how I'd noticed the audio signal buttons, how I'd attended workshops and street tours, but I'd never noticed before the unfolding dramas. That blind man...my eyes had fallen on him, and I was just a disinterested observer, noticing yet not noticing. Then I'd entered his scene. I'd empathized. I mulled "empathized" in my mind. *Empathy.*

*My client.*

She'd empathized with me. And I hadn't noticed. Regret churned in me, fluttering my skin from the inside. I floated towards Harbour Square Park and hovered over the railing at its edge. One or two people reclined on the benches behind me in the cool fall evening air. A few hustled past on the boardwalk. Gulls shrieked overhead. A brown female Mallard strutted towards me. She veered off to the bench behind me. *Looking for scraps*, I thought, as I read the city's inadequate sign telling people not to feed the birds. "Does the city fine anyone for feeding the ducks and birds?" I asked the air.

"You're asking questions," Shireen Anne said as she floated up to hover beside me.

I turned to look at her. I contemplated what she'd said. She smiled.

"It's a good thing," Blair said, drawing abreast. "Empathy. Asking questions. Heaven is about engaging."

I turned to look at her on my other side. She regarded me. "You've fought all your life against engaging with people and the world. But life after death rests on relationships."

"And relationships need engaging," Blake sang out behind me. She didn't startle me. I'd sensed her, no, I'd seen her, coming. "That's good. You're learning to use your new three-hundred-and-sixty-degree senses." She leaned against my back and propped her chin on my shoulder. "Isn't this view soothing? Your client is so lucky to live here."

I nodded. "Not precisely here at this park. Further down at a condo on Queens Quay and Spadina. She has a view of the Music Garden."

"Oh!" Blake exclaimed, leaping up and off me. "One of my favourite parks! We used to hang out there at night when you were sleeping, watching the water ripple against the boats, hearing the clinking music of their moorings."

I stared at her. She smiled back. "You know we've been with you for years. We told you that. Remember?"

I nodded. I remembered. But I hadn't thought about how they existed here, in Toronto, with me. I'd had this image of them watching me from Heaven, not walking the same streets as me, visiting the same parks as me, knowing my city better than I had—

I blinked up at her. "You know my city better than I do, don't you?"

"Yup!"

"That's because you're engaged with the world?"

She grinned and elbowed me.

"I've missed so much," I murmured to myself.

"You're not missing now!" Blake sang out.

I searched for Bailey.

Nihil asked, "Why are you looking for Bailey?"

"Where is she?" I answered.

Nihil's stony grey eyes, whose colour matched the rippling water of the November harbour, stared into mine. I turned to Blair. "Where's Bailey?"

Blair scrutinized me for a moment. "Noticing is part of your growth here. Noticing where people are and when they've left you."

"Oh." This felt unfair.

"How's it unfair?" Shireen Anne asked in her curious tone.

"How do I keep track of everyone in three-D with you all appearing and disappearing?" I grumbled.

"Your soul family is always with you. We," she emphasized, pointing at herself and Nihil, "may come and go, but those three don't."

I gawped at her. My head dropped as her words sunk in. I berated myself.

Blake said, "You don't need to berate yourself. You're learning!" She hugged me and let go, flinging her arms out to encompass the wintry scene.

I passed my right hand over my eyes. Had I shifted in time?

"Hey!" Blake chimed. "It's okay. I'll tell you."

Blair glared at her. "Hush!"

Blake continued blithely, "She's with your client. She wanted to make sure she's at home when you get to her condo."

"Oh." I spun in the air and thought, *Speed!* Instantly, I was zipping along the waterfront towards the quay next to the Music Garden and through the glass entrance doors of my client's condo. I braked. "Wait a minute," I said to Blake as she halted beside me. "How do I get to her penthouse?" This time, I'd opened my senses to keep track of everyone. They'd followed behind me like a line dance.

Blake smiled.

"You're not going to tell me?"

She shook her head, a happy grin filling her face.

I searched the empty foyer for an answer. *Oh!* I realized. *I can float! I don't have to use the elevator like I used to. I can go up to her penthouse from the outside!* I hastened back through the glass doors, reassured myself gravity doesn't hold me, imagined neutrinos like pink asters rising upwards, and jerkily rose. I circled the building, hunting for her condo. I slapped my head. *Of course!* She'd be in the one facing the Music Garden. That's when I spotted Bailey.

Bailey stood serenely, observing me from above.

"You found me," she said, then she smiled. "I know Blake told you."

I smiled back.

"Are you ready?"

"Yes, but..."

"Your usual question?"

I nodded.

Bailey pointed towards the Music Garden. "There are Blackbirds who live in those trees."

"I remember them. They dive bomb people in the spring to protect their nests. Dangerous birds." I shuddered.

"Go get them."

"What?" My mouth opened. I stared off towards where the Blackbirds lived. I clamped my mouth shut and shook my head. Bailey crossed her arms. "They're not nice," I said.

"They won't be nice with that attitude," Blair said. I ignored her.

"Your client lives here because the water grounds her. She goes to sit in the Music Garden to watch the Blackbirds, people, and other birds. She'll notice a Blackbird sitting on her penthouse terrace." Bailey nodded towards the condo. "She's in there, watching TV. She'll come out in a minute to look at the moon when it rises. Then she'll read. You need to have the Blackbird here by the top of the hour. The bird will stay here while she gazes at the moon. And will stay here when she sits to pick up her book. She'll notice the Blackbird then and work out that God is sending her a message."

"Oh." I contemplated this. "But then how is that reconciling with me?"

"Although you died two years ago in her timeline, you're the only friend or family who has in the last decade. She remembers you from time to time with sadness at what could've been. She'll go from knowing the bird is from God, to knowing her favourite bird is telling her you're safe and still alive."

"Still alive?"

Bailey nodded.

"She believes that?" *Do I?* I muttered to myself. *Do I believe I'm alive, not merely existing?*

Bailey nodded.

Nihil said, "Just because you didn't believe doesn't mean others don't."

I glowered at her. She lowered her lashes and regarded me through slitted eyelids. I didn't look away. Pain flickered through her eyes. I blinked. *Had I seen pain?* Her gaze hardened. I tried to dismiss my thought like I usually did. But I couldn't. I had seen it. I didn't know what to do with that knowledge, yet the new desire to engage kept me hostage. So I left for the Blackbirds.

I arrived at their tree.

I touched down on a far branch.

The Blackbirds fixed their beady eyes on me. Somehow they told me they were settling down for the night, and they'd pluck out my eyes if I didn't leave them alone. I had no idea how I was talking with them, but I pleaded. I needed one to go to my client's penthouse and stay with her until she knew I was still alive. One Blackbird strutted along a higher branch towards me, her fleshless feet disturbing leaves and shredding bits of bark. She shouldered past two perched on the branch between me and her. They fluttered their black wings in protest, their red stripes undergirded by yellow, capturing my attention. She stopped and lunged at me, her beak almost stabbing my nose. I reared back.

*She can't hurt me*, I assured myself. *But is she a Blackbird?*

She was brown, her breast like the marshy mouth of a river, grooving brown rivulets in sand. Lighter lines against the plain brown of a sparrow patterned her wings. Bright yellow washed the area around her eyes. Those eyes glared into mine.

*I'm no sparrow. I'll go*, she informed me.

The branch sprang down as she launched and flew straight to my client's condo.

I arrived as my client slid back her glass terrace door. The Blackbird strutted before me. My client's eyes were fixed on the moon shining a path on the black, rippling water. Streetcars screeched around the street corner below. The Blackbird fluttered up to the railing and landed a metre from her. My client turned her head and said, "Hello." The bird bobbed. My client smiled and returned her gaze to the moon.

Minutes stretched.

My client drew her hands and arms off the railing as she turned around. "Oh hello. You're still here," she said to the bird, who walked sideways along the railing towards her, her fleshless bird toes wrapping around the railing with each step. My client smiled. "You must be from God." She bowed her head. "Thank you."

She sat down in a wooden Muskoka chair, picked up an eReader lying on the small outdoor table beside the chair, pressed the on button, and began to read. The Blackbird flapped down and landed in front of her. I followed and faced her. The bird strutted between us, this way and that. My client laid the eReader on her lap. Her eyebrows drew together. "What are you trying to tell me?"

The Blackbird ran towards me, where I was standing a couple of metres in front of her. Then she strutted back. Back and forth she went. My client's brow lifted; her mouth made a moue. "Oh. Someone is visiting?" Her brow puckered. "Charlotte Elisabeth is here?" The bird stopped pacing and pecked at the terrace stone floor. My client gazed around. "Charlotte Elisabeth?"

I took a step towards her. The Blackbird stopped pecking.

"Charlotte Elisabeth. I'm glad you're alive, you're here." She nodded and smiled. "I didn't agree with your choice. It made me unhappy and angry. I've been reading grief books." She tapped her eReader. "This one is on helping survivors of suiciders. And though the law allowed another to kill you, it was suicide. We've failed people." Tears wet her eyes. They spilled over and flooded her cheeks. "I'm so sorry."

I reached towards her. I'd experienced her emotions and thoughts towards me during my life review, but her grief startled me. *How can she feel so much for me, her accountant?*

"We need to do better supporting people like you. Not endorse your suicidal mind, but help you live in love. With other people. We're bad at supporting each other." She stopped and contemplated the Blackbird. Words suddenly tumbled out of her like a dam's crack widening and widening until the whole structure explodes apart, cascading emotions and thoughts and words like a surging river.

"We've failed to walk hand in hand with God to protect the vulnerable. We've failed to help the hurting to heal like Jesus did when he walked the Earth. We pretend people know what they want so we can abdicate our role in bringing heaven to earth as God's collaborators." She wiped her eyes. "I'm so sorry, Charlotte Elisabeth. I didn't know how to help you, but I didn't advocate for better care, either, which would've helped you. Me and my church, all our churches and places of worship, talk about working with God, about looking forwards to a better world, and we forget our role while living here. Jesus is supreme, rules and saves us all. But that doesn't give us permission to watch from the sidelines instead of intervening, no matter the cost in popularity with the cool kids.

"Why? Why did I think more about being accepted by my progressive friends instead of doing what I knew Jesus wanted me to do?" She slapped at her cheeks with fisted hands. "I knew Jesus wanted me to do more, to speak up with my MP, my church, my friends at the temples, to fight against this horrid idea, the evil law that advocates for hopelessness, that shouts there's no help for people like you other than death. When it's not true!" she wailed, bending at her waist and straightening, bending and straightening, hugging her stomach.

Blake said, "I think she's hurting."

I frowned at her.

Blair said, "Guilt is vicious, ain't it?"

I backhanded the air between us.

"Hey! Don't blame the messenger!" Blake exclaimed.

My client hadn't paused for breath. "—not true! We should be paying for better care, not letting ourselves off the hook by believing murder is the only way to heal pain!" She hiccuped a sob and drew in a ragged breath. She stopped bobbing. "Even when I was hiding my real motives from myself, Jesus saw my thoughts and feelings for what they were. He convicted me. I cared more about what the cool kids, the progressives, would think than I did about saving a friend. I know you didn't see me as a friend—life had hurt you too much—but I was...I am your friend. I'm so sorry." She palmed her cheeks. "I'm so sorry," she whispered. "I'm going to change that. Starting tomorrow, I'm going to speak up against MAiD. I'm going to question doctor education. I'm going to bug my pastor and my spiritual mentors from other faiths...you know, I met Zoroastrians in my effort to know you better and befriend you. After you passed." She choked out a laugh. "They're an assertive bunch. But they also shied away from confronting the lie of hopelessness behind this evil legislation. I hope those judges are rotting in hell!"

She panted and rocked.

I thought back to Hell Track...

Catching her breath, she spoke to the Blackbird, "You're still here. You're still listening to me. I guess you're forgiving me?" She pondered the stones near the Blackbird's scrawny feet. "Jesus is the word, John wrote in his Gospel. Yet I haven't listened."

My client became motionless. We waited. The Blackbird pecked at an errant seed between the stones. Nihil sighed, *So much angst.* We waited. My mind wandered to once-painful memories of Mom nailing the lion's head, my father driving away, the disturbing questions in the Expanse, my regrets over spurning my client's overtures of friendship. *Am I healing? Perhaps reconciling does heal?*

My client's voice startled us out of reverie. "The word from love. I'd preferred to ignore the word and the unconditional love of our creator and listen to the temporary words of who is temporarily popular in this temporary time and place. I listened to the temporary instead of the eternal and expected I'd still reach heaven and live with my Lord and Saviour. How did I respond to that love?" She smacked her forehead. "How could I?" She lifted her eyes to stare beyond the bird.

I faltered backwards under the force of her gaze. *Can she see me?*

"How could I forget that when we listen to Jesus, when we obey the word, Jesus strengthens us and opens the way for us to walk hand in hand with God. We're not alone even if it feels like it because we can't see and hear Jesus or God with our physical senses. God-incidences are real. I've experienced so many, yet when MAiD became law, I had no courage and turned away from fighting it. We say every Sunday Jesus won the victory, but I don't think we believe it." She murmured, "The word "gospel" means the waiting between the victory and the arrival of the victor, and while we wait we work with the victor where we are. We don't wait until the Resurrection. We're all supposed to be resurrected at the end of the age; not just the "right" people, the ones we think are deserving. There's no rapture for the in-crowd, only Resurrection for us all." She nodded to herself as she mouthed, "God wants to resurrect us all."

She'd lost me, but I listened, experiencing her sorrow and empathy, facing her remorse and determination to change. *Am I determined, too? Or am I going with the flow?*

Her voice loudened, recapturing my attention. "We have priests and pastors, but we are all to remember Jesus already won our battles with death and defeat. Our church leaders are meant to walk hand in hand with Jesus and guide us, not be his special in-crowd. God sent the word to teach us that." She cried out, "I forgot we're not alone in fighting for justice for the vulnerable, the lonely and hurting. No political party represents the victor. No charming politician nor rousing one. No popular one. No autocrat with his followers. None represent Jesus here. Jesus represents Jesus alone. The word speaks for God, no one else."

*Am I in a lecture hall?* I gazed around. I laughed at myself. *She's lecturing herself, not me.*

"My new Zoroastrian friends and I argue over who their Saviour is. They told me about their faith's salvation story, and I exclaimed, 'That's Jesus!' They jeered. But I'm convinced. I love our debates. I imagined you with them, and how much joy it must bring to someone like you with your bright mind to engage with equally bright minds."

*Engage? Me? Bright mind? Debate? Why does she think I'd have liked that?*

She considered the stone beneath her feet. "And then I remembered. You always talked to me and behaved as if you're alone. So you probably missed out." She sighed. "Who am I? A progressive who speaks the right words? A friend who doesn't interfere? A health care professional who doesn't challenge the chronic mythos with curative innovations? A person who works with others to keep the status quo? A good church goer?" She smacked her cheeks over and over with both palms. "How could I get so sidetracked? My identity is child of God! Why did I trust love and the word and the spirit less than my colleagues, my church members, my friends? Why?" she screamed, grabbing her hair, yanking chunks. She panted. Her hands fell to her lap. "No one committed their very life to me more than Jesus, more than any human being. Why didn't I trust that sacrifice and that protection? Is that because I couldn't imagine doing what Jesus had, putting others' needs before my wants?" She dropped her head into her hands. "What was the point of my adult baptism? Of declaring my faith in Jesus, in accepting his love and protection and wisdom in leading me through dark paths? When I spoke and acted more to fit in with my peers than to ponder and listen every day in which direction I should go, what words I should speak, what I should learn, who I should act to help in ways that'd make me stand out and expose me to mocking disparagement, even yelling from you. Why do I fear for my life? My reputation? Those are not in my hands. They're in Jesus's. And he's guarding them for me. I will prevail because Jesus already did. Why do I fear as if I'm alone in this battle? All my battles? I hear the Bishop, our Rector, say I am a child of the Most High God. I nod, but my mind and heart don't believe it. God birthed me for a reason." My client stared at the Blackbird. Her voice faded away, but her thoughts spewed like a burst watermain geyser. *How could I forget? At one time, I knew in my heart I am God's child. When did I forget? When did I move from that knowledge? When did I start to follow a political party and to believe I belonged to them and their group more than I belonged to God?*

Her thoughts pierced me, and I stretched out a futile hand towards her.

"You know something, Charlotte Elisabeth," she said out loud. "I joined St. Paul's, that big church on Bloor Street. You know the one? Or maybe you don't." She frowned. "I think you were an atheist. Didn't know much about church. I've attended my whole life, but something made me leave my own lifelong church to move to St. Paul's. We don't pray collectively with Morning Prayer anymore.

That service taught us how to communicate directly with God. The ritual of communion has become required in fear of criticism. Even church follows popular trends, wanting rituals like others, instead of uniting us in teaching us how to talk to God." She grimaced.

Shireen Anne's whisper reached my ears as I watched my client drown her gaze in the Blackbird's beady eyes. "Belonging," Shireen Anne sighed like a moaning wind through bare branches. "In all the churches I tried, only the elders reached out to me. And when they died, no one did. Low church, high church, I belonged nowhere but virtual church."

I opened my mouth to ask, *Why?* when Nihil snarled, "See, I told you. A social club." and my client sat up, her eyes widening, her voice obliterating Shireen Anne's confession from my mind. "I met your sister, Charlotte Elisabeth!"

Startled, I reared back. A grin appeared and disappeared on her face. "I met your sister," she whispered. "But I didn't tell her who I was. We all knew what she was going through, but I didn't want to interfere. I'm going to now because it isn't interfering. It's...it's engaging. After all, it's been two years since I attended your memorial service. I'm going to go up to her next Sunday and ask her to join me in getting our pastor and the Anglican Church of Canada and all other faiths—and I'm going to talk to my Zoroastrian friends, too—to fight the scourge of hopelessness. We need to bring hope back into our health care. We need to wrench complacent doctors and ignorant politicians and advocacy societies out of their manage-but-not-heal mindset. We need to kick hopelessness out of our laws. I don't know how we can. Hope is so hard," she said, bending over and hugging her knees. "So hard," she whispered. "But I'm not alone. Walking hand in hand with God means Jesus is with me, will guide us, lead us, show us the way through God-incidences. You and I are not alone. You've learned that now, right? You want me to face my failure and repent through action. With your sister Sally," she said.

I wasn't sure I'd learned anything. A lot of what she was saying bewildered me. But her forgiving me for not responding to her friendship and her remorse driving new action ignited a desire in me to do the same. Like cells regrowing over a nasty scrape into scarless new skin, my new thoughts sewed up my regrets.

She let go of her knees, sat up, and palmed the wetness off her cheeks. "I get it. I'll do better." She exhaled and exhaled. "I hope where you are now you have friends and family to hold you up."

I leaned towards her, nodding. "I do," I croaked. The Blackbird nodded. "Chak, chak, chak," it answered.

My client smiled with her glistening eyes. "I'm so glad."

# Chapter Twenty-Four
# ISLAND WALK

*J*stumbled off the terrace and levitated above Queen's Quay. A streetcar screeched its way around the corner under me.

"Let's go for a walk," Bailey suggested, coming alongside me.

"Great idea!" Shireen Anne agreed, twirling around me. "I know the place. The Toronto Islands. The sky is clear, the moon is bright. No one will be out and about. Should be good for a confab."

"I was thinking more along the lines of using a walk to help her process all that her client said."

"By the way," Shireen Anne asked, "What's your client's name?"

"Marcia," I replied automatically. "Spelled M-A-R-C-I-A. Pronounced marsh-ah."

"Thanks!" She cocked her head and considered me. "You still have a problem with using names. It's almost as if...you fear once you call someone by their name, they'll want to know you, and you'll be required to know them. It scares you." She scrutinized me. "I thought after you beat the Expanse, got through the Barrier, managed the ghosts, reconciled with your sisters—"

"Half-sisters," I mumbled.

"—and your father, that you desired knowing people and them knowing you."

I floated in place.

"Come on," Bailey said, grabbing my hand.

I followed docilely as Bailey led us diagonally across the harbour and over to Ward's Island. We landed on the path that paralleled the island's shoreline on its Lake Ontario side. "This path isn't well-frequented," she said, letting go of my hand. She strode off. The others followed. I stayed in place.

"Where are we walking to?" I asked.

"Nowhere," Shireen Anne replied over her shoulder.

"What's the point of that?" I asked, frowning.

"Walking helps you think. Even in our energy form, physical-type movements help with mental processes," Bailey said.

"You've had a whole bunch of new things thrown at you, and Marcia's monologue didn't help," Blair replied. "Perambulating with a lake view will steady you."

"Besides," Blake said, skipping ahead. "It's a beautiful night. The moon is out. The stars are twinkling." She lifted both hands to the sky.

My eyes tracked her hands and rested on the night sky, its stars unconcealed by blinding-white city lights. The luminous moon attracted my mind.

Shireen Anne's "c'mon" tore my eyes from the heavens. I dragged my feet, and towed behind them along the shadowed path, with the waist-high concrete retaining wall on our left, trees stirring on our right, hemming us in. I didn't understand the point of this. *Going nowhere for the sake of going nowhere? What did my client, no, Marcia mean about 'Lord and Saviour'? The way she said it, it sounded different from the way my grandmother had said it.* My grandmother had shot out the phrase like an accusatory bullet, but Marcia had made it sound like...like a person...like a meaningful...personal...relationship, maybe? I wondered what that was like. Whatever it was, it had brought her peace that had softened her features. I contemplated the hard path. No, her face had reflected security, like she was talking about a big brother who had her back.

*I would've liked to have had a big brother*, I thought.

I watched my bare feet pad along the concrete, right, left, right, left. The rhythm called thoughts out of my mind. The rhythm drummed emotions in.

Confusion.

Upset.

Regret.

No, regret was marching out.

Wanting.

Desiring.

Pining.

*What am I pining for?* The answer arrived instantly from the locked box of my heart: I pined for what I'd seen on Marcia's face when she'd begun talking about Jesus. She'd so easily expressed her regret and admitted her mistakes. She couldn't see me, yet she'd known I was there, talked to me as if visible. *How?* The only person from my Earth life who could.

Pain.

Yearning.

*What am I yearning for? Life.* Startled, I raised my head and looked ahead. The others were walking a few metres ahead of me, silently. Yet their thoughts and presences were accompanying me.

Back in the Expanse, I'd admitted I wanted to live. But I didn't want to engage. Life is hard. It's terrifying. It's so lonely.

A sob birthed in my mind.

Bailey turned to look over her shoulder at me. I smiled and averted my gaze to the sky.

The shining moon lit up a rippling path on the lake to my left. Stars winked around the moon, like dust on black film. *You're not alone.* The thought dropped into my mind. I knew it to be true. I'd resisted it. I'd chosen to see myself as merely existing so I could remain aloof from people. I obeyed Samuel's instruction to reconcile so that I could flee back to Heaven's flower field. I hadn't expected that I could or that reconciling would open and lighten me. But Marcia showed me reconciling heals. *My regret is gone*, I marvelled. *I feel lighter!*

I dropped my eyes to my soul family and friends ahead of me. I couldn't fathom why Shireen Anne and Nihil wanted to be with me. How my soul family chose me remained a puzzle. *And who and why is Frederick?* People seeking a relationship with me confounded and scared me.

Shireen Anne smiled at me over her shoulder.

I'll have to learn how to keep my thoughts private. Yet somehow I didn't care that they heard everything I was thinking.

We walked off the end of the path into Centre Island. Ghosts haunted the empty rides and long pier. I jogged to close the gap between me and my family. *My family? Yes*, I thought. *Bailey, Blair, and Blake are my family.* My real family, not just my soul family, I realized, as if they're an arm's length from me and I don't belong to them. *I do belong to them!*

Blake jogged backwards and squeezed my arm. "Of course, you belong to us!" She hugged my arm to her side. "And we belong to you," she smiled at me before releasing me and skipping back to the group. "Don't worry about those on the pier," she called back. "They're star watchers. They come here every night. Sometimes I'd join them when you were sleeping."

I smiled and shook my head. My family really knew me. Maybe I can get to know them.

Pleasure.

Quiet joy.

Peace.

Maybe reconciling and developing relationships weren't so bad. Maybe I can learn more about Shireen Anne and Nihil, too. Shireen Anne jostled Nihil's arm, grinning. Nihil glowered at her as Scruffy trotted at her heels. I smiled at Nihil. Glowering was better than a dead stare. "Scruffy never leaves your side, Nihil," I called out.

She kicked towards him. "No matter what I do, Scruffy's there."

"For your Soul Track?"

"What's it matter to you?"

"I, uh,..."

I didn't know the answer. Another question popped into my mind: *Who is Jesus?*

"Are you ready to learn about him?" Blair asked me, turning to face me as she walked backwards.

We exited Centre Island and stepped onto the asphalt path of Hanlan's Point that wended its way between trees, beaches, and ponds. I had a sudden hankering to walk onto one of its small lakeside beaches. I ran ahead to the first boardwalk bridge to a beach. I pounded along it and jumped onto the sand. My bare feet sank into the particles as if I had physical feet. I realized that happened because my mind had expected it. I grinned. I savoured the experience of each sand granule rubbing its sharp edges against my feet's edges—unlike when I was alive—alive physically, I reminded myself. I'm still alive.

Life.

Living.

Relating.

I trudged across the sand, sinking into the granules, sensing every molecule of each granule, my mind absorbing all the details and sensations, awed at this novel life.

I stopped at the water's edge. Waves lapped through my toes. Water is transparent. *That means I can walk through it*, I realized. I sensed cold through sensing the sluggishly vibrating molecules. Lake Ontario, vast and deep, was never warm to swim in from my experience. But this cold didn't bother me. For me, the slow molecules stroked my mind, unlike hot ones, which bombarded my skin, zipping here and there. The moon reflected sunlight across the vast light-absorbing lake.

I raised my eyes to the stars.

Wondrous.

I soaked it in.

*Why would Marcia work with Sally?*

Gratitude.

Respect.

Amazement.

For the first time, I apprehended why MAiD was a life-and-relationship-killing choice. I hadn't realized that hopelessness killed the soul. *It kills you!* I turned that thought over. How had the medical profession—how had society—turned from curing and loving people to one preferring to rid themselves of challenging human beings?

*We're human!* The thought startled me. "I'm human," I breathed. "My life was valuable. It is valuable. But it was treated as not worth living in two different ways by the two doctors."

"Don't look for a cure," Nihil drawled. "Because there is no hope of one."

"But we cure cancer," I said.

"So what? That's cancer."

"I remember a cancer diagnosis being a death sentence. But now it's not."

Bailey nodded. "Hopelessness in the form of death by doctor."

Blake splashed into Lake Ontario. I blinked. *How'd she do that?* I squinted to see clearer, as if I needed to. She'd coalesced like in my father's office. My mouth formed an "O."

Bailey's voice recalled me to our conversation. "Your reconciliation gave Marcia the strength to change her mind, to decide to approach your sister and advocate to end what killed you."

"How will she do that? Won't it be tough? Why would she?"

"Because she follows Jesus and she doesn't want another to lose someone like they lost you."

I regarded her skeptically.

With enforced patience, Bailey said, "Jesus brought life to people oppressed by intense poverty, ill health, pain, and exploitation. People believe those with evil intent more than they do those speaking about Jesus. Talking about God's love gets one mocked and eyes rolled at. Demons and evil spirits possessing people are believable in K-Dramas and speculative fiction, but not in real life, meaning physical life. Why not?"

I had no answer to her question. But understood what Bailey meant about real life. Life after death feels more real, with its vivid sensations and complexities, than Earth life had. Yet until you die, you think real life is only what you can physically see, hear, taste, touch, and smell. *My pre-Earth life was two-D, yet I believed it complete,* I admitted to myself. *How stupid!*

"Hey!" Blake called across the water. "Don't shoot yourself down!"

"Marcia knows it'll be tough to go up against popular opinion—"

"Uninformed opinion," Blake shouted as she balanced on the wave tops.

"—to talk about God's love and warn against evil-dressed-in-nice-clothes seducing you. But engaging in that challenge to aid other people, to bring them life against the odds, makes one feel alive."

"Alive?" I asked.

"Yes," Bailey asserted. "Alive. We're social beings. God made us to walk hand in hand, supporting and loving each other. When we do that, we thrive. When we pretend we're individuals wholly independent of each other, we fall ill. She has the strength because facing up to where she erred and deciding to work with others reinvigorated her. More importantly, she knows Jesus is with her. She met him. You have, too. But meeting isn't sufficient. You must want a relationship with him. With God. The one the elder called, "Love." With the Holy Spirit."

I sagged. "Holy Spirit?"

Bailey nodded. "The Holy Spirit is God's spirit. Jesus's spirit."

"You're soaking in it, Madge," Blake sang out across the waves, giggling.

*Dishwashing detergent?* I hadn't heard that old ad jingle in decades. *What's detergent got to do with—?*

"It's a metaphor. You're soaking in Jesus's love, better than any detergent," Blair said. "All you really need to know is God is love. Jesus is the word that love used to create us, the universe. Jesus represented God to us in a way we could see, hear, and follow. The Holy Spirit is an energy being like we are yet not the same. The Spirit creates the web that connects us, and they exists inside us if we want that kind of close relationship. Closer than any spouse, parent, or best friend."

"Oh."

"If you fear relationships, you'll fear Jesus."

"Oh." I scanned their faces. "But what about Nihil?"

"What about me?"

"You don't believe in reconciling?"

"Is that true?" Bailey asked me.

I stared at her. I eyed Nihil, who averted her eyes and turned her back to me to study the still trees. Bearing relationships means getting to know another, feeling what they feel, understanding their thoughts, and desiring to spend time with them. In my Earth life, relationships scared me and brought control. I hated being controlled. So I withdrew. *But no one in this afterlife tries to control me. They let me be me; they accept me. Is this what a relationship is supposed to be like?*

*Yes,* Shireen Anne replied to my thoughts.

Blair added, "Working with Sally will connect Marcia to you. That'll energize her because it'll be like fighting for you even though in her current material form, you're gone. And working with Sally will strengthen both women. Sally will reevaluate her superficial approach, too."

"Two minds are better than one, you know," Blake crowed, throwing water into the air and laughing.

*I want to reconcile with Grand.* My eyes widened and wandered, seeking an answer to this sudden thought. *I used her name. I must want to reconcile with her, right?* To my astonishment, I did. I wanted to get to know her. To reconcile with her. I didn't know how, but it didn't matter. I'd learned how to use a butterfly, a bird, and possession that didn't control. I couldn't move objects. *Yet,* I thought. But that would come in time. I'd learn.

Learning suddenly excited me. Learning about my new existence. *No, my life! My continuing life. A life where friends seek me out, I reciprocate, and family love is real. Love.* I tasted that word. Sweet. Rich. Scented of roses. Soft. It felt neither false nor metallic. It contained no artificiality here in this place, in our energy forms. *Maybe I can trust love? I can trust Love aka God?*

"You can," Bailey said. "God formed all of us, all those stars you see, the moon, the earth, from love."

*Wow,* I thought. *How do I comprehend that?*

"You don't," Nihil said to the trees. "You let it exist."

"I guess," I said.

Nihil said, "Love doesn't let you go, even when you want it to. You let that exist, too."

Her words comforted me. Security entered my heart. I now understood what Marcia's face had expressed.

The beauty of the lake and the moon, the security of the stars sprinkling the night like cascading glitter, Blake dancing through the waves, drew my eyes.

I sat down on the sand, hugged my knees to my chest, and sighed happily.

# Chapter Twenty-Five

# BACK TO GRAND

The earth rotated on its axis. Night turned into day. Day into night. The clouds rolled in. And snow filtered from the sky. I opened my palm upwards, and a flake landed on it. It didn't melt.

I turned a quizzical face to Bailey, lying next to me on the sand. We'd all stretched out on this small, hidden beach for a time that didn't count. The lake susurrated froth up onto the sand, drifted back down, then up again.

She said, "You don't give off heat, so it won't melt."

I sat up straight and stared at the flakes accumulating on my hand. Each flake an art piece of languid water molecules. "Molecules are fascinating. The faster they vibrate, the hotter. The slower, the colder. Are we cold?"

"No," Bailey said. "We're energy forms, extensions of what our minds envision of ourselves. Before you enter Heaven, it's the latent energy version of your physical self with nascent abilities. Once you reach Heaven, then your mind connects one hundred percent with

God's Spirit, perceives it's detached from your brain, and starts learning how to be.

"It's like philosophy of mind. We're a thinking thing, and our thinking thing creates extensions. Our matrix-mind gathers and manipulates electromagnetic energy at an electron level, to create an outer shell—our skin—which traps atoms and molecules inside it. But like a house's skin, it isn't completely impervious. Atoms and molecules like oxygen and carbon dioxide can seep in and exhale out when you mimic the physical act of breathing. Your skin senses the material and energy worlds down to the tiniest quanta, and your mind reads that, just like your brain reads the messages from your sensory nerves. So you feel the atoms within you, but they're not you."

"Oh," I uttered, staring at the white flakes with their dagger points. "These aren't penetrating my skin."

"They're too light."

I nodded as if I comprehended. *What is mind? Why matrix-mind?*

*You're not ready to know that yet*, Bailey replied. She asked out loud, "Are you ready?"

I turned my head to look down at her as I dropped my hand down to the sand by my side. "Ready?"

"To reconcile with your grandmother?"

"Yes."

The rippling water before us thrust up wavelets and then waves. Surf crashed on the beach.

Unperturbed by this sudden change, Bailey said, "She's near the end. Her heart kept beating after her bout of terminal lucidity."

"I wonder if her hostile anger kept her going?" Shireen Anne mused from the other side of Bailey. She stretched her arms, palms facing the sky, to catch mounds of snowflakes.

Bailey sat up. "You're ready to visit the nursing home and reconcile with your grandmother on your own," she told me.

"My own?" I stared at her. "I thought you're always with me."

"We are. But growing up in this life after Earth life also includes becoming independent. It's time to see if you can fare on your own."

"Have you learned your lessons, she's trying to say," said Blake from where she floated on the surf.

"Oh!" I exclaimed. "The lake changed because I shifted us in my storytelling time to when I first visited Grand. That's three years after my death, right?"

Bailey smiled and nodded, then spoke to Blake's utterance. "I wouldn't put it like that."

"But it's the truth," Blair said.

"Yes."

Silence fell as pinhead-sized snowflakes scattershot across the air. My skin sensed the wind's pressure. I somehow knew its strength in Pascals; my skin, the shifting wind velocity in kilometres per hour and how it changed the air pressure. I revelled in these new sensations and measurement abilities.

"Do you remember the prayer the elder taught you at Heaven School?" Bailey asked me.

I nodded.

"Recite it."

I tore my attention away from Nature's forces gathering around us. I recited it. Word for word. Then astonishment hit me. *How did I do that?*

*Memory is perfect in life after death*, Shireen Anne thought to me.

*Handy*, I thought. *Yet scary. I don't want to remember the bad.*

*But you can't heal the bad without remembering it. Without memory, you can't salve the wounds. They're like the pea that pained the princess.*

I considered that.

"You'll need that prayer when you get to the nursing home."

"What do you mean?"

"The ghosts, as you call them, are waiting for her," Nihil said.

"Her?" *Weren't they waiting for me last time? I don't want to deal with them.*

"Yes, your grandmother. You have to," Nihil said. "We all had to learn how to keep ourselves safe."

"Remember, you can't save everyone or reconcile with everyone. Only Jesus can. And don't forget: be not afraid," Bailey added.

"What do you mean?" I asked.

"Jesus tells us over and over to fear not, for he is with us," Shireen Anne explained.

I raised my eyebrows. I looked around. I didn't see anyone but us.

Nihil rolled her eyes. "You're so literal."

"Experience will teach you," Bailey instructed. "Remember the prayer. Keep fear away and recite it when you encounter them. The rest is up to you."

"What happens if they get me?"

"They won't," Bailey said.

Somehow I believed her.

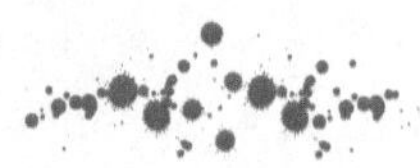

I STOOD INSIDE Grand's nursing home room. The ghosts gathered like a storm outside her window as Grand's breath rattled her lungs. Eyes shut, cheeks sunken, mouth pinched, grooved lines revealed her bitter anger.

The empty room heightened her aloneness. With a last exhalation, her physical form died, and her energy form rose out of her.

"You!" she said, pointing a sharp finger at me.

"Yes, me," I replied calmly. "I'm here to reconcile with you."

"Filth!" she screamed.

"And warn you," I replied. I'd perfected self-control, locking away my emotions, blanking my thoughts, in the face of Mom's control. I automatically reacted in my old Earth-life ways.

"Warn me? Me?" she mocked. She cackled, her eyes blazing triumphant hate.

The ghosts penetrated the window and crowded around me. Fear prickled my back, picking at the lock on my emotions. I strained to remember the prayer.

"I see you have company," she rasped.

"No, they're here for you, Grand."

"Are they? They're followers of our Lord and Saviour?" She nodded at them with satisfaction. They murmured assent, stroked her ego with their chorus.

I stuttered, "Je...Je...Jesus lov...lov...loves me."

The ghosts halted in their glide towards Grand.

"Love is with me," I recited.

They taunted, "You think those words have any effect on us? Silly girl!" They chortled. I resisted clapping my hands over my ears.

"Silly girl," Grand repeated. "You don't know our Lord and Saviour."

I ignored her. I shouted for her and for me, to whomever the prayer was to, "Protect us now!"

The ghosts wafted to the window.

I turned to face the angry, hissing horde. I spoke with all the authority I could muster as Grand scrabbled at my back. "Spirit guide me and buffer us from these who wish me ill. Buffer us from these ghosts! Protect us now!!"

Caterwauling and threatening, they fled through the window, fading into the snow-filled sky.

The sudden silence leadened the air.

"What did you do that for?" Grand cried, her harsh voice renting my mind. "How dare you call on spirit guides!"

"I didn't call on any spirit guides," I said as I turned to face her, hanging on to my control, threading my mind to the Holy Spirit in the way I'd seen expressed by my soul family. I captured her clawed hands in mine. "I called on the Holy Spirit."

"You don't know anything about our Lord and Saviour's Holy Spirit," she said venomously, dragging her hands out of my fingers. "How could you? You're her progeny. The atheist!"

I bit back my thoughts. I wanted to scream that I knew the Holy Spirit better than she did, but urgency gnawed at me, and smudges of that overwhelming unconditional love strengthened my control. A black mist rose behind her. I gasped. *Dark? Here in this world, on Earth?* I gripped her hands again. *I have to warn her; I have to reconcile with her before the Earth-Heaven Interdimensional Expanse draws her in. But how? She doesn't want to know me. How do I reconcile with her?*

Grand screamed and flailed her arms to snatch her hands out of mine. I clasped them tighter and straightened my arms to keep her away from me as I thought about how to help her. A zigzagging vertical seam appeared in the black mist behind her. The seam fissured like soundless lightning and widened to reveal Hell Track on the other side.

"Oh!" I exclaimed.

The Red Robes sat in their circle with their papers. The garbage dump had grown. And in the far distance, Hell Gates rose. Yet something was different...

I cocked my head. *Had that black mist risen behind me when I'd died, as well? But I'd gone straight into Dark Distortan, not Hell Track. Why Hell Track first for her?* Terror rippled my skin and crawled through my mind. My hands convulsed and tightened around hers. She screamed in agony.

I looked into Grand's wretched face. *Agony? How does she feel pain?* I stared into her wide-open mouth, her hate-filled eyes, and recognized this is my ancestor who needs my help. *No, whom I want to help.* I didn't understand where this compassion came from for someone I barely knew and who hated me.

*Love your enemies.*

*Who said that?* I concentrated on probing the entire space as I gripped Grand's hands. The room's emptiness except for the bed, nightstand, chair, and us, and the view of Hell Track, sang back loneliness.

"Grand, listen to me," I said, staring hard into her eyes.

"Why should I? Who are you to lecture—"

"Listen!"

Her head reared back as her mouth dropped open.

"You're going into Hell Track," I said. "I don't know why straight there. Something terrible awaits you there. Remember this! The light, the golden light of love will help you. Look for it! And if you find yourself in Dark, if you hear the questions 'Where are you going human-killer?' look for the light. Ask for Jesus's help."

"Jesus is always with me."

"Jesus isn't because you've rejected them: God, Holy Spirit, Love, the Word." *How do I know this?* I shook my head free of distracting questions.

Her mouth snapped shut; her eyes narrowed; her nostrils flared. She spat, "How dare—"

A vortex opened up, dragging her backwards, snatching her words. I clutched her hands so hard, she screamed. "You filthy whore, you're hurting me! How dare you hold me in your clutches!"

"I dare because I want to save you."

"You?" she spat without spit. The vortex yanked her feet up and back.

"Your hatred is what attracted those ghosts to you. Your rejection of what Jesus taught is why Hell Track is going to suck you in. Dark will claim you, if you don't listen and remember." I yanked her towards me as terror trembled my skin's adhesion. I shoved my face into hers, nose to nose. I lowered my voice and enunciated as one speaks to an obstinate child.

Her mouth shut, and she blinked up at me, her body horizontal, pulling me and her towards the black mist tornadoing her into itself. Astonishment blanked one part of my mind as another part spoke the last words I'd say to her. "Please remember Grand, to look for that light, to ignore Ignorance Distortan, which shows you what you want to hear and see. Don't believe Dark or Desire or Ignorance. Do not, whatever you do, put on the glasses that Ignorance will offer you. You lose Jesus if you do."

*Where is her soul family? She's going in there alone without support. How can that be? Why?*

Sadness and pity mingled and choked my breath. Grand's pupils contracted. She blinked rapidly. Something in Hell Track, something I hadn't encountered, crawled along my skin, its terror trying to splinter me. I fought its menacing message, telling me to let go, that I had no power, that my existence would be endless aloneness if I didn't let go of her. *No!* I exclaimed. *I won't let go! I have to reconcile with her. I must!! I must warn her. It's the only way I know how to reconcile with her.*

I yelled. I beseeched, "Remember Grand, don't put on the glasses. Don't believe what they tell you when it mimics your deepest desires and hatreds and fears. Look for the light way off in the distance and ask for help. Admit you don't know God."

The unknown terror within Hell Track wrenched her out of my grasp, and the mist imploded into nothingness. Confusion and hatred warring in her eyes were the last I saw of her.

# Chapter Twenty-Six

# THE LION'S REVENGE

*I*edged my way to Mom's front window and peeked in. The Lion was prowling around the living room. I jerked my head back. I'd expected to see Mom's lion head trophy nailed to the wall, but not its spirit. *What's wrong with your memory, Charlotte Elisabeth?* I remonstrated myself.

The Lion, no, Grandfather prowled past the window; I ducked.

I'd been so focused on reconciling with Mom, I'd forgotten about the grandfather lion. *What to do? What to do? Courage, Charlotte Elisabeth*, I told myself. The ghosts hanging around outside had scattered before my prayers. I smirked at the recent scene. They'd screamed and screeched as they'd fled. I'd added my own words to the ones Heaven School had taught me. *Jesus doesn't love you!* I'd called out, sticking my tongue out. I chuckled to myself. Sometimes being a child satisfies.

*Roar!*

I flattened myself against the wall under the front window. In my gloating, I'd forgotten about the Lion. *Does he know I'm here?* I

224

craned my neck to side-eye the living room. His furry rump and swishing tail greeted my eyes. I raised myself a little, squinted to narrow my focus, and scanned the room. The trophy still blighted the wall. Fear froze me; only my eyeballs moved to find Mom.

She lay on the couch, a cloth covering her forehead. She moaned. With her left hand, she raised her iPhone listlessly to her face. Unexpectedly, she sat up and punched the screen with her forefinger.

One ring, and the 311 welcome message began. Mom listened. Her shoulders twitched. She swung her legs off the couch and glared at her screen.

The Lion towered behind her and the couch. He turned his head. His predatory sight almost caught me.

Mom vaulted up and gesticulated, "Enough already! Get to the operator!!"

Toronto's 311 auto message was warning the caller to behave themself else the call would be terminated. I observed the automated threat escalating Mom, who was now about to throw her phone against the wall. I thought back to one client who offered security to places of worship. He'd talked non-stop on the phone, during our meetings, pausing only to listen to my explanations of his tax documents. I lost sight of Mom extending her arm back, knuckles white, as I remembered him lecturing on de-escalation and how he required all his employees to learn it. "Annual updating is the key," he'd said, raising his index finger. "Better than any threat to behave, just release the de-escalation tool, and in one minute, I guarantee it, the aggressor will behave."

The Lion's whiskers twitched upwards as Mom swung her arm forwards, fingers clenching the iPhone. Grandfather Lion rumbled, "Lawyers and zero tolerance. They escalate my meal for me, preparing it for revenge."

I couldn't even swallow.

Grandfather Lion thrust his head forwards; with his large, scraping tongue, he licked Mom from her sacral bone to her skull.

Mom screamed, and her arm dropped, clutching her iPhone. "A minute and a half of privacy notice and telling me not to yell and no operator yet!" She hurled the innocent iPhone across the living room. It smacked the wall and thudded onto the carpeted floor.

She plunked down on the couch, arms crossed.

Grandfather Lion purred, "Satisfactory. Wouldn't make my revenge easy if they answered within ten seconds and taught trainers to de-escalate." His blond eyes laughed at me and refocused on Mom. She collapsed against the couch's arm and slapped the cloth over her eyes. Fleeting images of a man in a priest's collar looming over filled her vision and mine. A doctor in a small room, a silent nurse next to him, as the priest instructed him and she lay on a bed, feet in stirrups. Mom moaned and rolled her head from side to side as Grandfather Lion energized the memories. Horrified, I tried to barricade my mind against them.

*What was it they had said? Fear not?* I uncurled myself. *I have to do something! But what?* I pulled my head back and gazed sightlessly at the opposite houses. They looked normal. No sign of recognizing the drama behind me. *How do I reconcile with Mom, who doesn't believe in God or the afterlife? With the lion she'd shot and the city's 311 escalating her frustration and resentments?* I didn't begrudge her atheism. I saw why she'd rejected the entire idea of God. Why she soured on people of faith. But I couldn't pretend I'm not alive.

*Alive.*

I savoured that word.

*I am alive*, I marvelled.

*Maybe I do have a second chance at life.*

I pondered that.

I wanted to give Mom that, too. But how?

I turned to look through the window again. Grandfather Lion's tail was swishing back and forth, back and forth, back and forth. Its hunter's rhythm hypnotized me. I shook my head free. I'd discovered the ghosts feared me; I had power they didn't have. *Is the Lion the same way?* No, I shook my head. *Grandfather Lion doesn't have evil intentions like those ghosts did.* Mom and my unknown grandfather had killed him violently. *Revenge is a state, not a person. Or in this case,* I thought, *an animal.*

*Isn't revenge an evil intention? A bad thought that leads to bad deeds?*

Where'd those questions come from? I swivelled, searching for the source. Was this voice my mind or...the Holy Spirit...or God? I considered the words. I conceded that maybe revenge is an evil intention. I glanced through the window at Grandfather Lion. He had stoked Mom's anger. He'd feasted on her low mood, her frustration, her need to control. *That feasting justifies his revenge, doesn't it?* Understanding catapulted itself into my mind. *Evil can influence animals, too. Pain can become evil intention or bad thoughts in animals, too. Which means love can vanquish it.* I gasped on that last revelation.

I lifted myself up. Levitated a moment. Then edged my left foot through the window behind Grandfather Lion's back. He didn't notice. I edged my other foot in and stilled myself at an angle. *I'm hovering at a forty-five degree angle,* I giggled silently. *I'm defying gravity with my lower half in the living room! I can enter upside down!* I clapped a hand to smother my guffaw. *Life after death is neat.* For a moment, I enjoyed the sensation and my new abilities.

Mom sat up. The cloth fell from her eyes onto her lap. She sighed. I bobbed myself upright and passed through the window, pausing just inside it.

Mom covered her face with her hands. Tears splashed through the cracks between her fingers. "How could she?" she moaned. "How could both of them leave me like that?"

Grandfather Lion roared, "How could they? Have you no insight? How could you take me from my pride?" He thrust his head close to the back of hers. Mom hunched in on herself as if terror had reached for her. I frowned. *Can she sense Grandfather Lion's presence?*

He turned his massive head and hypnotized me with his darkening blond-golden eyes. His whiskers twitched. I gulped. *Fear not,* I recited to myself. *Fear not.*

"She's mine," he pronounced. He padded around the couch and placed one massive paw on both of Mom's bare feet, resting side by side on the carpet. Through his transparent paws, I saw her toes curl in and her feet angle over each other. *She senses him! Or maybe,* I pondered, *he filled her with fear. If I take him away from her, she'll have relief. Maybe she'll feel less afraid and can reconcile with Sally.*

"You're optimistic," he mocked me. "Scurvy rots the soul."

*Scurvy?*

"She's deficient in love for others. It's rotted her like scurvy rots teeth."

*How do you know about scurvy?*

"I learned a lot being nailed to the wall," he growled.

I looked towards the wall where his physical head hung. *Had he felt his physical self being beheaded? Had he felt his head being stuffed and screwed onto a plaque and onto the wall?* I hadn't felt my physical body because Dr. V had numbed me with anesthetics. "A dignified death," he'd called it. But another human being killing me had interrupted my Soul Track, depriving me of learning I had relationships and could love. *Do animals have Soul Tracks, too? Had Mom shooting Grandfather Lion and that man beheading him, interrupt the lion's Soul Track, deprive him of carrying out his relationships to their proper end?* In a way, the medical profession, the Supreme Court, and governments had beheaded me. They'd split my mind from my life.

My heart burned and spurted sorrow towards Grandfather Lion. "I'm sorry they shot you."

He turned his massive head with its glorious mane to face me. His eyes narrowed, pinning me. He padded towards me, releasing Mom's feet. Her toes uncurled. He spat, "I don't need your pity!"

"I don't pity you," I said out loud, unmoved by his predatory thoughts. Unlike the ghosts, he could read my thoughts, I realized, but he spoke to me in growls and hisses and roars of words. I should respect his communication style. "I'm really sorry my family killed you and split up your relationships. You didn't deserve that."

His cheeks pulled up, exposing his sharp teeth. "It sounds like pity to me."

Mom stood up and swayed behind him. I tried not to notice, to hold his golden eyes on mine. His eyes pulled me in. I felt a predator's hypnotic stare immobilizing me. I blinked. Mom was tottering towards the door to the back hall. She was pulling down her shirt and wiping her face as the traumatizing memories sank back into her unconscious mind. I cocked my head. Yes, getting Grandfather Lion out of her life could help her. And helping her would be my way of reconciling with her. I'd avoided a relationship with her my entire adult life, never thought about how to engage her or pacify her like Sincerity had.

Grandfather Lion swung around and trotted after her. I ran after him. He pounced on her back, and she braked, shuddering. She crossed her arms over her chest and pulled her shirt collar points towards each other. Grandfather Lion thrust his snout into her skull and roared. She sank into a crouch, tucking her head in. He exited her skull; he tongued the back of her head.

Mom plunged to the floor, her right hand braking her fall, her legs bent underneath her. She panted; he panted above her, his front paws planted on her back.

I reached out a hand to grab his mane; all of a sudden, I knew physical-type violence was not the answer.

"I saw Shelagh and your collaboration partner!" I called out.

Grandfather Lion jerked his massive head around to face me, his orange-flecked golden eyes bored into me. "Starlight?"

"Starlight?"

"My collaboration partner. We lived together in Shelagh's pride."

"Yes, him."

"He tried to kill you for me?"

"No."

Grandfather Lion pawed off Mom and turned his entire body around to face me. "No?"

"No. He said little. He looked sad."

"Sad? What did you do?"

"Nothing," I exclaimed, raising my hands, palms facing him. "Shelagh and he found me." I emphasized my pronoun. "Shelagh told me your story, that's all."

He narrowed his eyes and padded towards me, claws deceptively sheathed. I forced myself to remain still. He lowered his head, his transparent mane filling my vision yet allowing me to watch Mom. She sat up and shook her head as if coming out of a terror-filled daze. I had to keep him occupied but also soothe him.

"I think your collaboration partner—"

"Starlight," he growled.

"Yes, Starlight...um, you know, I don't know your name. Mine is Charlotte Elisabeth."

"I know yours," he sniffed, halting in front of me, his eyes and whiskers and gleaming white teeth dominating my three-sixty vision. "I heard it every day. From her."

I nodded. *Fear not, fear not.* I rolled my shoulders back. "I'd like to know your name...please?"

"Moonlight."

"Was that because you were born under the moon?"

"Under the crescent moon. Starlight under the falling stars. Sunlight in full noon."

"Sunlight?"

"Our third brother. He died in the season before they shot me."

"I'm sorry."

His suspicious eyes scrutinized my face. His eyes widened. "You are," he said disbelievingly.

"Yes, I am." I straightened my spine. "They only want you with them. They're grieving your loss."

He snuffled me.

I swallowed convulsively. I squeaked, cleared my throat, wondering how I could have phlegm, and spoke again. "Why not counter what Mom and her father did, rejoin your family...I mean, your pride?"

He stepped one paw closer.

"Show them that they can't split you up. You're not a trophy. You're a cherished family member." I whispered to myself, "Like I wished I was."

Moonlight stepped back one paw length and contemplated me. "You were cherished," he stated. "She had murder planted in her soul and couldn't see it. But it doesn't matter she didn't see it. I will have my revenge."

I swiped at my eyes. "Doesn't revenge hurt?"

His eyes flickered. He glanced at her over his shoulder as she stood up shakily and planted one hand against the doorjamb to brace herself. He turned back to me. "Are you lying to me?"

I opened my mouth to say no and realized that once he got there, he'd know the truth. I'd avoided so many truths while alive on Earth. I couldn't anymore. I inhaled a skinful of air molecules and exhaled. I said, "Shelagh hates me. My friends and family got her to leave me alone."

He shoved his head into my face. I didn't flinch. "Yet you said Starlight was sad."

"Shelagh did all the talking, but I felt his emotions."

He examined my expression. His vengeful intent licked my thoughts. I asked against the fear screaming at me to flee, "How did Sunlight die?"

"Not your concern. Why was Sunlight not with Starlight?"

"I don't know. I didn't know there was a third," I replied.

He lowered his head and sat. He lifted his left paw up and licked it like a cat.

"I am a cat. A cat who lives with his brothers and moves from family to family. Your kind stole that from me."

"How long do you want to live in a perpetual state of revenge? How long do you want to be like Mom, filled with bitterness and misplaced betrayal...and traumatic memories?"

Moonlight stopped licking; his body a transparent statue. I kept talking. "Why not heal your own wounds? Shelagh and Starlight fear you'll end up away from them in Hell Track, never to see each other again. If you continue to prowl Mom, yes, you'll keep her terrified, always feeling betrayed, stuck in those horrid memories, separated from her own family. But is the price of you letting her and her father separate you from your family for eternity worth it?"

He lowered his paw.

"I think you know how to find them. I'm not sure how you get to Heaven, but maybe animals know that instinctively?" I asked.

He contemplated the carpet through his transparent paws.

"They're waiting for you," I breathed. "Go and be their healer." I said at a normal volume, "Go play with them, live with them like you used to, only better because no human being can take you away from them ever again."

I waited.

"It's only you now who's separating yourself from them. Starlight wants to see you."

"I need to find Sunlight," he grumbled. Moonlight lifted his massive head up, transfixed me with his gaze, then jumped over me, through the window, and vanished.

Mom straightened up. She let go of the doorjamb, yanked her shirt down, and strode through the doorway towards the kitchen.

# Chapter Twenty-Seven

# SINCERITY'S FALL

*Why is Sincerity standing at the bridge balustrade like that?* I knitted my eyebrows. I scanned the empty sidewalk east and west. I floated over the concrete-stone balustrade and peered down. A long way down. Dizziness assailed me, and I hastened back to land on the sidewalk.

Sincerity was resting her hands on the balustrade, her hair fluttering in the wind. Her fingers contracted.

*That must hurt,* I thought.

She planted her feet wide apart in a ready-to-jump stance.

My eyebrows shot up; my lips parted. *Why?!*

I jerked my shocked eyes around to look straight into her eyes. Tears created a glassy lens over her blank eyes. Salty water crystallized her bottom eyelashes together. I tuned in to her training, chaotic thoughts.

*Why did she die? I tried to help her. I wanted to be her big sister. We were too close in age, that was it. How could I be her big sister? How could*

*I go to that lawyer? Why did I listen to her? I didn't want to go see that lawyer. Why did I? None of this makes sense.*

Sincerity's tumbling thoughts shot guilt through me. *My guilt? No, hers. Why?* I braced myself and slipped into her body. Guilt fogged her memory. I dove into the guilt to follow its corkscrewing way through flitting thoughts. It crashed into the memory of that lawyer's visit; it snaked backwards in time to her meeting with her colleague.

*I should've spoken up,* Sincerity raged at herself in her mind. *I should've said no. Charlotte Elisabeth is my sister! I don't want her estate. I want her!*

*Me?* I tumbled out of her and stared as her thoughts careened into my mind.

*I tried so hard. But she died! She hated me, her life, all of us, she left us! Why couldn't she see I love her?*

A sob erupted and blasted my mind like water gushing out of a fire hydrant.

*I didn't try hard enough. Why should I live? What's the point? We failed her.* "I failed her," Sincerity suddenly shouted into a gust. The wind died, and Sincerity stared with open eyes towards Lake Ontario.

Snowflakes drifted from the silvery seamless sky and melted before they reached asphalt and concrete. Drivers accelerated across the dry bridge. A streetcar trundled by us, vibrating the bridge with its heavy passage. Sincerity noticed none of it. I saw it all as if I was a fisheye lens. But I didn't know the date nor the year. *Is this the same week as her last visit to the lawyer? A year later? Two years?* I waved my hand in front of my face. *Chronological time doesn't matter! I'm in storytelling time now. This is the next episode, scene, whatever it's called in my time.* I adjured myself, *Is time important anymore? Focus! How can I help her?*

*A butterfly! Maybe the first ones didn't reach her.*

*How did Calico teach me?* I concentrated on my memory of Calico's call for a white butterfly. Oxygen and nitrogen molecules buzzed; carbon dioxide molecules vibrated. I raised my face to the sky; a white butterfly was zigging and zagging with the wind towards Sincerity.

She didn't notice.

I gabbled to the butterfly. "Please tell her I'm here. I'm alive. I'm with her. She's not guilty of anything. She's not at fault. She tried hard enough. It was me who didn't. I regret it so much. I didn't think she'd suffer. I thought me and everyone else would be better off. I was such a burden to myself; how could I not be to her? Tell her she's better off without me. And I'm getting a second chance at life."

A voice sounded from above, beside, and below me. "Perhaps your second chance was meant to be while still in your first life. Perhaps your heart condition was meant to have you re-evaluate your choices and draw closer to Sincerity. Suicide ripples out like a contagion to those left behind. By doctor or by your hand it doesn't matter, for it is your own will that completes it. Your will moving another's hand instead of your own hand as Sincerity is doing now in traditional suicide."

I looked around. "Who is that?"

Emptiness answered. *Calico? Greeter?* No, it didn't feel like Greeter, that comforting dog who greeted me in the Earth-Heaven Interdimensional Expanse. The butterfly landed between Sincerity's trembling hands on the balustrade. It opened its wings, paused, and closed them. Opened them and closed them.

Sincerity didn't notice.

*She hadn't noticed me connected to her mind within her body. She isn't noticing the butterfly now. How do I get her attention?*

I sidled up to her. I placed my right hand on her left shoulder. I thought heavy thoughts. She glanced down at that shoulder. Frowned. And noticed the butterfly. She stared at it. It opened and closed its wings. "Go away," she muttered. "Aren't you supposed to be in warmth?"

I blinked. Sincerity didn't get it. *I wouldn't have, either, before I died my first death*, I admitted to myself.

*There's nothing for me here. Charlotte Elisabeth had the right idea.* My sister's thoughts captured my breath and convulsed my hand on her shoulder. I no longer thought of her as my half-sister, as if she and I were detached. She was and is my sister.

Sincerity leaned back on her heels. Her right foot rose; her shoulder ripped out from my hand; she landed on top of the balustrade in a crouch. The butterfly fluttered up to land on her nose. I gasped. Sincerity blew air upwards. The butterfly stuck. Both her hands gripping the balustrade held her in place; she couldn't use either to brush off the white butterfly.

"Why are you here?" Sincerity wailed.

The butterfly opened and closed its wings. I hastened forwards and clasped her shoulder again. I leaned in and whispered. "I'm alive, Sincerity. Alive! It wasn't your fault. That was some...some...thing...a ghost but not a ghost...I don't know what...it was evil making you go to the lawyer. Live, Sincerity! Have the courage to do what I didn't!"

A guitar strummed behind me. I whirled around. A tall man smiled at me. Grey highlighted his short white straight hair. A matching beard graced his chin. His glacier-blue eyes reflected blue sky and blue ocean. Calm soaked into me. He began to sing in harmony with the sweet melody of his guitar. I recognized it. "My Sweet Lord."

*Why are you here?* I asked him in my thoughts.

He stopped strumming the melody and stroked the strings. "My name is Duke. I'm here for the lost and suicidal. I felt her misery and came."

"You're dead?"

"I'm alive in God! I live because Jesus doesn't want to say goodbye."

I stared. Again, that phrase.

"Before my death, I believed in life after death, and, as N.T. Wright wrote, in life after life after death, for God so made the world that he sent his only son that whosoever believes in him shall never die. But I also couldn't believe that the Creator would want to give up his created children. No parent wants to lose their child."

I considered that. I remembered Mom at the hospital, wailing over my body, preventing anyone from coming near it. I reluctantly agreed. "I guess not." Keeping my hold on Sincerity, I straightened my back and said, "Mom wouldn't want Sincerity to die. She's already mourning my death and upset at Sally leaving her."

Duke began singing again as he strolled to stand beside Sincerity. The music's sound waves undulated towards her, reflecting off her head, her body.

"Why did they bounce off her? Isn't your music in an energy form she can't hear?"

He shook his head in concern.

Sincerity shook her head. "No," she spoke under her breath.

"She's closed herself off," Duke grieved. "I shall remain with her."

Sincerity shot herself forwards into the open air. I leaped and grabbed her around her middle. My hands clasped, and her body fell through them, ripping me apart from shoulders down to my hands. Bits of me flew in all directions, like mist being broken apart. Gravity's wave pulled Sincerity down as I tried to gather myself back together in desperate thought that somehow I could stop her fall.

Her thoughts streamed up to me: *No! I shouldn't have jumped! I want to live! I don't want to live without Charlotte Elisabeth. But I want to make it up to her!*

Duke dove after her, his guitar strapped to his chest. His guitar transformed into a banjo, and his hands fingered a lively melody that seemed to call on life-affirming life.

*Bluegrass!*

Sincerity bounced off a jutting branch of a tree. She pitched towards a shorter tree whose branches snapped underneath her, slowing her fall. She smashed through the lowest branch and broke through tall bushes to land on the ground.

Thump.

Air exhaled from her lungs. Her eyes teared at the sky above her.

I zoomed downwards.

A woman screamed from the path that ran beside the bushes and trees. We were in the Don Valley. Duke landed beside her, fingered the last chords, and coalesced, his banjo strapped across his back. I faltered. I rubbed my eyes, opened them again, and hovered above him. Blake had done the same thing. Duke looked human, like any other human on Earth, before death.

*How'd he do that?*

He glanced up at me and thought, *Resurrection is God's gift to us, the fulfilment of God's Creation plan. God's Grace gave this gift of a resurrected body to me for continuing my part of God's work on Earth.*

*Resurrection? Resurrected body? God's work?*

Duke eyed me. *Life after life after death. You'll find out when you're ready.* He turned his back to me and placed a gentle hand on Sincerity's shoulder. Her eyes moved raggedly within their sockets. She panted, her eyes beseeching his.

"Don't speak."

Shouts from the path caught my attention. A group was gesticulating towards us; one member pulled out their phone and called 911. The rest crashed through the bushes and stumbled to their knees beside her.

"Are you alive?" one whispered to Sincerity's terrified eyes.

Another asked Duke, "How is she? Did you see it?"

Duke replied softly, "Yes, I saw it. She's still alive. We can save her."

I stared around. No sign of her energy form. I looked back down at her body. *Is she alive?*

Sincerity closed her eyes and moaned.

"Oh, thank God."

The one with the phone, a man, raised it up and shouted, "They're not answering. What do we do?"

The woman closest to Sincerity shouted back, "I'm going to triage her. Call nine one one again and again until they pick up. You," she said, pointing at the other woman in their group, "call my partner. He lives close by and carries a full first aid kit. I've teased him about being ready for the apocalypse." She cried-laughed, "He was right." The other woman nodded and punched at her phone rapidly as the first woman leaned in to Sincerity and said with compassionate authority, "I'm a paramedic. You're going to be okay."

I drifted apart as Duke comforted and the group rallied to save Sincerity. No one in their cars driving by, seeing her ready to jump, had stopped to prevent it, but this group will save her. The white butterfly landed on her chest.

"Oh look," a man in the group said, pointing to the butterfly. "There's a message from heaven. Whoever sent it is okay. That's the message for you ma'am." Sincerity opened her eyes and stared unseeing up at him. He leaned down and said, "Whoever you're missing is okay. They're doing well in the afterlife. They want you to live. They sent that white butterfly to tell you they're okay and love you and want you to live. So live, okay?"

Sincerity closed her eyes.

"Don't fall unconscious on us," the paramedic shouted.

Sincerity opened her eyes as tears slipped out of their corners.

I collapsed onto the dead grass.

Calico appeared behind the group as the man still on the path was talking to 911. He took the phone from his ear and yelled, "They're overloaded. It'll be twenty minutes because they have to send a bus from the other side." No one seemed surprised. The paramedic and the others closed in to examine Sincerity. Duke removed himself a little way. And when unnoticed by the group, he transformed himself back into our mind-extension-energy form. Duke's banjo became a sitar. He sat cross-legged next to Sincerity, unheeding of the women and men moving through him as they hustled expertly to save Sincerity. Duke supported the sitar across his legs. Mourning mingled with joy as he played the complex instrument, calling life to stay within us all.

Calico called to me, "Charlotte Elisabeth. It's time to go. Sincerity will live. This group will look after her."

I sniffled, "I know." I watched the group help Sincerity.

"No, you don't," the cat reprimanded me. "You think I mean here. But I'm saying they won't leave her when she's recovering in the hospital. Not after. They'll become her friends; she'll join them on their daily walks. She'll learn about the afterlife and grow into herself because of their support. She has her second chance at life to finish her Soul Track. You've accomplished your reconciliation goal."

"I have?" I said, twisting my head to look at Calico, to confirm they were telling the truth. Behind Calico, a man loaded down with paramedic bags was running towards us. And then the scene vanished. Calico had whisked me away somehow.

"Time to go."

"But, but," I looked over my shoulder towards where I thought the Don Valley and Sincerity were.

"Humans! Contrarians every time," Calico meowed.

"What do you mean?"

"You're not the first one to finish reconciling and then want to stay after balking at first at Samuel's instruction."

"Oh."

"I'll lead you to Heaven. You'll traverse this direct path in the future, both future chronological time and the next scenes in your storytelling time."

"So I did it? I really made amends and reconciled with them all?"

"Yes," Calico purred.

We sped into motion. Earth receded into a blur.

# Chapter Twenty-Eight

# HEAVEN'S SECOND ENTRANCE

Chronological time left us. We moved forwards in my storytelling time. Space morphed, compressed and expanded, billowed and stalled. Yet we existed as ourselves. Behind us, the paramedic's colleague wrapped a neck brace around Sincerity's neck while they waited for the ambulance. Beside us, outer space spread in endless expanse littered with far-off stars or galaxies. I couldn't tell them apart. Ahead of us, a minuscule prismatic dot appeared.

"Hey!" Blake called out. "Wait for us!"

A mistral blew. And Bailey, Blair, and Blake drew alongside in their orb forms.

I blinked.

I'd forgotten about how they'd greeted me in the Dying with Dignity Suite.

I looked down at myself. Human shape. Naked. *Naked? Wait a minute!*

They laughed. Calico smirked as they led us ever quicker towards that dot.

"It's okay, Charlotte Elisabeth," Bailey said. "We've seen you in every form. You've now finished the Solar Age phase of your Soul Track. You opened your most intimate side of yourself."

"I have?" I wondered. *I didn't speak or think about every secret thought or emotion.*

"That doesn't matter," Bailey said, shaking their head. "You've begun the process. Once begun, there's no reversing. You're well on your way to discovering yourself. That's why Heaven has shed your Earthly clothes. You'll be given new ones for the next phase of your life."

"Next phase? What do you  mean next phase?"

"Hush," Calico scolded me.

I wished I'd worn my favourite outfit. My go-to suit. Camel-hair-coloured jacket, white shirt, and calf-length pencil skirt that matched the jacket. With pockets. I longed for my nude-coloured pumps.

Nihil said, "That's your favourite suit?"

I looked down at myself and gasped. I was wearing my go-to suit. Nihil rolled their eyes. They said, "It's endless here. Your mind growth continues whether you like it or not. God has infinite patience. Love is like that. It never gives up." She muttered, "I wish they would."

I faced Nihil. "You don't mean that. I'm glad Love didn't give up on me, so I know you're glad, too." Warmth towards Nihil stretched my lips upwards and crinkled my eyes.

They knitted their brows. Their grey eyes expressed confusion and rejection of an unwanted thought. Rainbows washed over them; lightwaves waterfalled down them, with photons winking on and off.

I stared.

"What?" Nihil muttered.

I pointed.

"Oh." After a moment, or maybe no moments, they said. "I saw that on my friend when we first returned to Heaven with Calico. They'd reconciled with their family. But I hadn't. I was returning because Jesus recalled me, said I wasn't ready. There was time—time on Earth—yet to finish my Soul Track."

*How had I finished mine, and they hadn't? Wait a minute! When did I start thinking in gender neutral?*

"You completed the Earth portion of your Soul Track," Bailey smiled at me. "That's why you see humans, not genders anymore."

I absorbed that before asking, "Why couldn't you, Nihil, complete your Soul Track?" I heard my voice emote unfamiliar gentle compassion. A new curiosity and emotion. I didn't dwell on this perplexing change. No one I'd known on Earth would recognize me! I suppressed a laugh. I genuinely wanted to know why Nihil, who started ahead of me in her growth, was behind me.

"I tried," she replied. "I was an orphan. No soul family greeted me when I died. Two of us died together." Nihil eyed me. A challenge. I sensed a lie in there. They huffed, "Okay, I wasn't an orphan. My family accepted me in public, ignored me in private." I nodded, not daring to show sympathy. "So I ran in a gang," Nihil shrugged. "Not a real gang, just a bunch of us who looked out for each other because our rich parents couldn't care less about us. We drove fast cars. Smoked. The usual thing." She hunched one shoulder. "Our parents didn't care when we crashed their toys. They paid off the cops and paid for new cars. They didn't care when we shoplifted. They paid off the stores with an extra on the side for their managers. Money, money, money made us—their troubles—go away." Nihil's voice wobbled.

I stayed my mind to listen as we sped along towards the growing polychromatic dot.

"One day our leader challenged me. We fought. She and her friend had brought knives. They knifed me and my friend. We died behind a bin in one of those old downtown graffiti-covered alleyways. Some homeless guy found us, picked our pockets of our cash, and left. A week later, the police found us. A year later, the police charged the rest of the gang. They pointed at each other, but the jury figured out who murdered us and why. The judge showed mercy in his sentencing. Pretty girls get the best sentences, right? They're out free now."

"It's been a while?"

Nihil side-eyed me and smiled mirthlessly. "I tried to reconcile, like Calico taught."

The dot became spirals of stars, surrounded by a light containing every hue and saturated colour. I frowned. I didn't recall photos of galaxies surrounded by prismatic light.

Nihil looked at it. "There's no justice!" they screamed.

I halted, startled. The others braked. We surrounded Nihil.

"There is justice," Shireen Anne said. "Just not the kind we want."

Nihil narrowed angry eyes at Shireen Anne. Charcoal clouds chased across her grey irises. "You keep saying that. It doesn't help."

Shireen Anne nodded. "I agree. Revelation, the vision Jesus gave to John, agrees with you. It says, 'I saw under the altar the souls of those who had been killed because of the word of God and because of the witness they had borne. They shouted at the tops of their voices. "Holy and true Master!" They called, "How much longer are you going to put off giving judgement, and avenging our blood on the earth-dwellers?"'"

"I'm not a witness," Nihil stated.

"You're here. You're a witness to the injustices on Earth. The prayer goes, 'on Earth as it is in Heaven,' yet it isn't, is it, it seems like? You were a teen, reacting to your family's neglect and injustice towards you. Scruffy greeted you when those girls interrupted your Soul Track prematurely. Scruffy is your family."

"I know. Why are you telling me?" Nihil's glacial voice sliced me.

"Because Charlotte Elisabeth doesn't know."

Nihil shot a coal-black glance at me.

I heard shouts behind us and looked. The group was calling the ambulance crew over to where the two off-duty paramedics were triaging Sincerity. *What an upside-down existence*, I thought. *How can this be? Earth saving a mortal life. Us saving a perpetual life. Them unable to see us. Us speeding away from them yet able to see them while not being seen.*

Nihil whispered in my face. "It never ends. The injustice. The pain. The scars rip apart each time I return...back there." She choked on the last two words. "But you...you reconciled with your family who didn't deserve it. How?! How did you do it?"

Their eyes burned with cold, pewter fire into my brown ones. I resisted moving my head back. "I don't know."

"Yes, you do."

Light spheres appeared and surrounded us. Peace emanated from them. Compassion. Overwhelming love. I choked. Tears streamed out of both our eyes. I blinked. I hadn't seen Nihil show this kind of emotion before. *What's happening?*

"You!" Nihil choked. "They didn't affect me before. But watching you broke me. Why?"

I pressed my lips against a sob. I wanted to soothe, wanted to comfort, but the light spheres' overwhelming love cracked apart my lips. Sobs erupted, stopping words and thoughts.

Nihil laid their head on my shoulder and wailed.

Shireen Anne moved close and patted our backs. Calico regarded us with slow-blinking eyes. My family hovered nearby with joy and gentleness glowing their orbs.

"What are those spheres?" I asked when my sobs calmed down enough.

"Angels," Shireen Anne replied.

"Angels? What are those?"

"Some are God's messengers. Some watch over their humans. God created them to serve their creation plan. They can look human like us but aren't human. They can appear and disappear. Interject in our lives by saving us from catastrophe, but sometimes God wills them not to. In Heaven, they live alongside us, but they're not on the same plane because they don't have free will. We do. Remember?"

I nodded slowly as I did.

"They're here to comfort Nihil because God emanated their will to Jesus, who instructed them to come here."

"Oh."

Nihil lifted their head. And I looked closer at the angels. "What are they made of?"

Shireen Anne laughed. "That's a good question. It's said we ate from the tree of knowledge, but we still don't know everything even though we now live with Jesus and can ask. Jesus still answers in those famous parable riddles."

My family's transparent orb forms swirled blue jetstreams with pink, yellow, or silvery highlights in a sine wave with rainbow photons sparkling within. I drew closer, moving past Shireen Anne. "Can I look like that?"

"When you attain your next form, yes," Shireen Anne replied.

I knitted my eyebrows.

"Resurrection," Shireen Anne said.

I strove to parse that word. Nothing. I said, "Duke used that word, too. What does it mean?"

"Jesus will explain it," Bailey replied.

"Who is Jesus, anyway?"

"We're made in the image of God."

"God?"

"Think of God like our matrix-mind."

My head hurt already.

"While God created our matrix-mind in their image, how our matrix-mind emits properties perceivable by others is like the Holy Spirit's role; and how our language of words and body communicate to others what we're like, so Jesus is the Word of God."

My matrix-mind spun like a demented washing machine.

Baily smiled. "It's like this. The Holy Spirit interacts with the physical world, and Jesus speaks to the psycho-physical world. Our matrix-mind's emittive properties interact with the physical world, and our language speaks to the physical and psycho-physical worlds."

*How is that clearer?* I grumbled to myself. "Okay," I acceded equitably.

"God, the Holy Spirit, and Jesus live in equirelationship, and our matrix-mind, physical appearance to others, and our language live in synergy—an image of God. And with others, we are also an image of God. We form a community that has certain properties and speak with a common language to other communities, and we as individuals are meant to live in equirelationships."

I stared at Bailey until their smile faltered.

"Are you ready to re-enter Heaven with the others?" Impatience tinged Calico's voice.

Calico recalled me to my conversation with Shireen Anne. I replied, "Not yet. What's your story, Shireen Anne," I asked them. Curiosity about my new friends and family overwhelmed me. Questions rose like geysers in my mind, questions with easier answers than who God is.

Shireen Anne laughed, joy and delight lining their face. "It's a long story. One for another time. Time. We have eternity yet none to get to know each other. I don't know everything about you, and you'll keep growing and changing like me as Earth spins on its axis and chronological time marches one millennia on after another."

I gulped at the thought. Yet excitement bubbled up in me. "Does that mean..." I hesitated. "Does that mean I can get to know you, my family, over millennia, too? You won't leave me?"

*Family*. I cherished that word and feared it lied.

Bailey rushed towards me, Blair and Blake alongside. They transformed into their human forms and hugged me. "We'll never leave you. We chose you, remember? We'll have times apart when adventures beckon, but we're always a thought, a request away even when far apart in space. Don't forget that, Charlotte Elisabeth! There's no abandonment or rejection or neglect in life anymore!"

I hugged them back.

Calico purred-growled.

I raised my head and smiled.

I blinked.

Behind Calico, a galaxy spun. A band of light enormous and shatteringly bright encircled it. Photons sped towards the encircling band. Every colour hue twinkled like stars sprayed across its surface, and primary colours—red, blue, and green—splashed vividly throughout its structure like a painter had gone wild with their brush. Ultraviolet rays shot out from the encircling band's depths, and infrared lazily waved in its outer shell. Microwaves hummed harmonies; the cosmic microwave background patterned the space around the galaxy with its prismatic band—and around us. Everywhere I spun to look confirmed my three-sixty perception wasn't deceiving me. Gamma rays pitched high like the prettiest near-zero-Kelvin violets, which prickled my form and sparked questions in my mind. Yet I was neither cold nor hot, dissatisfied nor impatient. I sensed temperature down to decimal places of degrees yet remained unaffected. Curiosity buoyed and delighted me in a way I'd never experienced, yet no impatience to slake my thirsty questions blackened it.

"What is that encircling band?" I whispered. "The pictures NASA shared of galaxies didn't show it."

Calico answered with a bored meow. "That's because no human eye or technology can see it."

I frowned at Calico. They blinked back at me. Then smiled like a Cheshire cat.

They said, "Only once you've reached life after death can you perceive what cosmologists call 'dark matter.' They only know it's there because of the gravity effect of billions of humans taking up quarters in Heaven."

"Oh."

"That's home," Calico added. "You'll learn more about it later."

*Home?* I smiled, contentment flowing through me. *Home.*

Sight and sound melded. Taste and touch and scents united. I perceived the entire colourful spectrum from violet-blue gamma rays to the blackest radio waves, seeing and hearing and sensing their frequencies.

"It's like John's vision in Revelation," Shireen Anne whispered in awe. They quoted, "I heard the number of the people who were sealed. After this I looked, and lo and behold a huge gathering which nobody could possibly count, from every nation and tribe and people and language."

I turned my head to look into Shireen Anne's brown eyes. They explained, "Our five senses are separate on Earth but God designed them to perceive different perspectives of the same, to appreciate their endless Creation in many ways all at once. Your senses can do that now, unlike in your first form." They leaned in to whisper, "Your final form—your resurrected form—I hear, will be even more skilled at perceiving the universes."

I returned my gaze to the galaxy behind Calico, with my new home surrounding it. My family let their arms fall from me as they turned to behold the amazing sight with me.

Spheres of light that absorbed my senses yet stayed separate from me left my new home's depths and zipped towards Earth.

"Angels on their God-ordered missions," Blair explained.

I swallowed against the magnificence.

"Isn't Heaven beautiful?" Blake breathed understatedly.

# Chapter Twenty-Nine

# AN ALLEY AND A SKY

*Meow!*

We startled as Calico's growl-meow burred through us. With our angel escort of light spheres, we resumed our flying journey through space-time, closing in on our life-after-death home while retaining position near the unearthly window to the rescue scene around Sincerity. As we drew closer to Heaven, a small section of its shell fluctuated.

"What is that?" I asked Bailey.

"It's the entrance to Heaven."

"Oh."

"Think of it as a doorway that lets us bypass the Earth-Heaven Interdimensional Expanse."

"Oh."

We streamed into the section of fluctuating shattering light, and my vision didn't object. Music sang harmonies that reverberated throughout Heaven's surrounding space, and my hearing didn't object. Furry softness brushed my mind's projection of skin, and my matrix-mind didn't shudder. Music tasted like caramel chocolate, and rainbow hues of violet, gold, aquamarine, and ruby smelled like summer wildflowers.

My family alighted, Nihil plunged, Shireen Anne floated down, and I somersaulted into my field of flowers, where I'd begun my Heaven's storytelling time.

Calico landed on all four paws and lifted one paw at a time, shaking each in turn. They raised their tail like a white, orange, and black flag and swaggered into the tall forest of daisies.

I stood up, lost. *What do we do now?*

"It's like entering an American supermarket cereal aisle for the first time, isn't it?" Blake chimed.

I glanced at them. My family had resumed their human shapes. I nodded. I looked down at my naked self. Embarrassed, I asked, "How do I dress myself?"

"The same way you did on our trip here. You think it," Nihil said.

I thought, *Blue skirt.* Nothing happened. I raised my questioning eyes at them.

Nihil said, "You didn't desire it, like you did your favourite suit."

My go-to suit covered my form, as I remembered it.

Nihil eyed me up and down. "I'd change your clothes, if I could," they smirked.

Shireen Anne contemplated my outfit. "It's strange. Your ideal world is a field of rainbow hued flowers. Every colour we can and cannot imagine. A variety beyond joy. Yet you wear beige and office blue. Why?"

"It's not beige!" I contested. "I felt good when I wore my go-to suit."

"I wonder why?" Shireen Anne returned their gaze to my face.

I squirmed like a bug under a microscope. "You don't have to like my favourite outfit, but you don't need to criticize me!"

"I'm not," Shireen Anne replied. "I'm curious, is all. Motivation, desire, needs, wants." They waved a hand. "I'm curious about all of it. I want to know more! More, more, more!" they grinned.

"Stop it," I huffed. I didn't want to admit it, but standing surrounded by reds and golds and blues in every nuance, I questioned why I chose a colour that blended me into the background. "Like sandy soil camouflage," I murmured to myself.

"Soil nurtures growth. Without soil, no flower can grow," Bailey said.

I smiled at them, grateful. But Shireen Anne had started me questioning my choice. I hesitated. "How do I change my clothes?"

"It's simple," Nihil said.

I waited.

Blake rolled their eyes. "If you're going to tell her, Nihil, tell her!"

"I already did."

I snorted. I closed my eyes against the sight of flowers and annoying friend and focused on clothing. My mind blanked. I mentally reviewed my closet. Out of nowhere, every dress, every skirt, every jacket screamed boring. I opened my eyes. "I don't know what to wear."

Shireen Anne chortled. "That's how I felt, too!"

The rest smiled, even Nihil.

"What's so funny?" Frederick's soft voice whirled me around. Their eyes leaked. Their head drooped. "What happened?"

"I cannot find my father." They didn't take my hand. My hand felt bereft.

*Should I take theirs?*

Shireen Anne nudged me.

I looked at them; they jerked their head towards Frederick. I stretched out my hand and hesitated. Shireen Anne hipped me. My hand jerked against Frederick's, and somehow I was holding it. They smiled half-heartedly down at me; their chestnut brown forelock flopped over their left eye. Frederick didn't push it back in place.

"Can we walk?" they asked.

I looked over at the others. They all nodded, and I said, "Yes."

We sauntered into the daisies dancing their petal-skirt heads. Pushing through their stems, we entered a forest of tall poppies; roses scented the air. "Is Heaven filled with flowers?" I asked.

"Your version is," Nihil called out from behind us. "It's boring."

"What's your version," I asked Frederick as unfamiliar calm flowed into me. *Where is this calm coming from? Me? Frederick?* But sadness drooped Frederick's face. I startled to a stop. Frederick walked a couple more steps until my arm, stretched to its full extension, yanked them to a stop. Frederick looked back at me as the others tip-toed to within two rows of poppies.

"What is it?" Frederick asked me.

I lifted wondrous eyes to their face and exclaimed, "I'm free of anxiety. I don't feel nervous or anxious or depressed or wanting to..." I swallowed. "Wanting to end my life. I feel light, like the burden of a thousand years vanished somewhere on our way from Earth."

"You're close," Bailey said, pushing their way through the poppy stems.

"Close to what?"

Frederick tugged my hand, and I trotted to catch up. Bailey and the others openly followed.

"Close to what?" I demanded.

"The Resurrection," Blake chimed, skipping up to me, squeezing between me and Bailey, and grabbing my free hand. They swung it, like we were two children skipping home. "The Resurrection. We're—"

"Not yet!" Bailey remonstrated.

Blake pouted. "I think, yet!" They grinned at me. My returning smile wobbled. "What's the Resurrection?" I asked.

"It's our final form. God's love through their creation made complete. It's the marriage between physical and energy. It's where your matrix-mind asserts its dominance, and we collectively live as one diversely within God's love, word, and spirit."

"My mind? Physical and energy? One diversely?" I sucked my lips in between my teeth. "But what about Duke who said they were resurrected. Does that mean you are? And why you and not us?"

Blake swung my arm way up high and back again. "Yup. It's how we can do things you can't." They grinned mischievously at me, let go of my hand, and said, "Let's see Nihil's Heaven!"

I saw my questions would remain unanswered, yet impatience didn't eat at me. I, too, wanted to see Nihil's storytelling time and space.

The flowers vanished. Concrete buildings hemmed us in on either side. A can clinked and clattered under a wind's direction. Ahead lay an endless alley enclosed by Toronto's original brick warehouses. Graffiti splashed squiggles of black and vibrant murals of reds and blues, the only colours under the drab sky and faded, pollution-dirtied brick. I halted and stared. "This is Heaven?" I whispered. "I thought Heaven was all light and fun and beautiful."

"No," Bailey said. "It's the emanation of our heart and memories. Of what our minds dwell on in their secret spaces. God harbours murdered people here. God comforts them with their unconditional, soul-soaking love. But God cannot change their mind's will to show beauty. That only comes after they've been able to heal and complete their Soul Tracks."

"Which includes reconciling with their murderers," I said slowly as understanding filtered in. I let go of Frederick's hand and walked into Nihil's endless alley. My pump-shod foot toed a discarded, crushed pop can. It rattled forwards over the cracked concrete. Asphalt ribbons criss-crossed the concrete as if the black tar-mimicking substance could heal the cracks. "Oh, Nihil," I gasped.

"What?" They crossed their arms and planted their feet to glower at me.

"Is this...this..."

"Where it happened? Yeah, so what?"

I stared down the alleyway. Like my field of flowers, the alley had no end. Graffiti blazed territorial and slogan messages; it dared passing eyes with murals. The lowering sky: the only sign of Nature.

I turned to Nihil. "Weren't you rich? Didn't you have flowers in your home? Or a garden you could hang out in?"

They shrugged. "That was for my mother's garden parties. We were only allowed to stay on the paths."

"Oh."

"This place," they extracted one arm to gesture, then recrossed their arms tightly, "was where we hung out in. This place was our home."

"Oh." I absorbed the alienation. "Yet you were murdered here."

"Yeah, so what?" Nihil's eyelids dropped halfway over stony eyes.

I squinted at Nihil. No, not cold, aggressive hostility, but pain. Excruciating pain, and something else. I surveyed the pollution-stained brick walls and tried to sort out the answer in the graffiti. The others stood silently around us, like a shield to our intimate conversation. I'd never talked with a friend like this before. *I didn't have friends before.* Yet it felt natural and safe and...

*Hope.*

That's what I'd seen hidden in their eyes. I looked at Nihil again. "Is this the first time you've felt hope?"

Nihil shrugged.

I stared down the alley, wondering why now. *What changed for them?*

A voice murmured into my mind. *You did.*

*Me?*

*Yes. Look. Look at the cracks. What do you see?*

I searched the asphalt beneath our feet. Cracks everywhere. So many! Like a shattered person. Pink caught my eye. I stepped forwards.

"Don't bother," Nihil said behind me.

I ignored them. I took another step. Yes, pink. I swivelled on my toes and reached for one of Nihil's hands, protected in their armpits. Through the armour of arms, I grasped their hand. I tugged, and Nihil's left arm dropped to their side as their right stretched towards me, their right hand enclosed in my firm grasp. "Come on." I dragged them towards the pink. I didn't give in to their resistance. I didn't acquiesce to their avoidance desire. I didn't know where I'd gotten this new initiative. Or this desire to help them. I kept out of people's business. I didn't get involved. Yet here I was, involved. Desperately, determinedly involved.

The pink coalesced into a shape. The shape morphed into a recognizable daisy. Its feeble stem struggled out of a crack. Its fragile leaves fluttered in the breeze. Its petal-encircled head lifted halfway to the weak sun filtering diffused rays through the dense clouds. The clouds' gunmetal grey mimicking Nihil's eyes.

I pointed down. "Look, Nihil. Hope!"

Nihil stared down at the daisy, their hand gripping mine. Their eyes glistened. They blinked the tears away. A small smile flashed and then disappeared.

I squeezed Nihil's hand.

"Therapeutic doses," Bailey said from where they'd remained standing.

"What do you mean?" I asked them over my shoulder.

"Nihil has had enough. Give them time to process this new growth. Let's see Shireen Anne's heaven."

"Oh no," Shireen Anne exclaimed. "I want to see Frederick's. I think Frederick needs us, don't you?"

Frederick fixated on the cracked concrete beneath our feet.

Bailey contemplated Frederick. "You're right."

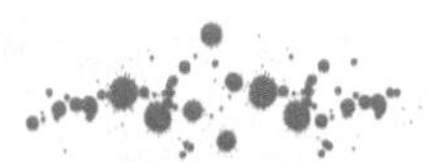

NIGHT FELL AROUND us. Blackness so absolute, it sucked our energy's light emanations. All of us had auras that bled into the night that surrounded us from under our feet to the sky above. Stars populated the dome that arched overhead. I searched for a moon. Low on the horizon, it hung, its light a dim opalescence.

"Where are we?" I asked Frederick, walking towards them, still holding Nihil's hand.

I clasped Frederick's hand but didn't let go of Nihil's. Nihil dragged their hand out of mine and went to huddle by my family and Shireen Anne.

Frederick didn't answer. I raised my eyebrows at Bailey for an answer.

"We're not in Frederick's heaven per se," they said. "We're in their state of mind. Their feeling of lost."

"Lost?"

"I didn't find my father," Frederick said.

"Oh, Frederick, I'm sorry." I heard the shared sorrow in my voice and wondered again at such intense emotion. My emotions had left their locked box and were growing like adolescents accelerating towards full adulthood. As I absorbed this remarkable change, I asked. "What happened?"

"I went to the bar that we were told about."

I nodded.

"My father wasn't there."

I frowned. "Isn't your father dead?"

"Yes, but he's not in Heaven. He'll be stuck in his own personal hell. But he's not in Hell Track. He must've become a ghost. Ghosts lurk where they're stuck. Or they gather together and go to each other's stuck places, haunting the living and the newly dead on their Soul Tracks." Frederick glanced down at me. "Like what happened to you."

I shuddered.

Frederick squeezed my hand reassuringly.

"You're safe. I'm safe. But my father isn't. How do I complete my Soul Track without reconciling with him?"

I noticed Frederick still used gendered pronouns while I no longer could. It was like an audible border one crosses when completing the Soul Track. I corrected myself. When completing the Solar Age phase, whatever that was.

We stood around silently, none of us knowing what to say.

I sensed a presence. *Frederick's father?*

Thoughts of pleasure, of joy burst out of everyone else.

A man yet not a man entered my vision. "Hello Charlotte Elisabeth," they said, their mellifluous voice brushing my being like a gentle hand comforting me. I stilled.

The man smiled. "My name is Jesus."

I stared. *Who is Jesus?*

I heard two voices, Grand's and Marcia's speaking at the same time in my memory: *Lord and Saviour.* I puckered my brow. *What does that mean?*

"I came to Earth two thousand years ago to show humanity God in their form. I taught and healed. My story is one that God's children study their whole lives. Know only that I am the word of God. Through me, you'll know God, and through me, God communicates with you. But God also loves you, and you can sense it at any time when you hold the desire in your mind to communicate with God."

My mouth formed a soundless "O."

Jesus smiled and touched my shoulder.

Jesus said, "Welcome Charlotte Elisabeth, I've been waiting for you."

I sank to my knees.

My hand fell out of Frederick's.

I laid my head on the ground.

Flowers sprouted up around me and underneath my forehead like colour cushioning my hurting head and soaking in my sudden tears splashing like Niagara Falls.

Jesus sank to my level and sat before me cross-legged. Jesus laid their hand on the back of my head as I wept. Golden energy flowed into me. Somehow, I saw Jesus, even though my hands covered my drowning eyes. Jesus stroked my hair. A trail of comforting ASMR followed their hand as their fingers drew light lines down my head over and over and over again. Their hand stopped, and their palm cradled my cheek. My tears stopped. Happiness and excitement burst out of my heart, and I raised my eyes, my mind overflowing with joy.

Jesus smiled into my vision, and the feeling of it collapsed my legs sideways, my hands stopping me from prostrating myself. I wanted to never stop looking into Jesus's eyes, never stop being in Jesus's presence.

And then I felt only myself within myself. It's like Jesus withdrew their energy back into themself.

Jesus turned to Frederick. "I came also to tell you I've noticed your diligence. You haven't given up in your search. I know where your father is, but you must find them on your own."

"How?" Frederick whispered, reaching a hand out to clutch at Jesus's arm. Jesus didn't recoil. Instead, they enfolded Frederick in a hug, and Frederick wept on Jesus's shoulder.

I blinked; I looked at my family. They and Nihil and Shireen Anne were all smiling at the tableau. *What's going on? Is this like one of those saccharine movies Mom scoffed at? Artificial and cheesy?*

"Nah," Blake replied. "It's not supersweet pap. It's the real deal."

"Look," Blair said, pointing.

I followed their finger.

*Love.*

Somehow, love appeared as energy, as magnetic, as photons and waves. Love flowed into Frederick from and through Jesus. Stars filled the surrounding night, and the moon brightened and rose from the horizon.

Jesus eased the hug and held Frederick a little way from them so that they could look into Frederick's eyes. "Sometimes you can't complete your Solar Age phase of your Soul Track and must wait for the cataclysm to try again before your own Resurrection. Or even after."

*Cataclysm?*

Frederick asked, "What do you mean?"

"There are other places the dead go, places you can't reach in your current electromagnetic form. They're too dangerous for you. You need to have achieved the rest of your Soul Track and, ideally Resurrected, to search those places, to be armoured and shielded as you enter the brief last-moment-of-faith-hope-love near the Lake of Fire before they're thrown into it."

Frederick mouthed, "Lake of Fire?" Frowning, they asked, "You mean second death? Are you saying, my father is dead forever?"

Jesus smiled a sad smile.

The night vanished. We hung suspended in water. Sunlight filtered its warming rays through the surface and deep into the midnight blue depths beneath us. Hues of aquamarine and turquoise coruscated above our heads as currents of purple-blues and brightening blues mingled and flowed around us. I breathed and didn't fear.

"It's time," Jesus said.

# Chapter Thirty
# POST-EARTH LIFE

"I thought time doesn't exist here," I said boldly to Jesus after they'd brought us into the water.

Jesus nodded. "You're right, it doesn't. You exist in your storytelling time, and we—God, me, and the Holy Spirit—outside it, as the creators of the universes and space-time. But you understood."

I admitted I had. I turned to Frederick. Their eyes, like dark roasted coffee, subsumed me. Their slight smile sparked an answering smile from me.

I spiralled lazily like a porpoise. We gathered together, floating in a circle around Jesus. Frederick's sadness weighed their features down. Bliss illuminated my family's. Curiosity and enthusiasm hummed Shireen Anne's face. Wariness and desire vied with each other on Nihil's.

Jesus, a man yet not a man, tall yet not tall, unperturbed by our varying responses, interrogated my eyes on a level plain. I could lay my head on their broad shoulders, and comfort would flow into me forever and ever.

I slapped my cheeks. Opened my mouth. Shut it. I thought, *Jesus? Yes?*

I rocked in the water, its buoyancy holding me in place, and somehow, without asking, Jesus knew my question.

"I was a man on Earth," Jesus said. "As it is written in John's gospel, 'In the beginning was the word, and the word was with God, and the word was God.'"

I let Jesus's words sink in. I revolved them in my matrix-mind. *Oh!* Here before me stood the word in human form yet in energy form, yet neither, yet both. Jesus appeared to me as I needed Jesus to manifest. I needed to see a man—and so that's what I saw. *Can I see Jesus as a word?* I contemplated that concept. Suddenly, I understood. Love begat Jesus as the word to communicate with the world of human beings. Begat, yet Jesus had already existed simultaneously with God.

*Wait. What? How did I think those thoughts? How did I know?*

I remembered Bailey, Blair, and Blake saying when we first met that they were with me, had waited for me, would always be with me. And here, in this perplexing moment, they swam over to support me. Again and again, they'd supported me. I squeezed my eyes against my blurring vision.

"You've matured, Charlotte Elisabeth. You've completed the Solar Age phase of your Soul Track and Frederick has theirs as far as they can. I'm proud of you both."

I bit my lips against a flood of tears. I wanted to cry and wail and bend. But I didn't. Our watery environs consoled and cushioned me against this bittersweetness.

Jesus turned towards Bailey. "You can tell Charlotte Elisabeth now."

I opened my watery eyes to look at Bailey. "Tell me what?"

Bailey said, "We're not only spirit beings. We're resurrected."

The inner edges of my eyebrows wrinkled up. "Resurrected?"

Nihil said, "Bailey means God graced them with their final form."

"Final form?"

Blair sighed. "Did you forget what you learned already?"

I shook my head and opened my mouth, but Blair interrupted. "Jesus rose from the dead. The Apostles, that is, the messengers sent by the Holy Spirit to tell the world about Jesus, taught that Jesus underwent the first Resurrection. The revelation to John—not the writer of the gospel, but another John—"

My thoughts swam as I tried to follow.

"—showed there'll be one thousand years of Satan locked up—"

"One thousand?"

"Not a literal millennium. Then Satan will be released to attempt anarchy; but the good will be separated from those who cannot let go of Satan's ways and of evil thoughts, words, and deeds; and after they, along with Satan, are thrown into the Lake of Fire, the good people will be raised. We'll all experience the communal Resurrection. But a few will experience it beforehand."

"Like you and Duke?"

"Yes," Blair replied. "But also some who'll be given a specific purpose during those thousand years."

I twisted myself in the general direction of Earth—though I didn't know how I knew its location—and pointed, "There's no difference there now as when I died then."

Bailey affirmed, "You're right. There isn't. But the church wasn't entirely correct."

"What do you mean?"

Blake said, "Matthew twenty-seven, verses fifty-two and fifty-three give a hint. Revelation twenty-one, too."

I frowned.

"Hey!" Shireen Anne said, bumping me with a grin. "Heaven has a library. Books and books, so many books! It's one of my favourite places. I'll show you! There'll be a book there that'll explain things."

I sank my upper teeth into my lower lip. *How do I tell Shireen Anne, with endless questions and conspicuous affinity for books, that I read accounting books and tax books but not much else?* "Why read," I replied, "when we can ask?"

Shireen Anne agreed, saying, "You're right! I love books. Bury myself in a book, lying under the covers, with a light on the words, is my heaven." Shireen Anne's chest heaved, and a grin drew mischievous lines across their face. "I kind of got banned for a little while from the story side of the library."

"Story side?"

Shireen Anne nodded. "I ask too many questions, and they got tired."

"Tired?"

"I mean, if you're a mind-matrix in energy form, how do you get tired, right?"

"Uh..." I wrinkled my brow.

Shireen Anne exhaled and exhaled. "Okay, okay, I didn't give them a chance to breathe." They lifted their head, eyes sparkling. "I was just so excited to hear all the stories."

"What stories?"

"Not what. Whose!"

My lips parted, but words died before forming.

Shireen Anne laughed. "You'll love this part of the library because you won't have to read. You can search in the library's system for the topic you're interested in, call it up, and you'll be able to select from the stories you like."

I became exasperated. "Whose stories?"

"Why, everyone's. Every human, dog, cat, rabbit, lion, elephant, dolphin, whale, you name it!" Shireen Anne threw their arms out wide. "Even ancient trees and the robins who nest in them! To gain a full understanding, God shares books through humans and stories through all their created beings! All sorts of books and stories with different perspectives—you gotta read them all!"

I quailed. My eyes bugged out. I gestured feebly towards my family and Jesus. "Yes, but..."

"There's need to know—like characters in some sort of American TV military cop show—and there's soaking in all the knowledge we can because time here is immaterial."

Resentment pushed upwards. I pushed it back. *Patience*, I reproached myself. My mind lifted, feeling better for the reminder. "I don't want to fully understand. I just want to know as much as I need to."

Shireen Anne raised their forefinger to tap against their lips. "You're like the person who needs to know as little as possible to get by."

"You know that about me."

"Yes, but I thought as you matured during this last phase of your Solar Age Soul Track that you'd realize time is meaningless and understanding is an infinite journey of exploration and fun discovery. Curiosity can never be satiated, yet it excites the drive to discover."

"That's your thing."

"Uh-huh." Grinning, they arched an eyebrow. "And it's yours, too."

I dropped my gaze. I had to admit curiosity had blossomed in me.

"So?"

"What?"

"Are you going to the library?"

"No."

"Why not?"

Blake giggled and fell against me, snickering, "You really hate Shireen Anne's hypercuriosity, don't you?"

"No, I don't," I denied. "Shireen Anne just needs to keep it from bothering others." I pushed against those words. "What I mean is, I want to hear what Bailey and Jesus meant."

"I do, too," Shireen Anne said.

"I thought you wanted to read about it?"

"Just because I want to read about it doesn't mean I don't want to hear about it first or after or both!"

I fluttered my lips into the water; a bubble formed. I followed the expanding bubble's trajectory, and Bailey appeared in my perception. They seemed to have grown taller than me; their energy form had changed to...material?

Bailey nodded. "I," they said, pointing at Blair and Blake, "I mean, we three are Resurrected. We didn't show you how we can take on material form earlier because you weren't ready. Only Blake showed a hint of it to help you reconcile with your father. And, of course, Duke revealed it."

Shireen Anne said, "Fascinating."

Frederick drew closer to me.

Nihil took a step back.

Jesus said, "Perfection is a process but not the goal. Seek first us—the foundational relationship—then you can live in harmony with God, me, other beings, and yourself. Relationships are the rock on which you live. You've matured into thinking, speaking, and acting in this way. Even now, when you find Shireen Anne grates against what you like, you quickly analyze and repair your thoughts towards the good. Love is what drives you now. Love doesn't mean liking everything about everyone and every living creature. Love instead drives you in the way you reacted to Shireen Anne. That's what God, our Holy Spirit, and I want to see when we decide who to Resurrect. You're not quite ready yet."

That felt right.

"Your next phase of your Soul Track will happen during the thousand years. Indeterminate time follows from here."

"So I can take a break?"

Jesus nodded.

"But wait a minute," I frowned. "If the next Soul Track phase is during Satan's thousand years lockup..."

"How are some raised today?"

I nodded.

Jesus smiled and spoke. "A farmer sowed seeds on their field. The soil had hardened on a quarter of the field. Rocks strewed across another quarter. A third quarter had been paved into a path. And rich loam filled the last quarter. As the seeds withered in the first quarter, struggled and died in the second, and were eaten before they could sprout in the third quarter, they thrived in the last quarter. But over time, the farmer tilled compost into the first quarter, rocks broke down in the second, dandelions thrust themselves up through cracks in the path, creating soil for the seeds to grow. Eventually, the farmer sowed and harvested across the entire field. But some seeds remained inert as if the soil had convinced them that they couldn't grow. Choosing death, they will be thrown into the fire. So it is and will be with God's children."

"Uh, what?"

"You will listen but not understand. Yet. You will see but not perceive. Yet."

I swallowed against Jesus's gentle rebuke.

Jesus said, "God will resurrect Shireen Anne."

"Really?" Shireen Anne exclaimed, bobbing in the sapphire water.

Jesus nodded, smiling.

Fear flared into Shireen Anne's excitement. "I don't know if I'm ready."

"God created humans for change, yet you all fear it. Fear not!"

Shireen Anne bowed their head.

I stepped back. Into Frederick. Their energy bounced me back towards Jesus. I slowed to a halt. I turned my head to look up and back at Frederick, feeling their strength buttressing me. My fear collapsed. It vanished, leaving only nervousness.

*What's next?*

I'd survived the Distortans, escaped the Red Robes' seduction in Hell Track, argued with Grand, reconciled with my birth family, said goodbye to them, fled ghosts, and fended off their strange leader who wanted to pull me away from my Soul Track. Jesus had said I could rest from following my Soul Track but not forever. I thought, *This adventure and my growing isn't over. I'm exhausted*, I whined to myself. *I want to lie down beside Greeter in Flower Track's field of flowers and never move again.*

Jesus smiled, put their hand on my shoulder, and squeezed it. With mouth closed, I stretched my lips upwards. Jesus let go.

"Frederick also will not be Resurrected. They cannot complete their father's search in this energy-mind form. When you are ready to accept that your father is speeding towards second death, Frederick, God will Resurrect you. Don't hasten before you're ready."

I blurted, "That's sad about their second death."

"It is," Jesus said. "We want to save all our children. We want them all to choose us willingly. But we can't force people to think the way we want them to."

"Why not?" I asked.

"Free will means something." Jesus's voice deepened and thrummed. "Why do you humans not understand free will means just that? You're free to choose badly, to follow death-leading paths, to harm others, to harm yourself. God, I, and the Holy Spirit try to communicate, to get you to listen. But you refuse."

I swallowed. Yet somehow I didn't swallow any of the water Jesus had suspended us in.

"It's like the wisdom of psychologists. They know they can only guide and lead their clients to health, but the client must choose it. Humans fear change. I tell you to fear not; yet you fear. You insist on fearing. But change—"

"Change is nothing but endless hard work," Nihil muttered.

"Yes, hard work," Jesus reproved. "But have I not said my yoke is light? Change is easy when you lean on me; my yoke excites you and lessens the burden of your pain." Jesus reached a hand out to Frederick, the water undisturbed. "Are you ready now to accept, Frederick?"

"I can't give up on my father," Frederick said. "Whatever the cost, I must continue."

Jesus smiled tenderly, sadly.

My heart broke; yearning engulfed my heart, a yearning to partner with Frederick in their search. I'd never felt this way towards anyone before. Its unexpectedness arrested me. I wanted to...

I chewed my lips. Frederick's eyes, so dark, sad, and determined, hooked me. *I must accompany Frederick! I cannot spend this indeterminate time before Satan lockup without seeing Frederick!*

I waved my hands as if treading water to swing towards Frederick, who grinned lopsidedly at me. *Does Frederick feel the same as me?* I held my breath. Frederick stretched their arm out, turned their hand palm up to invite me. With a frog kick, I reached Frederick's side, and our hands clasped. I looked down at our hands. Their twining so natural. I marvelled at the softness of their energy skin against mine, at the security of their long, strong fingers wrapping around my palm. *How do I feel material sensations when we're electromagnetic extensions of our matrix-minds?* I laughed at this incomprehensible mystery.

I smiled and smiled. *I'm not alone!*

Blake nudged me. *You're not alone.*

I flung back my head and laughed. Happiness jumped and danced within me.

Bailey said, "God, Jesus, and the Holy Spirit are with us always. They live in an equirelationship. They collaborate. The way they work is how we work."

I looked a question.

"Since we're made in their image, we're meant to work and live in equirelationship like they do. Collaboration is in our DNA, as they say."

I stared at her. *Equirelationship? That's a word? Bailey didn't mispronounce it that time? Equal relationship with whom?* I shook my head. That wasn't how I worked best. Mom dominated our relationships. I'd begun my accounting practice to get away from perplexing office relationships. Countless adults as I grew up had taught that one must have a leader to succeed. Perhaps they meant—

"Hey!" Blake exclaimed. "You're not alone, remember?"

"What about Nihil?" I asked.

"We're your friends. You can't get rid of us," Nihil stated.

*Friends?* I sucked on that word like a delicious candy. *Yes, Nihil, Shireen Anne, and Scruffy, wherever that mutt had gotten to, are my friends.* No qualm assailed me about that truth. Trust filled me. Betrayal and abandonment had left. No more would I hide my emotions or thoughts—although I had to learn how to keep some thoughts private! I knew Bailey would teach me. Then I could return to my accounting. Resume my work. Live smarter in those thousand forthcoming years.

Jesus interrupted my happy thoughts to say, "Wake up, Charlotte Elisabeth. When anyone experiences the kingdom and does not understand, the evil one comes and snatches away what was sown in their heart."

I opened my mouth, but no words came.

"Do you think you can return to your old life?"

"I was a diligent accountant. I served my clients well, and they were loyal to me."

"You still don't understand what is to come."

I frowned. "I understand I'm alive, not just existing. What else is there to know? Why isn't it okay to pursue what I'm skilled in, what I love doing?"

Sorrow filled Jesus's eyes. "It's time."

*Why is Jesus looking at me sadly? Time for what? My second death?* I shuddered, and chills raced through me.

Golden energy suddenly blasted my vision apart. Love so intense erupted joyous tears out of every particle of my energy being, electrifying the lines of my mind. This light, this love that surrounded and entered all of us, dug into me like an anthropologist excavating Neanderthal skeletons, ancient peoples, recent cultures. It revealed my self to myself. My particles, my matrix-mind thrummed, like a song of welcoming home, of praising their writer, of drawing in more and more of this unconditional love that didn't hurt anymore.

I vanished into it and became one with it.

My material birth so long ago winked into my memory.

Then, it was painful and jolting. I had hated leaving the warm nest. Now, this birthing stroked, entered, and encompassed me as the Holy Spirit became one with yet separate from my matrix-mind, like the entire universe had come into me and I had expanded into it. My self became exposed. Excitement filled me. Nervousness shook me as I watched Shireen Anne's transformation. That golden energy that surrounded and spoke love into us, rippled their form, consolidating it into material and changing their appearance as if forever thirty years old.

The life-changing energy faded upwards. We remained in the warm, blue water, Frederick, Nihil, and I appearing the same, but Shireen Anne utterly changed. I couldn't explain how.

Nihil breathed, "I understand now why Mary didn't recognize Jesus at first after God resurrected the man divine into Jesus's new form."

Curiosity crawled up my back and knocked on my mind. *What is Nihil talking about?* Perhaps visiting that library was in order, after all. Time to learn the stories. They'll answer my question: *What's my new post-Earth life going to be like?*

Frederick bent down and whispered into my left ear, "Let's discover."

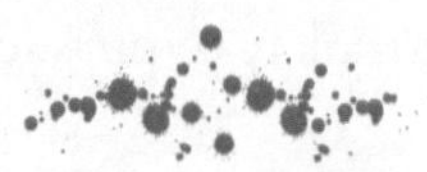

*THANK YOU* FOR reading this book!

If you enjoyed this tale, please encourage your friends, family, associates, neighbours, heck, anyone, to buy a copy or request a copy at their library so that they can enjoy it, too!

And if you have a moment, please review *The Soul's Reckoning* at the store where you bought it or the library you borrowed it from. **Help other speculative fiction readers choose *The Q'Zam'Ta Trilogy* by telling them why you enjoyed this visionary adventure into the afterlife.** I look forward to reading your review, and thank you so much for your support! I hope we meet again in the pages of another book.

**Find more information** at https://jeejeebhoy.ca

or **subscribe** at https://books2read.com/author/shireen-anne-jeejeebhoy/subscribe/66298/

**Please turn the page to read excerpts from four of my novels.**

# THE SOUL'S AWAKENING

chapter one

## DEATH

At the moment of my death, my life began.

I was upset. Angry. Horrified.

And confused.

Looking back to that moment in the Solar Age, I found the voices the most unsettling, certain my dying brain had created them and not daring to ask who they were.

I ran an accounting firm, my own one-woman office. I interacted with clients only when needed, saw my one-year-older sister as little as possible, attended my cardiologist appointments when required, and knew no one else. I didn't need anyone else. My existence had ended because I'd met a doctor who understood me. *Why then, voices?*

"Why is she surprised?"

Chimes, like tiny silver bells, slivered the air.

"You know why, Blair."

"I know, I know, Bailey. I'm frustrated with her decision."

"We're not here to decide for her."

"I know, I know."

I regained consciousness on the ceiling, hearing these two voices intermingled with chimes, as I spied below me my physical self lying in the bed under the blanket and sheet, the blanket's mounds outlining my legs lying straight together, my hands clasped over each other on my stomach while my head stuck out, denting the pillow, eyes closed, reminding me of a guillotined head. The face, my face, reflected peace. So still. I'd never seen such an unmoving face before. I squinted. *That's what death looks like.*

I smiled.

My last memory was peace.

The peace of drifting away into the perfect sleep.

Dr. Veritas had promised me that the sleep he prescribed his patients brought them only peace. It ended change's upheaval. It stopped having to explore a different way of living.

I'd liked my life the way I'd arranged it. I wanted it to continue in the familiar, predictable pattern of breakfast, work, news, dinner, and TV dramas. Toast, jam, orange juice, and breakfast tea to start my morning; followed by three hours of concentrated working on my clients' accounts; a lunch of tomato soup, omelette, and Red Rose tea to refuel; finishing my work day with four hours of client calls, emails, and resolving problems that had festered; suppertime news while I heated dinner—each night of the week had its standard fare—and, with dishes washed, three hours of television dramas and bedtime at 11 PM.

My diagnosis and the cardiologist's prescription had upended my meal routines and threw my work hours into chaos with the requirement to exercise. I didn't want to explore new recipes or a different way of living. Dr. V's prescription had filled me with relief, and his promise was true. He'd promised me I'd feel no more pain.

I didn't feel pain.

I frowned.

*Why was I up here, pressed against the ceiling?*

I thought about it. No answer presented itself as I played his last promise to me: "I will end your suffering. I will give you an end," he'd said.

*But I was not at an end! I was here! On the ceiling looking down upon him and his nurse pulling a sheet over my head.* Something interrupted her movement. Her eyes fastened on my peaceful face. Her brows drew down. She jerked her hands away. The sheet floated down, half covering my chin as she stared down at my face, eyes closed. The form of my body under the blanket lay there like an ugly sack of nothing.

Blonde hair—that dyed blonde hair Mom insisted I had to have, and I'd adopted. Dyeing it controlled my hair, except my bangs that waved over the faint lines on my forehead. My eldest sister Sally had mocked those faint lines. She'd pushed me to go for collagen injections or Botox. I'd covered them with bangs instead.

My skin waxed under the lamp's glow on the nightstand; across the bed, the nurse stood, scowling down at me. She'd been efficient, guiding me gently from the moment she'd met me at the Dying with Dignity Suite's reception desk. I'd recognized long experience in her practiced movements and soothing words. The receptionist had reassured me when she'd shared the nurse and doctor had started the Suite together as soon as the law had permitted it.

The nurse's small smile had comforted me, so why was she scowling now?

All of us in the Suite had wanted me dead, including her. Did she see I wasn't?

The nurse snapped herself upright and wheeled around to face Dr. V.

*Why am I here?* I yelled in my thoughts towards them. I reached up to feel my head. Energy surged in a magnetic force between my hands and my head. My hand flew back; I tried to breathe. But I felt...I didn't know what I'd touched. Atoms? Photons? My high school physics didn't explain this...this...peculiar sensation.

Lights appeared beside me; one of them chimed like the silver bells I'd heard earlier. I jumped away from them and gaped, frozen.

Three orbs hovered near me, blue energy encircling them like flowing jet streams around a transparent earth. Pink highlighted the flowing streamers on one orb, yellow the ones on the second orb in the middle, and silver that tinkled like bells on the third. The first one spoke, and my thoughts whirled inside my frozen form. *What's happening? I'm supposed to be dead! This is supposed to be the end! Dr. V didn't complete the job. He didn't put me at rest as he'd promised me!*

"It's okay," hushed into my brain. Except not a brain. Yet here I am conscious, on the ceiling, gazing at my blood-drained skin and dyed blonde hair and brown eyes hidden by closed lids. *That must be it. Dr. V thinks I'm dead because my eyes are closed.*

"Get a grip. We're here for you," said the orb with the yellow highlights.

"Hush!" commanded the pink-highlighted orb. "She's new. She doesn't understand we're here for her. We chose her."

*No one chose me!* I clamped down on the rising tide of panic. Dr. V had promised no more pain, and here panic came. My least favourite form of pain when my heart would thud against my ribs, my lungs solidified against inhaling, and every muscle tightened me into immobility.

"Dr. V, I'm not dead!" I yelled down at him as I shifted away from the three orbs beside me. Somehow, they remained locked in proximity to me. My heart raced, except I had no heart, I realized as I raised my hand to comfort it in long practice. Instead, energy magnetically responded out from where my heart should be towards my hand. I gulped. But I couldn't gulp. No throat contracted to meet my swallowing action. I whisper-shouted, "Dr. Veritas! Help me!"

"What we do here is important," he was snapping at the nurse.

I raised my voice to a louder whisper-shout. "Dr. Veritas, help!" They both ignored me.

"Oh, get off your high horse," she responded. "What we do here is save the health system a buck."

He drew himself up and stared down his beaked nose at her. "We started this Suite together because we both believed in this treatment. I," he pronounced, "am saving my patients from their pain."

"Are you? Why do you lie? You know as well as I do that the government gave us licence to kill so they could save a buck. Those progressive pantsy types are being taken in by blind greed."

"How dare you! What's wrong with you? Our patients are in real pain. There's no solution, no better health care than releasing them from their pain. I end their pain."

"End?! Is that what you call death?!" the nurse roared with laughter. "You've gotta be kidding me. You no more care about your patients than this...," she gestured to the machine that had delivered sweet medicine to my pain, the three tubes of drugs with their plungers standing at attention.

One drug to relax me, and it had. As I'd watched him push plunger one down, his eyes upon my own, relief had flooded my muscles. The second drug to put me to sleep. I smiled into his eyes as he'd pushed that plunger down. The last one to end my pain. I hadn't seen him push plunger three down. *That's why I awoke on the ceiling!* But I wasn't supposed to. Somehow, I must tell him.

The yellow-highlighted orb remarked into my ear, "You're dead."

"Hush Blair, she isn't ready."

"Okay," she replied. "You take the lead."

The pink-highlighted orb seemed to nod. I ignored them as I worried about how to tell Dr. V he hadn't ended my pain, how my life had survived because I'm still here! I tried to lower myself to his level, but I couldn't move. *Why am I on the ceiling, anyway?* I concentrated on that question. It made no sense to simultaneously exist on the ceiling and my body lie on the bed. I was supposed to be dead. *How could I still be existing unless Dr. V had failed to put me into my permanent rest?*

"After I administer the last medication, there is no more pain," Dr. V had assured me. "Because there's no more consciousness. Your consciousness is in your brain."

I'd nodded. I'd done some homework on the brain to verify his words. Stuff that made no sense, stuff about spirit and spirituality—what Mom had called nonsense. "You don't need to fill your head with nonsense," she'd glared at me. I'd agreed with her and, remembering that agreement during my search, had skipped past those results. Nonsense didn't deserve my time.

"Look. You and I are supposed to be partners in our patients' final moments. We need to provide a unified front to them. Can you still do that?" Dr. V grilled his nurse.

"Sure I can. Didn't I do that for this woman there? I've had enough, but I'll keep going. This woman didn't know she's the second one today, and you have ten more lined up. You really do know how to kill them faster than a hornet stings a human."

Dr. V growled. I wanted to retreat, but the ceiling wouldn't let me. "Listen up. I'm not a hornet! I do this to save my patients' dignity—"

"Dignity," the nurse scoffed. "What's so dignified about being executed? You think because she's not a criminal, that you killing her is dignified? Only if she was a criminal, then her execution wouldn't be dignified? Do you hear yourself, Doctor? I'm in this because I've crossed the killing line. I'm honest enough to know that when I see a patient coming in once again with the same old, same old chronic illness requiring vats of empathy I don't have, my first thought is: 'They're better off dead.' I'm honest enough to know what I really mean is I'm better off if they're dead. I don't have to deal with their complaints, their pain, their mental pain.

"We're controlling their physical pain, but there's nothing we can do about a society that leaves them to fend for themselves with too little money. Uh-uh, Doc-tor Ver-i-tas, we're not saving them pain and giving them dignity. We're making it easier on ourselves, and we can do that because the Supreme Court and Trudeau government gave us a licence to kill. Stop being so high and mighty. You and me, we've crossed the killing barrier. And we're never going back." With that, she turned back to the bed, grabbed the sheet and blanket, and yanked them over my head. "And I suddenly hate myself for it," she rasped.

Dr. V glared at her bent back. I'd never seen him like that before. Neither of them paid attention to my body. *How did they know I was dead? Because I wasn't dead. I couldn't be. I was still conscious. Feel my pulse!* I thought with all my might. My whisper-shout had gone unheard. *Maybe he'll hear my thoughts?*

"I have to check her pulse," he said. Relief flooded me. Somehow he'd heard my pleas. The nurse stepped back. He stepped forwards, lifted the sheet up near my right wrist, grasped my arm, and hauled it out. *Why is he so rough with me? He was always so gentle, reassuring me with a soft touch that I'd finally be at rest.* He held my wrist in his left hand as he watched the second hand tick around on his magnificent watch. Its gold band glinted in the soft lamplight. I held my breath;

I refused to contemplate there was no breath in me. I couldn't deal with that. Now he'd know he hadn't completed the job.

Dr. V dropped my arm. It bounced off the bed's side and hung down like meat. "I've cured another one. She has her dignity back. That's what they pay me for," Dr. V stated.

The nurse brushed past him and lifted my arm up to push it under the sheet. "Some dignity," she said sardonically.

The silvery-highlighted orb morphed and a hand shape emerged. Two fingers angled to the left, the other two fingers angled away from them, shaping a "V." I sensed the orb smirking with amusement. I didn't understand. Fear convulsed my shape.

"We're sorry," the pink-highlighted orb said.

"Forget them," the silvery-highlighted orb tinkled. "They don't understand."

*I didn't understand*, I thought. I sagged. *I wanted an end to everything. What had happened? Why had his fingers failed to feel my pulse?*

*Doctors know how to take pulses, right?* I asked myself. He hadn't ordered me hooked up to an ECG machine because he'd wanted to create a home atmosphere, a comforting one for my last minutes. I appreciated that. A doctor who understood me. A physician who'd grasped my desire—to die—and was willing to offer it.

Not like my cardiologist, who'd said that my heart disease was well controlled and all I needed was therapy for my suicidal thoughts. I could live a long, happy life with therapy. *I was sixty-one years old. What long and happy life? It'd been too long.* I disagreed with that arrogant man that I was suicidal. I knew what I wanted. The three-step medication prescription to pass me into the rest that Dr. V had promised me when we'd gotten talking at the Second Cup in the hospital cafe. That wasn't suicidal; that was me facing my reality of heart disease and choosing medication that worked for me instead of what the cardiologist had prescribed.

I remembered taking the pills the first time I'd received the cardiologist's prescription. I'd struggled to fight my way out of bed. Fatigue had transformed accounting from pleasurable flow to a persistent battle to focus on numbers instead of collapsing back into bed. I'd told the cardiologist that I needed to be alert and awake to calculate my long-time clients' budgets, to whip through theirs and occasional clients's taxes, to keep up with CRA's tax code changes. I shuddered at this year's sudden trust reversal a day before reports were due. *Typical Canada Revenue Agency move.* If I'd still been on the cardiologist's drug regimen, I wouldn't have been able to pivot to amend my last remaining client's tax return and email her before I closed down my practice.

"Your heart rate is down. Your blood pressure is under control. That's what matters," my cardiologist had said. I hadn't known what to do. *How could I work with that much fatigue? But he'd said I had to manage my heart.* I shook my head. His prescription wasn't the medication I'd needed.

I'd wandered out of the elevator on that thought and had spotted the mini-cafe near the hospital exit. I'd found the only available table after I'd bought my coffee. A few minutes later, a resonant male voice had asked me if he could sit at my table. I'd swivelled my eyes towards his voice, had nodded, and said nothing as he sat and placed his coffee cup on the round table with intense attention. Keeping his head lowered, he'd raised his eyes to mine, smiled, and gestured to my coffee, asking if it healed what ailed me. I heard myself talking. I never talked. None of my doctors, especially the cardiologist, had the time to listen. Years earlier, when I'd tried to talk, I'd discovered they were like Mom. They listened to the facts with one eye on the clock. My questions, and expressing the pain that camped in my head, led to being told off. Best to do what they say.

But Dr. Veritas had been different. He'd listened as I'd clutched my paper coffee cup with both hands, my black coffee cooling in the busy, echoing air. When I'd run out of words, he'd leaned forward and softly touched my arm. I remembered his gentle touch now, how it startled, because doctors didn't touch anymore and because it'd soothed. I'd grown used to not being touched to the point I retreated when someone leaned towards me. But his touch had been kind. He'd told me of another option. He'd told me about MAiD. I didn't know what MAiD was. Medical Assistance in Dying, or MAiD for short, he'd explained.

"Euphemisms are fun!" the silver-highlighted orb sung like chimes.

"Hush," the pink-highlighted orb remonstrated.

I barely registered either as the memory played in my head like a favourite film. Wonder had lit me up as I'd absorbed this new method to end my life-haunting pain. That's what I'd asked all my doctors for; all they'd done was tell me to go to therapy. But Dr. V hadn't. He'd offered me real health care. I'd snatched at it.

I blinked back into my present circumstances, except I had no eyelids to blink, yet for a moment black had obscured my vision. I glanced down. My body remained underneath me.

I existed in defiance of his promises.

Memories popped into my mind. Pop, pop, pop, like exploding bubbles. Empty promises doctors had uttered of controlling my heart disease as it worsened despite the visits and fatiguing prescriptions. *Dr. V's promises cannot also be empty!*

The pink-highlighted orb floated forwards. "We're here for you. We're your soul family. We came to help you."

*Help me?* The sole person able to help me had his profile to me, his face suffusing red while he and the nurse glared at one another. I didn't understand how Dr. V didn't know how to take a pulse, for I was alive, and my heart must be beating. No heartbeat, no life. I knew that.

"How can you help me?" I replied with no mouth or tongue to speak, confusing me even more. "How can you hear me when Dr. V can't hear me? How can I speak with no means to speak?"

A vacuum sucked at my back. Every atom of my being blew backwards, and the hospital's Dying with Dignity Suite where Dr. V and his nurse continued to argue disappeared like a car accelerating away from me.

# TIME AND SPACE

chapter one

## THE SNATCH

Forty. Tomorrow, I will be forty. That number echoes in my footsteps as I walk the familiar beat to work.

Time.

That's my name, and ... where did the time go? When did I get to forty? What does it mean?

Beat, beat, beat: my footsteps rap along the sidewalk in time to the music pumping into my ears from my iPod touch. My footsteps distract me. But only for a moment. I think: at my age, my mother still had not had me. That's why my mother and father had called me "Time."

"It was about time your mother got pregnant," my father would say often during post-Sunday-dinner coffee, as he leaned back in his worn armchair lighting his pipe.

"And it was about time you got out. You sat in there and sat in there and would not come out," my mother would retort to me.

"So we called you 'Time'," Father would say. Then he would end the story with: "Seemed logical."

"Seemed appropriate," Mother would counter as Father finally managed to pull a draw from his pipe and emit three puffs.

What a horrid name, I think, as I turn the corner onto Queen. Today, it's made me obsessed with time and with turning forty. I see a people-stuffed streetcar trundle by, and I sigh. It's been awhile since I gave up trying to catch the streetcar to work and reluctantly woke up earlier to get there on foot.

Peggy and Sue have this big birthday lunch planned for me tomorrow at our favourite restaurant. And the boss has generously—I roll my eyes at "generously"—given me two hours off so we can take our time. The whole thing is surreal.

Bzzzttt.

I take my iPod touch out of my skirt pocket and look at it. The screen is dark, and I press the Home button. No notifications. I turn it this way and that to find what created that strange noise. It seems okay. I shrug, slip it back into my pocket, and continue walking along my route.

The morning sun is slanting sharply along the sidewalk in front of me, toward me, pointing at me, that old woman turning forty. I want to hide from its edgy light, but no point in crossing the street into the shadowed sidewalk. I'll only have to cross back again. I hate walking.

Voices interrupt my thoughts, and I glance into a garishly-painted alley and think: Ford Nation has obviously missed this place. But perhaps there's so much graffiti in Queen West alleys, it's worn out Mayor Ford and his fans before they could erase it all. But there's no one loitering or walking in the alley, only solitary people like me hustling along Queen Street, coffee cups in hand. Suddenly, I stop. I look at my empty hand: I forgot to get my morning café latté, no whip, soya milk, half-sweet, grandé. I think of retracing my steps, but then I'll be late, and the boss doesn't like tardiness. He gets in a snit if I'm even one minute late. My feet resume walking.

And my thoughts resume churning.

At my age, my parents had been married twenty years. It would be another five before I was born. They'd both died a decade ago. I have no sisters or brothers. And since both my parents were only children, I had no immediate cousins. As a child, I met these strange adults my parents called "distant cousins" on special occasions like weddings, adults who embraced me in powder and perfume, exclaimed over how much I'd grown, making me squirm. But I haven't seen them since the funeral.

The last funeral.

I've been alone in the world for ten years, yet until today I hadn't dwelled on it, hadn't felt alone. I live in the house my parents lived in. I've been working at the same kind of job since I graduated from university with my English Lit degree and went right into a temping agency. Father tried to get me to think bigger, but what was I good for? I'm bad at math. Numbers confuse me. And science is gibberish. Only eggheads do science anyway. But then who'd want an English grad? I thrust away a stray memory of an interview with ... I can't even remember now. Father had said I'd sabotaged it; Mother had said never mind, I was born to type. And so type I did and have until this day. I thought it'd be temporary until I found my feet. Yet there they are, my feet, attached to the bottom of my legs, and they're taking me to my admin assistant job as they do every weekday.

"Her."

I hear a word faintly from ahead of me but ignore it. I am thinking about my bosses. I had a few different bosses at several different companies in the early days. Every time I landed a new job, I'd think: this time I'll have a better boss. This time he—or she will treat me like a person with a mind. But they're all the same. They boss you around, treat you like you can't think, dismiss your suggestions unless it's about what to get their spouse for their birthday or how to sort their endless paperwork. I stopped thinking for myself. I stopped caring about having someone else think for me. It's been a long time since I've used my brain independently. And so why do I care today? Why does it bother me now? I shake my head. I've been working at the same company, for the same boss, since two years before Mother and Father died. Father was glad I'd landed a job at a prestigious firm—if I had to be an admin assistant. Mother was glad whatever I did.

I think about Peggy and Sue. They work in the same pool area as I do. Each has her own boss, but our bosses all report to the same Director. Peggy and Sue welcomed me on my first day there, took me out to lunch, showed me the ropes. We've perfected the art of doing as little as possible while looking like we're typing all the time. Typing and emailing and phoning and filing. And organizing the bosses. Technology is great. I hate science, I hate computers—I won't have one at home—but I've learnt how to manipulate them at work so that the boss thinks I work hard when in fact it's the computer. He knows less about the tedious machines than I do, and it's so easy to hoodwink him.

Every month, Peggy and Sue and I go out to a new restaurant for dinner, one that *Toronto Life* recommends. We won't go for anything rated less than three stars. Sometimes we'll go to a show afterwards, something new from Broadway. Every Saturday I go to the library and borrow my week's worth of books. I often borrow books I've read two or four times because it's becoming harder to find new ones that interest me. And I won't buy books. It's not that I don't have the money, but that I want to support Toronto's great library system. Still, cutbacks may force me to buy books. I make a face at the thought. I used to like going to Abelard's or Britnell's, but a Starbucks claimed Britnell's elegant bookstore ages ago, and Abelard's has gone online. I hate the Internet and the endless emails too. I'm not going online to buy books or anything else. And the big chains feel impersonal every time I walk into them, which I haven't for awhile. They're not real bookstores. At least the librarian, when she's there, knows me and knows what I like in books. I smile as I remember last week's conversation when I told her I was turning forty. She'd sympathized and whispered that she'd find me some books about turning forty. At least books remain the same through time: solid, reliable, always there.

Peggy bought an e-reader a month ago, and daily, she tries to have me read it. But ebooks aren't real, aren't solid. They won't last, not like the hard covers I read with their sturdy covers and strong pages. E-readers will change because computers always do, and her ebooks will be gone. Ebooks are a fad, fuelled by those egghead science geeks. I think again about the librarian's promise and pick up my pace in anticipation of my weekly library trip and of those books she'd promised me and of snuggling down Sunday morning after my weekly waffles with a new book. I always begin reading my weekly book borrowings on Sundays. Each day of the week, each day of my life has its own routine—except for tomorrow. At least by Sunday, my fortieth will be a new, fading memory.

"Get ready."

The menacing voice interrupts my thoughts. The hair on my arms and the back of my neck stand to attention. I focus on the people hurrying to work ahead of me, each one alone. One of them must be talking into his Bluetooth, I tell my upright hairs. I hate this intrusion of technology into our world. I take my iPod touch out, crank the volume up, and keep it in my hand. Forty. I'm going to be forty, and there's nothing I can do about it. I cross another graffiti-strewn alleyway and yearn for my latté.

Suddenly.

Hands grab my shoulders, my arms, my waist. They twist my skirt up. A faint thuck-thuck sounds as my iPod touch clatters to the concrete from my shot-open hand. Shock silences my scream and freezes my arms and legs. The foreign hands drag me down the alleyway. Too late, my vocal chords vibrate, for we're not in the alleyway anymore. We're in a white place where the white walls hum into the space.

I scream.

I thrash.

The white walls wash into the space to vacuum the sound out of my throat.

The hands release me, and I stumble to the luminous floor.

The hands' owners step around me from behind to stand in front of me. I blink and scramble up and see three skinny twenty-something boys with double-espresso-latté-coloured skin smirking at me, their necks sticking up from skin-hugging white suits that cover everything but their heads and chestnut hair. They look identical. Yet as my eyes adjust to this bright place with its strange soughing and electric smell, I see they're not. One has a big nose; one a small one. One has cupid-bow lips; one a straight line. One has long lashes; one has thick brows.

They shove me backward, and a seat edge grabs my legs. I sit down hard. One reaches toward the wall closest to him and plucks out a limp piece of white fabric that hadn't been there before. Air catches in my throat. He throws it at me and tells me to put it on.

I almost drop it but make myself hold on. I look around and cannot see a door. They cackle.

"No escape," says one.

"No door you can find," says another.

They laugh harder. They're right. I see no door, no way out. I examine the limp fabric, and abruptly it's a suit hanging from my hands. I drop it in horror. They bend double, they're laughing so hard. My heart beats rapidly against my ribs. I gulp for air. I can't escape, and I dare not disobey. I pick up the suit with my right forefinger and thumb and eye it warily, trying to control my breathing. It doesn't change; it simply hangs from my finger and thumb. I take a firmer grip on it and nothing happens. I must do what they say. I inspect it and find its feet.

One stops laughing long enough to bark, "Put it on!"

I jerk. I glance up at him and immediately back to the suit. I don't know whether to keep my shoes on or not and then decide it's their stuff, what do I care if the heels of my pumps ruin it. I don't want to take them off. I let the suit fall out of my hand, button up my cardigan, retrieve the suit from the floor, find the legs of it, and insert my feet, right foot first. My shoe gets caught in the stretchy, shiny fabric, and I struggle.

They stop laughing and watch me maliciously.

I try again. Suddenly the right leg of the suit opens up and my foot slides down easily into the foot of the suit. I squeak but duplicate the movement with my left foot in its shoe. I stand up and start to pull the suit up. It's like panty hose, and my skirt's bulk is bigger than the suit. I try to stuff it in because I'm not taking my skirt off. As I stuff one section in to one leg, another section flops back out. The boys crack up, but thankfully the walls absorb the highest pitch of their cackles. I persevere, pushing more skirt into each leg of the suit, trying not to expose the ugly topside of my panty hose. The suit bulges unattractively; lumps and bumps sprout wherever I've been able to shove in my skirt. Finally I have the suit pulled up to my waist, and I'm exhausted. I pause to catch my breath. And I look down at the results of my effort. My skirt in the suit is like a muffin top and feels just as bloated.

The suit morphs.

The lumps and bumps disappear.

My skirt is sucked down into the legs.

I suck in air, suck in air. I scream and scream and scream. I cannot hear myself. I cannot even feel the screams in my throat. But I can't close my mouth or stop exhaling through my vocal chords. I want this awful suit off.

Suddenly I'm sitting down, the wind blown out of me.

One boy growls in to my face, "Finish."

I wipe my face from forehead to chin, stand up, and pull on the arms and shrug into the shoulders of the suit. I reach for the zipper to close the front, but there's no zipper, no buttons, no Velcro. I frown at this puzzle. I hear a choked guffaw and look up. They say nothing; they are too entertained by my perturbation. When I look back down to find some way to close the suit, I see the front edges of the suit moving toward each other, fusing, leaving no seam, making the suit into one fabric. My chest heaves hysterically.

"Watch."

I look up at the boys. They step back, and in sync, their upper eyelids drop slowly, deliberately, stay shut for shorter than a second but longer than a normal blink, then as they open, out of the back of the boys' suits arise hoods that pull over their heads, cover their faces, and fuse with their necklines so that the white fabric becomes one from their feet to their heads. Yet I can see the surfaces and edges of their faces clearly. My heaves turn into quick shallow breaths. One blinks again, that same slow blink. I feel something wispy cover my face. I reach up to touch my cheeks. I don't feel my skin. I feel something soft yet not there, something that prickles and lets my fingers sink into it so that I can feel the edges of my cheekbones. I see clearly, as if nothing is covering me, yet I know I'm as covered as they are. My lungs don't want to work anymore, my heart pounds to get out of its rib cage, and I become dizzy.

"Sit down."

He doesn't have to order me because my swimming senses have sat me down already. I can't breathe, and panic rules. From somewhere rises the thought: I must gain control of my breathing. I reach into my memory back to a friend during university who'd taught me deep breathing. I hear her instructions and obey. My breathing fights me, and I fight it. And as I struggle to gain control, one of the boys blinks that blink again, staring at me much like a cat at a mouse, and a shimmer appears before me and then is gone. They look at each other, laugh out loud, and start dancing. Or at least, I think that's what they're doing. It vaguely reminds me of football players celebrating a goal, no, a touchdown. Knees rising up to chests, arms flailing, heads chucking like chickens out of rhythm. I forget all about my breathing, for their contortions are too weird. This place is too weird. I must be in a dream, caught in a nightmare, thinking too much about my fortieth. I stare hard at the white walls, willing them to disappear and become the soft tangerine walls of my bedroom.

And that's when I notice that the walls don't actually end in corners. They're not round either. School-era geometry floats back into my memory from the past, and I think: maybe this is what the inside of an ellipse looks like. Smooth, never ending, yet beautiful as if it could cut the wind, creating no wave to show it's been there. Seats emerge from the walls here and there. On the other side of the dancing boys, the wall coruscates as if it's about to display something.

The boys stop and leer at me, their grins self-satisfied. They nod at each other, and I feel a faint lurch. And then I have the oddest sensation. I feel like I'm moving yet not moving. I feel like my thoughts are with me then behind me. I feel like every cell, no, every molecule is forming and dissolving and reforming in me. I feel as if the suit is the only thing holding me together. The walls and the boys become semi-transparent, as if every other molecule in them has disappeared. I want to rub my eyes but cannot move. I want to yell for help, even though there's no point, but cannot open my mouth. I want to run, but I'm fixated like a cobra's victim.

My boss is going to be pissed. Peggy and Sue won't have anyone to take to my fortieth birthday lunch.

# ABAN'S ACCENSION

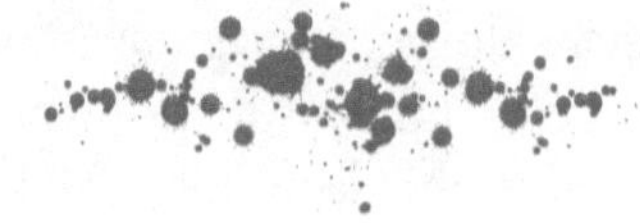

chapter one

## THE DREAM

A black sink. That's her first thought. A black sink. She squints down. The blackness is moving softly, its edges… there are no edges. A ping of fear rises in her, then settles softly back into simple observation. The empty deep swirls beneath her. She is hanging over and in it, its inky fluidic space sucking out the light from around her, vacuuming away all hope. Motion catches her eye to the left and behind her. She moves her eyeballs left and sees two creamy, ribbed things undulating toward her, slowly. Their blurred triangular shapes swim in a straight line. A second couple hoves into view: two by two they come. Maggots. She flickers her feet, trying to rise, to get out of their way, but she's stuck, gripped by an unknown force and the niggling thought of, does she really want to move? Aren't they fascinating, these effervescent couples with their soft bodies and hypnotic movement. She stops struggling.

The line is long now stretching into the unseen distance, growing like a scarf flying out of a magician's pocket. She's not sure if the line of pairs is above her or in front of her. Her eyes watch them while her mind disengages. It is so easy to disengage, to see them as having nothing to do with her. They're just maggots swimming by. The void beneath her feet does not exist.

They turn.

The front of the line has now gone way past her on her right, and so when they turn, they are on her front and right flanks. She doesn't like that. Her mind re-engages. She can no longer pretend that they have nothing to do with her. She wriggles; she flaps her feet; she stretches her neck, arches her head back. But it's hard to resist this formless place. Fear rises in her throat.

She wakes up.

And finds herself struggling with her sweat-dampened sheets, the bottom one all wrinkled, the top one holding her down, pinning her arms to her sides. Panic grips her until she wakes up enough to relax and release herself from the tight top sheet.

Her chest rises and drops heavily, up and down, up and down. Gradually, her hearing returns, her sight broadens. She hears: the cicadas singing outside in the sultry air. She feels: the air inside her bedroom sitting on her like a wet fleece with no breeze blowing in through the open window to bring relief.

She jumps out of bed to fill her mind with the busyness of brushing teeth and putting on her multi-pocketed, baggy army pants and favourite T-shirt proclaiming "The Secret is My Birthright."

# SHE

chapter one

# THERE WAS ONCE A WOMAN

Tires hiss against the road. A gentle bump bump at high speed wakes her up. She stretches against the confines of the seat belt and blinks open her eyes. Pitch night engulfs the car. The glowing numbers on the dashboard clock draw her eyes: 12:54.

"Wow, I can't believe the time." She yawns, "Did I really sleep that long? I can't believe it's that late. Did we run into heavy traffic? That sucks. I thought leaving so late in the evening, we'd miss the Toronto-bound traffic. I guess not, eh?" She smiles at the driver, but he looks stoically ahead. Her eyes drift past the clock again and suddenly widen. "Hey! Do you know what time it is? It's almost summer solstice time. How cool is that, being out in the country at the exact hour?" Still no response.

Sighing, she looks out her window and frowns. Not only are they late, but for that matter, where are they? This country road doesn't look like Highway 10. Pickets of a prim wooden fence fly by, the ground at its feet rising into view and disappearing. The fields beyond vacuum the meagre starlight, and the car's beams cannot penetrate into their depths. She leans toward her window and cranes her neck to look up at the sky. It's a moving charcoal surface with white glitter winking here and there. The moon is nowhere in sight.

She asks him as she continues to stare out the window, "Where are we?"

"I thought we'd take a shortcut."

"Meaning you don't know," she laughs. He smiles faintly as he continues to stare straight ahead, his hands resting in the ten to two position on the leather grey steering wheel of their car. The amber glow of the dashboard lights up the front of his face like some sort of eerie jack-o-lantern. She watches him for a moment.

"Well, I guess we're somewhere in the country. Traffic must've been bad, eh?"

He shrugs one shoulder. She sighs. She's fully awake now and sharing space with a statue.

"I guess it wasn't so bad for you that I dozed off, eh? Silence is golden and all that," she grins. "Well, I can be silent...sometimes." She chuckles and then stretches again. "That nap did me good. I feel so awake now and refreshed. I'm raring to go, and I can't wait till tomorrow, I mean today. I have all these song ideas bouncing around in my head. This was a great idea of yours, going on this road trip, it's got me going again, and I love visiting those cute Ontario towns." She twists round to the left to check out the back seat, to make sure all the goodies they bought are still there. Pies and jugs of maple syrup sit side by side with pints of fresh Bing cherries, her favourite. She untwists herself and settles back in her seat. She watches the hypnotic yellow line as it snakes ahead.

"I can't wait to dive into those cherries. They were my favourite fruit growing up. Did I ever tell you that? I used to look forward to the end of school because that's when Grandmother would buy them. And I'd make a big mess, and she'd get so mad." She laughs at the memory. "Now I can make as big a mess as I want." She falls silent for a moment. "I was thinking: they're too good to make pies with. I'd rather eat them fresh like that, but it's almost strawberry season. Maybe we can go up to Andrew's Scenic Acres and pick some berries. I'm in the mood for making strawberry rhubarb pies or maybe mixed berry pies if the blueberries and raspberries are out too. We have enough room in that chest freezer, I'm sure. I gave it a big cleanout the other day. What do you think?" she asks rhetorically. She savours the thought of a strawberry rhubarb pie with crumble topping. Those are always a hit. And they freeze so well. She can almost smell them baking and taste their sweet tartness. She smiles; her eyes focus on the road again.

She looks past the yellow line, past the boundaries of light the car beams create, into the darkness coming toward them, a forest on the right. The hairs on the back of her neck lift up; her stomach flutters.

"Uh, where are we really?" she asks as she sits up straight, tensing her body. He stays silent.

Her nerves feel taut. She urges, "We need to stop and turn around. Now, if you don't mind."

The car doesn't slow down. His eyes don't flick up to the rearview mirror or down to the speedometer.

Her chest starts to contract. "Look, I know you're all into exploring the side roads, but this doesn't feel safe, and it's really really late. Let's drive home on a faster road. Let's turn around and go to Highway 10."

He says nothing.

"Could you please just stop the car, turn around, and go back to Highway 10."

"We're fine." He stretches the word out. "Stop being so paranoid."

"I'm not being paranoid."

"You are," he replies. The slight put-down in his voice works. She feels silly. They're just trees.

Those trees are beside them; ahead their mates on the left loom. They fill the front windshield more and more. It's 12:56 a.m. She wants to be the one in the driver's seat badly; instead she's being driven inexorably toward the forest, where starlight cannot penetrate. She shifts her gaze back down to the road, to the familiar yellow ribbon and the dusty edges of the asphalt where road meets grass. But then the edges vanish into the shadows cast by the trees standing shoulder to shoulder, leafy branch merging into leafy branch, creating a light-sucking toothy maw. She feels the air hold its breath. Her breathing speeds up. His body remains still.

The trees close in on the other side, only a sliver of rectangular sky between the two forests breaks their starless black.

She leans toward him, her thick, shingled hair falling against her cheek, trying to get away from the trees on her right, jostling his arm.

"What are you doing?" he snaps at her.

"Can't you move closer to the yellow line?"

In response, he steers toward the right.

"Stop it!" She struggles to breathe evenly.

"I'll stop it when you stop being silly."

She leans forward to look up through the windshield, her hair gleaming in the reflected dashboard light, searching for that sliver of glittering sky, looking for the one opening in the lightless claustrophobia without.

"Would you get a hold of yourself. We're fine. Don't worry." He tries to nudge her away with his elbow, but she resists.

She cannot move back to the upright position; she just cannot separate herself from him. She looks ahead, focusing on the end of the forest, even though she cannot see it, where the fields re-emerge beyond the headlights, willing them to arrive there as fast as possible. But their speed drops to 70 kilometres per hour. She begins to see the individual trees, the shrubs sticking up among them, the rocks laying among their bases. The sky is morphing, undulating, changing degrees of grey-black shades. Clouds are rolling in.

"Why are you slowing down?"

He doesn't answer. "Of course not, why need he?" she thinks angrily. He's proving his point. He doesn't usually treat her this contemptuously. Her anger fades into loneliness as memories arise of how he used to always treat her with consideration and respect and love. She remembers the first time they shopped together, how he had insisted on carrying the grocery bags. Or how when she had lost her keys for the umpteenth time and was becoming mighty annoyed about it, he'd used his carefully modulated voice to calm her and focus her memory on those keys. Within minutes she'd found them. But lately, ever since his annual spring camping trip up near the Bruce Trail with his buddies, he's become moody. Grim. Many, many days, he has been his old cheerful self, making her laugh so hard that she snorts water out her nose, or he has run errands by himself instead of interrupting one of her songwriting sessions. But on this weekend's road trip, he'd once again become serious, become watchful of her as darkness inhabited his face. She doesn't understand this change in him and towards her. It's like he's decided that she has to prove her worth over and over again.

She wants to grab that wheel and take back control. But she can't. She's in his hands.

Sinking down into the shadow of her seat, still leaning on him, her eyes reach the level of the clock. It flips to 12:57 a.m.

The landscape flashes sickly neon green. The car heels to the left as a wind screams out of the forest like a ghastly, whirling Northern light, and slams into its right side then dances up on to the hood, on to the roof, down beside them. The car's back fishtails out. She squeezes her eyes and senses the car turn one way then the other. Even through her closed eyelids, she senses the chartreuse-yellow lightning inside the whirlwind. She squeezes her eyes tighter until they hurt. They're speeding up; they're driving to the left; they slow. She opens her eyes to see him manhandling the steering wheel until they're aiming straight down the road again, but the wind, with its ever-changing neon-green-bottom border, with its dancing gold-green veins, streaks alongside and in front of them. They can't outrun it. He presses the accelerator, trying anyway, as she clings to his right arm, as she puts her head between her own arms. Glass cracks in front of her. The cracks glow green. She scoots closer to him and squeezes her eyes so tight, she sees red. Cracks fracture her side window, and she can't help opening her eyes to look toward the sound. Air moves all around her, pushing at her, raising the hair on her arms, throwing up the hair on her head, fluttering her T-shirt, turning her skin sickly green. Suddenly she sees nothing. She closes and opens her eyes and still sees nothing. Panic attacks her. And then they shoot out of the trees and are between open fields. She sees again. Sobs rack her, and she can't stop them.

"There's a patrol up ahead. I have to pull over," he says.

Her sobs quit suddenly. She sits up, wipes her eyes, smoothes her hair off her face, straightens her Black Sabbath T-shirt. The car rumbles off the road to the gravel shoulder and crunches to a stop. He pushes the window button and his window hums down. A policeman with a bright wand in his right hand and a reflective vest walks toward them; the officer leans in, his eyes keen on them. She returns his look emotionless.

"Good evening sir, ma'am. How are you this morning?"

"We're fine officer. I wasn't speeding."

"No, you weren't sir. That's not why I pulled you over. We're the Akaesman patrol."

"The what?"

"Will you step out of the car sir, ma'am. We need to ask you a few questions."

She obeys. Or tries to. All her muscles seem to have seized up; she looks down puzzled, feeling old. Using her hands and her arms as leverage, she turns herself towards the open door, puts her feet on the ground, stands up, and leans on the open car door, apperceiving her balance, before straightening her flared black jeans and walking over to where the policeman has joined a woman standing a metre or so in front of what looks like the back of a white ambulance sitting next to the black and white police car.

"Did you drive through the forest sir?" the policeman asks him.

"Yes."

"Did anything happen?"

"Like what?"

"You tell me sir."

Slowly he shakes his head.

The policeman stares at him for a few seconds, and then turns to her.

"You ma'am. How are you feeling?"

She considers that for a moment. Shocked maybe.

The woman who had been standing there watching them walks over to her, while snapping on blue nitrile gloves. She takes a penlight out of her pocket and flashes it in her eyes. She flinches. The woman is unfazed. She reaches round and lightly squeezes her neck muscles, moving down to feel the top of her shoulders.

"Follow me."

She obeys.

"Please sit here," she gestures to the step at the back of the ambulance. From there, she can see the reflective letters on the side of the police car: "Akaesman Patrol. To Guard and Save." Weird.

She feels a cuff being fastened around her left arm, and then the rhythmic pump, pump as the woman inflates it. Air hisses out before the cuff is ripped off. A stethoscope is pressed against her chest and then her back. She finally looks at the woman as she straightens up and speaks to the policeman: "It's mild, but definitely."

He nods and faces her fiancé again.

"Sir, you did experience something back there, didn't you?"

She watches her fiancé stare back nonchalantly, but he's no match for an officer of the Akaesman Patrol.

"We might've."

"You did sir. I want to know what it was."

He told him all, even how she was whining about turning back.

"You should've listened to her sir. Stay here." He walks over to the patrol car, the gravel crunching under his dusty black boots. He opens the driver's door, gets in, and slams it shut.

They wait.

He gets out with a clipboard and walks over to her.

"OK ma'am, I'm sorry to have to tell you that you probably had a run-in with Akaesman. Now it doesn't look too serious, some sprains, but I must ask you to read this form and sign it. Then go see your GP tomorrow." He looks at his watch. "Today." He writes, his pen scratching the paper on the clipboard. Then he hands the clipboard over to her. The woman aims a flashlight at it, but it's too much to read. She must be tired, and so she pretends to read it. His finger extends into her view, pointing to where she should sign. She signs. He flips the page up and asks her to sign the copy. She signs and hands it back to him. He presses down on the clip handle and releases the top piece of paper. He hands it to her. She takes it, but he doesn't let go until she looks up at him.

"Go see your GP ma'am."

She nods.

He still doesn't let go. "See your GP, your family physician."

She looks up into his face and says, "I will."

He lets go. She carries the paper back to the car, where her door is still open. She gets in awkwardly and drops the paper on her lap, wondering why she has to see her family physician. She reaches back for the seat belt, and pain ratchets up her neck. She pauses and then turns her entire body right to get at the seat belt, pulls it toward herself, turns her entire body to the left, and stiffly aims for the seat belt clip. Click. She sits back, sighing. And waits, staring at her fiancé, yet not seeing him as he strides back to the car. She hears his door open, his booted foot twisting on the gravel, his jeans sliding against leather; she hears the slam of the door, the feel of the car softly rocking in response, the slither of the belt as it's pulled, the click of it going home, the key being turned, and the engine roaring excessively to life. They accelerate onto the asphalt, the wheels spitting small stones out, and drive for home.

# ACKNOWLEDGEMENTS

A clash of ideas birthed this book. Back in 2019, I got fed up with Christians and the general population focusing on the Passion Play and crucifixion with no equivalent attention to the Resurrection—the event that made Christianity Christianity. To me, it's like humans preferred celebrating torture and death over renewed life.

My first attempt to right this wrong (in my mind) was to write the Resurrection equivalent to the Passion Play. I reread the four gospels' accounts, paying attention to their similarities and differences. I read books on the Resurrection and discussed it and my ideas with several people. I owe a big posthumous thank you to Pastor Duke Vipperman who recommended N.T. Wright's books, particularly *Surprised by Hope*; to Rev. Adrienne Clements for her insights and references; and to Roger, who generously gave me a book on the *Gospel of Mary* and the *Nag Hammadi*.

Writing the play satisfied an itch, but then a trilogy introduced itself to my mind. A woman appeared. I knew book one began with her death, but when she told my mind how she intended to die, I objected. Vociferously. I didn't want to deal with the emotional heft of such a decision. Eventually making peace with her method of death, I wrote the award-winning *The Soul's Awakening* in November 2021, and I revised it in February 2022, by joining Prolifiko's 7-Day

Writing Sprint to initiate thought into action and to provide accountability.

Then life intervened.

For two years, I didn't write any fiction; when 2024 arrived, I doubted I could anymore. But with encouragement from writing summits and writing sprints, I finished the first novel, *The Soul's Awakening*, of *The Q'Zam'Ta Trilogy*.

As I edited the first novel, I again researched end-of-life and near-death experiences since I didn't want to rely on my memory from 2021 and 2022. And I studied *Revelation*, writing my thoughts down in Mind Explorer, a newsletter I started on Substack. I read books and articles on terminal lucidity, dark matter, dark energy, and Philosophy of Mind.

I wrote this novel in November 2024, the traditional NaNoWriMo month. Unfortunately, National Novel Writing Month, which made my book writing possible since 2009, was no more that year. And so I tried TRACKBEAR (trackbear.app). It, along with my long-time habit of binge writing in Novembers, allowed me to write *The Soul's Reckoning*. In 2025, I once again joined in Breakthroughs and Blocks (formerly Prolifiko) 7-Day Writing Sprints. Bec Evans and Chris Smith, who run the sprints, and my fellow writers kept me going through personally challenging times of my father's health failing and the novel's difficult topic of reconciling broken relationships.

I signed up for Autocrit's first-chapter critique. Katherine D. Graham provided insight and editorial comments that improved the opening scenes and gave me a blueprint of how to edit the rest of the novel. She'd recommended Maddy216 on Fiverr for beta reading for *The Soul's Awakening*. Maddy is quick, approachable, and generous in her insights; I turned to her again for this manuscript. She didn't disappoint. She also helped me understand the role of Shireen Anne (who suddenly popped up as I was writing this novel and demanded to be inserted into *The Soul's Reckoning*, much to my bewilderment—I obeyed).

I used Fictionary and ProWritingAid to check the structure and to facilitate editing. I know, I know, human editors are best. But as an Indie Author and not financially well off, I can no longer afford human editors, as much as I yearn to experience again the joy of working with an editor in polishing my manuscript. And so I must rely on my proofreading and copyediting training from my early working days, aided by these two powerful apps plus WordHippo instead of Roget's. Yes, they use AI to analyze, but all the writing, all the changes are my own words, from my own editing brain and imaginative mind.

Thank you to Ann Benoit for reading the final version and for her valuable insights. Ann has read almost all my manuscripts; not only does she discuss her comments with me, she also writes them down for me, and, as well, she pencils in copyediting notations where she catches grammatical and spelling errors. I can always count on Ann to tell me where the dialogue is monotonous or the action a little too tedious.

If monologues get a little too preachy, it's entirely on me, though I strive to add humour or break them up in some way to avoid the TV show preaching effect!

Thank you to Neda for keeping me on track. Brain injury destroys one's organizational abilities. Despite radical improvement in brain function and cognition, my ability to get things done still resists my own efforts. I rely on external motivators like the 7-Day Writing Sprints and my case manager to finish my novels and write my monthly *Psychology Today* posts. If you'd like to learn more about brain injury and my experience, check out the links and my two non-fiction books on it under Author Presence.

Marketing, which begins with an attractive cover and a captivating blurb, forms the bedrock of sales. I'm grateful to Adrijus of RockingBookCovers.com for the former and Rodney Hatfield from Reedsy for the latter. Both gave generously of their time, attention, patience, and expertise. They made the publishing process easier!

Mum, Dad, and Aunty Joan asking about my writing kept me eager about telling Charlotte Elisabeth's story. Talking about my ideas sparked my imagination, for which I'm hugely thankful. I apologize to anyone my memory refuses to remind me about. Know that I'm grateful to every person I've spoken with about *The Soul's Reckoning* and *The Q'Zam'Ta Trilogy!*

9 781738 678884